D0396955

WIFE
OF THE
GODS

KWEI QUARTEY

RANDOM HOUSE NEW YORK

WIFE

OF THE

GODS

a novel

M

Copyright © 2009 by Kwei J. Quartey

All rights reserved.

Published in the United States by Random House, an imprint of The Random House Publishing Group, a division of Random House, Inc., New York.

RANDOM HOUSE and colophon are registered trademarks of The Random House Publishing Group

Library of Congress Cataloging-in-Publication Data

Quartey, Kwei J.
Wife of the gods: a novel by Kwei J. Quartey.
p. cm.
ISBN 978-1-4000-6759-6
eBook ISBN 978-1-5883-6857-7
1. Detectives—Fiction.   2. Murder—Fiction.   3. Missing persons—Fiction.
4. Mothers—Fiction.   5. Ghana—Fiction.   I. Title.
PS3617.U37W54 2009
813'.6—dc22
2008032579

Printed in the United States of America on acid-free paper

www.atrandom.com

2 4 6 8 9 7 5 3 1

First Edition

Book design by Liz Cosgrove

To Papa.
He would have loved to see this.

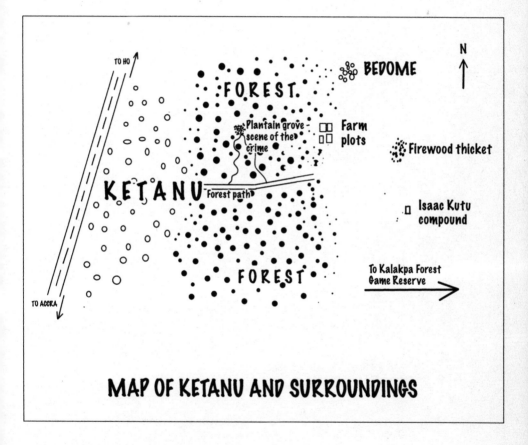

MAP OF KETANU AND SURROUNDINGS

AUTHOR'S NOTES

Glossary

Because of the rich collection of Ghanaian names, expressions, and locales in this work, a glossary is provided at the back of the book to enhance the reader's experience of the story.

Witchcraft

Although it may seem a fanciful notion to many Western readers, witchcraft still holds importance in Ghana, where belief in magical powers coexists with acceptance of modern science and medicine. For many people, concepts of ancestral influence and the spirit world are important in everyday life.

Trokosi

This controversial custom is found in isolated areas of Ghana's Volta Region and in neighboring Togo, with strongly opposed views on either side of the issue. Even the English translation of the word is debated (wife of the gods, slave of the gods, child of a divinity, and so on).

Traditionalists, such as the Afrikania organization in Accra, are in favor of the tradition and deny that slavery is involved. The Ghanaian government and NGOs such as the Christian organization International Needs decry the practice. Some of these opposing views are presented in the novel.

WIFE
OF THE
GODS

PROLOGUE

*T*HE FOREST WAS BLACK *and Darko was afraid to enter. The trees, covered from apex to root with dry, sloughing scales, beckoned him with their crackling, stunted branches. The forest floor erupted in a charcoal-colored cloud of dust as the gnarled, ragged tree roots burst from the earth and turned into massive, thrashing limbs. Swaying, the trees began to lumber toward Darko. He wanted to escape, but terror paralyzed him. He opened his mouth to scream but no sound came.*

"Don't be frightened, Darko."

He recognized his mother's voice at once. Relief swept through him and rendered him light and free. Joy swelled in his chest and knotted in his throat as he saw Mama emerge from the shadows. She walked toward him as if floating, her head held high in the assurance that she would allow nothing to harm her boy.

She held out her hand. "Come along. It's all right."

Her palm softly and completely cocooned his. He looked up. She smiled down at him, her eyes deep and warm and liquid. She was strong and beautiful. He loved the touch of her hand and the scent of her skin.

And she took him into the musty forest of putrefying trees that walked. The forest floor was carpeted with ashen, lifeless leaves and brit-

*tle twigs that snapped underfoot. For a moment, the trees stopped mov-
ing and allowed Darko and his mother to pass through silent as ghosts.*

*"You see?" she said. "They can't trouble us because we're not afraid
of them."*

*One of the trees moaned loudly—a hoarse, wrenching sound full of
the pain of approaching death. Roots flailing, its bulbous trunk took on
the distorted likeness of a face, eyes cruel and mouth bitter as quinine.
Darko shied away, but Mama held him fast.*

*"No, Darko, you can't go back now. I've led you here to find the
truth."*

"I'm scared to go on, Mama."

"Why, Darko?"

"What if the truth is more terrible than the forest?"

*At that very instant, his hand slipped from hers. She faded away,
and in the void she left, there was no answer. The tree with the face, suddenly luminous in the darkness, floundered in the soil as it lurched
closer.*

"Mama?"

His reaching hand touched empty space.

"Mama, where are you?"

*Darko turned in circles, straining his eyes to see, but Mama had
vanished. The trees grunted, scrabbling at the ground to gain traction
as they closed in.*

Darko Dawson the boy cried out. "Mama!"

Darko Dawson the man cried out. Gasping, soaked in sweat, he sat
bolt upright in bed. "Mama?"

The room flooded with light and he cringed. He felt arms wrap-
ping around him and he tried to fight them off.

"The trees," he said.

"No trees," Christine said. "No trees. Just me. In the bedroom, here
with you."

Dawson looked at his wife, startled for an instant before he recognized her. He sighed deeply and let the tension go as he leaned against her. She held him and wiped the sweat from his brow.

"The dream was different from before," he whispered.

"Was it?"

He nodded. "This time, Mama was in the forest with me. I think she's calling for me, Christine—no, I'm certain she is. She's ready for me now. She may have disappeared, but she isn't gone, and now she wants me to find her."

1

INSPECTOR MAX FITI had great significance in a place that had little. He was the head of police in Ketanu, a small town in the Adaklu-Anyigbe District of Ghana's Volta Region. All he had was a small police station as ragged as a stray dog, two constables, and an old police vehicle that ran erratically, but when there was trouble, people turned to Fiti.

Case in point: Charles Mensah, a fortyish man with a painfully thin body and a bulbous head like a soldier termite, had just come into his office this morning to report his sister missing.

"When did you last see Gladys?" Fiti asked.

"Yesterday afternoon, around three," Charles said. "Just before she left for Bedome."

"She went to Bedome? To do what?"

"You know she's a volunteer with the Ghana Health Service AIDS outreach. She goes to different villages to teach and so on."

"Aha, yes."

The village of Bedome was east of Ketanu on the other side of the forest.

"When she didn't come back home yesterday evening," Charles

continued, "I thought it was strange, so I rang her mobile and left a message. She never called back and I started to get worried, so then I rang Timothy Sowah, the director of the AIDS program, and he said he too had been unable to reach her on the mobile."

"Maybe she went to another village where the reception is poor?" Fiti suggested.

"Mr. Sowah told me Bedome was the only place she was scheduled to visit," Charles replied.

"Are you sure she actually got to Bedome? I mean, not that I'm saying something bad happened on the way, but—"

"I understand what you mean, Inspector. I got up early this morning—I couldn't sleep anyway—and I went to Bedome to check. Everyone told me yes, that Gladys had been there yesterday and she had left some time before sunset to go back to Ketanu."

True, less than twenty-four hours had passed, Fiti reflected, but he agreed this was all very troubling. Gladys Mensah was a serious girl—reliable, solid, and smart. And beautiful. Very, very lovely indeed. So, yes, Fiti took this seriously. He jotted some notes on a legal pad, sitting slightly sideways because his rotund belly prevented him from pulling up close to his desk. Fiti was approaching the half-century mark in age, and most of the weight he had recently been gaining had gone to his midsection.

"Something else I want to tell you," Charles said. "Maybe it's nothing, but while I was on my way to Bedome this morning, I spoke to some farmers who have their plots near the forest. They told me that while they were working yesterday evening, they saw Samuel Boateng talking to Gladys as she was on her way back to Ketanu."

Inspector Fiti's eyes narrowed. "Is that so?"

He didn't like the Boateng family much. Samuel, the second oldest boy, was a ruffian who had once stolen a packet of PK chewing gum from a market stall.

"Have you asked Samuel or his father about it?" Fiti said.

"We don't speak to the Boatengs," Charles said tersely.

Fiti pressed his lips together. "Don't worry, I'll go and see them myself."

2

EFIA WAS A *TROKOSI*, which meant that she belonged to the gods. Eighteen years ago, her uncle Kudzo beat a man to death with a branch from a baobab tree. Over the next several months, bad things began to happen to the family: crops failed because of drought, Efia's mother had a stroke, and a cousin drowned in a river. Everyone in the family panicked. Even though Uncle Kudzo had been imprisoned for his crime, it appeared the gods were punishing the family for what he had done. This was the only reasonable explanation for the horrible series of events that had been taking place, and who knew how many more catastrophes were to be meted out by the gods?

The family elders went to the Bedome shrine to consult with Togbe Adzima, chief and High Priest of the village. Adzima, who was an intermediary between the physical world and the spirit world, said yes, there was most certainly a way out of this predicament. The family needed to bring a female child to serve at the shrine. Efia, twelve at the time, was the perfect choice. She was handed over to Adzima to learn "moral ways." This would restore good fortune to the family. As a trokosi, though, she officially belonged to the gods and was to bear their children through Togbe Adzima. He had three other trokosi and nineteen children among them. The wives cooked for him, cleaned, made palm wine, and harvested crops. Every penny from the sale of foodstuffs went to him.

And there lay the heart of the matter. Whatever the supposed reason for the women serving at the shrine, despite their being sometimes loftily called "wives of the gods," they were the source of all Togbe's plenty, and that made life very good for him.

Whenever Efia looked back on the day her new life as a trokosi began, she flinched with the pain of the memory. She and the extended family had walked about sixteen kilometers from their home village to the shrine, bearing all kinds of gifts for Togbe. Efia didn't understand why she was being cleaved from her family. She cried and cried and could not stop.

The shrine itself was a low mud hut containing a large, brightly painted wood carving plastered with human and animal figures. The gods endowed this carved object with magical powers that the priest could summon whenever needed. That's why it was often called a "fetish object" and the priest a "fetish priest," even though many of the priests didn't like the word *fetish* used to describe them.

Efia remembered entering another hut close to the shrine while her family stayed outside. It was hotter than a northern desert in there, smelly and stifling. Efia knelt down in front of Togbe and two other priests. They poured libation with schnapps and drank up whatever was left in the bottle. Togbe, sweat dripping off his face and body, chanted magic words and waved an oxtail fly whisk over different shrine objects.

Every stitch of Efia's clothing was removed, and a female elder inspected her to make sure she was a virgin. As Efia bowed down in obeisance to the fetish objects, she felt as if she would be choked to death by the smoky heat and the alcohol breath of the men.

But she didn't die. She survived. Her family left her in Bedome and she began her life at the shrine. She never tried to run away. The gods would punish her for that, and anyway, where would she go? Once Efia had reached puberty, Togbe Adzima began to have sex with her. At the age of sixteen, she had her first child, Ama, who was now fourteen.

Efia had missed her period last month and she could tell she was pregnant again. She had suffered two miscarriages since Ama was born. Her second live child, a boy, had died of malaria before he reached the age of one.

Togbe Adzima would want to eat plantain *fufu* for lunch. Balancing an empty basket on her head without the aid of her hands, Efia walked through the thick bush of the forest toward the plantain grove. Her feet, broad and solid from years of walking, easily passed over the tricky terrain of low shrubs, dead leaves, fallen trees, and trailing vines. It had rained a little last night, and the moist earth was fragrant. Overhead in the trees, birds filled the crisp air with bright morning song.

As she came level with a palm tree, she caught a glimpse of an animal on the ground barely a second before she stepped on it. *Snake.* She jumped to the side with natural quickness. But when she looked now, she saw that it wasn't a snake. It was a human foot, toes pointing up.

Efia put down her basket and moved slowly around the palm tree. She saw a woman lying on her back partially obscured by the branches of a low shrub. She was fully clothed. Her legs were together, her arms by her sides. *Sleeping?*

"*Heh!*" Efia called out. "Hello?"

She came forward two steps, pulled the branches aside, and when she saw the face, the wide-open eyes and the gaping mouth, she recoiled and her blood went cold.

No.

"Gladys?"

In a way, Gladys seemed different, in another way she looked the same. Efia touched her and was shocked by how cold and rigid she was. Her eyes were open but unmoving and cloudy white, as though filled with coconut milk.

"*Gladys.*" Efia began to cry. "*Ao,* Gladys, wake up, wake up. *Gladys!*"

She got to her feet and whirled in a circle shrieking for help, but no one was close by. She began to run. Her vision darkened, her hearing deadened, and her feet lost sensation.

She burst out of the bush and spotted a man walking ahead along the Bedome–Ketanu footpath, and she ran after him screaming. He stopped and turned around, and as Efia got closer she recognized him as Isaac Kutu, the local herbalist and healer. His compound was not far away. She felt a surge of hope. *Healer. Maybe he can do something.*

"Mr. Kutu." She was gasping, trying to catch her breath. "Mr. Kutu, please come."

"What's wrong?"

"It's Gladys Mensah. *Hurry!*"

Efia turned and began to run back. She could hear Mr. Kutu keeping up behind her. The bush seemed thicker and more tangled now that her energy was so spent, but she knew the way well and got there quickly.

The body was still there. Efia stopped, pointed, and then leaned over with her hands on her knees to get her breath.

Mr. Kutu pulled aside the obscuring bush and drew back at the sight. He stared for a moment and then knelt down by the body. He touched it softly and whispered something Efia didn't catch. He looked stunned.

Kutu stood up. "Bring me something to cover her."

Several plantain trees, their leaves long and broad, were only a few feet away. Efia pulled on a branch and broke it off. Kutu laid it gently across Gladys's body. It seemed much better that way, so much more dignified.

"I have to go and get Inspector Fiti," Kutu said. "Can you wait here for us to come back?"

Efia backed away, shaking her head. "No. I'm afraid to stay with her by myself."

She turned and bolted back to Bedome without stopping or look-ing back.

Including the shrine, Bedome was a collection of a dozen scattered thatch-roofed huts. Yesterday's rain had stained the soil dark, but once it dried out, it would be the identical monotonous light brown color of the dwellings.

The normal morning's activities—sweeping, cooking, collecting water, the smaller children playing—had begun, but everything stopped as Efia came running. She collapsed to the ground wheezing with exhaustion, her face buried in her palms. The trokosi wives came to her at once, dropping down beside her. *What's wrong, what's the matter?*

Efia couldn't speak. She was paralyzed with shock. Nunana, the oldest, most experienced wife, her body worn and wiry and her breasts wrung dry by the toll of six children, pulled Efia up and led her protec-tively away.

"What happened?" she said softly. And suddenly more sharply, "Stop crying and tell me what's wrong."

As Efia was sobbing out her answer, Togbe Adzima came out of his hut shirtless and yelled, "What are you people doing standing around like cocoa trees?"

He was in his late fifties. He was oily and never looked clean, and his eyes were red and muddy from drinking.

"Nunana!"

She came to him quickly.

"What's going on?" he demanded.

"Please, Togbe. Efia says Gladys Mensah is dead in the forest."

"What?"

"She found her at the plantain grove."

"When?"

"Just now, Togbe."

He looked baffled. He beckoned Efia over, and the children of the shrine fell in behind her, eyes wide with curiosity.

"What are you saying, Efia?"

She repeated what she had told Nunana. Togbe Adzima frowned. "Are you sure?"

Efia nodded. She tried to wipe her tears away, but they kept pouring.

Adzima went into his hut and came back out buttoning his shirt. "I'm going to see for myself. Finish your work. Make sure my *akasa* is ready when I return."

The Boatengs' home was a ramshackle house on its last legs. When Inspector Fiti entered, Mr. Boateng looked wary and his wife was visibly nervous. She offered Fiti some water, which he dismissed as if she had suggested poison. Four of the seven children were at home, all of them in tattered clothing.

"Where is Samuel?" Fiti asked in Ewe.

"Please, Inspector, he went with some friends to somewhere," Boateng said.

"Find him," Fiti said. "I want to talk to him. Right now."

Boateng's eight-year-old son went to look for Samuel and came back with him a few minutes later. Samuel was nineteen, compact and wiry, the striations of his ropy muscles showing through his faded shirt. *Chale-wate* sandals clung to his muddy feet by threads. He looked suspiciously from the inspector to his parents.

"Sit on the floor," Fiti told him.

Samuel's face was fluid and mobile. His forehead creased and relaxed in rapid waves like a physical manifestation of his mind at work. He sat down looking both wary and defiant. The inspector moved closer and stood over him.

"Have you seen Gladys Mensah today?"

Samuel's brow furrowed. "Please, no, sir."

"What about yesterday? Did you see her?"

"Yesterday? No, sir."

"Don't lie, boy. Some farmers saw you with her."

"No, sir. It wasn't me."

"Hello, Inspector?"

Everyone turned in the direction of the voice. Isaac Kutu was standing at the door.

"Yes?" Fiti saw the grave look on Isaac's face. "What's the matter?"

"You should come, Inspector. Gladys Mensah is dead."

3

BAD NEWS SPREADS THROUGH any small town like fire through dry savanna bush. Kweku and Osewa Gedze first heard about Gladys Mensah's death as they were working on their cocoa farm. The golden ripe cocoa pods were particularly beautiful this year. Each was perfectly almond shaped with sculptured ridges that ended in a point like an erect nipple. One pod held thirty to forty fleshy seeds that were scooped out, fermented, and then dried for days before they were ready to be shoveled into sacks for shipping. It was back-splitting work, and for all of it Osewa and Kweku would probably never savor a single mini-square of the final product—chocolate. It all went to fancy stores in the big cities at prices that they could never dream of paying.

Kweku wiped the sweat off his face and watched his wife for a moment. She was on her knees deftly slashing the pods open with a cutlass. Fifty-one years old and nine years his junior, she was strong and skilled with powerful hands that wielded a cutlass or shovel better than most men.

They looked up at the sound of running footsteps, and Alifoe, their twenty-three-year-old son, burst into view. He was tall and beautifully built, with the deepest black skin possible, glossy and silky with its natural oils.

"Have you heard?" he said breathlessly.

"Heard what?"

"You know the Mensah girl who was going to be a doctor?"

"Yes, what about her?" Kweku said.

"They found her dead early this morning."

"Oh, no." Osewa dropped her cutlass and stood up. "Where?"

"In the forest not far from here. Everyone is going there. I'm going too."

He turned and started out.

"Wait for me," Kweku called out. "Osewa, we'll be back soon."

Moving quickly with Isaac Kutu, Inspector Fiti made a call on his mobile to his constable.

"Gyamfi," he snapped, "where are you—at the station? Eh-heh, good. Stop everything. Gladys Mensah has been found dead in the forest. . . . Yes, that's what I said, are you deaf or what? Go there now and secure the place. . . . You'll know where it is because everyone is going there. That's why you need to hurry before they destroy the scene. You hear? *Go!*"

He pocketed his phone and took a few trotting steps to keep up with Isaac, who moved as swiftly and easily as a river over its bed. The police station was closer to the scene than the two of them were at the moment, so Gyamfi would get there first. The forest was on the eastern edge of Ketanu. To reach it, Inspector Fiti and Isaac had to cross the breadth of the town. Its dwellings and shops sprawled along either side of the busy road to Ho, the capital of the Volta Region, twenty kilometers due northeast. In his time, Inspector Fiti had seen three new roads built in Ketanu as it had mushroomed in size, and many of the mango, banana, and palm trees in which the town had once nestled had gone the way of chopped wood and compost.

Bedome village was in turn on the east side of the forest, a well-beaten footpath connecting it to Ketanu. Fiti had been right—scores of people were breaking off into the forest from the footpath. As the inspector closely followed Isaac, he shouted at people to get out of the way, which they did. Everyone was familiar with Inspector Fiti's rough, gravelly voice. He was not a particularly patient man.

Gyamfi had already arrived by the time Isaac Kutu and Inspector Fiti made it there, and he had managed to mark off a wide perimeter using a length of rope wrapped around the trunks of plantain trees. Now he stood guard at the edge of the cordoned-off area looking as fierce as he could to keep away a gathering cluster of spectators. People sometimes teased him and called him Boy Constable Gyamfi, because even though he was twenty-four, he looked nineteen and still had no serious facial hair.

"Who is it there?" Fiti asked Gyamfi as they came up to him. "Is it really Gladys Mensah?"

The constable nodded. "Yes, sir. It's her."

Fiti lifted the rope and ducked under. Isaac was about to follow, but Gyamfi put a gentle restraining hand on his shoulder. "Please, when we're ready for you, we will call you."

Isaac stepped back, looking a little insulted.

"Where is she?" Fiti asked Gyamfi.

Gyamfi pointed to just beyond a palm tree and led the way. He pulled aside the bush, and the inspector looked.

"Oh," he said softly, shock in his voice. "Oh."

It was midmorning by now. The sun was already scorching and the first of the bluebottle flies had begun to buzz around frenetically, but Fiti didn't see a wound of any kind on Gladys's body. She was missing a shoe, though. The left one.

"Is this how she was when you first came here?" he asked his constable.

"Yes, sir."

"With the plantain leaves on her body?"

"Yes, sir."

"Did you find something else?"

"Yes, sir." He moved away about five meters. "Here, sir. Her shoe."

It was a russet-colored, open-toed shoe with a back strap and low heel. Why was it here and Gladys over *there*?

"Maybe someone dragged her body and the shoe got pulled off," Fiti speculated.

"I found another thing, sir," Gyamfi told him.

Moist dead leaves crunched softly under their feet as they moved ten meters farther along.

"Here, sir." Gyamfi pointed to a black leather briefcase soiled by mud and vegetation debris.

"*Aha.*"

Fiti opened the partially unzipped top of the bag and found papers inside clumped together in a soggy mass. They were flyers about AIDS—simple diagrams with arrows going back and forth. Man to woman, woman to man, woman to baby. Underneath those was the "ABC" campaign of Abstinence, Being faithful, and Condoms. At the very bottom of the briefcase was a mobile telephone just as soaked as the pamphlets.

Fiti left the bag exactly where he had found it. He went back to the rope, where Isaac stood waiting.

"You say a woman from Bedome found her?" Fiti asked him.

"Yes. One of Togbe Adzima's wives—Efia."

"Where is she now?"

Isaac shrugged. "Back in Bedome, I suppose. She ran away."

"But why did you let her?" Fiti demanded. "You should have told her to stay here."

"I did," Isaac said evenly, "but she was afraid to be here alone in the forest with a dead body."

Fiti pressed his lips together in some annoyance. "When you got here with Togbe Adzima's wife, those plantain leaves were covering the body?"

"No, I put them there."

Fiti scowled. "Why?"

"Respect for the dead, Inspector."

"But you didn't disturb anything?"

"No."

Fiti grunted and returned to the corpse. Gladys's clothes were spattered with mud from last night's rain, which had started after dusk. She had been—still was—wearing a fashionable blue and white blouse and matching skirt, both with decorative Adinkra symbols. In the old days, you saw Adinkra cloth only at funerals. Now anyone could wear it as fashion, and it was a tourist item as well.

Fiti leaned down. Gladys's color was changing—she was much blacker than she had been in life, with a greenish hue that repelled him.

"Help me," he said to Gyamfi. "I need to see her back. No, go to her other side and roll her toward you."

Gyamfi grasped Gladys's shoulder and pulled gently. She was heavier and more inert than he had anticipated, and she did not roll on the first try. The second time, he was successful. She moved in one piece, like a log.

Apart from the mud and twigs that soiled Gladys's back, there was nothing out of the ordinary. No blood, no visible injuries, and no tears in her dress. Her braided hair was still beautifully in place, so it was easy to see that her scalp was free from injury.

"All right," Fiti said.

They released her body and stared at it for a moment. Fiti didn't know what to make of it. *What had happened to her?* A healthy woman of only twenty-two years of age. And what had she been doing here? How did she get here?

"There's no mark on her," he said, mystified. "Maybe she was poisoned?"

Fiti heard a loud cry and whirled around. Gladys's mother, Dorcas, appeared from behind a flank of plantain trees screaming. *She already knows,* Fiti thought. Dorcas could barely hold herself up, her body ravaged by emotion. Her oldest son, Charles, was propping her up on one side, her husband, Kofi, on the other. Behind them was a long trail of family members.

Fiti and Gyamfi leapt up to head them off.

"Stay back," Fiti said, holding up his palms to them. *"Stay back!"*

But one or two in the group forcefully held down the cordoning rope, and the family surged forward across it shouting, pushing the inspector aside as if he had not been there at all. Gyamfi had a little bit more success holding off some of the family, but not much.

Dorcas fell onto her daughter, and her shrieks became animal-like. Kofi was frozen in place at the sight of Gladys's body. Charles turned away and vomited.

Fiti was furious. Until proven otherwise, this was a crime scene, and any policeman worth his salt knew it had to be preserved.

"Get them away from there!" he shouted at Gyamfi.

Together they began to try to pull and push people back with a combination of cajoling and physical force. Fiti put his hand on Dorcas's shoulder as she crouched over her daughter's body weeping uncontrollably.

"Dorcas, come away, eh?" He turned to Kofi. "Take her away from here, I beg you. It's too much for her, too much."

Dorcas resisted, but Kofi and Charles coaxed her to go with them to a spot under a mango tree where Gladys was out of her sight. This gave Fiti and Gyamfi some momentum, and they were able to urge the rest of the multitude—family and unrelated onlookers—back behind the cordon. While Gyamfi kept them at bay, Fiti, sweat pouring off his face and body in rivulets, got on his mobile. He liked everything in Ketanu under his control, but he knew when it was time to call in the big boys from Ho. He needed help.

4

DARKO DAWSON RODE a Honda Shadow Spirit so he could maneuver between vehicles and get to work much faster than he would in a car.

"I wish you wouldn't ride that thing, Dark," his wife said as he put on his helmet. "It's so dangerous."

"Not this debate again," Dawson said. "Christine, I'm not spending two hours sitting in traffic just to get across town, so until and unless they build an underground system in this city, it will have to be a motorbike."

Accra, Dawson's smoky, noisy hometown and Ghana's capital, had traffic jams rivaling the worst in the world. Christine, a primary school teacher, was lucky that her job was close enough to walk it, but Dawson worked at Criminal Investigations Department Headquarters, eight tortuous kilometers away.

He kissed his son good-bye. "Be good, Hosiah, okay?"

"Okay, Daddy," the boy said.

Hosiah, six years old, was their only child. At the end of a hellish pregnancy, he had emerged in perfect form except for one important detail: he had a hole in his heart, or more correctly, ventricular septal defect.

Dawson worried about his boy every single day. The doctors at the Cardiothoracic Center at Korle-Bu, Accra's largest hospital, had at first hoped that the defect would close on its own, as they sometimes did, but that did not happen, and the ill effects were now showing. Hosiah was beginning to suffer from fatigue and shortness of breath. It was painful to watch. He was taking two types of medicine to suppress the symptoms, but the only true cure was surgery. Ghana's fledgling National Health Insurance Scheme provided only for basic medical care and did not cover surgery for congenital heart disease. The operation was staggeringly expensive, far beyond Dawson and Christine's immediate financial reach, especially now, with the price of food spiraling up. They were saving money as fast as they could but they were nowhere close to the required amount, even with Christine working part-time on weekends.

Dawson had to force his mind away from Hosiah to concentrate on negotiating bumper-to-bumper traffic on Ring Road. He white-lined the double lane toward the Ako Adjei Interchange, dodging cars that suddenly cut in front of him while he simultaneously avoided the young, nomadic street hawkers who walked up and down the narrow space between traffic lanes selling pencils, TV remotes, DVDs, tennis shoes, gingersnaps, hairbrushes, apples, chocolate milk, and anything else one could think of. They stopped beside cars and *tro-tros,* waving their wares in the windows with astonishing persistence until it became obvious they were not going to make a sale. It was a tough life. After twelve hours in the broiling sun, these traders could expect to make a profit of less than a *cedi.*

Tailpipe exhaust invaded Dawson's throat and expanded in his lungs. He had tried covering his nose and mouth with a handkerchief tied across his face, but that seemed to smother him even more, so now he simply moved through the traffic as fast as he could. Every vehicle was his enemy. Taxis, ubiquitous and distinguished by their yellow front and rear panels, were the worst of them all. There was one chief rule about driving in Accra: always be prepared to give way to another vehicle at an instant. People drove with razor-thin margins between their vehicles and the next ones.

Tro-tros, the other means of transport for the masses, packed twelve to fifteen passengers into their rattling, smoke-belching frames. Dawson called them "Chariots of Fire." On the other end of the spectrum were the glittery Benzes, Lexuses, BMWs, SUVs, and the most ostentatiously obnoxious of them all, Hummers.

Once Dawson was past the Ako Adjei Interchange, he didn't have far to go to Police Headquarters. At seven fifteen exactly, he turned left into the parking lot, barely slowing down at the security gate as he gave a cursory salute to the armed guards. They had complained to him before that he charged in the entrance too fast. He locked up the bike and cut across the browning lawn and past the knee-high hedges to the side of the Criminal Investigations Department building.

CID was a specific branch of the Ghana Police Service. Although the headquarters was here in Accra, officers were stationed throughout the country. For a structure with such an official title, CID was a downright disappointing seven-story building that could easily have been an undistinguished apartment block. It might have once been off-white, but now it was the color of the dark sand of a less than pristine beach. In addition to an interior staircase, a flight of steps cascaded along the outside of the building's south end and provided free access to anyone wandering in and out. It seemed ironic that CID Headquarters was no high-security fortress.

Dawson trotted up the stairs to the second level and turned in to the narrow, dim corridor lined with office doors painted blue with yellow trim. A few other employees were coming into work just like Dawson, wishing one another "Good morning," a crucial ingredient of Ghanaianness: no "Hi," "Hello," or, God forbid, "What's up?"

He crossed the reception area, an inner courtyard with half a dozen worn wooden chairs on opposite sides and a handful of early-bird vis-

itors waiting to take care of their affairs. Regina, the glacial receptionist, was at her desk in the corner serenely setting up for work.

"Morning, Regina."

She looked up with her impenetrable, enigmatic smile. "Good
morning, sir."

Dawson worked in the Homicide Division and shared a small office with two other detectives, neither of whom had yet arrived, which
was just fine. Dawson preferred a quiet start. The cramped room had
three desks and not enough storage space. There were computers, yes,
but no matter how hard you tried, you just couldn't get rid of paper.
Some of it was stowed in file cabinets or on shelves the way it was supposed to be, but the rest was on the floor or any clear space on a table-
top. Dawson did his best to keep his desk tidy because he could not
think clearly with clutter around him.

His desk was closest to a louvered window with a view onto the
lawn and parking lot below. He turned on the ceiling fan in the hope of
staving off the vicious March heat, which would be in full force in another three or four hours. No luxurious air-conditioning here. He was
a detective inspector, still a "subordinate"—he disliked that word—
officer. When someday he got to detective chief superintendent or
higher, *then* maybe he would get a big office with the AC blasting.

Dawson sat down and logged on to his terminal, quickly running
through his emails. They were much of the same, as always, with the
usual edicts from the boss, Chief Superintendent Lartey.

Dawson turned to the bottom drawer of the file cabinet next to his
desk and pulled out a stack of ragged folders stuffed with papers—
court records, statements and documents from open cases, and the
miscellaneous laborious reports that were inescapable elements of police work.

As Dawson started on the first report, Detective Sergeant Chikata
walked in. He was about six years younger than Dawson's thirty-five,
muscular and impossibly handsome.

D.S. Chikata was good when he applied himself, but much of the

time he was as languid as a lion in the midday sun. It was hardly a secret around CID that he had got into the Homicide Division mostly on
the strength of his being Chief Superintendent Lartey's nephew. This
was also undoubtedly why the detective sergeant was so smugly confident that he would soon rise to Dawson's rank of inspector, and why
he was such a cheeky brat. He showed little or none of the customary
deference to his superior officers, and although Dawson was not a
stickler for protocol, Chikata's impudence could be irritating.

"Morning, Dawson."

"Morning. How're you?"

Chikata yawned long and wide, shaking his head as if to throw off
the lingering remains of the night's slumber. "Tired," he said. "Too
much beer last night. And women."

Dawson grunted. What did one say to that kind of information?

Chikata sat down at his desk, and Dawson mentally counted down
the time it would take his colleague to lean forward and switch on the
radio; he came within a second's accuracy. He'd do better tomorrow.

Chikata leaned back and propped his gigantic feet on his desk as he
listened to the call-in morning show on Happy FM. After a while, it got
on Dawson's nerves.

"Turn that racket down, Chikata."

The D.S. reduced the radio's volume. "Yes, sir, D.I. Dawson, sir,"
he said, with mock reverence, before resuming his repose position.
"We need to close some cases."

"Maybe we would if you actually did some work."

Chikata ignored the jab. "Can't we get some confessions by beating
up one or two suspects—like you did to that rapist when you were detective sergeant?"

Dawson swiveled in his chair. "Look, that's not what happened,
Chikata."

"Sorry. Then tell me."

"I caught the guy red-handed. He confessed. After I cuffed him, he
said all little girls deserved to have his *bulla* up their *totos,* so I punched
him in the face. That's all."

"Oh, I see. How many times did you punch him?"

Dawson shrugged. "I don't remember exactly. Two, three times."

"Three times at *least,* from what I heard. No disrespect, but I think your temper is too hot, Dawson. Why waste energy on a bleddyfool like that?"

"I'm not like you. Doesn't anything ever upset you?"

"Oh, yah. Not getting enough sleep."

"You would get some if you would go to bed by yourself every once in a while."

Chikata began to laugh so hard he capsized his chair, at which point Dawson could not help himself and broke into laughter himself. Chikata recovered and restored the furniture.

"Anyway, you'd better solve something before my uncle transfers you to some bush village somewhere," he said, only half jokingly.

"I'd like to see him try," Dawson said.

Perhaps he should not have spoken with so much bluster. That afternoon Chief Superintendent Theophilus Lartey called Dawson to his office. Lartey, around fifty-two, was a surprisingly tiny man for the amount of power he wielded. His soft leather armchair and expansive desk dwarfed his proportions, as did the room, which could have held at least three offices the size of Dawson's. It was luxuriously cool in here, with a powerful air conditioner purring from high up on the wall. The room was completely quiet, insulated from the hum and bustle of the outside world, where the weather was hot and stifling.

"Sit down, Dawson," Lartey said.

Dawson did so, feeling as he always did—like a pupil in the headmaster's office. One never went there unless there was trouble.

"You know Ketanu in the Volta Region?" Lartey asked.

"Yes, I've been there before."

"And you speak Ewe?"

"Yes. My mother is Ewe." He could not refer to her in the past tense. "Why, sir?"

"There's a situation up there," Lartey said. "A young woman was found dead in the forest day before yesterday. Suspicious circumstances for sure, so the local police called in a CID detective from Ho."

Ho was a minuscule city compared with Accra, but as the capital of the Volta Region, it was where small-town Ketanu would look for help in police or other matters.

"All right," Dawson said. "So CID Ho is investigating—"

"And where do we come in?" Lartey interjected. "The young lady, Gladys Mensah, was in her third year of medical school and was volunteering with the GHS under the Ministry of Health. The minister called me this morning. He insists someone here in headquarters take the case."

"What's wrong with the Ho detective?"

"Look, Dawson," Lartey said irritably, "don't ask me these questions. I have no idea why the minister doesn't want the Ho man to take the case. I'm sure it's something political, but what difference does it make? The bottom line is that I have to send someone there, and that someone is you."

"Why me, sir?"

"Use your head, Dawson. You're the only detective here who speaks Ewe and that's what they speak in the Volta Region, so you have a big advantage. What's that stupid look on your face?"

"This is a little unexpected, sir—"

"Life is full of surprises."

"When am I supposed to go, sir?"

"Tomorrow morning. You can take one of the CID cars. The MoH will make the arrangements for a place to stay in Ketanu, but your first port of call will be the Volta River Authority Hospital. The postmortem is being done there tomorrow, and I want you to attend it."

5

DARKO DAWSON'S FIRST VISIT to Ketanu had been twenty-five years ago. He was ten and his brother, Cairo, was thirteen when their mother, Beatrice, took them there to visit Auntie Osewa and Uncle Kweku. Papa couldn't go with them because he couldn't get any time off from work. That's what he said, but Darko didn't believe him. For some reason, Papa wasn't fond of Mama's side of the family.

Ketanu was about 160 kilometers away, the farthest Darko had ever traveled, and he was excited about the trip. They boarded a tro-tro at the Nkrumah Circle lorry park, a whirling dust bowl of people coming and going. Darko thought the tro-tro was packed enough to begin with, but the driver made two more stops in the city and the tro-tro conductor, or mate, squeezed in a few more passengers. Darko and Cairo had wanted to sit somewhere up in front, but Mama would not allow it.

"No, no," she said, shaking her head firmly. "If there's an accident, I don't want you flying through the windscreen. Nor me. We sit in the back."

Mama was very nervous about traveling in tro-tros. Darko noticed how tense she became, gripping the seat in front of her whenever the vehicle had to brake sharply.

Several cramped and bone-rattling hours later—the ride seemed endless to Darko—they arrived at a transit town called Atimpoku, on the Volta River, where they were to change tro-tros. The Atimpoku stop was a bustling trading place. Market women with trays of merchandise balanced effortlessly on their heads swarmed around arriving vehicles in aggressive attempts at selling sugar-bread and the popular "one-man-thousand," plastic bags packed tight with tiny crispy-fried fish.

Mama waved the traders off and firmly led Darko and Cairo away from the mayhem. They had a little time before the next tro-tro to Ketanu was to arrive.

"Come, boys," she said. "Let's stretch our legs. I'm going to take you to a secret place."

Darko loved exploring. "Where, Mama?"

"You'll see. It's a bit of a walk, so get your legs strong and ready."

"I *have* strong legs," Darko said.

"They're skinny," Cairo said. "Just like a girl's."

"They're *not.*" Darko hit his brother on the arm, and Cairo struck back and almost knocked him over.

"Boys, if you don't stop, I'm not going to take you there at all," Mama said sternly.

They managed to behave themselves as she led them away from the depot across the Adomi Bridge spanning the Volta River. The bridge bounced noticeably up and down with passing traffic.

"Why does it do that?" Darko asked.

"Because it's a suspension bridge," Mama said.

"What's a suspension bridge?"

"What we're walking on," Cairo said obviously.

"Look up, Darko," Mama said more kindly. "See all those cables that go up to the top? That's what's holding the bridge up—suspending it."

He gazed upward. "Oh. I see." After walking a little more, Darko declared, "I *like* this bridge."

"It's the only suspension bridge in Ghana," Cairo informed them. He knew a lot of things.

They stopped for a moment to look out on the expanse of the Volta, with its lush banks and islands of palm and mango trees. The sun reflected off its surface, silhouetting fishermen in their canoes gliding silently and smoothly over the water like spirits.

"Come along," Mama said.

At the other side of the bridge they went off the road and were soon going up an incline thick with vegetation. Birds sang, and bees and butterflies flitted from plant to plant.

"Just a little longer," Mama said over her shoulder.

"I'm thirsty," Darko said.

"Me too," Cairo said. "This hill is steep."

"Here we are," Mama said, breathing heavily. "We can stop here."

"Oh, look!" Cairo said. "You can see the whole river even better than on the bridge."

Darko stood on tiptoes while holding on to his brother.

"Come on, shorty pants," Cairo said, stooping down. "Get on my shoulders."

Cairo lifted him up for the full view.

"The Akosombo Dam is up that way," Mama said, pointing north.

"We learned about it in school," Darko said. "I'm sure I could swim across the river."

"No, you couldn't," Cairo said.

"Yes, I could!"

"No."

"I'll throw you both down this hill in a minute if you don't shut up," Mama said crisply.

Darko and Cairo collapsed in the bushes and laughed till their sides hurt.

It was getting late in the day when they alighted at Ketanu's small bus terminal off the main road and took a footpath in the direction of Auntie Osewa's house.

"Mama?"

"Yes, Darko."

"Do Auntie Osewa and Uncle Kweku have any children?"

"No, they have no children."

"Why?"

"Don't you know?" Cairo said brightly. "She's barren."

"Cairo!" Mama said sharply. "Who told you that?"

"Papa."

"What does *barren* mean?" Darko asked.

"Never mind," Mama replied quickly.

Darko looked up at her walking beside him. Everything about her gave him reassurance and comfort. He knew the touch of her hand and the fresh smell of her skin. He loved to sit on her lap with his head resting against her while he played with the gold necklace she always wore and never removed. The pendant was a little butterfly, because she loved butterflies.

The footpath took them past thatch-roofed huts and tin-roofed houses. Goats, sheep, and stray dogs shared their route.

"Are people *staring* at us?" Darko whispered.

They had indeed attracted some attention from the locals, who could tell they were from out of town, but it was out of interest and not hostility. Mama called out "Good afternoon" here and there. She had always said that politeness toward complete strangers was the highest form of courteousness.

The dwellings began to thin out, and in turn the forest became more evident.

"Look at that place over there," Darko said, pointing in the distance.

It looked particularly different from the other houses they had been seeing. It sat within a grove of trees, a comparatively large abode subdivided into three with a courtyard formed by an encircling wall.

"I wonder what they do in there," Darko said.

"They live there, of course," Cairo said.

"Here we are," Mama said, at length. "That's Auntie's house over there."

It had a rusted tin roof. The walls were marred with gashes and trailing cracks. A crooked screen door hung open with ragged mosquito netting curling off the frame.

Mama announced their arrival. *"Kawkaw-kaw!"*

Seconds later a woman came to the door. Darko could immediately tell she was Auntie Osewa, just from her resemblance to Mama.

"Woizo, woizo!" she cried in welcome.

She kissed Mama and then Darko and Cairo over and over again. She was younger than Mama by a few years and not as tall. Both were pretty, with heart-shaped faces and lovely skin. But to Darko, his auntie was only a close second to his mother. *No* one was prettier than Mama.

"How are you, Sis?" she said to Mama. "It's been so long—*too* long."

Darko felt the silken quality and the musical lilt of Auntie's voice. He had always had a peculiarly heightened sensitivity to speech. Not only did he hear it but he often perceived it as if physically touching it. He had on occasion told Cairo or Mama that he could feel "bumps" in a person's voice, or that it was prickly or wet. They were mystified by this, but Darko could not explain it any better than he could describe the process of sight or smell.

"Come with me," Auntie Osewa said. "Let's go and fetch Uncle Kweku. He went to the farm to get cassava."

They followed her around the small house to the back. The "farm" turned out to be a tiny plot of land. Uncle Kweku was bent over using a hoe to dig up the soil around the cassava plants.

"Kweku!" Auntie called. "Come along, they're here!"

He looked up, put down the hoe, and dusted off his hands as he approached. He was average in build, but his right hand and forearm were disproportionately large from years of wielding farm tools. Close up, Uncle Kweku seemed to Darko quite a bit older than Auntie Osewa, or maybe just more worn down. He was sweating profusely in the heat.

"Woizo," he said, his smile crinkling the corners of his eyes. He gave Mama a hug and lightly patted the boys' heads.

"How was everything? The journey was fine?" His voice was quiet, the texture of a wet loofah sponge lathered with soap.

"It was very good, thank you," Mama said, and Darko and Cairo secretly exchanged amused smiles because she had failed to mention how petrified she was of traveling in tro-tros.

"Come on," Auntie Osewa said. "Let's go inside now."

The house had only two rooms, a table and a stool and chairs in one, a bed in the other. It was hot and airless, and the two windows let in very little sunlight.

They sat down to chat, but Mama and Auntie did most of the talking. Uncle Kweku didn't say much, merely nodding and smiling at intervals.

Darko noticed a bundle of straw in the corner of the room.

"What's that for, Auntie Osewa?"

"I'll show you." She took him by the hand. "Pick a straw out. Any one, it doesn't matter."

He pulled one of the long filaments from the bundle.

"We get these off the tops of elephant grass," Auntie Osewa explained.

"Why's it called elephant grass?"

"Because it can grow as tall as this house."

He looked disbelievingly at her.

"I'm serious," she assured him.

"Really? I've *never* seen grass that tall."

She chuckled. "People use the pieces of straw to make rope and baskets."

"Can *you* do that, Auntie?"

"Of course. Watch."

Auntie bit the end of Darko's straw into two and split it along its length. She twisted each half of the split straw on the other by rolling it against her thigh, and then she combined the two strands to create a length of rope thicker and stronger than the original filament.

"There," she said, smiling. "See how we do it?"

"That's clever."

"You can have this piece. That's my little gift to you."

"Thank you, Auntie." Darko folded it carefully and put it in his pocket.

After that, Darko and Cairo began to get restless as Mama and Auntie Osewa conversed nonstop. Uncle Kweku excused himself for a moment and went outside, which led Cairo to ask Mama if he and Darko could do the same.

"Yes, but stay where Uncle Kweku can see you. And don't get dirty because we're going to eat soon."

There were a few huts nearby, and Uncle was standing next to one of them talking to a neighbor. Noisy weaverbirds were building their upside-down, trumpet-shaped nests in the trees.

"Let's go into the forest," Cairo said.

"But Mama said not to go far," Darko said.

"I know. We won't. Come on."

They passed several large mango trees just beginning to bear the season's fruit and then clusters of pawpaw and banana trees until they were in the forest proper. The ground here was thick with dead leaves and fallen branches, in the midst of which sprouted virgin palms and brand-new ferns and creeping plants. Cocoa trees here and there were not very tall, but the forest giants towered over them and let in only dappled sunlight. Darko loved it. There were no forests like this in Accra.

"Cairo," he said, "do elephants live in the forest?"

"Yes, and if they get you they'll pick you up with their trunks and throw you into the trees."

Darko cackled. "No," he said, but he half believed it.

A millipede crossed in front of his feet, and he knelt down to touch it. It rolled into a tight, impenetrable ball, and its million legs miraculously disappeared.

"Cairo! Darko!"

Mama was calling. They ran back out of the forest and saw her at the front of Auntie Osewa's house looking around for them. Uncle Kweku had gone inside.

"We're coming, Mama!" Cairo yelled.

Dinner was delicious. The soft plantain fufu Osewa had prepared was arranged in a bowl like a row of smooth, rounded pillows too perfect to be disturbed. Steaming, fluffy white yam was piled high on another plate. Chunks of goat meat, *okro,* and aubergine lay in rich palm nut soup like islands in an ocher sea.

As they ate, Mama and Auntie Osewa talked back and forth and laughed together. Uncle Kweku joined in a little, but the conversation still belonged to the women. Cairo and Darko sat next to each other and were mostly quiet, the way children were supposed to be in the presence of their elders, but they slipped each other a few inside jokes and giggled in secret.

A call came from outside the house, "Kawkaw-kaw!"

"Come in," Uncle Kweku said.

A man entered. He looked about Auntie's age—around twenty-four or twenty-five. His physique was thicker than Uncle Kweku's by far. His face was angular, with high cheekbones as sharp as mountain ridges, and his smoky black skin was as smooth as a woman's.

"Woizo," Uncle Kweku said, getting up to shake hands with him.

"How are you, Kweku?"

"Fine, fine." Uncle Kweku was beaming. "Come and eat with us."

"Thank you, my brother. I was passing by and wanted to greet you."

Darko listened to his speech. It had an uneven rhythm. His voice was not exactly rough, but it had cracks in it like the surface of a badly tarred road.

"Woizo, woizo," Auntie Osewa said.

She made space for him at the table and then introduced Mama, Cairo, and Darko. His name was Isaac Kutu. He was one of the local healers. He smiled at everyone. His eyes were dark and deep, and sometimes he looked to the right or left without turning his head.

"Mr. Kutu has been helping us," Auntie Osewa said, looking from her husband to her sister. Darko didn't know what she meant.

"Oh, very fine," Mama said.

"How is Papa Kutu?" Kweku asked.

Isaac looked troubled. "Not well at all."

"What a pity," Osewa said. "I'm so sorry."

"I am doing most of the work now," Isaac said. "He is too tired."

Osewa brought him a bowl of water to wash because he preferred eating in the traditional manner with his fingers—right hand only, left hand tucked securely out of the way. As they talked, it came out that the compound Mama and the boys had spotted on the way in belonged to Isaac's father. Papa Kutu apparently had great prestige as a traditional healer.

The discussion moved to farming and the price of cocoa and other unbearably boring grown-up talk. Darko didn't pay much attention to what they were saying, but for some reason he kept stealing glances at Mr. Kutu.

At one point, Uncle Kweku cracked a rare joke and the grown-ups burst out laughing. Darko didn't get what was so funny, and maybe Mr. Kutu didn't either because his chuckle seemed halfhearted or distracted. As Darko watched him, he saw something.

Mr. Kutu's eyes flashed sideways at Mama, who sat opposite him at an angle. It was very quick—again without turning his head—and Mama returned the look. But Auntie Osewa was quicker still, and she caught that glance between Mama and Mr. Kutu. It all happened in a tiny fraction of time, but Darko captured it like a photograph and he reacted strangely to it. His stomach knotted up and he lost his appetite and stopped eating.

"What's the matter, Darko?" Mama asked him.

"Nothing."

"Eat up then," she said briskly. "You don't waste food, hear me?"

Darko felt Mr. Kutu's gaze shift to him, but he never looked directly at the man again. He couldn't face the eyes.

Evening had arrived when Mr. Kutu left. Uncle Kweku brought out a game of *oware*, and they played by the light of a kerosene lantern. Auntie Osewa went up first against Cairo and was soundly thrashed. Mama challenged Cairo and went down in flames in the same way.

"Okay, let someone else play," Mama said. "Darko, play with your uncle."

Darko squirmed with discomfort. He wasn't terribly good at it—no comparison to his brother.

"Come on," Auntie Osewa said, "don't be so shy."

Darko did better than he'd expected, or maybe Uncle was just being nice to him. The contest between Uncle and Cairo was fierce, and it seemed like it would never end. When Cairo got squashed, he couldn't bear the defeat and challenged his uncle to a rematch. What intrigued Darko was the way Uncle Kweku had come to life with the game.

Laughing at the players' antics, Auntie Osewa got up, said she would be back in a moment, and went outside.

Cairo and his uncle went another round. Auntie had been gone longer than Darko thought she would be. When she returned, Uncle Kweku and Cairo were just about ready to finish up the game.

"Okay, I'm tired now," Uncle said. "Cairo, you're too good for me." He leaned back against the wall with a sigh. "Where did you go, Osewa?"

"I went to set the rabbit traps."

Darko, startled, looked sharply at her. Her voice had changed. It wasn't musical like before, and it shook slightly, like the tremor of a leaf in a brief stir of breeze.

"Those rabbits have been at our crops again," she added. Her eyelids fluttered very slightly. Darko saw that. It wasn't a mannerism. Auntie Osewa did not have such a mannerism. It was something else.

Whether a person's voice felt like silk or sandpaper to Darko, the texture did not vary much. The pitch could change, and so could the volume or loudness, but the way it *felt* to him stayed the same . . . *unless.* Unless the speaker was holding back an emotion or hiding something.

Or lying.

Why would Auntie Osewa lie? Darko's face grew warm, perhaps on her behalf, or maybe because such an embarrassing thought should even have entered his mind. No, she wouldn't lie—not his Auntie Osewa. *Would she?*

6

AT THE END OF THE workday, Dawson went to the CID garage to get his assigned Toyota Corolla and put away his motorbike in a secure spot. Before he went home, he had two stops to make. The first was to his brother, Cairo, who lived with Papa in Osu, a south-central district of Accra.

Once robust and naturally athletic, Cairo had been a paraplegic now for twenty-five years. Whenever he thought about it, Dawson experienced an eerie moment of unreality. He could still barely believe it. The accident had happened in Accra three months after the trip to Ketanu.

Mama sent Cairo to the corner kiosk to buy a tin of sardines. He was starting across the street when she remembered something. "Get some bread too!" she called out through the window. He turned at her voice, walking backward and sideways at the same time.

"What did you say, Mama?"

She screamed as she saw what Cairo never did. The oncoming car hit him hard. He went up over the roof of the car and down the back.

Within seconds, Cairo was paralyzed from the waist down. Yesterday the master of his own body, today immobile and dependent on the care of others. Mentally the anguish was immeasurable, and if anyone suffered as much as or even more than Cairo, it was Mama. Her guilt was a living torment.

Two years after Cairo's accident, she took a trip to Ketanu and never came back. She disappeared into thin air. Perhaps she could not bear ever to look Cairo in the eye again, but perhaps that was not it either. To this day, no one knew, and Dawson wondered about it over and again.

Jacob, Dawson's father, was in his early sixties now, and he was Cairo's sole caretaker except for the occasional member of the extended family who took over when Papa had to go out. Cairo made a little bit of money carving wood face masks—the kind popular with tourists. Dawson always felt guilty about how little he contributed to Cairo's everyday needs. The one rule he kept firm to the point of superstition was he never left town without first stopping by to see his brother. In any case, as if sensing Dawson's imminent departure, Cairo had called him on his mobile that afternoon to ask if he was going to drop in.

The house really wasn't far from CID Headquarters, traffic just made it seem so. Dawson made his slow way down Ring Road to Danquah Circle, where policemen were directing the flow. He got around the circle to the segment of Cantonments Road aptly nicknamed Oxford Street for its density of shops, Internet cafés, glitzy stores and banks, and restaurants serving anything from sushi to pizza. Once he got past Oxford, things lightened up a bit and he arrived at Papa's house and parked the car.

Cairo was in his wheelchair repairing a hole in the wood fence at the back of the house. He looked up and smiled.

"I thought you didn't love me anymore," he joked as they hugged.

"I do love you," Dawson said sheepishly. "I'm sorry. I have no excuse and I'm not going to make one up. How are you? You're looking good today."

In fact, with inactivity, Cairo had become overweight, and bouts of infection had taken their toll. It was often painful for Dawson to visit him, especially when Cairo was having a rough time. It left Dawson with a lump in his chest and moisture in his eyes. His mother gone, his brother maimed—these things still hurt.

Dawson was glad to help Cairo repair the fence. Doing something active with him made the visit easier and more cheerful. They chatted happily. As adults they were intellectually equal and compatible, but Dawson always regarded Cairo as his older, wiser brother and he was comfortable with that.

"Listen," Dawson said at length, "I have to go to Ketanu tomorrow."

"What's going on up there?" Cairo asked.

"Someone's been murdered." Dawson handed him a nail. "Lartey wants me to find out who did it."

"Just like that, eh?"

They laughed.

"So, back to Ketanu after all these years," Cairo said.

"The way it's grown, I probably won't recognize the place."

Leaning forward in his chair, Cairo deftly drove the nail home. "You might even need directions to Auntie Osewa's house."

"You know what I feel sorry about?" Dawson said.

"What?"

"That we've never visited her again over all these years. I mean, she was very good about writing every once in a while, sending us photos of the family, and so on. But after all that, it's not her invitations to visit that's taking me back there, it's official business."

Cairo shrugged. "Why should you or I want to return there? Ketanu took Mama away from us. At least, that's the way I look at it."

"I'd never thought of it quite like that," Dawson said. Cairo had a way of seeing things differently.

Papa emerged from the house into the yard. He acknowledged

Dawson without actually saying hello, and true to form he was short on conversation. He had always been that way, and Dawson could not remember him ever hugging them as children. For sure there had been lots of sharp, angry cuffs to the sides of their heads. Apparently that was the physical contact he had been most comfortable with. After all these years, Dawson didn't understand his father or like him much.

Papa watched while they got the fence patched up.

"Much better," Cairo said, beaming at the finished product.

They talked awhile longer, until it was dusk and the mosquitoes began to attack like dive-bombers.

"I'd better get going," Dawson said, slapping his forearm where he felt a mosquito attempting to steal his blood. "I'll need to get ready for tomorrow."

"Good luck up there, Darko. Be careful, eh?"

He hugged Cairo, but for Papa it was the usual handshake.

It was now fully dark, and Dawson headed for Nima, one of Accra's *zongos*. Nima Road was a vibrant thoroughfare, with Oxford Street's energy but none of its riches. The pedestrians who tramped the dusty roadside crossed the street willy-nilly, weaving in and out of stop-and-go traffic. With long stretches without streetlights, a visitor might find it unnerving, but Nima people knew how to make it work, even if with the narrowest of close shaves.

Dawson parked the Corolla beside a gutter filled with trash. He locked up and then walked several meters along a twisted, uneven walkway to a dense cluster of ramshackle houses. It became pitch-black as he got farther away from the lights of the main road. Good thing he had come armed with his small flashlight. He hopped over a pungent, dark-colored effluent trickling along the ground.

The man he was looking for lived in the back of one of the decrepit dwellings. The door was coming off the hinges, and Dawson didn't knock for fear that it would fall off completely.

"Daramani!" he called.

"Who dey?"

"Dawson."

"Ei! Dawson!"

The door went through several readjustments before Daramani could get it open.

"Hey, *chaley*! How you be?"

Dawson came in, and Daramani gave him a hearty handshake, ending with the customary mutual snap of thumb and third finger.

The room was tiny and cluttered. The single dangling, dim lightbulb was very likely using electricity siphoned off from someone else. In the gloom, Daramani was blacker than charcoal. When he grinned, his white teeth were blinding. He was thin and straight as a bamboo stick, but he could consume more food than two grown men put together. He was from Ghana's Upper East Region, and his mother tongue was Hausa, which Dawson didn't speak. Daramani in turn spoke Ga badly and Ewe not at all, so the two men had fallen into the habit of communicating in Ghanaian-English street slang.

Daramani had been a petty thief with a violent streak. Dawson had taken him down one night three years ago. His room had been full of stolen and contraband items that he had not yet sold, as well as a bountiful stash of weed. Dawson hadn't been able to resist and had pocketed some of it.

Marijuana was Dawson's Achilles' heel. He loved the stuff.

At his hearing, Daramani had stared at Dawson across the stuffy courtroom with a small, knowing smile on his face: *I saw you take the weed.* And Dawson had stared back: *And so what?*

The so-called justice system moving at the snail's pace that it did, Daramani had already served most of his prison time when he was finally sentenced. When he got out, it could hardly be said he was rehabilitated. Once a thief, always a thief. Dawson had picked him up again one night hanging around Makola Market. Daramani had acted quickly to avoid seeing the inside of a jail cell again.

"Dawson, I know people," he'd said. "Make I he'p you, you he'p me."

Half an hour later, Daramani was spilling the beans about a serial burglar working in the affluent airport residential area. As Dawson thanked him, Daramani slipped him some marijuana. It was just a little bit, but the quality was excellent.

"How much?" Dawson asked, avoiding Daramani's eye.

"No, I dey make give you."

Dawson became an ordinary citizen for a few seconds and stuffed some cedi bills in Daramani's pocket despite his flimsy objections. Now it didn't feel so much like bribery and corruption. What a joke. It was illegal any way you sliced it.

Now Daramani opened a large portmanteau on the floor and pulled out a green bottle.

"You wan' schnapps, my brodda?"

"You wan' waste my ear or what?"

Daramani grinned. "Yah, I know. Okay, I dey get dat ting wey you like am."

Daramani produced a small paper bag and held it to Dawson's nose. He nodded. Very good.

"Make same price?" Dawson asked.

"Dis one be too good for ol' price, my brodda."

"Den how much you dey make am?"

When Daramani told him, Dawson laughed and handed the weed back. "You craze."

"How much you pay?"

"Same like before."

"Chaley, you dey touch?" He was asking, *Are you insane?* "No fo' dis one. No you fo' do me like dat."

"Den forget."

"Okay, take am. Reglah price. I dey like you, dass why."

Dawson paid him. He took a couple of steps to the portmanteau and yanked the lid open.

"Wey ting?" Daramani said, surprised.

With the vision of a hawk, Dawson had caught a glimpse of something glittery in there. He reached in through the mess of plates, shoes, and other junk, and pulled out a gold watch. He held it up.

"Where you get am, dis watch?"

Daramani looked at him straight and steady in the eye. *Too* steady. "My friend gimme to make keep am fo' him."

Dawson felt Daramani's voice vibrate like a taut rubber band. "You lie."

"Oh, no, my brodda, I no lie."

Dawson flipped the watch over. It was engraved with someone's name and the inscription "M.D."

Dawson put the watch in his trouser pocket. "I dey make you one more chance. Where you steal am?"

"I tell you I no steal it, brodda."

Dawson kicked a stool out of the way as he closed in on Daramani so quickly the man barely had time to shriek and recoil. Dawson's long fingers encircled his neck, and he slammed Daramani up against the wall.

"Where you steal am?"

Dawson shook him like a doll and rattled his head against the wall.

Daramani screamed. "Abeg, abeg! Dawson, stop, please."

"Tell me now or you go for jail."

"Den where you go get good weed from?" Daramani said, eyes dancing and flashing with mischief. "Deh best weed, remember? And who go tell you where all dese bleddy fockin' criminal dey for Accra?"

Daramani grinned even as Dawson increased the grip on his throat. A smile crept to Dawson's face, and Daramani giggled.

"Steal anything more, I go kill you," Dawson said. "Understand?"

"Oh, chaley, no can kill me. You love me toooo much."

"I no love *you*, I dey love your weed."

He tried to keep a straight face, but at the very moment Daramani snorted, Dawson burst out laughing. He released Daramani from his grip.

"I go find dat person wey you dey steal dis watch and give am back," Dawson said, patting his pocket.

Daramani, chastened, was rubbing his neck. "Okay, my brodda. Sorry, I swear, never again. *Ei,* you break my neck, Dawson."

"Next time I go take your head with it."

Daramani began to giggle again.

7

DAWSON HEARD CONVERSATION COMING from the kitchen, and he knew Christine and Hosiah were already home. He was much less excited about the third voice—that of Gifty, his mother-in-law. Squashing his inner groan and making yet another failed attempt to persuade himself that she was really not so bad, he called out, "Hello!"

"Hi, Dark," Christine said in reply.

Hosiah came running out of the kitchen. "Daddy, Daddy!"

He stopped where he was, and Dawson smiled as the boy prepared to perform the customary welcoming exercise.

"Okay," Dawson said. "Ready?"

The boy leaned forward in the on-your-mark position, one leg forward and the other back. "Yah, Daddy, I'm ready."

"Set . . . *go!*"

Hosiah exploded into a run, his little feet pounding the floor with miniaturized power. Close to Dawson, he launched himself as high and far as he could into his father's waiting arms.

"Oh, that was a good one!" Dawson said.

"Yes!" Hosiah said, laughing. "I jumped higher than yesterday, didn't I, Daddy?"

"You certainly did. Getting better and better at it."

But in fact Hosiah was breathing more heavily than a boy of his age should for such a short burst of energy. Dawson kissed his son's perfectly round head. He had bright, shining eyes and a smile that could soften even the hardest heart.

In the kitchen, Christine and Gifty were at the table sharing a beer. Dawson put Hosiah down.

"Hi, sweetheart," he said, kissing Christine on the cheek. He smiled the best he could at Gifty. "Hello, Mama."

He kissed her with barely a touch of the lips.

"Hosiah had a nice day at Granny's, didn't you, Hosiah?" Gifty said without so much as returning the greeting.

"Yes, Granny."

"Where did Granny take you?"

"To the new zoo!" Hosiah said.

Dawson's jaw tensed, a tic matching the stab of irritation. He had planned to take his son to the brand-new and improved zoo this weekend, and Gifty knew that. She simply had to be one up on him.

"Really?" Dawson said. "And what did you see at the zoo?"

"Chimpanzees and monkeys and birds. And there was a leopard and a turtle this big." He spread his arms wide.

"Tortoise, Hosiah," Gifty corrected him in a tone that irked Dawson from his spine to his toes. He glanced at his wife, who was thirty-two, and at his mother-in-law, who was sixty, and wondered how they could look so alike yet be so dissimilar in character. Christine had inherited her mother's rich, dark skin, smooth and flawless as the petals of a black orchid. Her forehead was high, as were her lovely cheekbones, her nose straight yet flared, and her lips were rich. She never wore makeup except for the odd social gathering, and she had never relaxed her hair the way many Ghanaian women did to make it "straight."

Hosiah went back to playing on the floor with a model fire engine while Dawson looked in the fridge for something to drink.

"No more Malta?" he said, poking around.

Malta Guinness, Dawson's favorite drink, was nonalcoholic and made with malt, hops, barley, and too much sugar.

"Oh, Malta," Christine said. "I knew there was something I forgot. Sorry, Dark. I'll get some tomorrow."

"No worries."

He settled for a ginger ale as a distant second choice and sat down to drink noisily from the bottle. He knew that got on Gifty's nerves, so he did it deliberately and with gusto. She sent him one of her sharp looks, which he ignored.

"How was work?" Christine asked him.

He didn't want to talk about Ketanu with Gifty present, so he simply shrugged and gave the standard male answer, "Same ol' thing."

"Time for your bath, Hosiah," Christine said, clapping her hands briskly. "Go and get your clothes off and call Mama when you're ready."

"Okay. Can I have a bubble bath with plenty bubbles?"

"Yes, but we won't spend too long, all right?"

"Okay."

Hosiah scampered out of the kitchen.

"Did he get tired walking around the zoo?" Dawson asked Gifty.

"He—"

"Because if I'd been there, I'd've carried him on my shoulders when he got out of breath."

"He was fine," Gifty said with a tense smile. "You know I wouldn't do anything to harm him."

"Not what I'm saying," Darko returned. "I'm saying as his condition gets worse, we have to be careful."

"I realize that. Darko, I care about Hosiah as much as you."

"Of course, Mama," Christine came in just before Dawson could. "No one denies that."

"Thank you, love," Gifty said, looking satisfied. "So now, here is my question: How are the savings going for the operation?"

Darko shook his head. "It's a lot of money."

"And meanwhile he's getting worse," Gifty said pointedly.

"We realize that," Dawson said icily.

"I just want to know what you're doing," she said without flinching, "besides sitting around waiting. Waiting never gets you very far, you know?"

Dawson gritted his teeth and tapped his bottle on the table a couple of times. He looked at Christine for inspiration, anything to stop him from wringing her mother's neck.

"Mama—" Christine started.

"I'm not trying to cause trouble," Gifty said quickly. "I sincerely want to help, and I mean that from the bottom of my heart. I've been thinking about it a lot, and I have a suggestion I'd like the two of you to seriously consider."

Dawson looked at her sideways, skeptical and suspicious.

"What's that, Mama?" Christine said.

"I think we should take Hosiah to my healer."

"What healer?" Dawson said sharply.

"Augustus Ayitey. He's a famous traditional practitioner. He even works with the doctors at Korle-Bu. He gives me medicine for my arthritis, and he's healed many people with heart problems."

"Hosiah needs surgery," Dawson said curtly.

"But just listen to what I'm saying, Darko," Gifty said. "Hear me out, for once. Maybe Hosiah won't need surgery after he sees Mr. Ayitey."

"How would he know what Hosiah needs or doesn't need?"

Christine was looking back and forth between her husband and her mother.

"Look," Dawson said, "traditional healers might have some good herbal medicines for problems like your arthritis, but this is an actual physical hole in Hosiah's heart."

Gifty recoiled. "Such a horrible way to put it. Hole in his heart. Awful."

"What do you want me to say? That's what it's called—at least in layman's language."

Gifty turned her palms upward and gesticulated. "We are trapped. National Health will *not* pay for this. None of us is rich. We just don't have the money, plain and simple. And this dreamy idea that someday you're going to save up to that level—why, Darko, by the time that day comes around, if ever, Hosiah may be in *terrible* shape. Don't you see what I'm saying? My goodness, you barely have any *choice* but to try an alternative. You *owe* it to Hosiah. I know you love him. Now act on it."

Dawson closed his eyes, his jaw clasping and unclasping as he rubbed his left palm hard with his right thumb. He hated this. He hated the bind they were in, hated his mother-in-law pointing it out so eloquently, hated her intrusion . . .

"Mama, I'm ready!" Hosiah yelled from the bedroom.

"I'm coming, Hosiah." Christine got up, and so abruptly did her mother.

"I have to go," she said. "The taxi is waiting."

Dawson smiled to himself, knowing the real reason was that Gifty would rather not be left alone with him.

"Bye, Darko," Gifty said. "Consider my idea, okay?"

He didn't answer. Christine saw her to the taxi and returned once her mother had left. She squeezed Dawson's shoulder.

"She doesn't mean any harm," she said. "She just has her beliefs. She's of a different generation."

"And a different planet," Dawson muttered sourly.

Christine gave him a soft but emphatic whack on the back of his head.

"Ouch." He rubbed his scalp. "That hurt."

"Apologize."

"Okay, sorry."

Hosiah appeared in the kitchen door naked as the day he was born.

"I'm ready, Mama!"

She laughed. "Come on, you rascal."

She scooped him up under her arm, and he squealed with laughter and kicked his legs like a pair of drumsticks.

"Still true, though," Dawson called after her. He loved having the last word. "Definitely from another planet."

8

ONCE HOSIAH HAD GONE to bed, Dawson and Christine sat down to dinner and he broke the news to her.

"What?" She dropped her fork. "*Keṭanu. Why does it have to be you?*"

"None of the other guys speak Ewe."

"Wait a minute," Christine said fiercely. "Ketanu is in the Volta Region. Don't they have their own CID people in Ho?"

"Minister of Health personally called Chief Super and told him he wants an Accra detective to go up." Dawson shrugged and chortled. "Apparently the honorable minister thinks we're superior."

Christine let her breath out like steam escaping a valve. "How long do you think you'll be there?"

"Two weeks, maybe? It could be more. I don't know how complicated this case is going to be."

"Can't you refuse to go?"

"Sure, and Lartey sack me on the spot? Right now's no time to be out of work."

She frowned. "I don't like that man."

"I know. You've made it plain."

"A murder in Ketanu?" Christine said, ignoring his dry comment. "Isn't that rare in a place like that?"

"Has to be."

Christine seemed lost in thought for a moment.

"What you thinking?" Dawson asked.

"Just wondering. Dark, do you think . . . do you think this is a chance for you to reinvestigate what happened to your mother? She went to Ketanu and never came back, right? Maybe you might come across a missed clue or something. You know what I mean?"

"I do. And you read my mind."

"You mean you'll look into it?" Christine said eagerly.

"Yes, I will. If that last dream I had means anything, I *have* to do it."

Dawson packed a small suitcase and put it in the trunk of the Corolla along with a cricket bat, his only weapon. Detectives in Ghana did not carry firearms.

He turned in and slept poorly, thrashing about and dreaming he was chasing Gifty around Ketanu's village square waving a butcher's knife while Hosiah trailed behind begging him to slow down, panting and wheezing until he fell to the ground with exhaustion.

His eyes popped open, and he sat up sucking air into his chest. Yet another nightmare. Sometimes they recurred night after night for weeks. Other times they left him alone to sleep in peace. He got out of bed. Christine didn't wake up. She could sleep through a thunderstorm, whereas the smallest nocturnal murmur from Hosiah's room would have Dawson out of bed like a bullet out the barrel.

He went to the kitchen for a drink of water, then moved to the sitting room and sat in an armchair with his head resting in the palm of his right hand. Dawson was an insomniac just like his mother had been. For her, it had started after Cairo's accident.

Please God, turn back the clock and let me do everything over.

That had been Mama's prayer. She could shake off neither the replaying of the accident in her mind nor the torture of self-blame. She never again slept a restful night. Darko often heard her, and occasionally Papa, tending to Cairo—turning him in bed, giving him sips of water, keeping him clean. One night Darko padded after Mama and found her in the sitting room silhouetted against the moonlit window with her head bowed in her hands like a collapsed stalk of maize.

She was so still it frightened him.

"Mama?"

She jumped. "Darko. What are you doing up?"

He came to her. "I couldn't sleep. Are you sick, Mama?"

"No, my love. I'm all right." She lifted him onto her lap. "Sometimes we grown-ups think too much at night."

"You're thinking about Cairo, aren't you?"

"Yes," she said. Her tears moistened his neck.

"Mama?"

"Yes, Darko."

"You take care of Cairo and I'll take care of you, okay?"

She kissed him. "All right, sweetie. Thank you."

He suddenly had an idea. "I'm going to make you feel better right now. Wait here, okay?"

He skipped off her lap and trotted to his room. Mama had given him an eight-note *kalimba* for his last birthday. It was a small handheld wood box mounted with long metal strips of different lengths. Plucking them with fingers and thumb produced harplike tones that lingered beautifully and died out slowly. He had tinkered with it a little bit, but he was no master yet. He went back to the sitting room with kalimba in hand, switched the table lamp on, and hopped onto Mama's lap again.

"I'm going to play you a tune. Ready?"

She was delighted and charmed. "Yes, I'm ready."

He had a false start. "No, wait, wait."

He tried again, and this time the soft notes more or less made out "Twinkle, Twinkle Little Star."

He remembered that night clear as crystal and thought of it as the closest of moments with Mama. It was about six months afterward that Auntie Osewa wrote with wonderful news. After years of being barren, she had become pregnant. She asked Mama and all the family to pray that the pregnancy would carry through successfully and bring a child into the world, preferably a son.

After another seven months, collective prayers were apparently answered in the affirmative. Osewa had given birth to a baby boy they had named Alifoe. She invited Mama up for the celebrations. Mama hesitated at first, worried about leaving Cairo, but Papa urged her to go. Cairo had been doing well at the time. Papa would stay home with him and Darko. It would only be for two or three days.

So Mama left for Ketanu and stayed for five days with Auntie Osewa, Uncle Kweku, and Alifoe, who was a beautiful and healthy baby. When Mama returned home to Accra, she told stories of how every family member loved to hold and cuddle him.

Mama must have enjoyed her visit tremendously, because three months later she went back to Ketanu. Six days passed, eight, and then ten. Mama didn't return. Darko and Cairo began to fret.

"When is Mama coming home?"

"Soon," Papa replied, which was meaningless.

After another two days, however, Papa was as worried as his two sons were. Like most people in Ketanu, Auntie Osewa and Uncle Kweku did not have a phone, and so Papa had no choice but to take a trip up. He asked one of his two sisters to stay with the boys while he was gone.

When he got to Ketanu, Auntie Osewa and Uncle Kweku warmly welcomed him but wondered why he hadn't come with Beatrice.

"What?" Papa said. "Beatrice is not here with you?"

Auntie Osewa and Uncle Kweku were dumbstruck. "She was here for only four days," they said. Osewa told Papa she had accompanied Beatrice to the tro-tro stop to say good-bye to her when she was leaving.

"Did she tell you for certain that she was headed for Accra?" Papa asked.

"But of course," Auntie Osewa said. "Where else would she be going?"

They stood staring at each other in astonishment. Somewhere between Ketanu and Accra, Mama had disappeared.

9

ANUM BINEY, CHIEF PHYSICIAN at the Volta River Authority Hospital, could perform any operation, from an appendectomy to a facial reconstruction. He had to. The hospital served the entire population within a hundred-mile radius. Dr. Biney had the help of residents from the medical schools in Accra and Kumasi, but in truth he was on call twenty-four hours a day, seven days a week, 365 days a year.

And over the years he had become known for his skill at autopsies, much of it self-taught. With only about twelve pathologists available for the entire country, most of them at Korle-Bu, it was only natural Dr. Biney had become a much-sought-after postmortem guru. That would explain why he had a constant backlog of autopsy cases. He had added on an extra Wednesday evening to try to catch up.

The single-story cream-and-mahogany buildings of the hospital were nestled among trees, green lawns, and clipped hedges. Its sections—the male and female surgical wards, the children's ward, and so on—were connected by long open verandas. This was no scruffy place fallen on hard times. Taking good care of it was revenue from the Akosombo hydroelectric dam on the Volta River, just a few kilometers away.

Dr. Biney crossed the expanse of tended grass in front of the morgue, the only building at the hospital not connected to the rest. Perhaps logically so: the wards were for the living, the morgue for the dead. Biney was weary, having been up practically the whole night with various calls, including one for a victim of a vehicle crash. He wore exhaustion like his clothes—he was aware of it, but he didn't focus on it.

The morning was working up to the sweltering day it would become, and already the air was close on the skin like a cloak. Dr. Biney walked past the standby generators that ensured there would never be a failure of refrigeration in the morgue should there be a power cut. True, the Akosombo Dam was near, but blackouts did occur.

He unlocked the rear door and entered the mercifully air-conditioned morgue, first through the anteroom, where the bodies were washed, and then to the autopsy room itself. There were two postmortem tables. On busy days, every day really, Biney would finish one case and go almost immediately to the second table for the next.

He looked around for a moment, thinking he really must get the missing tiles on the wall replaced and get rid of that old defunct table in the corner that they needed to cart away somewhere.

He went looking for Obodai, the attendant, and found him scrubbing down the stone floor in front of the gleaming bank of aluminum storage drawers. There were twenty of them in columns of four. They were at full capacity and unable to keep up with the number of bodies arriving weekly. It was time to add some more drawers.

"Morning, Obodai."

Obodai stopped his work and practically stood at attention.

"Good morning, sir." He gave an imperceptible bow, a gesture so slight one might fail to spot it, but it was there—a show of eternal deference to his boss. Obodai had been working at the morgue for ages. He was wizened and wiry, loyal and unflappable. Whether you needed his assistance at five in the morning or eleven at night, he would be there. He was always the first to arrive and the last to leave.

"We'll be doing the case of the young woman from Volta Region," Dr. Biney said. "First priority."

"Very good, sir. When do you wish to start, sir?"

"We're waiting for a detective from Accra. He'll be witnessing. Should be here soon."

"Very good, sir. Everything will be ready."

Approaching Akosombo, Dawson slowed down at the security gate, but the guards waved him on. They had an instinct about who was legitimate and who was not.

Just a little way past the gate was the Volta River Authority Hospital. Dawson parked and went in through an open-walled reception area. About fifteen patients, some with children, were waiting to be called in for treatment. As Dawson paused, wondering where Dr. Biney's office was, a young woman with a brilliant smile and expensively braided hair approached him.

"Good morning, sir," he said. "Are you Detective Inspector Dawson?"

"Good morning. Yes, that's me."

"Welcome to the VRA Hospital, sir."

Dawson shook hands with her as she introduced herself as Victoria, Dr. Biney's administrative assistant.

"He is expecting you," she said warmly. "Please come this way. Did you have a safe trip up from Accra?"

He followed Victoria through a double door into the skylit, air-conditioned corridor within. Dr. Biney's office was the third on the left, and his assistant showed Dawson in.

"Dr. Biney, Detective Inspector Dawson has arrived."

As always in new surroundings, Dawson took a quick snapshot of the room. A full-scale model human skeleton in the far corner, bookshelf bursting with medical texts and journals, stethoscope and ophthalmoscope on the desk, piles of folders and papers everywhere, including on the floor. An outgrown office space of a busy man with too much to do and too little time in which to do it.

Biney rose from his desk. "D.I. Dawson, welcome!"

He was a hearty man with a voice to match, standing at least six two. He was taller than Dawson and heavier by far. He had a neatly cropped head of hair and an amazing salt-and-pepper mustache that sprouted straight out to the sides. When they shook hands, Biney's palm dwarfed Dawson's.

"Thank you for coming, Mr. Dawson. I trust the journey was fine?"

"Excellent, thank you, Doctor."

"Can we get you anything? Some refreshment, maybe?"

"No, thank you. I'm okay for now."

"Come along, then. Shall we proceed to the morgue?"

They suited up—gown, apron, gloves, face shield, and shoe covers—and moved on into the autopsy room. Dawson had somehow imagined a long row of tables, but there were only two, and upon one of them lay the body of a young woman. *Must be Gladys Mensah.*

Arranging a tray of instruments nearby was a man in a heavy-duty apron and thick, knee-high rubber boots.

Dr. Biney introduced him. "Obodai is my most trusted assistant, and without him, this place could not run."

Obodai laughed bashfully and offered a feeble denial, but Dawson had no doubt that Dr. Biney's declaration was true.

"Are we ready to go?" Biney said.

"We are ready, sir," Obodai said.

Dr. Biney turned to the body, standing to its right side as a doctor always does. Obodai stood at the head, near the sink, and Dawson took his position on the left. He looked down at the body. A courier had delivered the police file last night, complete with photographs of the body at the crime scene, but the Gladys Mensah now in front of him looked waxy and strangely unreal. He could tell she had been lovely alive, and he was trying to imagine her speaking, moving, animated.

Dawson lightly touched Gladys's arm. "So cold," he murmured. "Once she was warm and breathing."

It was what he could never quite get his mind around—not just how complex life was, but why it was so easy for life to leave a person once so complex.

"Only twenty-two years old," Biney said gently. "It seems a shame, doesn't it, Detective Inspector Dawson?"

"It does."

Biney took a deep breath and let out a sigh as if to say, *Be that as it may, we have work to do*. He first brought his face closer to Gladys and examined her slowly from head to toe. He did not touch her yet.

"In medical school we were always taught to listen, look, and *then* feel a patient," he said. "It's no different dealing with a dead person."

Dawson watched him, trying at the same time to spot anything on Gladys's body that might be significant. She was lean, with perfectly smooth skin that had likely been the color of milk chocolate before death had darkened her.

"Anything catch your eye, Mr. Dawson?"

"Not yet."

"Measurements, Obodai?" Biney said.

"She weighs fifty-two kilos, and measures one hundred and seventy-three centimeters long, sir."

"Mm-hm. Thank you. No stab or puncture wounds that I can see so far. Nor contusions, or ecchymoses. No evidence for fractures of the skull or long bones . . ." He checked her fingers. "She kept her nails short—they look clean, but get clippings later, Obodai, would you?"

"Very good, sir."

"Roll her up?"

Obodai smoothly and expertly turned Gladys's body on its side so Biney could look at her back.

"Ah, Inspector Dawson, take a look. Here we see blanching at the shoulders and buttocks, indicating that she was lying on her back for some time postmortem. The weight of her body compresses the blood vessels in the areas in contact with the ground, preventing accumulation of blood there. I still see no wounds of any kind. The posterior scalp's clear of contusions or hematomas. Interesting."

"Let her back down, Doctor?" Obodai said.

"Yes, please. And we'll put her on the head block now and open the skull."

Obodai lifted the body at the shoulders and slid the wooden block underneath it. As he did that and Gladys's neck became slightly more exposed, Biney seemed to notice something. He went closer and peered at her chin.

Dawson followed his lead. "What do you see, Dr. Biney?"

"It looks like an abrasion," he said, with a tinge of excitement in his voice. "I've seen it before, in another case. The victim is being strangled, she lowers her chin to protect her neck and gets a bruise from the assailant's hands. Strangling someone is not as easy as people think."

"*Strangling,*" Dawson echoed.

"Indeed. Change of plan, Obodai."

"Dissect the neck, sir?"

"Yes, let's postpone the skull for the moment."

"Very good. Your scalpel, sir."

Dr. Biney began at Gladys's chin and made a long, clean incision straight down the middle to the sternal notch. There was very little subcutaneous fat, and the muscle layer popped into view after minimal dissection.

"Do I see subtle hemorrhages in the soft tissues around the right sternomastoid," Biney said, "or do my eyes deceive? I don't want to be premature, but I think we may have something here."

He continued carefully with short, precise incisions with the scalpel, peeling away the layers covering the larynx.

"Ah."

"What is it, Dr. Biney?"

"Fractured thyroid cartilage. Gracious. Do you see it, Inspector Dawson? Let me show you. This is the thyroid cartilage. It looks like a roof we're viewing from above. This is one side of the roof sloping up, this is the other, and where they meet is the prominence everyone knows as the Adam's apple. We can't see them, but the vocal cords are behind the cartilage—underneath the roof, so to speak. Got it?"

"Got it."

"Look at the left side of the cartilage here. It looks smooth. When I poke it, it moves in one piece. Now look at the right. I depress it firmly, and what happens?"

"It bends in the middle."

"Yes. Why?"

"Because it's cracked."

"Ten points. There you have it. Fracture of the thyroid cartilage."

"Besides strangulation, is there any other possible cause of a thyroid cartilage fracture?"

"There are—such as falling against something and striking the front of the neck," Biney said. "The armrest of a chair, for instance. Another would be a karate chop to the neck. But fractures of the larynx in circumstances like this mostly result from strangulation, and my finding of perilaryngeal focal hemorrhage—in other words, bruising—is consistent with this. I wonder if the hyoid bone was damaged as well."

He returned to Gladys's neck and moved upward from the thyroid cartilage to the apex of the throat.

"Dissecting around the hyoid bone now," he said. "It's a much harder structure to fracture because it's protected behind the lower jaw."

A few minutes later, Dr. Biney said, "It's intact. No fracture. *But,* there's swelling and hemorrhage around it. Again, consistent with considerable force applied to the neck over some sustained period."

Dawson gazed at Dr. Biney, and their eyes met. It was, quite frankly, breathtaking.

"What you're saying is—"

"That's exactly what I'm saying, Mr. Dawson. In the case of Gladys Mensah, the cause of death is asphyxiation by strangulation. Manner of death is homicide."

10

Victoria typed up the official autopsy report in no time at all and gave Dawson a copy.

"Would you like to meet my wife and have some lunch before you set off to Ho?" Dr. Biney suggested as he saw Dawson out. "We have a place on the water and a floating gazebo on the river, and my wife makes an exquisite grilled tilapia."

It was certainly tempting, but Dawson declined with thanks. "I should get to Ho without delay," he explained.

"Very well—perhaps another time. You are always welcome."

They exchanged calling cards as they continued on to Dawson's car.

Just as he was about to open the door, Dawson thought of something. "You know a lot of people, Dr. Biney. Would you mind taking a look at this?"

He dug into his pocket and fished out the gold watch he had confiscated from Daramani. "Stolen item, seems it belongs to a doctor. Do you know this name?"

Biney looked at the engraving on the back plate. "Good gracious," he said in surprise. "I most certainly do know this fellow. He and I were classmates in med school and we're still in touch."

"Any idea where he lives or works?"

"In Accra. As a matter of fact, I have to be in Accra in two weeks and I can see to it personally that he gets it back—if that's okay with you, that is."

"It's a million times better than okay. A huge relief, really—one less thing to do."

"Consider it done, then."

"Thank you, Doctor. For everything."

"You're most welcome, Inspector Dawson. If there's anything I can help you with, please don't hesitate to call. Good luck, and drive safely."

To get to Ketanu from Akosombo, Dawson went south again to Atimpoku and took the Adomi Bridge across the Volta River. He fiddled with the radio dial until he found a station playing hip-life music—something to keep him company for the hour-long journey. Much of that time was taken up by slowing at police checkpoints. Togo, Ghana's neighboring country, was not far away, and as Dawson knew only too well, the Volta Region was a hub for illicit drugs going back and forth across the border.

No drug-sniffing dogs at the checkpoints, thank goodness. Dawson had a little marijuana on him, and though his CID badge would get him easily past the human police, nosy canines were another matter altogether.

Traffic was light up to Ketanu. Along the road, pedestrians trudged between one town and the next, and not for the first time, Dawson marveled at the stamina of even small children carrying firewood or buckets of water on their heads.

By the time he reached Juapong, he was good and hungry and kept thinking about Dr. Biney's alluring invitation to dine on grilled tilapia. Dawson would have to settle for something gastronomically simpler, and he pulled over to buy golden-roasted plantain and groundnuts from a roadside trader.

On the way again, Dawson noticed how the vegetation began to change from open bush with isolated skyscraper trees to denser semi-deciduous forest, but that in turn gave way to buildings as Dawson approached Ketanu. He passed a sign announcing YOU ARE ENTERING KETANU and slowed down over the brain-rattling speed strips.

If Ketanu had been an impressionist painting, it would have been dots and daubs of tan and brown. Buildings were a cream color or darker, and the rusted tin roofs exactly matched the color of the ground. Tro-tros and taxis plied the streets, and shops and trading kiosks lined the roadside with entertaining appellations like Nothing but Prayer Electrical Goods and the God Is Great Hair Clinic. Dawson loved these names.

He was looking for something recognizable from long ago, but nothing familiar had struck him so far. Even the road he was on was newly constructed and not the same one he had traveled with Mama and Cairo.

Dawson was to meet an Inspector Fiti at the police station. The directions were in his head. He turned right onto a fitfully paved road, drove slowly up a small incline, and pulled up to a small, stand-alone square building painted the signature dark blue with the words GHANA POLICE SERVICE—KETANU across the top in white.

Before the entrance itself, there was a small covered veranda, where three people were seated on a wooden bench. As he walked in, Dawson saw a counter at the front with space to fit no more than two people behind it. To his left, down a couple of steps, were two small jail cells, and to his right was an office whose door was shut.

Two constables in the standard GPS gray-and-black camouflage-like uniform were behind the counter doing some paperwork. The younger, round-faced one, who looked to be in his mid-twenties, looked up inquiringly.

"Good afternoon, sir. You are welcome."

"Good afternoon. I'm Detective Inspector Dawson, Accra CID."

The constable stood up even straighter.

"Yes, sir, Inspector Dawson, sir. I'm Constable Gyamfi." They shook hands. "That is Constable Bubo over there."

"Good afternoon, sir," Bubo said, standing up with an acknowledging nod.

"I will let Inspector Fiti know you are here, sir," Gyamfi said, coming around from behind the counter. He knocked on the closed office door, opened it, and put his head in.

"Please, sir, Detective Inspector Dawson from Accra is here."

"Who?" Dawson heard the inspector say.

"D.I. Dawson, sir. From CID, sir."

"From *Accra,* you say?"

"Yes, sir."

There was silence for a moment. The door opened fully, and Inspector Fiti emerged. He was probably in his late forties, pointy-faced with a thick neck and sweat rings at the armpits of his olive shirt, which was coming undone from underneath his paunch. He seemed both puzzled and wary as he approached Dawson.

"Good afternoon, Detective Inspector," he said. "Can I do anything for you?" His voice was coarse and sticky, like freshly laid asphalt.

Now it was Dawson who was puzzled. "I'm here regarding the murder case? Gladys Mensah?"

Fiti looked blank. "I was expecting someone from Ho."

"I don't know much about that part," Dawson said. "All I was told by my chief super was that the minister of health wanted Accra CID to be in charge."

"Who is your chief superintendent?"

"Theophilus Lartey."

"Oh, yes. I know him."

A trim, clean-shaven, baby-faced man had been hovering behind Fiti in the doorway of the office, but now he approached Dawson.

"Welcome, Detective Inspector," he said, shaking hands. His voice was gentle but resilient, like the sensation of soft, wet grass on bare feet, and his inflection hinted at some significant stay in England. "I'm Timothy Sowah, program director of the Health Service AIDS program in the Volta Region. Gladys Mensah was doing volunteer work with us. She was the best. These past three days have been horrendous."

"Excuse me one minute," Inspector Fiti said brusquely, returning to his office and shutting the door.

"He doesn't seem very happy I'm here," Dawson said, lowering his voice.

Timothy made a face. "No, he doesn't."

Seconds later they could hear Fiti on the phone asking someone at the Ho station what was going on.

"Can I have a word with you outside?" Timothy said to Dawson.

They stepped out.

"Don't let this on to Inspector Fiti," Timothy said, "but I had a lot to do with your being here instead of the chap from Ho."

Dawson was surprised. "You did?"

"Yes. Look, I was worried. I wanted to be sure we got someone really good on the case. I know the CID chap stationed at Ho, and I'm sorry, I'm not impressed. I couldn't take the risk. I really want this murder solved. So I called the minister, and he agreed to have Accra handle it. So here you are. Trouble is, I'm sure everyone thought everyone *else* was going to inform Inspector Fiti, and so it ended up no one did. I apologize if I've caused a bit of an incident."

"It's all right," Dawson said. "At least now I'm clear how it happened."

"Let's go back inside."

Inspector Fiti had emerged from his office again. "Accra CID is always doing this," he said bitterly. "They think we can't handle our own affairs."

"I'm sorry to have caught you unawares, Inspector," Dawson said. "I'm here to help, that's all."

Fiti heaved a sigh. "Okay. Anyway, you can come into my office."

It was small and jumbled, as untidy as Inspector Fiti himself. Tilting stacks of papers on the desk were gathering dust, and there was more chaos on the floor. There were only two chairs, and Fiti asked Constable Gyamfi to bring in a third. It was hot and airless in the room despite the whirring ceiling fan. Squashed close to the other two men with the door shut, Dawson felt suffocated.

His first order of business was to let Sowah and the inspector know the latest, and he told them about the autopsy on Gladys.

"*Strangled,*" Timothy said, looking stunned. "Strangled, my God."

"Do you have the autopsy report?" Inspector Fiti asked.

"Yes, I do," Dawson said, handing it over to Fiti, who read it in silence.

"I see," he said curtly when he was done. "I would like to make a copy."

"Of course," Dawson said.

Fiti got up and removed some papers from the top of a small photocopy machine.

"Can you give me your version of the chronology of the events around Gladys Mensah's death, Inspector?" Dawson asked as Fiti began to copy the first page.

"Chronology," Fiti said slowly, as if considering the nuances of the word.

"When the body was found and so on."

"Yes, I know what the word *chronology* means," Fiti said.

"I apologize, Inspector."

"Today is Tuesday. Gladys went to Bedome on last Friday in the afternoon. She was killed sometime during the evening or night of Friday. On Saturday morning, Gladys's brother Charles came to report her missing, and on the same morning, Efia, a woman from Bedome, found her body. Crime scene unit came in the afternoon and took their photographs and all those things, and then the body was taken to the VRA morgue on Saturday night to await the postmortem."

"Did the crime scene guys say when they'd be ready with their report?"

"They said next week," Fiti replied with a shrug. "They always say next week. It could be next year."

"You're right," Dawson agreed. "Back to Gladys, though. What was she doing in Bedome?"

"She was a volunteer with the GHS AIDS outreach program," Timothy explained. "We provide voluntary counseling and testing—VCT—in both urban and rural areas, and we have a limited supply of antiretroviral medicines to dispense to HIV-positive people, especially for pregnant women."

"You use a lot of volunteers?"

"A few. We have an arrangement with the medical schools. Every year they provide us with three or four medical students who do their electives with us. Gladys was one of them. Ketanu and Bedome were on our VCT list this year, and she picked those."

"Was she the only volunteer for the two towns?"

"Yes."

"Might there be anyone in Ketanu or Bedome who didn't like what Gladys was doing?"

Timothy took a breath. "Unfortunately, yes. She clashed badly with Bedome's head priest—name's Togbe Adzima—over this trokosi business. Have you heard about it, Inspector Dawson? These women they call trokosi? Supposedly wives of the gods serving at a shrine as penance for a family crime? They're often brought to the shrine as girls as young as nine, and once they reach puberty, the fetish priests begin to have sex with them."

"I thought all that had been outlawed."

"Technically, yes. There's a law on the books, but not a single person has ever been arrested in connection with trokosi."

"Why is that, exactly?"

"Good propaganda is one reason, if not the only one. The fetish priests—who, by the way, don't like being referred to that way—insist trokosi is an age-old tradition that should be respected. And if anyone tries to eradicate it, they say, the gods will be angered and take revenge in some way. That scares away even the police. And then there's AfriKulture."

"Afri-who?"

"AfriKulture. It's an organization dedicated to saving aspects of Ghanaian culture and tradition that it claims are under attack from the

Western world, trokosi being one of them. I'm loath to admit it, but their campaign is gaining strength. You can hardly get to a shrine without going through AfriKulture."

"What does AfriKulture say about the girls taken into the shrine?"

"That they're privileged young women who will learn the ways of morality. They deny that any of them are cast into perpetual servitude."

"I take it you think that's a load of nonsense."

"Yes, I do. Look, this thing might have worked centuries ago, but it doesn't fit with modern times. I think these so-called priests are con artists enslaving young women under the guise of a so-called tradition."

"Togbe Adzima being one of these con artists, in your opinion."

Timothy nodded vigorously. "Without a doubt. Gladys felt the same way."

"She confronted Adzima?"

"Not just confronted. She went head-to-head with him. I told her she had to tone it down, but she wouldn't. She kept telling him she was going to bring down the hand of the law on him, and he kept invoking the power of the gods against her. Told her she would be struck down by them if she continued in that fashion."

"And now she's been struck down," Dawson said.

"Yes," Timothy said bitterly. "It really gets to me."

"At any rate, it would seem to make Adzima a suspect. What do you think, Inspector Fiti?"

"I think Togbe Adzima believes in his gods," Fiti replied. "He really would trust them to destroy Gladys on their own power, and so I think he would leave it for the gods to do and not kill her himself."

Interesting point, Dawson thought.

"The one I really suspect is Samuel Boateng," Fiti went on.

"Who is he?" Dawson asked.

"This boy Samuel—he was constantly pestering Gladys to be his girlfriend and, according to Charles Mensah, some farmers saw him talking to her near the forest the last evening she was seen alive."

"You say 'boy.' How old is Samuel Boateng?"

"He's nineteen, something like that."

"You've questioned him?"

"Yes, and I'm going to arrest him. I believe he became very angry that Gladys was rejecting him and he killed her soon after he was spotted with her that evening."

Dawson nodded. "I see. What about Gladys's family members?"

"All of them loved Gladys," Fiti said, "and they were proud of her because she was going to be a doctor. Only one thing—there is some bad talk about her aunt Elizabeth. Some people say she killed Gladys using witchcraft."

"Witchcraft," Dawson echoed in surprise. "Why do they think that?"

"She's a widow," Fiti said, "she has no children, she's an older woman, and she makes money. Those things make people suspect her."

"The profile of a witch, so to speak. Did she have a motive?"

"Witches don't need any motive," Fiti said witheringly. "Elizabeth's husband died in his sleep years ago without any explanation, and people accused her of the same thing."

"I don't know if you've ever been to this part of the world before, Inspector Dawson," Timothy said, "but belief in witchcraft is very strong around here."

"Believe it or not, I was here twenty-five years ago."

"Oh, is that so?" Timothy said. "What brought you, may I ask?"

"I came with my mother to visit her sister. She still lives here."

"What's her name?"

"Osewa Gedze."

"Oh, yes," Fiti said. "I know her. Kweku's wife."

"Maybe later you can show me to their house," Dawson said. "I'm not sure if they live in the same place, and Ketanu has grown a lot since I was last here."

"Constable Gyamfi can take you there," Fiti said.

"Did you also visit Bedome when you were here as a kid?" Timothy asked.

"No, I didn't. How far is it from here?"

"About a kilometer away on the other side of the forest. Shrines prefer to be somewhat obscured by bush or forest."

"Makes sense," Dawson said. "Especially now with all this scrutiny."

"Indeed," Timothy said. "Where will you be staying while you're here?"

"The MoH guesthouse," Dawson answered. To Fiti he said, "Are you all right with my being in Ketanu with the investigation?"

"Look, it's no problem," Fiti said. "Anyway, when we go and arrest Samuel today maybe it will be all over and you can go back to Accra and live in peace ever after."

He suddenly grinned at his own verbiage, showing a set of yellowed horse teeth, and Dawson couldn't help smiling himself.

"Before arresting Samuel," he said, "can we go to the scene of the crime?"

11

TIMOTHY SOWAH LIVED IN Ho, and he had to get back. Dawson walked him to his car, a sleek, silver Audi 80. Timothy opened the trunk and pulled out a bag containing two bottles of liquor. Dawson took a peek. One was Beefeater London dry gin and the other was German schnapps.

"Good heavens," Dawson said. "Look at the size of these things."

Timothy affected a rueful look. "Standard gifts to take to a fetish priest. Besides, I want to make sure Togbe's tongue gets loosened."

"Thank you," Dawson said. "Very thoughtful."

They exchanged calling cards.

"I'll put my personal mobile number on the back," Timothy said. "Just in case you need me."

"Left-handed, I see," Dawson commented as Timothy wrote it down.

"Yes," Timothy said. "Is that of particular interest?"

"Yes. My mother was left-handed, and my brother is ambidextrous, so I tend to like lefties."

"Oh, thank you," Timothy said, looking pleased. "I certainly hope we'll meet up again soon in less unpleasant circumstances, Detective Inspector. Best of luck."

"Thanks, Mr. Sowah."

"Oh, please—do call me Timothy."

Dawson and Inspector Fiti set out into the forest. The midafternoon sun had fled from a mob of black clouds building up in the northeast corner of the sky.

"We have to be quick," Fiti said. "The rain is coming."

They picked up the pace. Dawson caught sight of a compound in a grove of trees in the distance to his right, and immediately his recollection of it swept in. *Isaac Kutu's place.* He remembered it clearly, and Isaac as well. Deep, dark, flashing eyes with secrets in them.

"Does Isaac Kutu still live there?" Dawson asked, pointing with his chin.

"Yes. Do you know him?"

"I met him at my auntie's house the time I visited with my mother."

"We can go and see him tomorrow if you like," Fiti said. "He knew Gladys Mensah very well."

They turned left off the Ketanu–Bedome footpath into the forest. What resembled a trail soon disappeared, and as the sky darkened, the vegetation thickened around them and slowed their progress. Now Dawson remembered the same padded and insulated quality of the forest that he had experienced when here as a boy. Sound was quickly muffled by the trees and undergrowth. Every footfall, every scrunch of dead leaves or crack of a branch had a kind of nearness isolated by the cocoon of the forest's stillness.

After several minutes of tramping along, Fiti stopped, put his hands on his hips, and looked around. "I think I'm lost."

He turned one revolution, getting more confused. "Which way did we come?"

"That way," Dawson said, pointing with his chin. "Southwest headed northeast."

If he had been blessed with one attribute, it was the ability to tell direction with compass precision, which few Ghanaians concerned themselves about. Fiti frowned at him as if he had spoken Greek.

"Let's go back," he said.

This time Dawson took the lead.

"Ah, *here!*" Fiti suddenly exclaimed. "This way—I remember now."

He made a direction change—due west, Dawson noted.

After another few minutes, Fiti said, "Yes, it was near here."

They went a little farther, and then Fiti stopped. "This is the place. She was lying just past this palm tree under that bush."

Dawson stooped down. "In what direction?" He had studied the photographs but wanted to be sure he had his bearings.

Fiti made a forward and back gesture. "Like that."

"And the shoe that was missing—where was that?"

"Over there." Fiti pointed a few feet away. "And then the briefcase she was carrying was farther up. It had a mobile inside, but the crime scene people say the rain completely spoiled it, so they have to see if they can get it to work again."

Dawson nodded. All Gladys's items found at the scene were now at the crime lab in Accra.

"You didn't notice any footprints around?" he asked.

Fiti shook his head. "No."

Dawson looked around. "A lot of banana trees," he commented as he stood up.

"These are plantain," Fiti corrected.

"Ah." Dawson went closer and saw fat green bunches of the fruit hanging. "Yes, I see."

Fiti was amused. "City man doesn't know how plantain tree look."

Dawson smiled absently. He took a few additional steps, searching some more.

"What are you looking for?" Fiti asked him.

"Nothing in particular."

Dawson penetrated some way into the plantain cluster and kept going without knowing why. At length, he found something curious: a collection of fifteen or so rounded rocks piled on top of one another to form a pyramid about two feet in height. Dawson knelt down in front of it.

"What is this?" he called out to the inspector.

Fiti came up behind him and stared at the pyramid for a moment. "Maybe some kind of juju to chase away evil spirits or witchcraft."

"Why here?" Dawson said. "Spirits like to be around plantain trees?"

"They can be anywhere, Inspector Dawson," Fiti said charitably. "People put juju near their farms so their farming won't be spoiled, understand?"

Dawson reached for the top rock of the pyramid, but Fiti deflected his hand.

"*No!* Inspector Dawson, I'm sorry, but you don't touch something like that, sir. Something could happen."

"Happen like what?"

Fiti sighed and shook his head. "Please, I'm just telling you for your own good—don't touch it."

Dawson shrugged. "All right. Where would someone get those rocks?"

"There is a stream not far away that has some like that."

The forest had grown dark, and the sky was black. Lightning, flittering from one horizon to the other, lit up the juju pyramid, and a rumble of weighty thunder lumbered through.

"We have to go now," Fiti said. "The rain won't wait anymore."

It began to pour before Fiti and Dawson made it back to the police station, and they were soaked enough to need a change of clothes. Dawson grabbed a shirt and pants from his bag and changed in Inspector Fiti's office.

They talked about the case, and Fiti told him about the Mensahs. It was obvious how much admiration he had for them. They were relatively successful people who ran several different enterprises, and their talent was clear: Kofi, the patriarch, and his wife traded in cocoa, palm oil, and cassava. Charles, the oldest son, helped with the farm as well, but he was also a carpenter who could put up anything a hundred times faster than any government-sponsored project. Kofi's sister, Elizabeth, was a seamstress and cloth trader, and of course, Gladys, the star, had been a medical student. Her becoming a doctor would have been the pinnacle of the family's successes.

In contrast, Fiti had nothing but distaste for the Boatengs, particularly Samuel, whom he accused of petty theft in the recent past. Fiti was determined to arrest him, and he wanted to do it before dark. It was now going on five in the afternoon.

"The rain is stopping," he said, rising from his chair. "We can go now."

Dawson took Gyamfi in his car, and they followed Fiti and Constable Bubo in the official police vehicle. It was impossible to drive right up to the Boatengs' house. A gutter ran directly across their path, and the rain had swelled it with mud. They parked the cars just in front of the gutter, jumped over it, and walked the rest of the way. It was barely drizzling now, but there were huge puddles and broad patches of sticky mud in their path.

"That's the house," Gyamfi said, pointing.

It was constructed of mud brick and a rusty corrugated tin roof. The outer walls were eroded away by rain at their junction with the ground, making the house sit on steadily thinning support.

Fiti led the way and went in unannounced. There were six people in the front room, one sleeping, three of them playing a boisterous game of cards, and the two most senior, whom Dawson assumed were Mr. and Mrs. Boateng, were chatting. In the corner was a woodstove, cold at the moment.

"Boateng, where is Samuel?" Fiti asked.

Mr. Boateng—Dawson's guess had been right—jumped to his feet.

"Good evening, sir." Thick voice, something like treacle.

"Good evening. Where is Samuel?"

"Please, he's not here, sir."

"Where did he go?"

"Please, I don't know, sir."

The adjoining room was small, windowless, and dark. Fiti switched on his flashlight and took a quick look inside. No one was there.

"We'll find him," Fiti said. "Split up. Gyamfi, stay with Inspector Dawson, Bubo is with me. Come on."

Outside, the two pairs went in opposite directions.

"Where might he be?" Dawson asked Gyamfi.

"He can be anywhere. Probably with his friends going around looking for girls."

Gyamfi described Samuel to Dawson so he would recognize him. After about ten minutes of trudging around, they hadn't spotted the suspect anywhere.

Suddenly they heard running footsteps approaching and then a shout, *"Stop him! Stop him!"*

A man was coming toward them fast, running for his life, bare feet kicking up mud. Close behind him was Constable Bubo, and Inspector Fiti brought up the rear.

"Catch him!" Fiti yelled.

The man saw Dawson and Gyamfi, and sharply veered away to avoid them. But Gyamfi was nimble. He sprang as if out of a cannon and cut back at an angle to intersect the man's path. They collided and spun to the ground like wrestlers. Bubo got to them a second later. For a moment there was a lot of thrashing around and shouting, but out of it Constable Bubo extracted the screaming man and yanked him up. As he did that, Inspector Fiti came galumphing, belly wobbling with the exertion.

"Hold him well!" he shouted.

A crowd was gathering fast. Both constables had a firm grip on their captive, who was putting up a healthy struggle. Dawson now saw that he was only eighteen or nineteen. *Samuel Boateng,* he realized.

Inspector Fiti came up to him, face twisted with anger.

"Stupid boy!" he screamed. "*Stupid!* You think you can get away from us? Heh?"

Samuel's shirt had been ripped off in the struggle. His chest was heaving and his skin ran with sweat.

"Take him away," Inspector Fiti ordered with a furious backhand swipe through the air.

Some of the crowd began to hoot as the two constables hauled Samuel off to the police car. His feet dragged as he tried to resist. Mr. and Mrs. Boateng trailed after the constables and pleaded with them to let their son go.

Fiti hitched up his pants. "Go home!" he yelled at the crowd. "Foolish people. What are you looking at?"

They laughed as they turned to slink back to their houses. Terrific entertainment this evening.

Gyamfi rejoined Dawson and Inspector Fiti while Constable Bubo kept an eye on Samuel in the backseat of the police car. Fiti ordered everyone out of the Boatengs' house.

"Only you in here with us," he said, pointing at Mr. Boateng. "You hear?"

"Yes, sir."

The dark of early evening was approaching. A kerosene lantern hanging from a hook on the wall provided dim, shadowy illumination in the main room of the house. It was the smaller adjacent sleeping room that was of greater interest to Fiti. On the floor was an assortment of mattresses, sleeping cloths and mats, clothes in several piles, and a tiny radio. There was a large battered portmanteau next to the door.

"Aha," Fiti said, handing the flashlight to Dawson, who trained the beam on the portmanteau while Fiti lifted the lid and looked inside. He rummaged around, removing items—a few tins of sardines, evaporated milk, and two bags of *gari*—and dropped them on the floor. Fiti grunted as he got to the bottom of the portmanteau without finding anything significant.

"Boateng," he called out. "Come here."

"Yes, sir."

Fiti took the flashlight from Dawson and shone it full in Mr. Boateng's face. He flinched and blinked in the beam.

"Which one is Samuel's sleeping cloth?" Fiti asked him.

Boateng pointed to the opposite corner.

It was dark brown and rolled up in a neat bundle. Fiti unfurled it with his free hand, and something fell out. He pounced on it.

"What's that?" Dawson asked.

Fiti showed him. It was a small plastic pack of three individually wrapped condoms.

"So now we know he was having sex," Fiti said.

"Maybe, maybe not," Dawson said, but Fiti didn't appear to have heard him, or more likely, he was ignoring him.

He beckoned to Mr. Boateng.

"Yes, sir?"

Fiti showed him the condoms. "You see now? You see what your son was doing?"

Boateng looked mortified with embarrassment.

"Did he sleep with some girls here?" Fiti said.

Boateng was appalled. "*No,* sir."

"With whom was he sleeping?"

"Please, I don't know. No one, sir."

Fiti smirked and waved the condoms in Boateng's face. "He's your boy but you didn't know he had these prophylactics. So how do you know he wasn't having sex? Don't try to be clever with me because you aren't clever enough, you hear?"

Boateng looked away, and Dawson saw his jaw muscles working with suppressed anger.

"Was your boy trying to sleep with Gladys Mensah?" Fiti snapped. "I'm talking to you, Boateng. I say, was he trying to have sex with Gladys?"

Boateng shook his head. "No, sir."

"We'll see about that," Fiti said. "I don't think you know what kind of person your son really is, and if you do, then you're trying to protect him." He turned to Dawson. "Let's go. Samuel will spend the night in the jail. In the morning he will be ready to talk."

12

THERE WAS NO MORE police work for the day. Dawson was tired and wanted to go to his lodgings, but before he did that, he wanted to pay his respects to Auntie Osewa and Uncle Kweku. He asked Gyamfi to show him the way to the house.

The flickering kerosene lanterns of night traders lit up the evening like a constellation. The kiosks and chop bars had electricity, but many homes were still using kerosene lamps as their light source. The air smelled of smoke and the tantalizing aroma of *kelewele,* fried fish, and red-hot meat stews. The flying termites that always appeared after a rain shower were fluttering around whatever fluorescent lights they could find, irresistibly drawn to them but rendered flightless the instant they made contact with the bulbs.

It was a torturous route to Auntie Osewa's. Dawson followed Gyamfi through alleys and over gutters and muddy paths. Ketanu had grown and sprawled so much since Dawson had been here that so far nothing was familiar to him, and the darkness did not help.

Suddenly, though, as they walked a little farther, Dawson was struck with déjà vu that raised goose bumps on his skin. He recognized where he was, and yet he didn't. Houses and huts occupied the space that Dawson had known as trees and bush, and the edge of forest he and Cairo had explored had been pushed far, far back.

"There it is," Dawson said to Gyamfi. He had spotted Auntie Osewa's house, but some sixth sense must have enabled him, because although there was a hint of light coming from within, there was practically no illumination of the exterior.

Gyamfi switched on a powerful flashlight and gave it a panoramic sweep. Now Dawson could see the original dwelling had been added on to. There were two small additional single-room houses built around an open-air courtyard strewn with firewood, stone stoves, pots, and pans.

A woman came out of the house with a lantern. *Auntie Osewa?*

"Who's there?" she said, squinting into the darkness.

Dawson came close enough to see better by the light of the lantern. It *was* her.

"*Fien na wo,* Auntie Osewa," he greeted her in Ewe.

"*Fien,*" she replied pleasantly, but Dawson could see the puzzlement still in her expression. "Do I know you?"

"Yes, you do."

He was giving her a chance, but she still wasn't making the connection.

"Auntie, it's me, Darko."

Her expression changed. "*Darko?*"

"Yes, Auntie."

She let out a cry, put down the lantern, and rushed forward to throw her arms around him. Now he towered over her, and the top of her head reached only to his chest. It felt strange because, after all, the last time she had hugged him, years ago, she had had to bend down to his level.

"Woizo, woizo!" She stepped back to gaze at him in disbelief. "Look at how tall you are! Oh, Darko, why did you wait so long to come back?"

"You're right, Auntie Osewa. It's been too long and I'm sorry."

She placed her hand over her chest, and her eyes welled up. "Oh, Darko, my dear. I've thought of you so often."

"Come on," he said, hugging her again. "No need to shed tears. I'm here now."

"Yes, you're here now, and that's all that matters." Her voice still felt like silk after all these years, just at a slightly lower register. "Come, come inside. Uncle Kweku is home. Ei, Constable Gyamfi, is that you?"

"Yes, madam."

"Come in too, both of you come in. Woizo."

She led Dawson by the hand. It must have seemed natural to her, but Dawson felt awkward. Inside, the house was lit by a combination of a lantern and one small electric lamp. He knew this was the same place they had eaten Auntie's masterpiece meal and played oware, yet everything looked different and much smaller.

Auntie Osewa also seemed smaller in stature than he remembered. Whether it was the effect of age on her or his false memory or both, Dawson couldn't say. For certain, though, she had kept her looks and her smooth, lovely skin. Her eyes were a little less bright, or perhaps it was wisdom Dawson was seeing. In a way, through Auntie Osewa, Dawson had a fair idea of what his mother might have looked like by now.

Uncle Kweku was sitting at a small wooden table carefully writing something in an exercise book.

"Kweku, you will never guess who is here," Osewa said excitedly.

He looked up over a pair of glasses halfway down his nose. That and the gray-peppered hair made him look like he had aged much more quickly than Auntie Osewa, and he was now a fraction of the size he used to be.

"Don't say anything yet," Osewa told Dawson. "Just stand there for a moment. Kweku, who do you think this is?"

He frowned. "I don't think I know him . . ."

"Yes, you do. This is Darko, Beatrice's boy."

Uncle Kweku's mouth dropped open, and he took off his glasses and rested them on the table.

"That's Darko? *Ei!*" He rose. "I don't believe it!"

He began to laugh as he pumped Dawson's hand and then embraced him strongly, which surprised Dawson.

"How long has it been?" he said, looking him up and down. He too was now much shorter than Dawson.

"Twenty-five years."

Kweku shook his head in disbelief. "It doesn't even seem possible. Woizo, woizo back to Ketanu. We're very happy to see you."

Kweku now noticed Constable Gyamfi hovering in the background.

"Constable!" He chuckled. "Come in, come in, never be shy, sir."

"Yes, please sit down," Auntie Osewa said. "Darko, you have to tell us everything about you."

Uncle Kweku immediately offered Dawson his chair and drew up a stool each for Osewa, Gyamfi, and himself.

"Our son, Alifoe, is not here right now," she told Dawson, "but he'll be back soon so you can meet him. You remember we had a son?"

"I do remember," Dawson said. "I know what a blessing it was to you."

"Oh, yes," she said, glancing at Kweku with a smile. "Truly. And Darko, how is Cairo doing?"

"Very well at the moment, Auntie, but sometimes life is a struggle for him, you know."

"Yes, yes," she said, inclining her head in sympathy. "We often feel for him. And your wife?"

"Christine—she's fine, thank you. She's a teacher."

"Oh, very good. And how many children do you have now?"

"Still just one. Hosiah is six."

Auntie Osewa was beaming at Dawson with such intensity he had to avert his eyes for a moment.

"Wonderful, wonderful," she said. She was sticking to Ewe, being much more comfortable with it than English.

"Will you take some beer?" Kweku asked. "I'm sorry, it's not cold."

"No, thank you, Uncle Kweku. I don't drink at all."

Gyamfi politely said no as well.

"What about some fresh coconut water, then?" Osewa offered.

"Yes, please. That would be nice."

She went to the nearby kitchen, leaving Dawson, Uncle Kweku, and Constable Gyamfi to talk. Dawson was glad to have Gyamfi there, because he would have felt a little awkward alone with Uncle Kweku. Unlike with his auntie, Dawson had never felt a personal connection with Kweku and had thought him aloof. But he began to relax now as he found Uncle to be much more affable than he'd expected or remembered.

Dawson stole a glance at Auntie Osewa working in the kitchen. She expertly chopped off the top of a coconut with a cutlass. She was still extraordinarily strong, and the muscles of her lean arms had remained well defined. She poured the coconut juice into two glasses and brought them to Dawson and Gyamfi.

"Thank you, madam," Gyamfi said.

"Oh, come on, Constable," she said playfully. "You can call me 'Auntie' too."

Gyamfi laughed. "All right, Auntie."

"If you want more coconut, just tell me and I'll bring some more." She sat down next to Dawson at an angle so she could easily make eye contact with him. "So, Darko, what brings you here to see your poor old auntie, eh? The one you've neglected for all these years?"

There was laughter all around. She was teasing, of course, but it was still uncomfortable for Dawson, because the truth was he *had* neglected her, and there was no easy explanation.

"Auntie, it's not that Cairo and I didn't often think about you and Uncle Kweku," he said, deflecting the question a bit. "In fact I was telling him just yesterday how much I regretted our not having come to visit you from time to time. I promise I won't let it happen again."

"All right," she said, smiling. "Constable, you are my witness."

More laughter all around.

"So how do you know Constable Gyamfi?" Uncle Kweku asked Dawson.

"We've just met," Dawson said. "You know, I'm with the police now. I work for CID in Accra."

"Oh, is that so?" Uncle Kweku said, looking impressed. "So you're a big, important man, eh?"

Dawson smiled. "Well, I'm not so sure about that, but thank you."

"Inspector has come to help us with the investigation of Gladys Mensah's death," Gyamfi said.

Uncle Kweku clicked his tongue with regret. "It's terrible what happened to her. We've heard so many rumors. Some people say she fell down in the forest and hit her head, some others are saying she died from witchcraft."

"I don't know much about witchcraft," Dawson said, "but for sure we know now she was murdered."

"*Oh!*" Kweku said, shocked. "Who could do something like that? She was such a good person. She came to see us one day, not so, Osewa?"

She nodded. "She did."

"Really?" Dawson asked with interest.

"Yes," Auntie Osewa said. "You remember Mr. Kutu?"

"Very well."

"Maybe you don't know, but he helped me to bear a child through his herbal medicines. Gladys Mensah, well, she wanted to learn about those kinds of medicines—how she could use them to help more women who could not have children, or something like that. So one day she came with Mr. Kutu to meet us."

"How did you find Gladys to be as a person?"

"Oh, just a very fine young woman," Auntie Osewa said. "Very fine. She sat and ate with us, and we talked about many things."

"How was she with Mr. Kutu?"

"What do you mean?"

"How did they behave with each other?"

Osewa shrugged. "I think everything was okay. What do you think, Kweku?"

"Oh, yes," he said. "I saw that they liked each other very well."

Dawson caught a movement from the corner of his eye and turned to see a young man in the doorway.

"Alifoe!" Osewa said. "Come and greet your cousin."

Their son was not as tall as Dawson, but his shoulders were much broader. He moved easily and had a bright, spontaneous grin. Dawson stood up, and Alifoe embraced him and then stood back at arm's length to gaze at him.

"So, finally I get to meet my cousin in the flesh," he said, smiling.

"Welcome back to Ketanu, Darko," Alifoe said. "How is Accra?"

"Big and dirty," Dawson said.

"But you like it?"

Dawson turned his palms up. "It's home. I complain about it all the time, but I'm not leaving."

"I want to live there," Alifoe said. "I like the big city."

"Alifoe, do you want some coconut?" Osewa said suddenly, and Dawson found the interruption striking.

"No, thank you, Mama," Alifoe said. He fell silent, Kweku looked away, and Dawson felt tension spring out of nowhere like water from a hidden underground stream.

"Darko, you and Gyamfi must eat with us," Osewa said, hurriedly filling in the lull.

Darko's salivary glands squirted into action at the thought of Auntie Osewa's cooking.

He looked at Gyamfi, who nodded enthusiastically.

"We would love to," Dawson said. "Thank you, Auntie."

13

THE MINISTRY OF HEALTH kept a guesthouse in Ketanu for the occasional stay by a minister or one of his or her deputies. It was small but comfortable, with a kitchenette and bath. The bedroom–cum–sitting room had one small table, an armchair, and a desk. The two beds were narrow and firm.

Dawson immediately took a cold shower—cold was the only temperature available. The water pressure was low, but it still felt good. In the bedroom he opened the window louvers to get in as much air as possible. He wanted to call Christine, but he would first have to recharge the battery of his mobile. He plugged it into the wall and hoped there wouldn't be any surprise electricity cuts within the next hour.

Ever since that night twenty-five years ago when he had first stumbled through a tune for Mama on the kalimba she had given him, he had loved the instrument and continued to practice. It soothed him whenever he played, and it connected him to his mother. He now had quite a collection of kalimbas, and he had selected an eight-note to bring along to Ketanu.

He sat and played for a while, both improvised tunes and ones he had composed, and then he rolled a joint and smoked. He needed it. The kalimba had taken away some of the tension the day had built up but certainly not all.

He thought about Gladys Mensah. She must have been quite someone to know, a force to be reckoned with, and that might have been exactly the problem. *Someone feared her or hated her enough to kill her. Or loved her and was rejected by her.*

He began to think about it in a circular way. Round and round until it no longer made any sense. He knew it was the THC infiltrating his brain. Tetrahydrocannabinol. What a cold, clinical name for stuff that soothed him with silky, molten warmth. He felt it infusing like rainwater saturating thirsty soil. His muscles started to relax, and his body felt light and floating. He sighed. It was very good, this feeling.

The world seemed to expand when he smoked. Sometimes that gave life more meaning, but on other occasions it only made it seem more mysterious. Marijuana had a sense of humor too. Dawson stared at the bed, and it looked longer, wider, and higher, but in an odd, distorted way. The angles seemed all wrong, and he giggled at how ridiculous it appeared as a piece of furniture.

He sobered again. Christine loathed his habit. She knew he smoked, but they never talked about it, and he kept it strictly away from her and Hosiah. This trip was ideal for getting some good marijuana in—far from home and CID Headquarters.

Possession and use of marijuana was illegal in Ghana, but it didn't bother Dawson that he was breaking what he considered a silly law.

He finished his joint, lay down on the bed, and returned to thinking about Gladys. Who would kill her? Togbe Adzima? Maybe. She had evidently infuriated him. Samuel Boateng? Perhaps. Dawson didn't know enough about him yet. What about family members themselves? Inspector Fiti had discounted that proposition, but even as a boy, Dawson had learned that a detective should never overlook a "loved one" as the victim's possible slayer.

As soon as Papa had returned from Ketanu, he went to Accra Central Police Station to report Mama officially missing. It was two weeks

before anyone got back in touch with them. A plainclothes policeman
came to their house. Darko stared at him. He was about Papa's age, late
thirties, neat, and *small.* Darko had always thought policemen had to
be big.

"I'm Detective Sergeant Daniel Armah," he said to Papa. "Is Beatrice Dawson your wife?"

"Yes," Papa said.

Armah shook hands with him and then with Darko and Cairo, who
was in his wheelchair.

"So," Armah said. "She's still missing?"

"Yes."

"I see." Armah's gaze was flat and steady, and Darko couldn't tell
what he was thinking. At first he thought the detective simply wasn't
that interested in Mama's case, but when Armah sat down and took a
long and painstakingly detailed report, Darko realized he had been
wrong. Armah took his time and asked Papa a lot of questions—sometimes the same question twice—and wrote everything down. After
more than an hour, the detective left. Darko stood at the door and
watched him walking away, oddly wishing he could stay longer. Suddenly Armah turned around and waved to him as if he had felt Darko's
gaze.

Papa stayed in the house, and Darko played in the yard with some
friends. Cairo sat in his wheelchair watching them. After a while they
got together and pushed him careening around the yard while he
laughed at the top of his lungs.

Darko looked up as Detective Armah appeared again at the side of
the yard and beckoned to him. He walked a little way with Darko out
of sight of the house and stooped down face-to-face with him.

"You want your mama back, eh?"

Darko nodded.

"She's a good mother to you."

"Yes, sir."

"And your father? Is he good too?"

Darko hesitated too long. "Yes, sir. He is good too."

"He never beat your mama or threatened to do something to her?"

"No."

Armah asked him a few more questions like that—actually the same question in different ways. At first, Darko couldn't understand why he kept doing that, but then like a flash of light in the dark, he realized what the detective was after. That was Dawson's first, chilly lesson that, in murder cases, those closest to the victim could well be prime suspects. It took Darko's breath away. It had not even entered his mind before now that Papa could remotely be involved with Mama's disappearance. It was a terrible, awful thought. Darko began to tremble.

"When will you find Mama?" he said, close to tears.

"I will try very hard, Darko, okay?" Armah said. "I promise you."

His voice was firm, but he held Darko surprisingly softly. Darko didn't know that kind of touch from his father, and he hadn't realized a man could be so gentle.

Armah kept his promise. Month after month, he stayed in close contact, bringing them news even when there was little to be brought. Every answered question seemed to raise a new one, and there was more information on what had *not* happened than what *had*. For instance, on the day Mama left Ketanu, no tro-tro collisions between Ketanu and Accra were reported. That practically ruled out Mama having been in a vehicle crash, but it still didn't help determine where along her journey she had disappeared, nor the how and why.

Armah had shown Mama's picture to dozens of people at the bus stop at Atimpoku. One fish trader had remembered spotting her the day she had been in transit with Darko and Cairo, but not on the day she had disappeared. Armah had also been up to Ketanu twice. Yes, people had seen Beatrice, Osewa's sister, but no one could shed any light on what could have happened to her.

Armah had quickly eliminated Papa as a suspect because his alibi, much of it provided by Darko and Cairo themselves, was airtight. Still, Armah continued to come up with more questions about Mama, and sometimes it seemed he had a promising lead. Nothing materialized, but Armah never showed any sense of hopelessness.

To this day, Dawson remembered the exact moment he looked at Armah and thought, *I want to be like you when I grow up.* The sun was setting at the time, and Armah had been at the house for a few minutes. For a moment the detective turned his head to one side, and the living room window framed his profile in sharp outline against the vermilion dusk. His nose was sharp and strong. He was looking downward with heavily lidded eyes, and he seemed to be wishing for something—maybe that he could find Mama, maybe that the world would not be so cruel so much of the time.

In the end, Armah never did find her. He kept in touch, yes, but time passed and the trail grew cold. He began to visit less and less frequently, and Darko could see he was more despondent each time. Almost a year to the day after he had first appeared at the doorstep, he came for the last time and announced that he was being transferred to Kumasi.

Darko's heart plunged, and he felt sick and faint.

"I'll write to you, okay?" Armah was saying, his hand on Darko's shoulder.

Darko nodded dumbly, scared to say anything in case he burst into tears. He was a big boy of thirteen now, and he wasn't supposed to cry.

Two weeks later a letter arrived in the mail addressed to "Master Darko Dawson." Darko feverishly opened it and immediately felt his chest swell with pride. It was Armah writing to him in his methodical, looped handwriting. He wanted to know how Darko was, how school was going, and how Papa and Cairo were doing. But he hadn't written to Papa or Cairo, he had written to *him,* Darko.

Then and there, he sat down to write a very long and careful reply, and the enduring pen-pal exchange between him and Detective Armah was born. His last line of the letter was "When I grow up, I want to be a detective just like you."

A father to me, Dawson often thought, and more inspiring than the real one by far. His respect for Armah was undiminished by the detective's failure to solve Mama's disappearance.

From afar, Armah had followed Darko through secondary school, and once, on a rare visit to Accra, he came by the house and was astonished to find the teenager had surpassed his height and appeared to be getting even taller.

"Still want to be a detective?" Armah asked him.

"Yes." The answer never wavered.

Armah would smile quietly and nod. Darko liked that. Just a small gesture, but so affirming. In contrast, Papa thought being a detective was a "stupid" career, but by then Darko was used to his father's disapproval of practically everything.

Armah had been present for Dawson's graduation from the National Police Academy. He didn't have to say how proud he was. Dawson could see it shining in his eyes.

Years after Dawson's graduation, Armah took early retirement from the police force and set up his own private detective agency in Kumasi. "When you get tired of the grind," he told Dawson, "come and join me."

As little as Dawson was inclined to leave Homicide for now, he would never categorically refuse an invitation from the wisest, most perceptive man in the world. Indeed, it was Armah who had told him that everyone, no matter how nice or respected, has at least one enemy. Perhaps Gladys Mensah was proof of that.

Darko drifted off and then woke with a start. He looked at his watch. He had been asleep for more than an hour. His phone was charged enough to ring Christine. A smile wide as the Volta River broke out on his face when she answered.

"Well, it's about time, Detective Inspector," she exclaimed. "We thought you'd forgotten about us."

"Forget about you?" He laughed. "Impossible."

14

DAWSON WOKE EARLY THE next morning, took a shower, threw on some fresh clothes, and sat down to study a map of the region. As Timothy Sowah had mentioned, Ketanu and Bedome were about a kilometer apart. Separating the two places was the forest in which Gladys's body had been found. The footpath Dawson and Inspector Fiti had taken the day before tracked through the southern tip of the forest. Most important, it was the same route Gladys would have taken back and forth between the two towns. Approximately halfway between the two, but closer to Bedome, Gladys's crossing had been interrupted by either herself or someone else and she had ended up dead some distance north of the path.

Bedome was east of Ketanu, and some fifteen kilometers east again of Bedome was the Kalakpa Reserve, the only remaining undisturbed forest in the Volta Region.

When Dawson had visited Ketanu as a boy, the forest bordering the eastern edge of the town had been denser, but years of tree felling and burning, most of it illegal, had thinned it out. In fact, much of the Volta Region's forestland had suffered in this way.

The Bedome end of the footpath was visible from Isaac Kutu's compound, which was about three hundred meters away. Dawson visualized the compound, the footpath, and the village of Bedome as forming the three points of a right-angled triangle.

Some distance from the footpath, perhaps a hundred meters, a cluster of farmers' small plots bordered the edge of the forest. Reportedly, some of the farmers had spotted Samuel Boateng with Gladys on Friday evening.

So what could have happened? Samuel lured Gladys to the plantain grove and killed her there? Dawson wondered what sort of compelling ruse would have got her to follow him into the forest.

He turned again to the police file and studied the photographs of the body and the surroundings in which it had been found. *Strangled to death in that pretty blue and white outfit adorned with little Adinkra symbols.* Dawson tilted his head, and then turned the photograph ninety degrees clockwise. There was something too neat about the way Gladys was lying. In his mind he saw the violent struggle until she was finally still. As Dr. Biney had said, strangling another person to death is not that easy. Then the murderer dragged her to lie beside this palm tree. Did he rearrange her clothing—make it neat, rest her arms by her sides? Undoing, it was called. Dawson preferred his own term: killer's remorse. *You've just murdered your spouse or parent or child, and now you're trying to reverse it by making everything nice and pretty.*

Dawson looked up at a knock on the door. He crossed the floor in three steps and opened the door to find a magnificent woman dressed in shimmering, swirling *white*, with a matching headdress. A white outfit in dusty Ketanu? Next to her, dwarfed by her size and splendid appearance, was a fortyish man with a vanishingly thin body and large head.

"Morning, morning," the woman said.

"Good morning."

"Are you Detective Inspector Dawson?"

"I am."

She thrust out her hand. "I'm Elizabeth, Gladys Mensah's aunt."

She had a firm grip, but her palm was butter smooth.

"This is my nephew Charles, Gladys's brother."

Dawson shook hands with him as well and invited them both in. He watched Elizabeth as they entered. She looked to be in her early fifties. She was tall and plentifully built, and held her chin at just the right angle to give her carriage a regal air.

"Please have a seat," Dawson said. "Apologies for the lack of space."

"Quite all right, Mr. Dawson," Elizabeth said, casting a quick look around the room. "It's not your fault the Ministry of Health is so stingy with their accommodations. They could have done better."

Dawson smiled at the sharpness of the criticism. Elizabeth took the chair, and Dawson and Charles sat on a bed each.

"We heard yesterday that you had arrived in Ketanu to investigate my niece's death," she said, "and we wanted to talk to you as soon as possible."

Her voice had the texture of rich, warm velvet.

"First of all, my condolences," Dawson said. "I know this isn't easy."

"Thank you," Charles said softly. He was despondent, his shoulders slumped. "I still can't believe it happened. I keep thinking it's a nightmare I'm walking through, and on the other side of it, Gladys will be there with her smile and her laugh and her cleverness."

"Yes," Dawson said. "I know that feeling well." And he did. "When you say her smile and her laugh and her cleverness, I begin to get a picture of her personality, and I'm grateful to you for that because I've been wondering what her spirit was like, and who Gladys the woman was."

Elizabeth's eyes became soft. "It's very hard to put into words, Inspector Dawson—even for Charles and me, or any of the family who was close to her. And if you had met her, you would have the same difficulty expressing it."

"She made you want to be around her," Charles said. "So magnetic, so full of energy and love, and she gave it out freely for everyone to experience."

"And a quick and brilliant mind," Elizabeth said. "Sometimes she talked so fast she would lose people, but when she wanted to pass on her message—about AIDS, about life, about anything—she came down or rose up to whatever level she needed to be. People sometimes said she had a hot temper, but that wasn't it. It was that she was a *passionate* person. That's what you have to understand about her."

Dawson nodded.

"It seems almost too easy to take a life like that," Elizabeth said. "It shouldn't be that way."

The tears welling up spilled over onto her cheeks. She dabbed her eyes and face with a handkerchief. Charles put his hand on her arm and squeezed.

"I'm sorry," she whispered.

"It's still early," Dawson said gently. "The wound is fresh."

"Still," Elizabeth said, "I hadn't exactly intended to subject you to this display, Detective Inspector." She laughed ruefully through her tears.

Dawson smiled. "When was the last time you saw Gladys?"

"Late Friday afternoon, when she left the house for Bedome," Charles said. "People say she was there till just before sunset."

"I see," Dawson said. "So, between five thirty and six Friday evening, had all the family except Gladys returned home?"

"Yes. I had been in Ho and returned around five, and Auntie Elizabeth came from the shop about an hour later to help Mummy with the cooking."

"And your father?"

"He had been at the farm, but he went home early in the afternoon because his gout was troubling him."

"I know why you're asking these questions, Mr. Dawson," Elizabeth said. "There's no one, *no* one among us who didn't love and cherish Gladys, and not one of us would ever want to hurt her, let alone kill her."

"I'm sure that's the case. Then let's talk about who *would* want to kill her."

"Togbe Fafali Adzima, the fetish priest at Bedome, for sure," Charles said at once. "He hated her, and I kept warning her to be careful with him."

"Sometimes it's not so much the nasty people like Adzima you have to worry about," Elizabeth countered. "Their bark is worse than their bite, if they have any bite at all. No, it's sneaky people like Mr. Isaac Kutu who pretend to be good but are rotten on the inside. Those are the troubling ones."

"I've heard Gladys was interested in Mr. Kutu's herbal remedies," Dawson said, "and I was told they got along well. Do you think otherwise?"

"They may have been okay with each other for a while," Elizabeth said, "but everything changed the day he thought she was stealing from him."

"How did that come about?"

"This is what Gladys told me," Elizabeth said. "She went to Kutu's compound to see him, but he wasn't there. She wanted to see some of his herbal treatments, and she persuaded his wife, Tomefa, to show her. When Kutu arrived later on, he found Gladys writing everything down that his wife was telling her about the various herbs."

"He wasn't happy about that," Dawson said.

"Not happy?" Elizabeth snorted. "Inspector Dawson, he was *furious*. He started screaming at them both. Tomefa ran away, and I wouldn't be surprised if Kutu punished her with a beating. He accused Gladys of stealing his ideas to profit from them."

"So he was angry. Enough to kill her?"

"Charles doesn't think so, but I do."

"What about lust or love or jealousy somewhere in their relationship?"

Elizabeth clicked her tongue. "No, not at all. Gladys would have told me that. She told me a lot of things."

"By any chance, did she mention anything about Timothy Sowah? Any romance?"

"She liked him, that's all I know," Elizabeth said. "I once teased her that she looked like she was in love, but she pooh-poohed it and reminded me Mr. Sowah is married. Why do you ask?"

"No special reason."

"I heard Inspector Fiti has arrested Samuel Boateng," Charles said. "Is that true?"

"Yesterday."

"Fiti the bully," Elizabeth said contemptuously. "Picking on the weakest of the bunch. The boy doesn't even have murder *in* him. But Fiti? He doesn't care, so long as he gets his scapegoat."

"Did Gladys have any feelings for Samuel, do you think?" Dawson asked.

"I don't think she found him anything more than amusing, if not immature," Elizabeth said.

"I understand from Inspector Fiti that some farmers working near the forest on Friday evening said they had seen him with Gladys as she was returning to Ketanu from Bedome."

"Yes, that's correct," Charles said, "but from what the farmers told me, Samuel imposed on her rather than the other way around."

"If that did happen, might it have upset her?"

"I doubt it, really. Gladys took things in stride."

"I'm changing the subject somewhat," Elizabeth said, "but there's something else you really should know, Inspector."

"Yes?"

"Gladys always kept a diary, a journal of everything she did every day, her feelings and thoughts and philosophies. It had a black cover— or maybe dark blue—about fifteen by ten centimeters in size. It's missing. We've looked for it in her room at our house, and yesterday when we went to her hall at the university to collect her belongings, we didn't find it anywhere there either."

"Did she ever share the journal with you?"

"No, and I never tried to read it. She made it clear that it was private."

Diaries fascinated Dawson. Each was unique to its owner, intimate, full of deep secrets, and they never lied. Even more important,

Gladys's diary might have borne information implicating her murderer.

"And there's one last thing, Inspector Dawson," Elizabeth said.

"Yes?"

"She wore a silver bead bracelet on her right wrist. She never took it off. That's missing as well."

"And there was no mention in the crime scene report of anything like that being found," Dawson said. "You've looked everywhere possible?"

"Thoroughly. It's nowhere to be found. So there you have two things—the bracelet and the diary. Both of them are gone."

15

OSEWA HAD RISEN EARLY, long before Kweku and Alifoe were up. The morning was cool as she went down the road to the communal water pump. People in Ketanu no longer had to walk miles to fetch water in buckets on their heads. Osewa remembered those bad old days. Things had changed. Just imagine, many of the houses in Ketanu now had running water *inside*. She would like that, she thought. Maybe someday.

At the pump she talked and laughed with the other women who were waiting to fill their various containers. Men never collected water. That was women's work. Once her bucket was full, Osewa lifted it onto the roll of cloth padding on her head and walked back home with it balanced perfectly and without spilling a drop. Just one of those things you learned to do as soon as you could walk.

In their small courtyard, she began to prepare the breakfast. Kweku was going off to Ho this morning, so she wanted to be sure his was ready. He liked akasa, but Alifoe preferred rice water with lots of sugar and Ideal evaporated milk if they were lucky enough to have some.

Osewa had two cooking stoves, each a circle of three or four large stones in the middle of which went the firewood. She bent over one of the stoves and fanned the fire to full blaze.

Kweku came out of his room, grunted good morning, and went off to the latrine. When he came back, he washed his hands in a large calabash of soapy water and then rinsed them off with clean water from a second gourd. He didn't waste a drop. He sat down on a stool opposite Osewa and waited for his akasa.

"I hope I get somewhere today," he said, voice still thick with sleep.

Osewa nodded. "I hope so too," she said as she handed him his bowl of gruel. She didn't really have much hope, though. Kweku was trying to wrestle a loan from a credit union run by a cocoa-farming cooperative. They needed the money because the prior cocoa season had been so lean, but getting their hands on the loan was difficult. Kweku had been to the Ho center four times in the last six weeks, and there still was no sign of his application being approved. Osewa had given up on the idea, but Kweku kept doggedly trying.

She brightened as Alifoe came out for breakfast. Unlike his father, he was awake the minute his feet touched the ground.

"Morning," he said, vigorously pulling his stool up to sit next to his father.

"Morning, morning," Osewa said, smiling. "Did you sleep well?"

"Mama, when do I *not* sleep well?"

"True," she said. She stirred his rice water and mixed in some milk.

Alifoe rubbed his hands together in anticipation. "Do we have sweet bread?"

"A little bit. You ate most of it yesterday, remember?"

"Oh, yes." He laughed.

She handed him his bowl and the last piece of the loaf she had bought two days ago. No bread till next week. That was that.

Alifoe dipped a chunk of bread in the rice water and slurped it up into his mouth.

Osewa chuckled. The relish with which her son ate could make even the most ordinary meal look spectacular.

"Are you going to Ho today?" he asked his father.

"Yes." Kweku swallowed the last spoonful of akasa. "Can you work with the cocoa while I'm gone? All the beans need turning."

"Yes, of course, Papa."

Before the cocoa beans could be bagged and shipped, they had to be thoroughly sun dried until they turned a rich, even reddish brown.

"I just hope it doesn't rain today," Kweku fretted. "We are already behind with the drying."

"It will be all right," Alifoe said. In English he sang, *"If you wan' roll with deh thugs tonight, well it's all right, baby it's all right . . ."*

Osewa wanted to smile because she liked to hear him break out into song, but she was uncomfortable when he sang this ugly modern stuff kids were listening to now—hip-hop, and the Ghanaian variety they called "hip-life," in which they sometimes mixed English with the vernacular. She had once stopped at a chop bar in town, and a bunch of boys were watching something on TV where men and women—*Ghanaians*—were dancing to some of this new music. Osewa was shocked to see the women so scantily dressed and shaking their buttocks in the men's faces. It was disgusting.

She worried more and more these days about losing Alifoe. She could sense he was becoming restless. Several times he had wondered aloud about living in Accra, and she knew that was why he had asked Darko so pointedly about it. Osewa would be loath to see him leave home, and please no, not to Accra. But the young folks weren't interested in cocoa farming these days. They wanted the fast city life. They always claimed they could get more work in the city, but Osewa knew for a fact there were countless young men and women loitering around the streets of Accra with absolutely nothing to do.

She didn't know what she would do if she didn't have Alifoe. It would kill her. Sometimes, when she looked at her son, at his tallness, his strength, his beauty, she felt a jolt, a shock as she realized that she had him and that he was real and not just a vision. He was her jewel. He made her heart hurt. When he was growing up, she had never put her hand to him, even though Kweku had done so several times. No, she would not ever do harm to the greatest blessing of her life.

Life had been much different before Alifoe. Twenty-five years ago, Ketanu had been a small place with no paved roads or running water. It was as lacking as Osewa was childless. The rains were heavier and more frequent then, and the forests were thicker and greener. Clear as a photograph, Osewa remembered the eve of her visit to the healer. The weather had been foul, and it had been pouring for three solid days. The tin roof, which Kweku had not been able to repair, was leaking everywhere.

Osewa shuffled around an assortment of calabashes and weather-beaten buckets to keep up with the shifting leaks in the roof. Inert in a corner of the room, Kweku watched Osewa play her drip-chasing game.

She went into the rain and collected the tin bucket she had set out to collect rainwater. It was full now and quite heavy, but she was strong and carried it easily back into the "kitchen," a tiny space off the main room with a stove and a stack of battered pots and tin plates. The floor was made of earth, but years of natural foot trampling and daily sweeping had made it as good as a concrete surface.

Osewa began to prepare dinner. She poured water from the bucket into a large cooking pot before beginning to make the fire. The matches were soft from the humidity in the air, but she got one lit and held it to the kindling in the aperture of the stove. Once she had coaxed the flame alive and fanned the firewood red and hot, she put a frying pan on the grate and scooped in a handful of palm oil left over from the last meal.

The plantains, almost black with ripeness, begged to be scorched crisp in searing oil. She peeled them carefully and saved the skins for the compost pile.

"Osewa!"

She barely heard him above the din of the rain.

"Yes, Kweku?"

"Come here."

Her hands were still moist and sticky from handling the ripe plantains. She knelt beside him.

"Yes?"

"Have you conceived this month?"

"No, Kweku."

He gestured impatiently. "I plant my seed in your soil and still you cannot bear fruit. Dry as the deserts of the north."

She lowered her head.

"Tomorrow I take you to Boniface Kutu," he said.

She nodded.

"If he can't heal you, then no one can and I will have to sack you from this house and take another wife. You hear? You are disgracing me. I'm tired of it."

"I'm sorry," she whispered.

He dismissed her. "Go and cook my food."

Osewa went back to the kitchen. The oil was ready now, and when she dropped in a test morsel of plantain, it sizzled and skittered across the surface like a nimble water spider. Her eyes misted. The oil spat and popped as tears rolled down her cheeks and fell into the pan. *Oh, God. Give me a child. Please, give me a child.*

Boniface Kutu had been a traditional healer for sixty years. His health was failing now, but people from Ketanu and all around still spoke reverently of him. He could diagnose and cure illnesses that had baffled other healers for years, and he was a master of the detection and cure of witches.

His compound was between Ketanu and Bedome. Osewa and Kweku arrived early in the morning. A scrawny young man politely asked them to stand in a corner and wait for Boniface to come out. Without complaining, they stood there and waited, and waited, and waited. The area was a completely enclosed space with several inward-facing rooms containing white calabashes, iron pans, wrinkled goat bladders, herbs and roots, feathers, snake skins, and porcupine quills.

They watched women going back and forth between the rooms. Others came from outside the compound with farm produce or firewood balanced easily on their heads. One was cooking at a wood-burning stove. Boniface had two wives, four daughters, and three sons, of whom Isaac was the only one who had not left home for the big cities.

At last Boniface appeared, and Osewa was shocked. She had heard that the old man wasn't well, but she had had no idea it was this bad. He walked with a cane in his right hand, and Isaac supported him on the left side as he took each labored, gasping step. His face was bloated, and his eyes were bloodshot. His ceremonial cloth, rolled down to his waist, exposed an oozing torso. Engorged legs, dimpled like orange peel, drained a yellowish liquid from a thousand distended pores. He was a healer. Why couldn't he heal *himself*?

Isaac guided Boniface to his chair, helped him sit down, and then wiped his dripping forehead with a sweat-stained rag.

Osewa's eyes flickered to Isaac's face and then guiltily away. He had fine, smooth features, eyes shadowy and deep, glistening skin blacker than night, and a tight, compact body packed with power. He beckoned to Osewa and Kweku, and they came forward. She knelt on a straw mat at Boniface's feet while Kweku sat on his haunches to one side.

Boniface leaned forward with some effort and peered at Osewa, his face so close to hers she could smell his foul, wheezing breath. He traced her facial features with his fat fingers. His palms were saturated with the dark color and odor of herbal medicines. Osewa found Boniface Kutu repulsive in a way that made her believe in him.

"So, Kweku Gedze," he said. "Tell us why you have brought your wife here."

Kweku cleared his throat. "Please, Mr. Kutu, she is barren."

"Eh?" Boniface said, craning forward to hear.

"Speak up, my friend," Isaac prompted.

"She cannot bear fruit from my seed," Kweku said more loudly.

"Have you taken your wife to a healer before?" Boniface asked.

"Yes, please. Many."

"And what did they do?"

"They gave her medicines to change her desert into a rich soil. And also a tonic for the blood."

"And what happened?"

"Please, nothing."

"Stand up," Boniface said to Osewa.

She did as she was told. Boniface placed his hands on her belly and began to press upon it. It was an experienced touch, firm and sure. He suddenly stopped and stayed completely still, as though he had felt something or caught a sound. Then he took his hands away and signaled to his son to perform the same inspection.

Isaac knelt on one knee in front of Osewa. She thought his inexperience and physical strength would render him rough and coarse, but the instant he put his palms flat upon her belly, she felt such a thrill race through her she almost gasped. He did not have anything approaching the hardness of his father. Instead, his hands were soft and light, his fingers long and flowing as they glided over her skin like a warm stream. She had never been touched like that.

Osewa looked down at him. His head was level yet his eyes were turned up at her, dark and burning. Her face grew fire hot, and her heart raced as he held her gaze.

"What do you feel?" Boniface said.

"Something is there . . . ," Isaac said, his voice trailing into doubt.

"No," Boniface said with a sigh. He sounded tired. "There is an absence, not a presence."

Isaac nodded. "Oh, yes."

"Don't make things up. If there is no water in your calabash, do not tip it as if to pour. Do you understand?"

Isaac looked embarrassed. "Yes, Papa."

Boniface turned to Osewa. "Do you know what is wrong with you?"

Osewa dipped her body in a slight curtsy. "Please, Mr. Kutu, no, I don't know."

"Little woman, you have no womb."

Osewa reeled.

"No womb?" she whispered. "How is it I have no womb?"

"It has been stolen from you."

"By whom? Who stole it?"

"Most certainly a witch."

Osewa stared at him in disbelief. "A *witch*?"

"Yes. Do you have any problems with your in-laws?"

"No," she said, with a sidelong glance at Kweku.

"How many sisters do you have?"

"Two."

"Are you fighting with them?"

Osewa shook her head. "No."

"Is one of them a troublemaker? When she was a small girl, was she disrespectful to her elders? Tell the truth."

"Yes. You are right."

"What is her name?"

"Akua."

"Is she jealous of your beauty?"

"Beauty?" Osewa was surprised both by the question and the compliment it held. "No, Mr. Kutu, I don't think so."

"I suspect her. Bring her here. I will try her by an ordeal that will tell us whether or not she's a witch. If she is, and she confesses to stealing your womb, then we can get it back. Then you will regain fruitfulness. Do you hear?"

"Yes, please. I hear."

"You will need to bring three hens with you for the trial."

Osewa, twenty-five, was the middle of the three sisters. Akua was younger by about three years, and Beatrice, thirty, was the oldest. As Osewa had predicted to Kweku, Akua ridiculed the idea that she might be a witch and resolutely refused to go to Boniface Kutu's compound to be "tried." Kweku made the decision to take her there by force. It took him three days to arrange for this. Two friends of his agreed to help kidnap Akua.

Boniface had told Osewa that she would have to attend the ordeal. After all, it was *her* womb that was to be restored. When she saw Akua being hauled in by Kweku and his friends, Osewa's stomach turned. She had feared there would be a struggle, but this was horrible beyond imagination. Akua was writhing and screaming like a beast. Her clothes were torn and twisted around her body, and her face was drenched with sweat and frothing saliva.

Kweku had brought the requisite three hens. The trial was a nasty affair, in which Akua had to partially slice each hen's neck and release it to run around blind and crazy for a few dying moments. When it finally staggered to a stop and collapsed, the question was whether it had died breast up or down. The first one died with its breast up.

"And what does that mean to you?" Boniface asked Isaac.

"It means that the gods approve of the woman."

"*No.* It means they approve of this one sacrifice and *only* this one."

"Oh, yes, Papa. That's what I meant to say."

"Does she have more chickens?"

"Two more, Papa."

"Carry on."

Akua's face was twisted and her eyes bloodshot with revulsion. Covered in blood, feathers, and beastly excrement, she looked at Isaac as if she would slice *his* neck if she got the chance.

She killed the second chicken, and then the third. Each did its strange dance of death, half running, half staggering, with its head flapping about like an appendage. The second one died with its breast upward like the first, and the third died on its side but more up than down.

"Come here," Isaac said to Akua.

She approached shaking like a leaf in a stiff wind, and Isaac turned her to face Boniface.

"The fowls have all died breast upward," Boniface said, new

strength in his voice. "That means all your sacrifice has been accepted by the gods. They would not approve of it if you were a witch. Therefore, I declare you not guilty."

The verdict barely registered with Akua. She was in a daze. Isaac rubbed powdered clay over her arms and shoulders and gave her a piece of white clay as a token.

Much later in life, Osewa was to have mixed feelings about the trial experience. She was glad it had happened because that was how she had met Isaac. At the same time, the memory was anguishing and sad because Akua never forgave Osewa for conspiring to subject her to the most humiliating experience of her life. Akua and her husband had to move away from Ketanu because rumors kept surfacing that she really *was* a witch, and Osewa never, ever heard from Akua again. The tragedy of it was that Akua had been the best sister Osewa had.

16

AFTER HIS MEETING WITH Elizabeth and Charles, Dawson's first
stop that morning was to have been the police station, but Elizabeth insisted he visit her fabric shop before that. Instead of the usual
religious reference, she had named it simply Queen Elizabeth's Dress
Shop, and Dawson smiled to himself and thought how fitting a name it
was. It was a cozy space packed with clothing, rolls of beautiful fabric,
and that unmistakable smell of fresh new textiles.

"This is really nice," Dawson said, looking around.

"Thank you," Elizabeth said sweetly. "Would you like to choose
something for your wife?"

He picked out a kente stole. "I think she'll like this one. How much
is it?"

"It's a gift, Mr. Dawson. I would not dream of charging you for it."

The station was quiet. Constable Gyamfi was at his desk taking swigs
from a bottle of Malta Guinness. Dawson's eyes lit up. Goodness, energy, vitality, as the label proclaimed.

"Good morning, Constable Gyamfi."

The young man jumped to his feet with a beaming smile. "Morning, sir."

They shook hands cordially.

"Inspector in?" Dawson asked.

"He'll be here soon, sir. Please, you can have a seat. Will you have some Malta?"

"Yes, *please.*"

Gyamfi poked around in a space under the counter and extracted a bottle. He popped open the top and handed the bottle to Dawson.

"Thank you. Cheers," Dawson said.

He clinked bottles with Gyamfi and then took a swig. It was warm, but no matter. Malta was good whichever way. Dawson let out a satisfied sigh.

Gyamfi smiled at him. "You like it, sir?"

"Very much. Even though I know it's too sweet."

Gyamfi laughed. "That's all right. Do you enjoy beer, sir?"

"Not at all."

"Oh, sir," Gyamfi said in mock regret. "I'm sorry to hear that."

It was Dawson's turn to laugh. He clinked bottles with Gyamfi again. "How's the prisoner doing?"

"Fine, sir."

"No need to call me 'sir,' Gyamfi. Just call me Dawson."

"All right, very good, sir. I mean, Mr. Dawson."

"Did he have something to eat this morning?"

"Yes. He ate some porridge."

"Good." Dawson took a sip and savored the taste. "You think he killed Gladys Mensah?"

"Well, you know—whatever Inspector Fiti says . . ."

Dawson nodded, wondering why he'd asked the question. Gyamfi wouldn't contradict his boss.

"How long have you worked here, Constable Gyamfi?" he asked.

"Almost two years now. I was in Sekondi before here."

"What about the other constable?"

"Bubo? He's been here less than a year." Gyamfi dropped his voice. "He doesn't like it."

Constable Bubo walked in at that very moment.

"Morning, Bubo," Gyamfi said, self-consciously clearing his throat.

"Morning, Gyamfi. Morning, sir." His voice was slightly hoarse, like a sharp-edged river reed scraped across the palm. Bubo took a sullen look at a couple of folders on the desk, turned around, and walked out again.

Gyamfi looked at Dawson and shrugged. "I don't know what's wrong with him. He doesn't like to talk much. He stammers sometimes—maybe that's why."

Minutes later they heard Inspector Fiti addressing Bubo outside. "Where are you going?"

There was a not quite audible reply from Bubo, but Dawson detected the stammer.

Fiti loudly objected to the constable's plans, whatever they were. "No," he said sharply. "Forget about that. Go and get Samuel Boateng from the jail. We're going to interrogate him."

"Yes, sir."

Constable Bubo returned ahead of Inspector Fiti, who faltered when he saw Dawson. Perhaps he had forgotten the CID inspector was going to be present for the interrogation.

"Morning, Inspector Dawson," he said heartily, recovering. "I hope you slept well."

"I did, thank you."

Bubo unhooked a large bunch of keys from his belt and disappeared around the corner and down to the jail.

"Elizabeth and Charles Mensah came to see me this morning," Dawson told Inspector Fiti.

He looked both surprised and somewhat annoyed. "For what reason?"

"To talk about Gladys. They told me something interesting. She had owned a diary, but they can't find it among her belongings. She had also had a silver bracelet, and that's missing too."

"I see." Fiti's brow furrowed. "There was no diary in her briefcase and she didn't have a bracelet at the scene either. But you know, people lose things. Maybe she lost them."

"Anything is possible, you're right, but if she didn't lose them, their absence could be connected to her murder."

Fiti nodded soberly. "We will ask Samuel if he knows something. Gyamfi, you will take notes."

"Yes, sir."

They heard the cell door clang shut. Bubo returned, guiding Samuel ahead of him. Samuel's head was bowed, and he looked wretched. He hadn't been provided any new clothes, so he was still shirtless, and his pants were filthy and almost coming off his lean frame.

The interrogation room was small with splotchy walls, a bare table, and four chairs. Fiti and Dawson sat at one side, opposite Samuel on the other. Gyamfi stayed behind Samuel, closer to the door.

Fiti cleared his throat and began. "Samuel, I'm going to ask you about the killing of Gladys Mensah."

"I didn't do anything, sir," Samuel said, his gaze down.

"The evening before she died, she was walking from Bedome to Ketanu and you were following her, is that not so?"

"I wasn't following her. I was talking to her. Sir."

"About what?"

"I asked her what she went to do in Bedome."

"And what did she say?"

"She told me she has been teaching the people about the AIDS disease. And I asked her if I could walk with her to Ketanu and she said yes. And so we were talking and walking. Like that."

"Tell me everything you talked about."

"She asked me if I knew something about AIDS, and I said no, so she told me about it and gave me a paper to read."

"Where is that paper? What did you do with it?"

Samuel looked uncomfortable. An undulating wave traveled across his brow.

"What did you do with it?" Fiti repeated.

"I looked at it, but later I threw it away in the bush because I felt shame to take it home."

Fiti took the pack of condoms from his shirt pocket and held it in Samuel's face. Samuel jumped as if jabbed with a live electric wire.

"But you're not ashamed to take these home?" Fiti said.

Samuel looked away.

"How many condoms have you used already?" Fiti demanded.

"None, sir. There were only three."

"Where did you get them?"

"She gave them to me. Gladys, I mean."

Fiti's eyes narrowed. "Why would she do that?"

"For protection—"

"You had sex with her?"

Samuel was incredulous. "What do you mean? I didn't want to have any sex with her—"

"She gave you the condoms and you decided it was your chance and so then you tried to force yourself on her—"

"*No.*"

"When she wouldn't allow you, you attacked her and dragged her into the forest. Did you rape her? You put a condom on and then you raped her?"

Samuel's voice rose. "No!"

"Did you steal a bracelet from her?"

"I don't know what you're talking about."

"Did you steal her diary? A blue diary?"

"I didn't steal anything, and I didn't go into the forest with her. Ask Mr. Kutu if you don't believe me."

"Ask Mr. Kutu what?" Dawson said quickly.

"He saw us from his compound while Gladys and I were talking," Samuel said heatedly, "and he came and told me not to be worrying her or he would report me to Inspector Fiti. He acted as if I'm some kind of bad person and told me to get away. I was annoyed with him."

"And what did you do after he told you that?" Dawson asked.

"I went back to the farms to work."

"Did you look back to see if Gladys and Mr. Kutu were still there?"

"Yes, they were standing there talking," Samuel said resentfully.

"Did you see them go into the forest together?"

Samuel shook his head. "No."

"Was that the last time you saw Gladys?"

"Yes." His eyes clouded over, and he tried to blink the moisture away.

"Do you remember what time it was?" Dawson asked.

"About five thirty, something like that."

"But you decided to hide behind a tree and watch Gladys and Mr. Kutu, not so?" Fiti said.

"No, I didn't hide anywhere. I went back to the farms like I told you."

"And when they had finished talking, you went back to Gladys and took her into the forest to kill her," Fiti said.

"*No.*"

"You're lying," Fiti said. "I know a liar when I see one. I can *smell* a liar. Do you know what a liar smells like?"

Samuel didn't answer.

"I'm talking to you, Samuel. Do you know what a liar smells like?"

"No, sir," he whispered.

"Then smell yourself and you'll find out, because you smell just like one."

Samuel shrugged brazenly.

"Okay," Fiti said with a smirk. "You don't care now, but wait until you start to rot in the jail and we'll see if you don't care anymore. Take him back, Gyamfi."

"*Why?*" Samuel said. "What have I done?"

"Come on," Gyamfi said, taking him by the arm. "Let's go."

He marched the protesting Samuel out.

"He will talk," Fiti said.

"Why are you so convinced he did it?" Dawson said. "Just because of the condoms?"

" 'Just because'?" Fiti snapped. "Nothing is 'just because,' D.I. Dawson. I suspect him because so far he is the one with the strongest motive and he also had very good opportunity. Don't believe what comes out of this boy's mouth. You don't know him the way I know him. He is one of the biggest liars I've ever seen."

"Isaac Kutu also had opportunity," Dawson pointed out, "and he may in fact have been the very last person with Gladys."

Fiti shook his head vigorously. "But, *no*. Isaac would have no good reason to kill her. Gladys was his passport to getting his herbal medicines licensed, don't you see? Who knows, maybe he was even going to make a lot of money through her."

Unless, Dawson thought, she planned to sideline him. Was that the kind of person Gladys had been?

17

NUNANA HAD BEEN MORE shocked by Gladys's death than she had let on. This "old bag of bones," as she sometimes called herself, maintained a tough exterior, belying the distress she really felt, and she did it for Efia. The poor thing was shattered enough without seeing her elder fall apart. Yesterday, Nunana had sat Efia down under a shady mango tree and given her a talking-to.

"Gladys has left us to join our forefathers," she said. "I know you loved her like a sister, Efia, and I know you are sad, but have you ever heard the saying that the true character of a person is revealed when something terrible happens? You have strength. You just have to let it come out. Gladys is gone and now the beat of the drum is different, and so you must change your steps according to the new rhythm."

Nunana had had great respect for Gladys when she was alive and maybe even more now that she was dead. Nunana had had an eerie fear that something terrible like this was going to happen. As clever as Gladys was and as much as she knew about that horrible AIDS sickness, she did not realize how much she was scaring Togbe Adzima, and when that man was scared, he lashed out. That's what had made

Nunana fearful of what might come next. She did not believe Togbe had laid his own hand on Gladys, but she was certain he had cursed her through the forest god and in that way brought on her death.

Nunana was one of Togbe Adzima's trokosi, and to that she was resigned. She would be here in Bedome till the day she died. She didn't say Togbe was good or bad. He was just Togbe, a fact of life like the sun rose and rain fell. He shouted at the wives, he shouted at everything, even goats and chickens. Nunana was yelled at too, but as the senior wife, she did earn a certain level of respect from him.

For one thing, she was the only one allowed to clean his room. No one else was permitted in his hut except by his express invitation. She made his bed every day. It was a thin foam mattress falling apart and supported on planks of wood lying on plastic crates. She swept the room. He had few clothes, but she knew which ones were clean and which ones were ready to be washed.

Hidden in the bottom of Togbe Adzima's box of gin and schnapps was a locked, rusty tin. At least it was *supposed* to be hidden, but like most women, Nunana could find anything that a man thought he was concealing. When she had first discovered it, more than six months ago, she'd quickly put it back and felt flustered and guilty, but its being locked had made her all the more curious. What was the metal she heard when she gently shook the tin? Jewelry? Coins? Maybe some gold?

She had forgotten about it for a while until last night. Togbe had got drunk, stumbled over his own feet, and fallen on the floor of his hut. He had lain there for a while, eyes half closed and bloodshot, foul mouth open and saliva trickling from one corner.

Nunana had picked him up and pulled him onto the bed. He would never know or remember. She had just been set to leave Togbe's hut when she saw the mystery tin on the floor. Drunk as he was, Togbe must have accidentally left it out.

Nunana had looked over at him to be sure he was completely unaware, and then she had tried the tin. *Open.* Hand shaking a little, she had examined the contents. Safety pins, a few cedi coins, a watch, and a silver bracelet. Again, she'd glanced at Togbe and then at the door of the hut to make sure no one was coming in.

The watch meant little to Nunana, but the bracelet was really beautiful. She had never seen anything like it. Even in the poor light of the hut, it had glinted and sparkled when she turned it this way and that.

Where did he get this?

She'd jumped as she heard Togbe stir, and hurriedly she'd put the bracelet back, closed the tin, and returned it to its so-called hiding place.

It had been only four days since Efia had discovered Gladys dead, and the memory of it was still too vivid to bear. Every so often, it stabbed Efia like a red-hot dagger and she jumped visibly. The first morning after that awful day, she had risen with a leaden heart to begin chores. She could barely move, as though she had suddenly aged to a hundred. The night before, her daughter, Ama, had found her staring vacantly into the distance when she should have been attending to the meal she was cooking for Togbe. Tears were streaming down Efia's cheeks.

"Mama?" Ama said. "Mama, don't cry. Please don't cry."

They had embraced, and soon both of them were quietly weeping, until Togbe Adzima spotted them and yelled at them for doing nothing when they should have been working.

Efia would never think of the forest in the same way. Now it seemed like a place of darkness and wickedness, and she walked through it with a new wariness. She couldn't bear to go back to the plantain grove where she had found Gladys dead. There was another one just about as plentiful, but it was farther into the forest, and Efia had been to it only once.

She thought she remembered the way well enough, but within a few minutes, Efia realized she was lost. She wiped her forehead with her palm and flicked the moisture away, sweating from both the pitiless afternoon heat and annoyance at herself. She stopped and looked around, trying to figure out where she was. The forest was particularly thick here—foot-snarling undergrowth, dense clumps of bushes, and tall, exuberant trees.

Efia heard something. It might have been an animal, but she wasn't certain. Following the direction of the sound, she thought she saw a bit of a clearing ahead to her left. She made her way there and found she had been right—the area was relatively free from the dense vegetation she had just tackled. Someone had recently set a fire, and it was still smoldering.

Efia heard that same sound again, this time closer. It sounded like the moan of a woman. She was just about to step into the clearing when she saw something that made her draw in her breath sharply and jump back.

There was a little hut—actually it was nothing more than four wooden sticks a couple meters in length with a roof of woven branches. Underneath that were two people lying on the ground. He was on top of her, hips moving rhythmically. They were dressed, but her garments were pushed up to her waist and his trousers were un-done to free his loins, and she had opened her thighs to receive him.

Efia backed away, revolted, her hand clamped over her mouth. *In the forest?* She almost threw up. It was offensive, horrible. People should never, ever do this in the forest. The gods would be furious, and so they should be.

A second realization struck Efia before she even had time to recover from the initial revulsion. She knew who the two people were. The man was Isaac Kutu. The woman was . . . what was her name? She was a cocoa farmer, she and her husband. She groped for the name and found it in a corner of her memory.

Osewa Gedze.

18

CHRISTINE WAS TO HAVE a late day at school because of a staff meeting. She dropped Hosiah off at her mother's house early in the morning and would pick him back up in the evening. That meant Gifty would have her grandson for the whole day, and she was happy to take him. She started by serving him a breakfast of sugar-frosted flakes and squares of toasted sweet bread spread thick with butter and pineapple preserves. By the time Hosiah was done, his cheeks were gloriously smudged with food.

After that, Hosiah unpacked his red and yellow plastic suitcase of toys and played on the sitting room floor while Granny watched. He was a sweet, sweet boy. She cared about the child every bit as much as Christine and Darko did. It was tearing at her heart that Hosiah's "sickness" was gaining its strength as it took his. And what were his parents doing? Saving up for surgery. *Saving up.* How did that help?

There were times when an older, wiser family member must step in. This was the strength of the Ghanaian family—that *everyone* took care of the children and that the elders advised the young parents. Sometimes it meant taking charge. Gifty felt it was her responsibility, her bounden *duty,* to help Hosiah. Yes, in the short term it might offend or annoy his mother and father, particularly his father, but in the end it would be for the best. She was convinced she was right on this one. There had been times in her life when she had been uncertain of herself. This was not one of those occasions.

Gifty had considered a couple of alternatives. She could take Hosiah to an herbalist like Augustus Ayitey, or she could take him to a "fetish" priest or priestess. Both were types of traditional healers. A fetish priest was a powerful intermediary between mortals and the gods, but Gifty thought Mr. Ayitey, with his wondrous array of healing potions, was a better choice still, and today was a perfect time to see him. She had Hosiah for the entire day, and Dawson and his over-controlling personality were away in the Volta Region. It was now, or never.

"Hosiah?"

Preoccupied with pushing his bulldozer across the floor, he answered without looking up. "Yes, Granny?"

"We are going out to see a nice man."

"Who is he, Granny?"

"His name is Mr. Ayitey. You know how there's something wrong with your heart?" She had his full attention now. "Mr. Ayitey can help your heart get well and you'll feel much better. Would you like that?"

"But Daddy and Mama aren't here."

"Hm?"

"Daddy and Mama said they'd be there when the doctor fixes my heart."

"Oh, *that* doctor. I see what you mean. But Mr. Ayitey is another kind of doctor who can fix your heart better, and he won't even have to do an operation on you."

Hosiah stared at her, trying to figure things out. Then he returned to his toys without further comment.

"We have to go now, or else Mr. Ayitey won't be there." She stood up and held out her hand. "Come along."

"Okay. No, wait, I have to take some toys, Granny."

"Choose two, sweetie."

She waited while he made the difficult selection, and then she took his hand and led him outside. There was no need to lock up behind her since her houseboy was there.

Gifty didn't drive, so she had a taxi waiting for them.

"To Madina," she told the driver.

Hosiah sat on Gifty's lap in the rear seat and watched the scenery go by for a while, then he got bored and entertained himself with the intricacies of his action figures. Gifty loved the feeling of his little round head in the hollow of her neck.

They took the pristine, six-lane Kwame Nkrumah Highway out of Accra, past glinting glass office blocks and luminescent hotels that had sprouted like well-watered plants. Yet more new buildings were going up, shadowed by the graceless skeletons of cranes. Accra's skyline was changing radically by the day.

Madina was twelve kilometers out of Accra, a little beyond the University of Ghana. It was a dense town—tens of thousands of people packed into the place like tinned mackerel. Gifty's trusty taxi driver already knew their destination. He pumped the horn every few seconds to nudge pedestrians aside as they crossed the street without any regard to vehicular traffic. The pavement was dusty, the markets were teeming, and the sun was scorching.

Small businesses lined the roadside so densely they were on top of one another, sometimes literally: dozens of Internet cafés, the Heavens Motor Driving Academy, Mobile Max's Phones and Accessories, and the Gowin Natural Health and Computer Clinic, offering instant computer diagnoses and cures for chronic diseases. Gifty's favorite, the All Shall Pass Beauty Salon, specialized in manicures, hair weaves, and wigs. She had bought quite a few fine wigs there.

They turned off into an unpaved lane and bounced along a few meters, stopping outside a dull green house with AUGUSTUS AYITEY's HERBAL INSTITUTE AND CLINIC emblazoned on the front in red lettering.

"We're here, Hosiah," Gifty said cheerily. "Come along."

The taxi would wait for as long as it took.

Gifty took Hosiah's hand.

"Granny, where are we going?"

"This is where the doctor is," she explained. "He's going to make your heart better."

❚ 19 ❚

SAMUEL BOATENG HAD CLAIMED Isaac Kutu had seen him talking to Gladys the last evening she was alive and had shooed him away. That story had to be checked, and after that Dawson planned to approach Togbe Adzima.

As he and Inspector Fiti left for Isaac's place, Dawson tried Christine's mobile. She answered on the second ring.

"I must be standing right underneath the satellite," he said.

She laughed. "How are you?"

"Fine. Where're you?"

"In between classes. We have a staff meeting tonight—what joy."

Dawson smiled. "Hosiah at Granny's?"

"Yes. He's doing fine. How are things going up there?"

"Still feeling my way, tell you more later. I'm off to question a couple people."

"Be careful."

"I will. Kiss Hosiah for me."

His next call was to Chikata. Incredibly it went through smoothly to his desk phone, and even more amazingly, Chikata picked it up.

"Chikata. I need a favor from you. The medical student who was murdered here, name's Gladys Mensah, she had a room in the women's hall on the University of Ghana campus. I need it searched. We're looking in particular for a diary the family says belonged to her."

"Any description?"

"I was told fifteen by ten centimeters, black or dark blue cover."

"Okay, I'll look into it. You owe me one case of Club beer for this, D.I. Dawson."

"You're dreaming."

"If I can't do the search today, is tomorrow okay?"

"That'll be all right, but no later than. Clear?"

As they walked to Isaac Kutu's compound, Dawson felt the awkwardness between him and Fiti, and searched his mind for a neutral topic to help break the ice. He noticed plumes of black smoke rising from the forest in the distance and gratefully latched onto that.

"Do people start many fires here?" he asked. "I see some smoke over there."

Fiti followed the direction of his gaze.

"They burn the bush so they can get room to farm, or sometimes just before the rain to make the soil rich. It's against the law, but they still do it."

Isaac's compound came into sight. Comparing it with the memory he had, Dawson could see it had been modernized. For one thing, the wall enclosing the compound had been rebuilt with good-quality brick. Outside, a woman with bare shoulders was lifting a bound stack of firewood off her head and transferring it to a pile on the ground. She saw Fiti and Dawson approaching and waited for them, greeting them as they came close. Fiti introduced her to Dawson. She was Tomefa, Isaac's wife. Dawson recalled Elizabeth mentioning how Isaac had blown up on discovering Tomefa giving Gladys information about his herbal remedies.

"Is Mr. Kutu in?" Fiti asked her in Ewe.

"No, he's not here right now."

She was exceptionally tall, her face dripping with sweat and her glistening arms lean and muscular from physical labor. She looked to be in her early thirties. Dawson sensed a quiet strength and dignity of character in her.

"When will he return?" Fiti asked.

"I don't know. Maybe soon."

"Thank you."

She nodded and smiled and then went into the compound.

"We can come back," Fiti said to Dawson.

"To Bedome now, then? I'd like to talk to Togbe Adzima and the trokosi who found Gladys, what was her name?"

"Efia. Okay, we can go now."

They had walked no more than a few meters when Dawson spotted a man coming out of the forest toward them. His belly tightened. *Isaac Kutu.* Twenty-five years since Dawson had first laid eyes on him, and yet it could just as well have been yesterday. The walk, the carriage, the solid build, and the powerful forearms were all still there.

Fiti too had caught sight of Isaac and waved at him. The healer raised his hand in reply but kept his pace the same as he approached—long, confident, and measured.

"Good afternoon, Kutu," Fiti said.

"Afternoon, Inspector! How are you?"

Dawson wondered what was inside the canvas bag Isaac was holding. He was possibly even handsomer than Dawson remembered him, as if the older face had taken on a richness that had not graced the younger. The eyes were still those dark, unfathomable pools, but there was more buoyancy to them now.

No sign yet that he recognized Dawson.

"I've brought someone to see you," Fiti said as they shook hands.

Isaac looked at Dawson with mild interest. "Is that so?"

"Do you know him?" Fiti asked.

Isaac studied Dawson for a moment. "I don't think so," he said slowly.

"Twenty-five years ago," Dawson said.

He saw the exact instant when the realization hit Isaac because the questioning look suddenly cleared and was replaced with a smile.

"Darko," he said. "How are you?"

"I'm well, Mr. Kutu."

They shook hands.

"I never thought you would grow so tall," Isaac said.

"Nor I."

They laughed.

"What are you doing here in Ketanu?"

"I'm here to help investigate Gladys Mensah's death. I work for CID in Accra."

"Ah, I see. So you're a policeman now. A detective?"

"That's right."

"I see. Very good," he said, but he seemed neutral. "How are your brother and your father?"

"Doing fine, thanks," Dawson said. "We just met your wife, Tomefa. She's very nice."

"Thank you. Are you married?"

"Yes," Dawson said. "I have one boy—he's six."

"Aha. I have five children."

Dawson smiled. "I have a long way to go, then."

Isaac laughed but then grew serious. "I heard about your mother. I am so sorry."

"Thank you."

"I went to get some herbs from the bush." Isaac indicated the bag he was holding. "Where were you two going?"

"To Bedome," Fiti said, "but we wanted to ask you some questions."

"Is that so?"

"Yes. About Gladys Mensah. The last time you saw her."

"She was right around here," he said.

"By herself?"

Isaac shook his head. "That boy Samuel Boateng was talking to her. I saw them from my compound. And so did the farmers who were working over there at that time."

Isaac gestured in the direction of the farm plots near the edge of the forest—the same ones Charles Mensah had described to Dawson. At the moment, two workers were bent over busily tending to the soil.

"What did you do when you saw Samuel and Gladys together?" Dawson asked.

"I went to them and told the boy to leave her alone."

"Why did you do that, Mr. Kutu?"

"He was troubling her."

"She said so?"

"No, but I know Samuel. He's no good."

"So you told him to go away, and did he?" Dawson asked.

"Yes."

"And left you alone with Gladys."

"Yes."

"And what happened next?"

"Nothing. We talked small-small, and then she went on her way."

"Back to Ketanu?"

"Yes."

"Did you follow her?"

"Follow her? No, I went back to my compound."

"And you didn't see Samuel return to Gladys at any time?"

Isaac clicked his tongue. "No. I scared him too much."

"How did you like Gladys?" Dawson asked.

"She was a good woman."

"I understand she was interested in your herbal medicines."

"That's true."

"Let me ask you something. Was she trying to steal them from you?"

"I don't think so. Who told you that?"

"Would it have angered you if she was?"

"Of course. But she wasn't trying to steal anything. Look, if you want to find who killed her, don't waste your time with people like me. You must look for a witch."

"Why?"

"Because a witch kills the way Gladys was killed. Without making any mark on the body."

"How do you know there was no mark?" Dawson asked sharply.

"I saw the body, and I know she was not touched."

"I see. You're wrong, but anyway, who do you suspect is the witch who killed Gladys?"

"Her aunt. Elizabeth."

"Why do you think it's her?"

"There are certain things healers know. Hard to explain."

"Just because she makes money and she's a widow?"

Isaac looked at Dawson in some surprise. "So you know something about it."

"Not really. I heard it said."

"Do you believe in witchcraft?"

"I've never experienced it, so it's hard for me to believe in it."

"You *think* you've never experienced it."

"How do you mean?" Dawson said.

"Your son," Isaac said, "or your wife. Is everything fine with them?"

"Not everything, no."

"It's your boy, not so?"

Dawson swallowed. "He has a heart problem, yes."

Isaac nodded. "Do you know for sure that it's not the work of a witch?"

Dawson laughed. "Please, Mr. Kutu."

"Have you ever woken up with a headache or pains in your neck or back?"

"Yes."

"That could be because a witch has been kicking your head around like a football, or banging on your neck with a hammer while you were sleeping."

"What are you talking about? I would wake up even before she could get close to my bed to kick me in the head."

"You don't understand because you think things happen only in the physical world," Isaac said. "At night your astral body leaves the physical body and enters the astral plane."

Dawson looked at Fiti. "You understand what he's saying?"

Fiti smiled. "Just open your mind and listen."

"Do you ever dream you are flying?" Isaac asked Dawson.

"On occasion."

"That's when your astral body is either leaving you or coming back to the physical body. The astral body of a witch also leaves her at night, but while you cannot function in the astral world, she can. That is how she carries out her malice. In the astral world, we have ethereal forms that are exact copies of the physical, only more delicate. If the witch kills your ethereal body in the astral plane, your physical body will die in the physical world. You understand?"

"Yes, but why do you need such complicated explanations when there is something much simpler? Someone in the physical world comes and kills someone else in the physical world. Finished. The deed is done and no one needed to travel to any kind of astral plane anywhere."

"Of course it can happen that way too," Isaac said, "but you aren't listening. What I'm saying is that the ethereal form is so delicate and filmy, the witch can easily kill it without deforming it. That way, in the physical world you will see very little sign of how it happened, or none at all. That is the case with both Gladys and Elizabeth's husband. What is the single connection between those two deaths? Elizabeth."

Isaac's reasoning made a bizarre kind of sense to Dawson.

"So, Darko," Isaac said, "what do you think now?"

"I accept your explanation of witchcraft, but I don't think Elizabeth is guilty of anything."

"Ah," Isaac said with a knowing smile. "That's because she has charmed you. That too is something witches do very well."

20

ABOUT A DOZEN PEOPLE WERE standing around outside the entrance of Augustus Ayitey's house. Gifty was not going to be dealing with the long wait that 99 percent of these clients would have to endure. She was a VIP customer who got preferential treatment, especially since she gave Mr. Ayitey and his assistants a nice dash every year at Christmastime.

Gifty confidently walked up to the front screen door and knocked. A few moments later the head of the assistant poked out, and as soon as she saw who it was, she invited Gifty and Hosiah in.

Mr. Ayitey practiced in his rear courtyard, where there was a collection of makeshift enclosures and overhead canvas coverings. People were standing or sitting around being treated or waiting to be. There was a strong smell of herbs and animal flesh. Gifty and Hosiah were shepherded into one of enclosures and asked to sit on the wooden stools.

Gifty hugged Hosiah. "See? Isn't this interesting?"

He looked around, eyes wide. There was a mat on the ground and a pot boiling on a stove in the corner. "What's that, Granny?"

"That's where they make some of the medicines."

"Oh." He wrinkled his nose. "It stinks."

"That's because the medicine is very strong."

It was another thirty minutes before Mr. Ayitey came in. He was a big, bald man with a wide, vertical scar on his left cheek. Gifty felt Hosiah flinch and press back into her.

Ayitey smiled broadly. He had a large gap between his upper front teeth.

"Madame Gifty! How are you on this fine day?" He spoke Ga, and his voice came out of him like a slingshot.

"Very well, Mr. Ayitey, thank you." She laughed pleasantly.

Ayitey sat on the stool opposite them.

"Every time I see you, you look better and better," he said to her. "Are you getting younger?"

"Oh, stop," Gifty said, enjoying his playfulness.

"So this is the boy you told me about," Ayitey said.

"Yes, this is Hosiah, my grandson."

Ayitey held out his hand to Hosiah.

"Greet Mr. Ayitey," Gifty urged, giving him a gentle push.

Hosiah shook hands the way he had always been taught, but he was staying very close to Granny.

"And you say he has some heart trouble?" Ayitey asked her.

"Well, the doctors at Korle-Bu say he has a hole in the heart."

"Eh-heh. I see. Come here, little boy." He held his hand out.

Hosiah looked up at Gifty.

"It's all right," she said.

He moved tentatively toward Ayitey.

"He's not going to hurt you, Hosiah," Gifty said.

Ayitey pulled Hosiah's shirt up over his head and gave it to Gifty. He put his ear to Hosiah's chest. She watched intently. The herbalist, *her* herbalist, turned Hosiah this way and that, listening to his chest and stomach, touching him all over, from head to limbs.

"When he runs," Ayitey asked Gifty, "he can't breathe well?"

"Yes, that's right."

"Eh-heh. I see." He flicked his fingertips along the bottom of his chin as if his skin was itching. "What trouble is in the family?"

"His father's mother disappeared many years ago—no one knows what happened to her. And the boy's uncle is paralyzed."

"Do you know of any curse on the family?"

"I am sure there's no curse on my side, but as for his side, I don't know."

Hosiah came gladly back to Gifty as she waited patiently for Ayitey to give his diagnosis.

"No, it's not any hole in his heart," he said abruptly.

"Is that so, Mr. Ayitey?" Gifty was thrilled. "I *knew* it!"

"Evil spirits are disturbing the boy," Ayitey went on. "They have entered his chest because that is a favorite place for them to stay. So when he is trying to run, they are taking his air."

"*Ao, mercy!*" Gifty exclaimed under her breath.

"Also, the evil spirits like to go in and out of his heart; that's why it is making some noises there and not beating well."

Gifty was nodding slowly. "Can you sack evil spirits from his body?"

"Yes," Ayitey said. "First thing is we wash the boy with water in which we have put *abatasu* leaves from the Shai Hills. That will take the disturbing spirits away."

"Yes, I see."

"Then he will drink the ashes of the *nereyu* plant with hot water. That will repair the damage done to his heart."

"Thank you, Mr. Ayitey, thank you."

He went out to get the treatments ready. A few minutes later, a young woman assistant brought a large metal pan of water wide enough for Hosiah to stand in. Ayitey came right behind her with a bunch of the dark green abatasu leaves in his hand. He dropped them in the water and stirred them around.

"All right," Ayitey said. "Now take off the rest of the boy's clothes."

"Granny, what are they going to do?"

"They're just going to give you a bath with that special water," Gifty said, starting to pull down his pants.

He clutched at them and tried to stop her. "But I had a bath this morning, Granny," he protested. "I don't want another bath."

She took his face between her hands. "Sweetie, we have to do this because Mr. Ayitey knows it will make you better."

"No," Hosiah said. "I don't want to. Can we go home now, Granny?"

"We have to hurry up a little bit, Madame Gifty," Ayitey said, impatience creeping into his voice. He ordered the assistant to help.

Gifty yanked Hosiah's shorts down, and the assistant pulled them off completely. Hosiah began to cry.

"Shh, shh, come on now," Gifty said. "It's just a little bath, Hosiah."

He pulled away from her. "*No!*"

She swept him up in her arms, but he executed a trick that all children know, stretching his arms above his head and kicking his legs straight out so he became like a stiff board that slid out of her hands like butter. The instant his feet touched the ground, he backed away to make his escape, but Ayitey and the assistant were ready for him. He grabbed Hosiah by the arms, and she took his feet. He was screaming and kicking as they got him to the pan. For a moment, the assistant lost hold of his feet.

"*Hold him!*" Ayitey yelled at her.

She got him back.

"Put him inside," Ayitey grunted. "*Inside.*"

They pushed him into the water in the pan, and Hosiah bucked and kicked. Ayitey pressed his head down and leaned on his shoulders.

"*Wash his body, wash his body, quick,*" he shouted at the assistant.

She struggled to rub him down with the water, but the wetter Hosiah's skin became, the slicker it was. From where Gifty stood, the fight was a blur of small, flailing limbs.

Hosiah came up coughing and choking. He took a deep, desperate breath that sounded like a *whoop,* and then he looked at Gifty standing by and his eyes asked her, *Why don't you help me?*

"Okay, okay," Ayitey said desperately. "We've washed him enough. Now we give him the nereyu."

They picked Hosiah up bodily. He was slippery and difficult to grasp as his legs kicked like little pistons. They brought him down to the mat.

Ayitey looked appealingly at Gifty. "Madam, we need your help, *please.* Hold his legs."

Gifty's stomach lurched. She knelt down and held on to her grandson's ankles. She heard herself saying, "Mr. Ayitey, I want to stop. It's enough, please."

Ayitey either ignored her or did not hear her. He told the assistant to proceed. She reached for a small calabash beside the mat, swirled it around a few times, and poured a dark grainy liquid into a spoon. She held Hosiah's head tight in preparation to force-feed the medicine down his gullet. She suddenly snatched her hand away, and her eyes went wide as she saw blood in her palm.

Gifty would always remember that moment. The world turned dark and cold as she realized what had happened. Sometime during the struggle, Hosiah had struck his head against the metal pan. Now she saw the gash in the soft skin of his scalp, and from it rivers of blood flowed down his face like bright red paint.

21

WHEN DAWSON AND FITI got to Bedome, chairs were being set up in an open area, apparently in preparation for some kind of ceremony.

"It may be there's a *durbar* today," Fiti said. "Or maybe a new trokosi is to be given to Togbe Adzima."

Bedome was a village indeed. The ground was uneven and reddish in color. The houses were really huts made out of mud brick and covered with thatched roofs. It intrigued Dawson that Bedome should be so far behind booming Ketanu, just on the other side of the forest.

A few children were playing with one another, running about and rolling around while goats munched placidly on whatever it was they ate and chickens pecked at invisible nourishment on the ground.

As they passed through the village, Dawson and Fiti greeted anyone who eyed them with curiosity. All the women seemed to be doing something—sweeping or carrying water in large bowls on their heads—but there was a good supply of men sitting languidly around doing nothing in the "life is boring" kind of way, not the "life is good."

But one of them redeemed himself and got up to approach Dawson and Fiti. He was thirtyish, with a broad, open face and huge eyes, dressed in a button-down teal shirt and dark trousers.

"*Ndo,*" he said in greeting, but he switched to English. "Good morning, Inspector Fiti."

"Good morning, John."

They shook hands, and Dawson wondered how they knew each other.

"Welcome, sir," John said. "You have come to see Togbe?"

"Yes. This is Detective Inspector Dawson from Accra."

"Oh, yes. Good morning, sir. You are welcome."

"Thank you."

"Please, come with me."

They followed John. He gestured ahead. "There is the house."

Though small, Togbe Adzima's house was the only one in the village made out of cement blocks. It was dirty brown with a single badly framed window.

"Please, wait here for one moment," John said. As he turned to go into the house, a rap tune sounded from his pocket and he fished out a mobile and flipped it open to his ear. Dawson blinked. *A mobile phone in the middle of a village with no electricity or running water. Amazing.*

"Who is John?" he asked Inspector Fiti.

"He does different things in Ketanu—odd jobs, carpentry, selling mobile phones, and so on, and he also acts as an assistant to Togbe."

"I see." Enterprising man, obviously.

John came back out. "Please, he says you should wait a little."

"Thank you."

John disappeared for a while and then returned with two women, one carrying a stool on her head and the other a large animal skin, probably that of a gazelle. They put the stool down and the animal skin in front of it. Evidently Togbe Adzima was to take his "throne" there. Two more women brought a wooden chair each for Dawson and Fiti to sit directly opposite the priest.

A small, curious crowd had quickly gathered. The adults stared, and the children fidgeted and giggled. Unlike in a jaded big city like Accra, the smallest distraction was of intense interest in a village. Dawson had forgotten that. This public assembly wasn't exactly what he had envisioned.

"We won't be able to question Togbe Adzima closely with this kind of audience," he commented to Fiti.

"Don't worry. Everything will be fine."

Adzima finally emerged, and Dawson realized he had been expecting a bigger, heartier man. In fact, the priest was quite average in stature. He was dressed in traditional cloth wrapped around the chest and thrown over one shoulder, and he wore an odd straw hat shaped like an upside-down tumbler.

He took his seat on the stool and arranged himself and his cloth. Only then did he look up. He wasn't in good shape. His eyes were bloodshot, and several teeth were missing or decaying behind slack, pendulous lips stained red with kola nut.

John formally introduced Dawson and Fiti, taking much longer than an introduction needed to. Then he came over to Dawson, which was the cue to present the drinks. Dawson gave up the Beefeater first, and then the schnapps, and John chanted something in Ewe and raised each bottle skyward, presumably so God or the gods could take a good look, after which he stood the bottles on a small table to Adzima's side. He opened the schnapps, poured a little out in a shot glass, and presented it to Adzima, who took a sip and handed it back. Now it was Fiti's turn, and then Dawson's, both taking a swig from the same glass. Dawson tried not to pull a face as the schnapps seared his mouth and sent a shot of fire down his throat. The stuff was ghastly. If only he had some Malta to wash it down.

Still in Ewe, John asked them the standard question on Adzima's behalf: "What is your mission here?"

"We are investigating the death of Gladys Mensah," Fiti said. "Detective Inspector Dawson here has come from Accra."

John recited this to Adzima, who rendered the reply back through John. "What is it that you want to know?"

"Togbe Adzima," Fiti began. "We understand Gladys Mensah used to visit Bedome on occasion."

Again through John and back.

"Yes. Correct."

"And we understand she was here on the evening before she was found dead," Dawson said.

"Maybe so. I don't know what evening that was."

"Friday."

"She was here many times."

"Do you remember speaking with her on Friday evening?"

Adzima signaled John, who came over and held a whispered conversation with him. John nodded, turned, and abruptly asked the crowd to leave. They looked sullenly at him for a moment and then reluctantly straggled away. They had evidently been hoping to witness the entire exchange.

Once everyone had left, Adzima beckoned Dawson and Fiti to come closer, and then he dispensed with the formality of speaking through John, although John stayed close by. This was where Dawson's ability to speak Ewe came in handy, because he could address the priest without an interpreter and catch any subtle shades of meaning.

"So back to my question," Dawson said. "Did you have any kind of discussion or argument with Gladys on Friday evening?"

Adzima shook his head. "Why should I argue with her?"

His voice was like the warty, slimy surface of a toad's back. Dawson was not enamored of toads.

"Did you have any problems with her?" he asked.

"What kinds of problems?"

"She told you she didn't like the way you treat your wives, isn't that true?"

Adzima shrugged. "And so? I paid no attention to her."

"She was against you and against the trokosi tradition."

"Yes, and that's why she has died."

"What do you mean?"

"I told her, I warned her—if you try to go against this tradition that has been in Ghana for so many thousands of years, if you try to stop it, the gods will take action against you. And you see now? Look at what has happened." Adzima shook his finger at Dawson. "Don't play, I say, don't *play* with the words of a High Priest in his shrine. If I warn you about something, take heed."

"Did you tell Gladys that on Friday evening?"

"Not just that evening, sir. Don't you understand what I'm trying to tell you? I told her a hundred times! Every time she was here, I tried to warn her. I told her, look, the gods do not like this. Be careful. We have a peaceful life here, Inspector Dawson. We have no problems. We don't need anyone to come and tell us how to live."

"Togbe Adzima, when Gladys left to go back to Ketanu, did you follow her?"

Adzima looked genuinely surprised. "Follow her for what?"

"Yes or no. Did you follow her back to Ketanu?"

Adzima leaned back and began to laugh softly. "Oh, Mr. Detective Man all the way from Accra. You are funny. No, I didn't follow her."

"Where were you around that time?"

"I was inside," Adzima said, gesturing to the house.

Dawson looked at Inspector Fiti to see if he wanted to ask anything, but Fiti shook his head.

"The girls who are brought to your shrine," Dawson said, "do you think they're happy to come here and be separated from their families?"

He felt a poke in his side and from the corner of his eye saw Fiti glaring at him.

"Aha!" Adzima said, smiling crookedly. "I knew you were going to ask me that, because it's what you kind of people from Accra always do. You see, this is our tradition. In our religion, these girls come to the shrine to learn godly ways, and they are the *blessed* ones. That's what you don't understand. And these white people who come all the way from *abrochi*—Denmark or U.K. or somewhere—to tell us our customs are bad and the women at the shrine are slaves and all this kind of nonsense. What about white people too and their ugly ways? Men having unnatural relations with other men. What about that, eh? *Kai,* what nastiness!"

Adzima spat a long stream of phlegm, and it landed on a rock with deadly accuracy.

"Do you treat your wives well?" Dawson said.

"Oh, yes!" Adzima said indignantly. "I treat them like queens. I have to. If I didn't, do you think the gods would not have punished me by now?"

"I don't know. You're the expert."

Adzima laughed. "True. I am the expert. Look, if you want, you can come and watch our trokosi ceremony today. I will get a new wife today."

He grinned his toothless, red, rubbery smile, and Dawson wanted to slap it off his face.

"Thank you, Togbe Adzima," Fiti said.

"But we need to talk to the wife," Dawson chimed in quickly, "the one who found Gladys."

"Efia?" Adzima said. "No problem. I can call her right now and she can tell you everything."

"In private," Dawson said.

"Eh?"

"We need to talk to her in private. Alone."

"Oh, no." Adzima shook his head adamantly and clicked his tongue. "She is not authorized to talk to you if I'm not also with her. She belongs to this shrine, and I am the High Priest of this shrine."

"But *we* are authorized to talk to her in private," Dawson said evenly.

"Authorized by whom?"

"The attorney general of Ghana and every rank below him."

This did not impress Adzima, who shrugged his shoulders. "I'm telling you she won't talk to you if I am not there with her."

Dawson felt another jab in his side, and Fiti said hurriedly, "Togbe Adzima, thank you for seeing us."

"You are welcome." He stood up. "Just one thing, Detective Inspector Dawson."

"Yes?"

"Never underestimate the striking hand of an angry god. No one can escape, not even you. I hope you will heed my words better than Gladys Mensah did."

22

THE TROKOSI CEREMONY WOULD not be for a couple of hours, so Dawson and Fiti killed some time by returning to Ketanu to get something to eat at a noisy, popular place called Light Up My Life Restaurant, where Dawson had spicy hot chicken and rice, and Fiti ordered *banku* and *kontomire*.

"How are we going to talk to Efia alone?" Dawson asked Fiti. "Any ideas?"

Fiti thought about it while munching on a mouthful of food. "While the ceremony is on and Togbe Adzima is occupied," he said at length, "we will try to talk to her."

"I don't want to get her in trouble," Dawson said.

"We'll do our best to protect her."

It was a facile answer that didn't make Dawson any more comfortable. Somehow he seriously doubted Adzima's claim that he treated his wives like queens.

When they returned to Bedome, the trokosi ceremony had begun. A large crowd had formed a wide circle, at the top of which three sweating, bare-chested men were pounding *sogo* and *kidi* drums. A group of women sang, clapped, and swayed in tight unison.

Dawson and Fiti made their way to the front rows. Togbe Adzima, dressed conspicuously in white cloth, sat diametrically opposite the drummers with village elders on either side of him.

The circle broke open, and a slow procession came through toward Adzima. The girl heading the procession, no older than fifteen or sixteen, carried a dappled black-and-white stool on her head and wore a black-and-white cloth bunched above her breasts.

"This will be Togbe's fifth wife," Fiti said.

And she's well into puberty, Dawson thought, which meant he might have sexual relations with her as immediately as tonight. Dawson's skin crawled at the thought of the hideous little toad touching this teenager.

Right behind the trokosi, the women of her extended family brought in cloth, gin—*yet more gin,* Dawson thought—kola nut, and money in large bowls balanced on their heads, but the men, solemn and silent, carried nothing.

The trokosi stopped in front of Adzima and curtsied to him as she placed the stool at his feet. He did not appear moved by the gesture, nor did he acknowledge the family members as they laid the bowls of goods in front of him.

All the women began to sing and clap joyfully as the trokosi performed a ceremonial dance around the circle. From Dawson's point of view, she moved as if she had feet of lead. Her face seemed contorted with sadness. She wept all the way through the dance, but Adzima watched her with a hint of a smile.

Dawson studied the trokosi's face and wondered what her name was. Last week she might have been chatting with her friends the way all teenagers do, unaware of the fate about to befall her. Completely innocent, she may not even have known about the family crime for which she was supposedly the atonement.

Abruptly, Adzima stood up and began to leave the circle, followed by other priests and half a dozen village elders. The young woman continued to dance until they were all gone. Then she stood still while family members crowded around her and unwound the first layer of cloth from her body, exposing her plump breasts. She was wearing beads around her waist and between her thighs, and there were white markings on her legs down to her bare feet.

The family ushered her forward in the direction the fetish priest had gone, and the village crowd followed.

According to Fiti, the new trokosi would go on to a series of private shrine initiation rites in the presence of Adzima and a few other priests. They disappeared into a small, smoky hut reputed to contain fetish objects before which the wife would bow. The public part of the ritual was over, and it was Dawson's and Fiti's chance to get to Efia.

They circled the perimeter of the village, and under cover of the bush they spotted the "old" trokosi wives preparing Adzima's wedding feast behind a cluster of huts. Some were pounding fufu in large mortars to the rhythm of their singing, others were stirring soup in pots over woodstoves. The children played with one another, and undernourished dogs hovered for scraps.

"That's Efia over there," Fiti said, pointing one of the women out. She was in the center deftly slicing plantains with a large, sharp knife. "And that one, the old one, that's Nunana. She's been here a long time."

"We have to get Efia away from there, but how?" Dawson said. "A diversion—that's the only way."

Fiti thought about it for a second. "I know what to do. I'm going to the other side. Once I cause a commotion, go and get Efia. You have to be fast."

Dawson nodded. He was ready.

Fiti disappeared, and Dawson waited and watched for him to reappear somewhere, but he didn't show. Dawson frowned. Where was he?

Suddenly Fiti's voice shrieked from somewhere in the bush, *"Snake! Snake!"*

Dawson had to admit it was brilliant. Nothing created more pandemonium than a long, slithery reptile with no legs. In seconds, men came from all directions yelling and waving sticks and cutlasses. Some children and women scattered, but a few were drawn to the direction of the screaming man.

"Snake! Help! Snake!"

Dawson kept his eye on Efia. She was moving back and forth and peering up and down, apparently searching the stampeding crowd for something or someone. The minute she spotted what she was looking for, she sprang forward, and in seconds she had extracted a girl from the mayhem and pulled her away. As she withdrew with the girl, she became relatively isolated and Dawson saw his chance.

He didn't run because he didn't want to alarm her, but he moved quickly, with an extralong stride.

Efia and the girl looked up at him, and he realized they were mother and daughter.

"Ndo, Efia."

"Ndo."

"Don't stand here," Dawson said. "The snake might get you. Come with me where it's safer."

Efia hesitated for a moment but then followed him with her daughter in tow. He moved quickly behind the cover of some trees, where they wouldn't be observed.

"Are you all right?"

"Yes, fine, thank you, sir." She spoke softly. Her voice was like the gentle stirring of air on the skin, light as the tone of a flute. Her shoulders were bare, and she wore a long, wrinkled, dark blue cloth bunched above her breasts and a curious necklace made out of straw. She was one of the loveliest women Dawson had ever seen.

"My name is Dawson," he said. "I'm from Accra."

"You are welcome, sir," she said with a hint of a curtsy as they shook hands.

"This is your daughter?"

"Yes, this is Ama."

He shook her hand as well. "How are you, Ama?"

"Fine, thank you."

Dawson could hear the men still beating the bushes hunting for the elusive snake, but he knew he had to hurry. "I work in Accra for the police, and I'm here in Ketanu to try to find out what happened to Gladys Mensah."

Efia's eyes widened.

"Don't be afraid," Dawson said. "I just have some simple questions to ask you, and I will never tell Togbe, okay?"

She nodded uncertainly.

"Was Gladys a good person to you?" Dawson asked.

Her eyes were downcast. "Yes."

"She wanted to help you."

Efia nodded and looked up at the sky while she tried to blink tears away.

"I'm sorry," Dawson said.

Ama was holding her mother's hand. Efia tried to pull herself together.

"I know Togbe doesn't want you to talk to me," Dawson went on, "but I'm begging you to help. If we're quick, you can go back to the cooking and no one will know I spoke to you. Can you help me? Not just for my sake, but for Gladys's and her family's."

Efia touched Ama's shoulder. "Go and stand over there and wait for me."

Her daughter obeyed and walked out of earshot.

"The morning you found Gladys Mensah, can you tell me what happened?" Dawson asked Efia.

She told him how she had been going to pick plantains for Togbe Adzima. "That's when I saw her lying there."

"Did you see anyone else around?"

"No, no one, sir. I was shouting for help, but . . . no one. Only after I came running out of the forest did I see Mr. Kutu."

"What happened after you came back with him?"

"He wanted to go and call the inspector, and he told me to stay there until he came back, but I was afraid and I ran away."

"You came back to Bedome?"

"Yes, and then I told Togbe what had happened, and he went to the place to see for himself."

That grabbed Dawson's attention. "Togbe went there alone?"

"Yes, sir."

"How long was he gone?"

She shook her head. "I don't know, sir."

"Okay, no problem. Efia, did Gladys teach you about AIDS?"

"Yes."

"And what else?"

"She told us how women can do so many things. Like being a doctor."

Dawson smiled. "What do you think about that?"

"I believe it, because Gladys herself was like that."

"Did she want to find a new life for you and Ama?"

"Yes, sir."

"When was the last time you saw her alive, Efia?"

"The day before I found her in the forest, she came to talk to us in the village. Everyone wanted to hear what she had to tell us, but Togbe wouldn't allow us to listen to her."

"What happened next?"

"He and Gladys, they had a bad quarrel. I saw them shouting at each other behind his house."

"Did you hear what they were saying?"

"She told him how she didn't like how he treats us, and she said she could call the police to come and take him away. And he became very angry with her and told her to get out of Bedome. He told her . . ."

"What, Efia? What did he tell her?"

"That she was going to die. The gods would kill her, he told her."

"And what did she say to that?"

"She laughed at him and turned her back and left."

"Did Togbe follow her?"

"No. I think he just went into the house to drink." Efia looked around nervously.

"No one can see you," Dawson reassured her. "Do you know if Togbe came out of the house a little later?"

"I don't know, sir."

"I have just one more question. Gladys's family says she was wearing a silver bracelet the last time they saw her. Did you notice if she was wearing one when you found her?"

Efia cast her mind back. "I'm not sure."

"Or have you seen a silver bracelet in Bedome? Somebody wearing one?"

She shook her head.

Just then there was a rustling in the bush, and a man appeared carrying a loaded sack on his head. Efia drew her breath in. The man paused in his tracks, stared at them for a moment, and then continued on.

"He knows me," Efia said, panic gripping her voice. "He knows me. I have to go. Ama, come. *Come!*"

And grabbing her daughter's hand, she left Dawson without his being able to thank her.

No snake was ever found, of course. It was concluded that the creature had got away. So after the excitement, things settled back down to normal and the women finished up cooking while more drumming and dancing began.

Dawson smiled approvingly at Fiti as they met up again. "Good job. I wouldn't have thought of that."

Fiti tossed his head and looked pleased. "Did you have a chance to talk with Efia?"

Dawson gave him a verbatim account of his conversation.

"As far as I'm concerned," he said, "Togbe Adzima is our prime suspect. I think he's clever. He threatened Gladys that the gods would bring about her death and he deliberately said it loudly enough for others to hear. He set it up so when he killed her himself, people would be convinced the gods were responsible, because that's the kind of thing people believe in. And I think he has that bracelet too. We need to search his house."

Fiti seemed uncomfortable. He looked away, chewing on his lip as if wrestling with a problem, and for a moment Dawson couldn't understand what could possibly be the matter. Then it hit him. Consciously or subconsciously, Fiti was afraid to antagonize Adzima. Timothy Sowah had mentioned that even some in the police force were fearful of interfering with the trokosi tradition because the fetish priest supposedly could invoke some terrible punishment by the gods. Here in front of Dawson was that fear in living color.

"I can go in there alone if you like, Inspector Fiti."

Fiti drew his shoulders up. "No problem. I will go with you."

The wedding celebration was in full swing. Adzima sat smiling and swigging down schnapps as he watched young women performing the *Agbadza* dance. Dawson waited by one of the huts as Fiti went up to him and shouted in his ear above the din. Looking annoyed, Adzima rose from his seat and followed Fiti to where Dawson stood.

"Inspector, I am very busy," Adzima said.

"It won't take long," Fiti replied.

"Togbe Adzima," Dawson said, "as part of the investigation into Gladys Mensah's murder, I'm informing you that we will be searching your house."

Adzima drew back. *"Never."*

"I'm not asking you," Dawson said evenly. "I'm telling you."

Adzima was livid. Schnapps and gin had loosened his tongue. He unleashed a tirade while Fiti tried in vain to placate him, but Dawson, who had no patience for this kind of inebriated nonsense, turned and walked in the direction of Adzima's house. Technically he should have obtained a warrant from the district magistrate, but Dawson needed to search the house now, not later, and quite frankly he didn't care about the rules where this odious fetish priest was concerned.

As Fiti followed Dawson, Adzima trailed them with an unsteady gait and slurred speech. When they reached the priest's house, he stopped for a moment with arms akimbo and said in English, "I don't care, you moddafockas. Go and search it. I don't know what you're looking for, but you won't find it."

23

TOGBE ADZIMA HAD BEEN right—there wasn't much to his living quarters: one room with two wooden stools, one small table, and a deteriorating foam bed mounted on planks and old crates. He kept his clothes in a cardboard box or hanging from nails in the wall. There was a pair of sandals near his bed and a selection of alcoholic drinks, mostly gin and schnapps, in another box. The place smelled musty and pungent.

Adzima leaned against the doorjamb and glowered at them as they searched. Fiti looked desultorily underneath the foam mattress while Dawson checked the sleeping cloth on top of it. If only he could find that silver bracelet, get a confession from Adzima, and wrap this case up. He would love that.

He went through the priest's few clothes, digging in pockets. Fiti leaned against the wall and folded his arms, apparently done with his search, and Dawson reluctantly admitted to himself that he was about done too. He looked around. There had to be something.

"Are you satisfied now?" Adzima said with a slight smirk.

"No," Dawson said. He was staring at the box of booze and thinking it reminded him of the way Daramani kept his own stash of toxic elixirs in a portmanteau. He hid things in there too—stolen watches, for instance.

And so might Adzima.

Dawson reached into the box and began pulling the bottles out—gin, schnapps, whiskey. Fetish priests and village chiefs received an impressive amount of alcohol as gifts.

Ah.

Under the Beefeater gin, Dawson found a small, locked, rusty tin. He shook it gently, and it rattled.

"What's inside?" he asked Adzima.

"Coins."

"Would you open it, please?"

The priest gave Dawson a slow, seething look before removing a small key from his pocket. He unlocked the box.

Dawson found some coins, safety pins, and a watch. No silver bracelet. Disappointing, very disappointing. He gave the box back. "Thank you."

Before he and Fiti left, Dawson said to Adzima, "We'll be back."

He liked telling suspects that. It kept them off balance.

Dawson and Fiti walked back to the dancing circle, and Togbe Adzima returned to his spot. As Dawson watched and listened, he saw in action the Ewe people's long-held fame for the drumming tradition, and he made a mental apology to the village of Bedome for having dismissed it as underdeveloped. In the realm of drumming and dancing, Bedomeans were unmatched by anything Dawson had seen before. He was not the only one impressed. Many in the thrilled audience had evidently come from Ketanu and other surrounding towns.

Dawson spotted John in the crowd, and as he smiled and waved, he saw something else out of the corner of his eye. A man appeared next to Adzima and whispered in his ear. Dawson's heart stopped. It was the same man who had passed by while Dawson was talking to Efia in the bush. The man cast a furtive glance at Dawson, and the priest followed his lead. Dawson looked straight ahead, as if he had not seen them.

The man slipped away. Adzima rested his chin casually in his palm, but his narrowed eyes glinted with anger. *He knew.*

He got up and left abruptly.

"I'll be right back," Dawson told Fiti, and he quickly cut a path through the crowd. Not quite fast enough, because Adzima had disappeared from view. Dawson picked up the pace. As he passed by the wives cooking, he saw that Efia wasn't there, and his stomach plunged. He began to run.

As he got to the priest's house, he heard two voices.

"Didn't I tell you not to talk to them?" Adzima was saying. "Eh? Didn't I?"

Dawson heard the first strike and Efia's cry. He charged into the room. Adzima had her cowering against the wall with her hands raised defensively. He hit her across the face.

"Leave her alone," Dawson said.

Adzima jumped away from Efia and swung around. Dawson reached him quickly and hit him hard in the face with an open palm. The impact sent Adzima's head whipping to the side as if unhinged from his neck. He reeled and toppled, but before he fell, Dawson got him by the throat and lifted him off the ground. Adzima kicked out, but found only air. He swiped and groped uselessly as Dawson dragged him across the room by the throat and drove him into the wall with the force of a wrecking ball.

Dawson pushed his thumb into Adzima's gullet and increased the pressure until the priest's eyeballs began to jut blood red from their sockets. A short gurgle escaped his open mouth.

"This is how it feels to die," Dawson said. "Do you like it?"

The priest's eyelids fluttered and his body slackened. Dawson released some of the pressure on his neck and slapped him again across the face. Adzima's body shuddered.

"If you ever hurt her again, I will finish killing you. Do you hear me?"

"Please, I beg you," Adzima whispered hoarsely.

"Did you hear what I said?"

"Yes, yes, please . . ."

Dawson released him with a shove, and the priest collapsed to the floor like a sack of yams.

Dawson turned to Efia. She had stood up but was still pressed against the wall.

"Are you all right?"

She was trembling violently. "I'm fine."

"Let me look." He lifted her chin to check. Her left cheek was swelling up rapidly, but her flawless skin had not been broken. For a moment their eyes met and held. Dawson found her so vulnerable, so achingly lovely. Their bodies were almost touching, and he drew back, startled by what he was feeling.

Inspector Fiti came into the room and looked in puzzlement from Dawson and Efia to Adzima and back again. "What's happening?" he demanded.

The priest staggered to his feet, screaming, "He tried to *kill* me!" He pointed a shaky finger at Dawson.

"What do you mean he tried to kill you?" Fiti said.

"He *did*!" Adzima cried, indicating his throat. "Look, look. Do you see? He strangled me!"

Fiti, nonplussed, frowned and looked at Dawson. "What's going on?"

"He was beating Efia up," Dawson said tersely. "So I took him away from her."

"But is it true you strangled him?"

"He *did*!" Adzima shouted again. He was now almost weeping.

"I think *strangle* is an exaggeration," Dawson said.

"Come outside with me for a moment, please," Fiti said, looking grim.

Dawson beckoned to Efia to come with him. He certainly was *not* going to leave her behind. She stood a discreet distance away as the two men faced each other.

"What are you doing?" Fiti asked Dawson.

"Someone saw me talking to Efia, and he reported it to Togbe,"

Dawson said. "He was beating her up for that, so I came to her defense."

"You hit Togbe?" Fiti asked in disbelief.

"Yes."

"A man can beat his wife if he wants to, Inspector Dawson. Don't you know that?"

"Togbe was beating her because she talked to me. I won't allow that. She deserves our protection."

"You could have stopped him without beating him up. He is the High Priest of Bedome!"

"There wasn't any time to be nice about it."

Fiti dropped his head and rubbed it as if nursing a headache.

"They insist on sending someone from Accra instead of our own man from Ho," he said, almost to himself. "Our own man from Ho is no good. And so whom do they send? You. *You.* Beating up a priest of this shrine. I just can't believe it."

Fiti went over to Efia and had a few words with her. From where Dawson stood, the inspector at first seemed sympathetic to her, but when he waved her away, the gesture looked callous. She looked once at Dawson, and he could see she was crying.

Suddenly she came back and clasped his hands. "Please, Mr. Dawson, sir. Take my daughter away from here to live a good life. Please, I beg you."

Then she turned and ran away.

Nunana noticed how silent and downcast Efia was as she scooped the pounded fufu into a pot.

"What's wrong, Efia?"

Efia shook her head, but she didn't say a word.

Nunana touched Efia's left cheek, and she flinched. "He beat you?"

Efia nodded.

"Why?"

She shook her head.

"Come here," Nunana said. "Come."

She led Efia away so they could have some privacy.

"What happened?" Nunana pressed her. "You might as well tell me. I will find out in the end anyway. Why did he beat you?"

"Because I talked to the policeman from Accra."

"About what?"

"Gladys."

"But why did you do that?"

"I thought we were safe—but someone saw us and told Togbe."

"Ao, Efia!" Nunana said. "Don't you know you have to be careful? These people who come here from Accra just do their business and go home and never think of us again. You don't know that? Don't talk to them!"

Efia nodded, wiping tears away.

"What did he ask you?" Nunana said. "The policeman."

"Just what I saw that day. You know—how I found Gladys. And what Togbe was doing that evening she came here and if they were quarreling, and if he went somewhere after she left."

"And what else?"

"If I've seen a silver bracelet they say Gladys was wearing before she died and now it's gone, and I told him I haven't seen anything like that."

Nunana's blood ran cold, and at once she knew what had happened. After Efia had rushed back to Bedome to report Gladys's death, Togbe had gone to the plantain grove to "see for himself." He must have arrived there before anyone else, and when he saw that bracelet on dead Gladys's wrist, he just could not resist taking it. Nunana's lip curled. What kind of man steals jewelry off a dead body?

Just then she had another thought that took her breath away and left her matchstick legs unsteady. What if . . . what if Togbe had taken Gladys's bracelet even *before* that? Say, at the time she was killed? In other words, what if Togbe had murdered Gladys?

24

NOT A GOOD DAY.
Inspector Fiti, in a state of high distress and agitation, had kicked Dawson out of Bedome. Like a chastened schoolboy, Dawson had obediently returned to Ketanu, which was bruising to his ego but probably the better part of valor.

He lay on the bed in the guesthouse and stared at the water spots on the ceiling. Now that adrenaline was no longer suffusing his brain, now that he was calm enough to think, he wondered exactly what had happened. He didn't remember anything clearly beyond the point at which he'd entered Togbe Adzima's house. After that it was a clouded memory, like a river laden with swirling silt. This wasn't Dawson's first such experience. It had been the same when he had beaten up the rapist for his disgusting comment about little girls. He didn't recall striking him or how many times, but at the end of it all, someone's face was a bloody mess and it wasn't Dawson's.

The eeriness of it was that he couldn't physically feel anything while he was in attack mode. Was he outside himself watching his shell, or was he inside completely insulated from sensation? What was the explosion that went off inside him? Did he get it from his father?

Now he was annoyed that he was spending time and energy trying to figure himself out when he should have been contemplating the case.

His mobile rang, and he fumbled for it in his pocket.

"Hello?"

It was Christine. "Dark, I've been trying to reach you for hours."

Dawson heard the tremor in her voice, and he sat up rigid.

"What's wrong?"

"It's Hosiah."

Dawson's heart stopped.

"He's going to be okay, Dark, but he's been hurt."

"What happened?"

"Mama took him to Augustus Ayitey this morning."

"Who?"

"Augustus Ayitey, the traditional healer she mentioned the other day."

"Go on."

"They were trying to make Hosiah go through some kind of cleansing ritual—don't ask me what—but he was putting up a fight and while that was going on he hit his head against the tub or bowl or whatever it was and burst his scalp open."

"But he's all right?"

"Apart from being terrified and having to get stitches in his head, yes."

"I'm coming home right now."

"Please be careful driving. I don't want anything to happen to you."

"Nothing will."

It was just after dusk when Dawson got home. He had broken every possible speed record getting back to Accra. Hosiah burst into tears the moment his father walked in. Dawson scooped him up in his arms and sat down on the sofa next to Christine.

"Daddy's home now," Dawson said softly. "Daddy's home."

He rocked Hosiah back and forth for a while and then took a quick look at the scalp wound. It had been neatly closed up, but there was still a little dried blood around it.

"Eight stitches," Christine said. "Mama took him to the University Hospital."

"Does it hurt?" Dawson asked Hosiah.

"Yes," he said, sniffing his tears away.

"You want Daddy to check it and see if it's all right?"

"Okay."

"Here, wipe your nose."

Hosiah messily scrubbed at his face with a tissue Christine had ready. Dawson made an elaborate show of peering at Hosiah's scalp and turning his head this way and that.

"It's almost all better already," he said brightly. "Soon you won't even know it's there."

"What does it look like, Daddy?"

"You want to see? I can show you if you like."

Hosiah agreed, and Dawson took him to the bathroom, where he used a hand mirror and the mirror over the sink to show Hosiah a reflection of his injured scalp.

"Oh," he said.

"See?" Dawson said. "It's not that bad, is it? And when they take the little stitches out in a few days, everything will be healed up."

"Why do they have to take the stitches out?" Hosiah asked in alarm.

"They can't leave them inside your head, Hosiah. You know how Teddy Bear has sewing in his head?"

"Yah?"

"You want to have a head like Teddy Bear?"

Hosiah giggled. "No."

"All right then, so that's why they have to take them out."

"But will it hurt?"

"It might a little bit, but not as much as it hurt today."

Christine and Dawson gave their son a bedtime snack of warm, sweetened akasa and then took him to bed. Before Hosiah went to sleep, though, they had the painful task of explaining that Daddy would have to go away again in the morning and would not be there when Hosiah woke up. This caused more crying and clinging, and it took quite some time to get him to settle down for his bedtime story.

Unlike on an ordinary night, Hosiah wanted Daddy to stay with him for a while, so Dawson lay down next to his son until Hosiah's breathing turned rhythmic and he was fast asleep. Dawson left a night-light on, went out to the sitting room, and sat down next to Christine. She was staring morosely at the floor.

"I don't know what could have got into Mama," she said.

"She gave you no clue at all she was going to do this?"

"None."

Dawson leaned back with his eyes closed and rubbed his forehead, trying to work away the throbbing in his skull.

"She's been phoning me all afternoon," Christine said, "and she called again just now while you were with Hosiah."

"To say what?"

"She's in a state, a complete mess. Crying, saying she's sorry again and again, begging me to let her come over. I told her we should postpone that for now."

"I'd like to talk to her, though."

Christine was surprised. "You would?"

"Yes, I would," Dawson said.

He got up and slipped on a pair of tennis shoes from the rack by the door.

"Where're you going?" Christine asked nervously.

"To see your mother."

"Don't you think we should wait until we're a little calmer?"

"I *am* calm."

"But I know how angry you are inside, Dark, and sometimes you snap and that's what I'm afraid of."

"Don't worry," he said, "everything's under control."

"Dark, *please.*"

But he was already gone.

He knocked softly on Gifty's door. She opened it and expressed no surprise that he was there.

"Come in," she said resignedly. "Christine rang me to warn—to say you were coming."

She was makeup-free now, although still wearing one of her many posh wigs. Her eyes were red and puffy from crying. She asked Dawson if he would like to have a seat.

"No," he said, "I won't be staying long. I just want to know what happened."

Gifty's face creased with pain. "I would never want to hurt Hosiah, you know that. I just wanted the best for him. We're all one big family, and I love him so much."

"Why didn't you tell Christine or me that you were planning to do this?"

"I wanted it to be a nice surprise, to please you, to help you out because I know it's so hard to save the kind of money needed for that operation. And I wanted to help little Hosiah too."

"No, none of what you've said is the reason. Shall I tell you the reason?"

Tears began to roll down her cheeks, and she turned away from him. "I don't know. Do whatever you like."

"Look at me, Gifty," Dawson said sharply. "I'm not going to talk to your back."

She turned around again but could not meet his gaze.

"I said, look at me," he said.

Her gaze fluttered jerkily to his face, eyeballs twitching and bouncing.

"Here's the true reason," he said. "You want to compete with me. You never liked me that much, and you want to steal my son in revenge for taking your daughter."

"No, it's not that. You don't understand."

"I *do* understand. When you took Hosiah to the zoo, you knew I had been planning on it. You wanted him to think *Granny is much better than Daddy because she took me to the zoo first.* And now you wanted to be solely responsible for curing his heart disease so again he would look at you as his heroine and give you all the credit. *Granny is better. I love Granny more.*"

Face in her hands, Gifty began weeping uncontrollably. Dawson put his arms around her, and she flinched. "Don't hurt me, please."

"I'm not going to."

"I'm sorry," she said. "I'm so very sorry."

"You can't compete with me for Hosiah," Dawson said, squeezing her more tightly, "and as long as I'm alive, you will never steal him away no matter what you fantasize. Now, you won't be seeing him at all for a while. Christine and I will let you know when you can."

Her crying grew louder, and Dawson felt a stab of anger at her sniveling. She disgusted him. He held her even more firmly as he felt her trying to push away from him. His fist closed slowly over her wig, and he wrenched it off her head. She shrieked and made a grab for it, but Dawson easily moved it out of reach. Gifty's real hair, which Dawson had never seen, was short, thick, and gray. She suddenly seemed vulnerable, weak, and much older. She made another unsuccessful dive for the wig, then tried to hide her head with her hands.

"Be yourself for a change, Gifty," Dawson said. "Look in the mirror, see the real you, and stop hating yourself."

He dropped the wig on the sofa and walked out.

When Dawson returned, Christine was reading in bed, or appearing to be.

"Hi," he said.

She didn't reply. Dawson began to get undressed and then sat on the edge of the bed next to her in his underwear. "For the record, I didn't hit your mother, if that's what you were worried about. I wouldn't do that."

She kept her eyes on the page.

"You're ignoring me?" he said.

Still no answer.

He tried again. "You're annoyed because you thought I should wait and I didn't?"

She put the book down. "This is a family affair, Dark. She's my mother, you're my husband, and Hosiah is our son. This is the worst crisis we've ever had. To exclude me from a discussion between you and *my* mother is just wrong. It's disrespectful and very, very upsetting. You're supposed to be this modern, progressive man—equality of women and all that—but in the end it's the same old male supremacy rearing its ugly head, isn't it?"

He stared at the floor without seeing it. She went back to her pretence of reading.

"You're right," he said. "I'm sorry. I didn't listen. I was angry."

"I seem to remember saying something to that effect."

"Yes. You did."

Christine put her book down again. "I see you driven by anger so often, Dark. You can't continue like this. It makes you so irrational, so . . . *crazy*."

"I get it from my father."

"Oh, come on. You're a better man than he is. So rise above it for God's sake and stop blaming him."

He nodded. "But what you said about male supremacy? I want you to know that it didn't enter into this. Anger, yes. Hardheadedness, yes. But not male supremacy. Please."

"All right," she said. "I accept that."

Dawson stood up. "I'm going to take a shower."

"Okay."

He kissed her on the cheek. "You know I love you, right?"

She sighed. "Yes. For better or worse, I know that."

"You still love me?"

"No, not at all. Go away and have your shower."

"Really? You really don't love me?" He nuzzled her neck. "Not even a little bit?"

She was unbearably ticklish in that spot, and she squealed trying to hold her laughter back. When she attempted to get away, he followed her until they were stretched out on the bed together.

"You really don't love me?" he said, kissing the top of her forehead. "Mm?"

He kissed between her eyes, and she closed them. He kissed the tip of her nose. When he got to her lips, she didn't resist. She wrapped her arms around him.

25

DAWSON COULD NOT SLEEP that night. At two, he got out of bed and went to check on Hosiah. He was sleeping peacefully. Dawson went to the kitchen for a drink of water. He was aware of the battle within—seething over what Augustus Ayitey had done to Hosiah, but also trying to not let his anger "drive him," as Christine had put it.

While she slept like a baby, Dawson silently put on some clothes and left the house. When he got into the car, he hesitated just an instant as an internal voice told him to do the right thing—*go to the police as a regular citizen, report what happened to Hosiah, and let them handle it.* But he didn't want to do it that way. It was too passive. He turned the key in the ignition and started the engine up.

The sound of the car cut through the silence of the night, and the headlight beams slashed the dark as Dawson dodged Madina's potholes. He knew eventually he would find Ayitey's place just by cruising around, but he was lucky to spot a lone night watchman standing outside the locked gates of a house. In Accra, if you had some money and any semblance of a luxurious home, two vital accessories were a private watchman and decorative but functional bars on all the windows.

"Good evening, sir," Dawson said.

The watchman had a head shaped like a bullet. "Good evening."

"Do you know where Augustus Ayitey lives?"

"The herbalist? Down there." He pointed. "Take a right turn at Jesus Is Lord Chop House."

Dawson stopped the car just after the chophouse, locked up, and went the rest of the way on foot. The watchman outside Ayitey's house saw Dawson approaching and trained a flashlight on him.

"Who goes there?"

"Detective Inspector Dawson."

"Stop."

The watchman scanned him up and down with the powerful beam and then approached warily, armed with a club.

"Show me your ID."

Dawson held it out, and the watchman examined it.

"Detective Inspector Dawson . . . Yes, sir, how can I help you, sir?"

Dawson explained he needed to question Ayitey about a case that couldn't wait till morning. The watchman listened carefully, nodded, and then opened the gate to let Dawson in.

He banged on Ayitey's front door. A couple of minutes later, a light came on inside the house.

"Who is it?" Male voice.

"Police."

There was a pause, and then two locks were released before the door opened a crack and two eyes peeped out.

"Yes?"

"Detective Inspector Dawson, CID." He showed his badge. "Are you Augustus Ayitey?"

"Yes?"

"Open the door, please."

"What is this about?"

"I need to speak with you. Open up, please."

Ayitey undid the latch on the door and it opened into a sitting room furnished with fat leather sofas and armchairs. There was a washroom and toilet in a short hallway to the right. Ayitey, in ice blue pajamas, eyed Dawson with wariness and curiosity.

"What is this about, Officer?"

Dawson hated being called "Officer."

A woman's voice called out from the next room. "Gussy? What is going on?"

"Nothing," he replied over his shoulder. "Go back to sleep."

"Do you know a woman by the name of Gifty and her grandson, Hosiah?" Dawson kept his voice soft, trying to modulate his anger like the escape valve on a pressure cooker.

"Yes, I know them," Ayitey said cautiously. "Why?"

"You recall they came to see you yesterday?"

"Yes, I do."

"And you remember the boy suffered a blow to his head that cut his scalp open?"

"That's why you're here in my house in the middle of the night?" Ayitey spluttered. "It was just an accident! What, you think I was trying to hurt the child?"

A middle-aged woman appeared at the bedroom doorway in a colorful dressing gown. "What on earth is going on, Gussy?"

"This Detective Inspector—Dawson, is it?—says he's here at this time of the night because of the minor incident we had yesterday at the clinic. You know, the boy who bumped his head while we were washing him."

The woman came up to Dawson. "Detective Inspector? I'm Penny, Mr. Ayitey's wife. What exactly is the problem? Perhaps I can help."

"No, I don't think so."

"We don't understand what you are doing here, Inspector," she said more sharply. "My husband has done nothing wrong, and why in heaven's name could this not wait till daylight?"

"Augustus Ayitey, I am Detective Inspector Dawson. I'm arresting you for assault and battery, abuse of a minor, and fraudulent medical practice."

Ayitey gasped. *"What?"*

Dawson touched his arm. "I'm going to be handcuffing you. Turn around with your hands behind your back, please."

"Look, I don't know who in hell you are or what you think you're doing here," Ayitey snapped, "but I'm an upstanding citizen and you don't have any authority to come barging into my house in the middle of the night."

"Turn around, please."

"I will not."

"Gussy, Gussy, please," Penny said hastily. "Mr. Dawson, who is in charge of your division?"

"Chief Superintendent Lartey."

"But we know him so well," she said sweetly. "Perhaps we can go to him in the morning and discuss the whole problem with him. I'm sure we can work it out."

"Turn around, please, Mr. Ayitey. Hands behind your back."

Penny's tone changed abruptly. "You are going to get in trouble for this. We know the chief superintendent, we know members of Parliament, we even know the president, and so you'd better think carefully about what you're doing."

"I am." Dawson gritted his teeth. He had been patient, but his restraint was dwindling like water draining from a kitchen sink. "Turn around, Mr. Ayitey."

Penny squeezed her husband's arm. "It's okay, Gussy. Don't fight it. Just go quietly. I'll have you out by morning's light. Mr. Dawson, you don't need to handcuff him. He won't give you any problem."

Dawson weighed the options. "You agree to that?" he asked Ayitey.

"Yes, yes, all right," Ayitey said, but he was seething. "I need to put on some proper clothes."

Dawson had not planned on all this fuss. He should have walked in, cuffed the man, and marched him out in his pajamas.

"Bring him something to wear," he said to Penny. "Stay right here, Mr. Ayitey."

She brought him a shirt and a pair of trousers.

"I would like to change in there," Ayitey said, pointing to the wash-room.

Whether Ayitey was stalling for time or just demanding special treatment, it was getting on Dawson's nerves.

"No. Change right where you are."

He watched as Ayitey sullenly put on his clothes over his pajamas.

"Don't worry, Gussy," Penny said. "I'll take care of everything. Mr. Dawson will regret he ever stepped into this house."

"Let's go," Dawson said, falling in slightly behind "Gussy." What an annoying name. Everything about the man annoyed him.

"Three o'clock in the morning and you come to my house to disturb me," Ayitey muttered truculently. "If the stupid child had just behaved properly, he would not have wounded himself."

Dawson's emotional wire, already stretched to its limit, snapped. He grabbed Ayitey by the neck and kicked his legs out from under him. The herbalist went down like a felled tree, as heavily and just as loudly.

Penny let out a shriek. Ayitey was dazed as Dawson rolled him onto his belly and snatched his hands up behind his back. The cuffs clicked them in place. He grabbed Ayitey by the collar and dragged him to the toilet.

"What are you doing?" his wife screamed. *"What are you doing?"*

"Dose of his own medicine," Dawson said.

Ayitey began to struggle.

"Kneel in front of the toilet," Dawson said.

"No, please, I—"

"I said *kneel.*"

Dawson straddled Ayitey, lifted his shoulders to the rim, and pushed his head into the bowl until his face touched the water. Ayitey bellowed like a wildebeest in the jaws of a crocodile, and Dawson felt a surge of satisfaction.

"You almost drowned my boy," Dawson said, raising his voice. "This is what it's like."

He flushed the toilet and held Ayitey's head underwater as he bucked and kicked like a goat.

Penny ran to the front door and began to scream. "Watchman, *help*! *Watchman!*"

The watchman came running in.

"He's trying to kill him!" Penny shrieked.

Dawson let Ayitey's head up for a moment and allowed him to catch his breath.

The watchman seemed paralyzed.

"Do something, you fool!" Penny yelled at him furiously.

"Madam, he's a policeman," the watchman said helplessly. "What can I do at all?"

The water in the toilet reservoir had replenished itself.

"One more time," Dawson said.

He flushed again as he held Ayitey's head down in the bowl and the torrent of water engulfed it to overflowing.

"Okay. Get up now."

He helped Ayitey up, moaning and choking and staggering while his wife screamed uncontrollably.

"Let's go," Dawson said. "We'll find some room at the jail for you."

As Dawson marched him out the door, Penny ran after them like a small flying insect.

26

Dawson came home a little before five, after booking Ayitey into Madina station. Christine stirred and asked where he had been.

"Taking care of some loose ends," he said.

She grunted, muttered something, turned over, and went back to sleep.

Dawson checked on Hosiah, took a catnap for an hour, and was up again with the sun. He got dressed and shook Christine gently. She started awake.

He kissed her. "Have to go, love. Don't get up."

She propped herself on an elbow. "Be careful, Dark."

"I will."

He stopped by Hosiah's room and gave him a kiss as well. His son's smooth breathing pattern did not alter and he didn't stir.

Before Dawson started the car up, he speed-dialed Chikata's number, and it rang four times before he answered, voice thick with sleep.

"Wake up," Dawson said.

Chikata cursed fluently in Ga.

"Did you have a chance to go to Gladys's room?" Dawson asked, ignoring the profanity.

"I'll do it today, Dawson."

"Don't worry. I'm going to take care of it."

"Where are you?"

"In Accra, but I'll be returning to Ketanu later on."

He headed for the University of Ghana campus at Legon. Since it was on the way to Madina, he took exactly the same road he'd been on just a few hours ago. Same road maybe, but Legon was a very different world from Madina. Oh, that Dawson could afford those six-bedroom homes in East Legon.

As he approached the arched front entrance of the university campus, a guard stepped forward and held up his palm. Dawson pulled up next to him and showed his CID badge.

"Carry on, sah."

The campus was built on a hill whose pinnacle was topped by the vice-chancellor's residence. Dawson drove past the buildings with their signature orange-tiled roofs. It was the end of March, a few days before the short Easter break. Students had begun moving to class, although Dawson imagined a few were still in bed trying to squeeze in another fifteen minutes of sleep after pulling an all-night cramming session. He could pick out the first-year students. Their faces were fresher, more eager and purposeful, and they walked faster. The third-years sauntered while affecting a bored look.

The clock in the tower of the pagoda-style Balme Library began to chime eight, sounding like Big Ben. Past the post office, Dawson turned right to the women's hall and parked in front of the steps leading up to the entrance. At the top of the steps a sign read, PLEASE STOP AT RECEPTION FIRST.

A young, well-dressed receptionist was behind the counter.

"Good morning, sir," she said with a bright smile. "You are welcome. Can I help you?"

"Good morning. I would like to see the warden, please. Is she here?"

"I'll see if she's available," she said, picking up the phone and punching in four digits. "May I tell her who's calling?"

"My name is Detective Inspector Dawson."

"Oh," she said, her expression changing.

Dawson smiled. "Don't worry. She's not in trouble."

"Oh, good." She looked relieved. "Hello? Good morning, madam. This is Susan at reception. There's a gentleman here to see you. A Detective Inspector Dawson. Yes. Of course. Thank you." She cradled the phone. "She'll be happy to see you. I'll show you the way. Do you mind signing in first?"

Dawson scribbled his name, arrival time, destination, and purpose of visit in the large sign-in book on the desk.

Susan came around to the front and led him into the courtyard of flowering jacaranda trees, bougainvillea trailing up the walls of the dormitory buildings, clipped hedges, and neatly potted plants around a center fountain. It was pretty. So, for that matter, was Susan. Dawson had not let on, but he had already taken in her small waist and lovely, ample buttocks, which moved so succulently underneath her rather short skirt. *Mercy. It should be against the law to torment souls in this way.*

"What is it like working as a detective, Mr. Dawson?" she said sweetly as she walked alongside him.

He shrugged. "It's all right. What's it like working as a receptionist?"

She laughed. "I'm sure it's not as stressful as your work. It must get very tense for you sometimes."

"Sometimes."

"Her office is just over there." She pointed ahead a few meters to the warden's clearly marked office door.

"Thank you, Susan."

Her hand touched his and moved lightly up his arm. "It was a pleasure meeting you, Detective Dawson."

"And you."

"Let me know if there's anything else I can do for you."

He smiled and winked at her and stole one more glance at her lovely rear as she walked away. *Anything else I can do for you.* Several possibilities skipped devilishly through his head before he mentally slapped himself back to reality.

The warden, Mrs. Ohene, was Susan's corporeal opposite. She seemed as wide as she was tall, and the fat had filled out all her curves so that she was squared off like a small bungalow. She had an attractive hairdo and wore a pleasant, light perfume. Her office-cum-residence was nicely furnished, and she had obviously been at work at the computer on her desk. They sat opposite each other at a comfortable distance.

"I'm sure I'm not wrong in guessing you're here about Gladys Mensah," Mrs. Ohene said.

"Yes, you're not wrong."

"What a loss, what a terrible, awful tragedy. Her brother and her aunt Elizabeth were here the day before yesterday to retrieve her personal effects. It was sad, so sad."

"Elizabeth tells me Gladys kept a diary or a journal that has gone missing. Do you know anything about that?"

"She asked me about it too—but no, I knew nothing about the diary."

"Could I take a look at the room Gladys occupied, Mrs. Ohene?"

"Yes, you can," she said, hesitating, "although nothing of hers is left and another student has taken her place. There's a huge demand for space, so it's a matter of only a day or so before a vacancy is filled."

"Of course. It's just for the record. I'll need to include a full description of the room in my report and say that I conducted a reasonable search."

"Oh, I see," she said. "Come along, then."

Like most university dormitory rooms, this one was tiny. There were two narrow wood-framed beds and a small desk and chair at the foot of each. Mrs. Ohene stayed discreetly in the doorway while Dawson looked around. He opened the doors of the shared built-in closet packed with clothes. He checked the top shelf, where four books had been stacked, and he lifted each of them to see if the diary was hidden underneath. Nothing. He quickly flicked through the pages of each book—just in case. He didn't expect to find anything, and he didn't.

Dawson left the books the way he had found them and turned to the desks.

"Which side of the room was Gladys's?"

"That one," Mrs. Ohene said, pointing to the right.

"And none of the furniture has been changed since she left?"

She shook her head. "No reason to."

The desk on the right had a single drawer that couldn't hold very much—pens, paper, and a few folders. It had a flimsy lock, the type whose key is so small it's barely worth the trouble, and Dawson noticed something wrong with it. The metal catch was up, in the locked position, and the corresponding slot in the underside of the desk was splintered apart. The drawer seemed to have been forced open. Interesting. He checked the drawer's contents for the diary. Definitely not there, no matter how much he wanted it to be. Had someone broken in and taken it? He opened the drawer of the other desk. No diary there, either, but significantly, the lock on that desk was intact.

He lifted the mattress of each bed to look underneath and checked under both beds themselves, on the floor and on the wood planks that supported the mattresses. Nothing.

Dawson stood with arms akimbo and looked around.

"That's about it, I think," he said. "Not much to search, really. Can you think of anywhere else?"

Mrs. Ohene shook her head. "No, I'm sorry. I don't have any brilliant ideas."

Dawson was rubbing his chin.

"To your knowledge," he asked her, "did anyone besides Gladys's brother and aunt come to this room after her death?"

"Not that I know of."

"I signed in at the reception desk. Do all visitors do the same?"

"Because it's a women's hall," Mrs. Ohene said, "I instituted that process for the security of the residents, and everyone *is* supposed to sign in, but I know people slip through from time to time."

"Can I see the book?"

"Of course."

They went back down to reception, where Susan was busy at the computer. She jumped up and came to the counter, eager and willing.

"Hi, Susan," Mrs. Ohene said. "We need to look through the sign-in book."

"All right, madam."

The pages were much longer than wide. Each was headed by the date, with columns for name of visitor, time in, destination, purpose of visit, time out. Most were garden-variety family or friend visits, a few were to Mrs. Ohene.

"The room number is K-sixteen, correct?" Dawson asked. He had noticed the number on the door.

"Correct," Mrs. Ohene said. "K is Gladys's block."

Dawson ran his finger down the page and stopped at his target. "Here's Charles Mensah's sign-in. Tuesday, eleven thirty in the morning. Let's go to the day before."

Susan was watching with interest, and Dawson suddenly realized how stupid he was not asking for her help.

"We're looking for visitors who went up to Gladys's room Sunday, Monday, or very early Tuesday, the twenty-fifth," he explained to her. "It would have to have been before Charles and Elizabeth arrived. Do you remember anyone in particular?"

"Tuesday, I was off," Susan said. "Monday I was here, but . . . no, sorry, I can't think of anyone."

"Any kind of visitor that seemed out of the ordinary," Dawson persisted.

She pondered again but drew another blank.

"All right," Dawson said patiently. "Let's try something else. How about *any* unusual visit to *any* part of the residence, not necessarily to Gladys's room? Anyone, going *any*where."

She shrugged, taking a stab. "The only thing I can think of was the man from the Ministry of Health who came on Monday, but Mrs. Ohene knows about that already."

Mrs. Ohene's head snapped around. "What man from the Ministry of Health?"

Susan froze. "Didn't you ask for someone to come and take care of a rat problem?"

"*Rat* problem! What rat problem? What are you talking about? We do not have rats in my hall, young lady." Mrs. Ohene was appalled. "Someone came from the Ministry of Health and you didn't notify me?"

Susan's eyes went wide with something approaching terror. "Madame Ohene, I'm so sorry. He said he had already talked to you about it earlier in the morning and that I didn't need to bother you." Her voice was shaking.

"The Ministry of Health does not handle this sort of thing, Susan," Mrs. Ohene said witheringly. "They deal with serious national problems, like AIDS and malaria control, *not* campus rats. The campus has its own pest control. Isn't that something you should know?"

"I do know that, I do, Madame Ohene," Susan said, "but this man, he said he was from the Pest and Parasite section of the Ministry of Health."

"*Pest and Parasite!*" Mrs. Ohene exclaimed. "That's the most ridiculous thing I have ever heard."

Dawson knew they were onto something now. "You say the man was here on Monday, Susan?"

"Yes."

Two days after Gladys's body was found and the day before Charles and Elizabeth had been here.

Dawson went back a couple of pages to Monday and quickly scanned the sign-ins.

"Here it is. 'H. Sekyi, oh-nine-twenty, K block, MoH Pest and Parasite.' " He looked at Mrs. Ohene. "He went to Gladys's section."

She stared at Dawson, mystified. "Who on earth is this man? What did he want?"

"Did he show any identification?" Dawson asked Susan.

"Yes. A badge that said 'Ministry of Health' and his name. He said there were complaints about rats in several rooms in the wing. He was very convincing."

"Pest and parasite indeed," Mrs. Ohene muttered.

"He asked you for a key to Gladys's room specifically?" Dawson asked Susan.

"Yes," she said, looking anguished. "He told me that's where the complaint had originated and that he would send the rat catchers out with special equipment."

Mrs. Ohene cringed. "*Rat catchers?* Oh, my goodness gracious me. Now I've heard it all."

"Do you remember what this Sekyi man looked like?" Dawson asked Susan. "Tall, short, slim, fat?"

"Not tall, but slim. And quite young. Boyish."

"Clean-shaven?"

"Yes."

"Wedding ring? I'm sure you noticed."

"Yes," she said a little sheepishly. "He did have one."

"Any distinguishing marks? Tribal scars on the face, for example?"

"No. Completely smooth skin."

"Glasses?"

"No glasses."

"One more thing. Try to picture him in your mind signing the logbook. Think carefully before you answer. What hand did he use to sign?"

"That's easy—I know it was his left because that's how I saw his wedding ring."

"You're brilliant," Dawson said. "Completely brilliant. Thank you."

"I am?" She was both relieved and incredulous, while the warden looked utterly unconvinced.

"Look at it this way," Dawson said. "If you'd called Madame Ohene, this man probably would have bolted, but instead now we have a name, and—I'm praying—I can find him at the Ministry of Health."

27

D AWSON'S DRIVE BACK TO Accra was painfully slow, with traffic particularly heavy on Independence Avenue. Lost in thought about the case as he inched along, Dawson paid little attention to the opulent buildings in this part of the city—the excessive presidential palace glittering in the sun like a diamond, the Mormon temple with its golden statue atop the tower, and the luminous College of Physicians and Surgeons.

He came back to earth as he turned left on Liberia Road and then left on the Kinbu extension to the ministries. He found parking next to the Ministry of Manpower and crossed the lot to the Ministry of Health, a cream-colored building with peculiar faded mauve trim. He started his search at the front lobby. If he had thought he would have an easy time looking for someone in a large government office, he would have been mistaken. Fortunately, he had readied himself mentally and physically. He went to a total of six departments looking for an employee by the name of H. Sekyi, each section directing him to the next.

He ended up in some kind of personnel office—or one of several, he wasn't sure. The bulky man at the desk was tapping away at a computer keyboard.

"Good morning, sir," Dawson said.

"Good morning," the man said, giving him a quick glance and returning to his screen. Apparently he was finishing up some pressing document.

"I need some information, please."

The man finished typing and looked up. "Yes? What kind of information, sir?"

"I'm trying to find an employee by the name of H. Sekyi."

"And you are?"

"Detective Inspector Dawson, CID."

"Let me check for you, Inspector." He changed the window on his screen. "Is that Sekyi with *k-y-i* or *c-h-i*?"

"*K-y-i*," Dawson said. The other spelling would be the anglicized form.

The man shook his head and got up.

"Let me try here," he said, pulling a large ring binder from the shelf. "You don't know what department he is?"

Dawson resisted the temptation to say "Pest and Parasites." "No, I don't know."

"I can't find any H. Sekyi," the man said. "Please, Inspector, if you can wait a little bit for Agnes, my co-worker, to come back. She will know."

Said Agnes walked in about ten minutes later, sucking on a Fan Milk strawberry ice, which, in the gathering heat of the day, looked very inviting.

"Agnes, this is Inspector Dawson. He's looking for one H. Sekyi he says works here."

Agnes, who obviously knew her way around, shook her head and clicked her tongue with regret. "Humphrey Sekyi? He used to work in Archives up until about six months ago, when he was sacked, and then only about one week after that, he was killed in a car crash. Poor man."

"Killed," Dawson echoed, drawing back in surprise. "He's *dead*? Could there be another H. Sekyi?"

"Not at all," Agnes said. "There's Ruth and Kwame Sekyi. No H."

"Who sacked Mr. Sekyi?"

"The Archives supervisor."

"Is the supervisor still here?"

"No, he was transferred to Ho to be in charge of the Ghana Health Service AIDS program in the Volta Region."

A smile of disbelief crept to Dawson's lips. "Transferred to Ho. Do you remember his name?"

"Of course," Agnes said. "I don't forget such things. His name was Timothy Sowah."

28

AFTER THE TOWN OF JUAPONG, Dawson continued past Ketanu on the Accra–Ho road. Both sides of the route became less forested, giving way to open bush. Under an hour later, the REDUCE SPEED NOW sign marked his arrival in Ho. It was of course a much larger town than Ketanu, but to Dawson it was still quiet and slow, like a kite lazily catching an updraft rather than an airplane taking off.

He had to get fuel and pulled up to a Total station.

"Do you know where the Ghana Health Service office is?" he asked the attendant as he filled the tank.

"I think it's somewhere near the Community Center," he said.

"And where is the Community Center?"

"Past the Municipal Assembly."

Dawson grinned. No doubt all perfectly correct, but he still didn't know how to get to the GHS office.

After some clarification and a little wandering around, Dawson found the Community Center, and the Ghana Health Service regional office was indeed adjacent to it. He parked and crossed the stretch of unpaved ground to the entrance.

Not one of the newfangled buildings in town, it looked rather rickety on the outside, but it was blissfully air-conditioned on the inside. The four employees busy at their computers were a lucky bunch.

"Good afternoon," Dawson said.

They chorused back the greeting, and one of the men asked how he could be of help.

"I'm looking for Mr. Timothy Sowah," Dawson said. "Is he here?"

"No, he hasn't come yet."

"Any idea when he'll be in?"

Everyone shook heads and said no.

"Do you know where he lives?"

One of the clerks came out onto the street with Dawson and pointed south along the road with instructions like "next to the My Savior Barber Shop" and "turn where you see the petrol station."

The directions took Dawson to a more residential area. Once he thought he was in the vicinity, he got out of the car and started asking around for Sowah. A streetwise teenage boy said he could take Dawson to his house.

They walked some distance past a group of shacks and a woman at a stand selling eggplants and tomatoes, then down a craggy lane with mosquito-friendly puddles of water. On the other side, the teenager pointed. "That is it."

Dawson fished in his pocket and gave the boy a dash. He scuttled off jubilantly.

Timothy's house was a cut above most. It was painted a sensible bronze color that masked the dust, and with its neatly shuttered windows, it looked like one of those perfect little square houses children draw. Outside, two teams of girls were deep into a game of *ampe*.

He knocked on the screen door.

"Come in," a female voice called out.

Dawson found a young woman breast-feeding her baby in the front room.

"Good afternoon. I'm Detective Inspector Dawson. Is Mr. Sowah here?"

The woman hitched her baby up a little closer to her bosom. "No sir, he's not here."

"What about Mrs. Sowah?"

"She went to market with the children."

"I see. Are you a relative?"

"I'm his niece." Her name was Charlotte, and her baby was four months old.

"She's a beautiful little girl," Dawson said.

She smiled shyly. "Thank you."

"Do you know when Mr. Sowah will be back?"

"I think he will come soon."

Soon could mean almost anything. Dawson debated what he should do.

"Thank you," he told the niece. "I'll come back."

He set back out for the Ho Magistrate Court, a salmon-colored, single-story building he had noticed while he had been looking for the GHS office. It took him about an hour to obtain the search warrants he needed. Not bad at all.

When Dawson returned, Charlotte was watching television while her baby slept on her lap. Timothy hadn't come back yet. Dawson had no inclination to sit around waiting, so he showed the warrant to the young mother, who read it and nodded uncertainly when Dawson told her he was going to search Timothy's bedroom.

The hallway beyond the front room was dim. There were two doors off either side and one at the end, which Dawson correctly guessed was Timothy's room. He pushed the door open, stepped in, and looked around. Compulsively neat and well organized—exactly what Dawson would have expected from Timothy Sowah. Nonfiction books were in one bookcase, on the left side of a shiny mahogany desk, and fiction was in another bookcase on the right. Dawson noticed they were arranged alphabetically by author. Atop the desk was a nice-looking laptop. Judging from that and his fancy Audi, Timothy Sowah was not a man without means.

Dawson turned to the desk, which had a column of four drawers on either side. He wanted to search quickly and efficiently, and preferably finish before Timothy, his new suspect, returned. Primarily he was looking for Gladys's diary, but he was also on the lookout for anything else relevant.

Timothy's drawers were arranged as meticulously as his bookshelves—paper in one, stationery in the next, a third with AIDS information pamphlets. Nothing was out of place.

Dawson found no diary. He checked the underside of the desk, where people often hide items with the aid of tape. Nothing there.

Dawson began to go through every book on the shelves. Perhaps Timothy had slid the diary between them or within one. He found nothing.

He spun a few revolutions in the chair, which was fun but made him dizzy. As he waited for the room to stop spinning, he noticed a recessed handle at the *side* of the desk. He pulled on it, and it tilted out to reveal a wedge-shaped space deeper than it was wide. Dawson's hand shot in and retrieved two items. They were both identity badges for the Ministry of Health. One belonged to Timothy Sowah, Supervisor, Department of Archives. The other belonged to Humphrey Sekyi.

"Ah," Dawson sighed. How utterly rewarding.

Two minutes later, voices drifted in from the front of the house, and Dawson recognized one of them as Timothy's. Hurried footsteps approached until Timothy made his appearance in the bedroom doorway.

29

"CAN I BE OF assistance, Inspector Dawson?" Polite but icy.

"I certainly hope so."

Timothy moved into the room like a wary cat. "May I ask what you are doing here?"

"I need to ask you one or two questions."

"Charlotte tells me you have a search warrant. May I see it?"

Dawson handed it to him. He read it quickly and gave it back.

"What is it you're searching for?"

"You were a supervisor of the Archives Department at MoH in Accra?"

"Yes. That's correct." Still wary. "Why do you ask?"

"Do you remember Humphrey Sekyi?"

Timothy's eyes flickered. "I don't recall that name."

"You should. He worked under you in Archives until you sacked him."

"Oh, yes, yes, of course. It slipped my mind. I fired him for theft. Why your interest in him?"

"It appears a Humphrey Sekyi from the MoH went to the women's hall at the University of Ghana and got into Gladys's dormitory room."

"Good gracious," Timothy said. "How? Or why? What would he want there?"

"*He* wouldn't want anything there, because Humphrey Sekyi is dead."

The side of Timothy's face twitched, and his Adam's apple bobbed up and down like a rubber ball. "All right, but what does this have to do with me, or with your being here in my room, for that matter?"

"Everything. The man who went into Gladys's room matches your description exactly. Including being left-handed. When you sacked Sekyi, he turned in his badge, which came in very handy when you needed someone to impersonate."

"You can't prove any of this."

Dawson held up both the badges he had found, and Timothy's eyes almost jumped out of his head.

"Do you want to modify your story now?" Dawson asked.

Timothy slumped into a chair behind him, sighed, and put his head in his hands.

"You forced open Gladys's desk drawer and took her diary, didn't you?" Dawson asked.

Timothy nodded. "Yes."

"Why did you do that?"

"Mr. Dawson, I must be honest with you. The trouble is . . . the problem is I was having an affair with Gladys. I was in love with her."

"Go on."

"The diary— Well, I had never read anything from it before Gladys's death, but she always told me it had her deepest and most secret thoughts. I was curious, but out of respect when she was alive, I never trespassed. When she died, I panicked because I knew the family would soon be picking up all her belongings, and they'd be able to read everything. I couldn't afford it getting out that I was having an affair. So, yes, I hurried to her dorm room and was relieved to find the diary was still there, and I took it. I wanted to be completely certain no one could track me, so I used a dead man's identification. I thought I was being clever."

"Where is the diary now? What did you do with it?"

Timothy's jaw was working rhythmically. He did not look at Dawson.

"What did you do with it, Timothy?"

He took a deep breath. "I burned it."

His voice warbled badly, and Dawson smiled inwardly. *Timothy Sowah, you are lying to me.*

"What was in the diary?"

"She wrote every day—sometimes a little, sometimes a lot. She talked about everything."

"About you?"

"Yes. How she felt whenever she was with me—here in town or out in the rural areas. We snatched moments here and there."

"Did you write love letters to each other?"

"When she was away at school, we did. She was more inclined to write than I was."

"Did you save the letters?"

"For a while, yes."

"But then you destroyed them too."

"I did."

"Did you love Gladys as much as she did you?"

He hesitated. "I don't know. Well, probably not."

"For instance, you would not have left your wife to marry her, would you?"

"It would have been impossible, Inspector Dawson."

"Was Gladys pressuring you to do just that?"

"I had to explain how unrealistic it would have been."

Timothy looked up and faced Dawson's gaze unflinchingly for a moment, and then he looked away. "I miss her. Badly."

"Perhaps too much to destroy her diary."

Timothy started. "Pardon?"

"The diary is not in this house because having it here would risk its being discovered by your wife," Dawson said, "but I don't believe you've destroyed it. The diary is like a part of Gladys's soul. It contains

Gladys's essence. She's been murdered, you miss her terribly, and now you'll set her soul alight and burn it? I don't think so. You're not that kind of person. Where is the diary, Timothy?"

"Inspector Dawson," he said, "I've told you the truth."

"We'll see about that," Dawson said. "Let's pay a visit to your office in town."

As Timothy Sowah sat sullenly in a corner, Dawson began to strip the GHS office down. First he emptied every drawer and checked that none had a false bottom. Then he started on the bookcases, flipping through every volume of mind-paralyzing GHS documents.

There was a locked gunmetal gray cabinet along the rear wall of the room. "What's in here?" Dawson asked, rattling the door.

"Old files and things like that," Timothy said.

"Would you open it up, please?"

"As you wish."

The cabinet contained more daunting rows of folders, ring binders, and large envelopes. Dawson did not show it, but he was beginning to lose some of his confidence as he searched each item and found nothing. He turned away.

"I hope I've been able to help," Timothy said as he locked the cabinet again.

Dawson said nothing. He scanned the room and reflected what an extraordinarily ordered person Timothy Sowah was—the type who, as a student, was always the first to get his textbooks and label them neatly with his name.

Once upon a time in primary and secondary school, the more compulsive pupils would design jackets to protect the covers of their new textbooks. Some jackets were fashioned most intricately, with precisely folded edges and self-locking corners. Plain wax paper and brown paper were common, but a colorful or unique jacket was prestigious. One made from old newspaper was laughable and considered bush, as in unsophisticated. Timothy would have been the type who made superior book covers.

Book covers.

Dawson inclined his head and stared at the cabinet.

"Something wrong, Inspector?"

"Unlock that again, please."

On the top shelf, four ring binders. Dawson transferred them to Timothy's desk. One of them had a white plastic jacket. Dawson pulled it off and looked at the edges of the binder's hard covers. The back one was thicker than the front, and its edge seemed to have been tampered with. He pressed his fingertips into the edge and wiggled them in until the cover began to separate into two layers. He grasped with both hands and pulled hard. The binder's cover came apart. A dark blue, embossed leather diary was tucked securely within.

Timothy's head fell forward as if he had been guillotined.

In the center of the diary were two folded, handwritten letters. Both began with "Dearest Gladys" and ended with "Love from Tim." One paragraph in one letter, written in February, stood out to Dawson. Timothy had written:

> I love you, dearest, but I hope you understand I still have a family to take care of and I do have obligations. I can't just leave my wife. My love, I'm not rejecting you, I'm just trying to explain the reality we're facing.

Next, Dawson flipped through the pages of the diary. Gladys had made an entry almost every day, with few gaps. She gave accounts of her journeys and AIDS teaching sessions, but in other entries she poured out her feelings about AIDS, poverty, superstition, and ignorance.

> Thursday, 20th March. I left him a message on his mobile. I told him he has to meet me tomorrow by the forest footpath after I've finished my work at Bedome, and that if he shuns me, he *will* regret it because I will be paying his wife a little visit. "Heaven has

no rage like love to hatred turned, nor Hell a fury like a woman scorned."

Angry. Very angry. A side of Gladys that Dawson was seeing for the first time. She was found dead two days later, on Saturday morning, but she was most likely murdered on the evening of *Friday,* the twenty-first, the day she'd wanted her lover to meet her at the forest path.

Timothy was staring at the floor with arms tightly folded across his midriff. He was rocking gently back and forth. Dawson came to his side and put his hand on his shoulder.

"Timothy Sowah, I'm arresting you on suspicion of murdering Gladys Mensah."

30

MR. BOATENG HAD REQUESTED permission to visit with his son Samuel in his jail cell, but Constable Gyamfi was busy at the police desk, so Boateng had to wait. No one could visit a prisoner without an escort.

Finally Gyamfi beckoned to Boateng to follow him back.

"Tell your son to eat," Gyamfi said. "He's not taking anything, and that's foolish. His bones are beginning to stick out even more than before."

Boateng saw the evidence for himself. A plate of rice lay untouched on the floor, not far from the filthy plastic bucket into which Samuel was supposed to empty his bladder and evacuate his bowels. The place stank, and the small barred window high up on the wall did nothing to improve ventilation.

Samuel was lying on his side, facing the wall with knees drawn up.

"Samuel, you have a visitor," Gyamfi announced.

No movement.

"Samuel."

He stirred and lifted his head.

"Get up. Your father is here to see you."

As his son slowly stood up, Boateng's stomach swooped. Samuel had changed drastically. His cheeks were sucked in, his eyes were bloodshot, and his ribs were sticking out like the slats of a louvered window. The boy was starving. He didn't move to the jail bars in one easy stride as he normally would have. He took three shuffling steps, holding on to his trousers so they wouldn't slip off his sparse hips.

Gyamfi stood discreetly to one side.

Samuel leaned against the bars, and his father tried to smile at him. The bars weren't far enough apart to admit a full hand, so they shook fingers.

"How are you?" Boateng said softly.

"Fine, Papa."

"They say you're not eating."

"Mm. Not hungry."

"You have to eat something. What about if I bring some food for you?"

Samuel shrugged. "If you like, Papa."

Constable Gyamfi spoke up. "No outside food allowed. Sorry."

"Oh, okay, sir," Boateng said.

"Papa, have you talked with Inspector Fiti?"

"I haven't seen him."

"Try to talk to him today," Samuel said weakly. "Ask him when he will let me go."

Boateng swallowed. "Samuel, have you told them everything? Have you told the truth?"

"Of course."

"If there's something more to tell, you should tell it."

"There's nothing more."

"They said you were talking to the girl near the forest. That evening, I mean."

"Yes, but I went away and left her alone. I would never do anything to hurt her."

"All right."

It seemed Samuel had all of a sudden grown up into a man.

"Time up," Gyamfi announced.

"I'll come back tomorrow," Boateng said. "But you have to eat, Samuel. Please. Look at your bones. They are poking out like sticks."

Just before noon, a visitor arrived at the police station. Gyamfi knew Osewa Gedze fairly well. She was quiet and law-abiding, attractive in a full-blooded, mature way—*not like some of the young girls these days who relax their hair and bleach their skin.*

Mrs. Gedze asked for Inspector Fiti, and Gyamfi told her he wasn't in the office.

"Maybe I can help you with something?" he offered.

"It concerns Gladys Mensah, Constable," Osewa said.

"You can report it to me and then I'll tell the inspector."

He saw her appraise him quickly, and then she nodded. "All right, that's fine. Maybe what I have to tell you is not important, or maybe it is. The evening before Gladys was killed, I saw something."

"Go on."

"I was collecting firewood to take home. First I saw that boy Samuel following Gladys. They started to talk, and then Isaac Kutu the healer came and he and the boy started to quarrel. He told the boy to go away, and after some time Samuel obeyed him. Then Kutu and Gladys conversed before he went back to his house. At that time, Gladys began walking back to Ketanu."

"Yes? Continue."

"I was finishing up tying the firewood, when I saw Samuel come out of the bush and again he started to walk and converse with Gladys."

"And then what happened?"

"He tried to hold her hand and put his arms around her, but she didn't let him. But after a while he went into the bush with her."

"Did he force her?"

"No, she just followed him."

"And you? Did you follow them?"

She looked puzzled. "Why should I follow them, Constable?"

"I'm just asking."

Gyamfi looked up, and Osewa turned around as Inspector Fiti came into the station. He stopped when he saw her at the desk.

"Mrs. Gedze," he said. "It's been a long time. How are you?"

"I'm fine, thank you, Inspector."

"She has something you should hear, sir," Gyamfi said.

31

TIMOTHY SOWAH WAS BOOKED into the Ho Central Prison. Dawson tried several times to reach Inspector Fiti on the phone. The line was busy until his seventh attempt, when he got through and told Fiti about Timothy's arrest.

"You're making a mistake, Inspector Dawson," Fiti said coldly. "Why would Mr. Sowah do such a thing?"

"Because he was having an affair with Gladys. She wanted it to be more serious than he did, and she began to threaten him."

"Inspector Dawson, that happens every day. It doesn't make him a murderer. I'm warning you, okay? Sowah knows people in Accra. You could get in big, big trouble."

"So be it."

"You sound so confident. Maybe you won't be when I tell you your aunt Osewa has just come and told us she saw Samuel and Gladys going into the forest together that evening. That may have been the last time anyone ever saw Gladys."

Dawson was momentarily stunned. "Auntie Osewa told you this?"

"Yes, sir. I tell you, this boy Samuel is guilty—no one else. He has done the thing. Mark my words, he will confess."

"Inspector Fiti, I hope you remember that you can't hold Samuel longer than forty-eight hours without charging him."

"He will confess today, and he will be charged today. And my advice to you is to release Mr. Sowah before—"

At that point, the connection was lost.

At the other end of the line, Fiti shook his head as he hung up.

"They say we need someone from Accra to help us investigate," he muttered, gesturing at the phone as if Dawson was still there, "and this is the fool they send. Forty-eight hours. Okay, you will get your forty-eight hours."

Constable Bubo, who was manning the desk while Gyamfi went on an errand, said, "What's wrong, sir?"

"Never mind," Fiti said. "Bring Samuel up to the interrogation room and lock him inside until I'm ready to question him."

"Yes, sir."

Inspector Fiti went back to his office and studied Osewa's signed statement. Gyamfi had written it out for her, and she had signed her name to it. Fiti had never had any problems with the Gedzes. They were honest, hardworking people.

The statement was very detailed. The most important item was that Osewa had seen Samuel *return* to Gladys as she walked along the pathway toward Ketanu. Samuel had tried to embrace her or something like that, and then they'd disappeared together into the bush. This was crucial. Osewa didn't use a watch, but the description of the sun's position in the sky put it at around a quarter to six. Osewa had even described what the two had been wearing. Fiti believed her. She had stuck to the facts and had not changed any of the details, even when questioned repeatedly.

There was no doubt in Fiti's mind that Samuel had killed Gladys. He just had to get that confession out of the boy.

Bubo knocked and put his head in.

"He's ready."

Fiti nodded. "Let him be there for a while."

The more uncertain and anxious Samuel became, the better. It was only a matter of time before he broke down.

On the way into the interrogation room, Inspector Fiti called Constable Bubo to assist. The man was not as good a constable as Gyamfi, but he was big and intimidating and useful for generating fear when needed.

Fiti sat down opposite Samuel at the interrogation table, but Bubo stood behind Samuel, deliberately just within peripheral vision. It was more nerve-racking that way.

Samuel had become gaunt. His eyes were oversize full moons in his face, and his cheekbones were knife-sharp ridges.

"Samuel," Fiti said softly, "I want to talk to you about what you did to Gladys Mensah."

"Please, sir, I didn't do anything to her."

"Listen to me. Someone saw you go into the forest with her, and that was the last time she was seen."

Samuel sat up straight. "Who said that? It's a lie."

"Stop calling people liars and tell the truth yourself. If you continue to lie, the gods will curse you and something bad will happen."

"Who is the person who said he saw me with Gladys? Let him come here and say that to my face."

"We know what happened. After Mr. Kutu chased you away from following Gladys, you came back and accosted her as she was on her way to Ketanu. Not so?"

"No, Inspector. You have to believe me, please."

"And then you made her go inside the bush with you."

"No, no, no."

"You wanted her to be your girlfriend, we know that already, and you tried to force yourself on her, and when she refused, you killed her."

Samuel put his face in his hands and groaned over and over, as if in physical pain.

"Look at me, Samuel," Fiti said. "Stop covering your eyes and look at me."

Bubo stepped behind Samuel and pulled his hands away from his face. His cheeks were moist with tears.

"He's crying," Fiti said to Bubo. "Crying like a girl."

Bubo laughed.

Fiti pushed a pen and a sheet of paper in front of Samuel.

"If you sign this, we will stop questioning you and you will feel better."

Samuel frowned at it. He could read and write English, but this thing they were showing him was beyond his comprehension.

"What does it say?" he asked.

"It just says everything that happened. You only have to sign on the bottom."

Samuel shook his head.

"If you don't sign it," Fiti said, "I'll throw you in jail and keep you there until you rot. But if you sign it, I can tell the judge who takes your case to pardon you and then they will set you free."

Fiti could see Samuel was thinking hard about what to do. He looked confused and afraid, which was perfect.

"If you don't confess and sign this paper," the inspector went on, "I will have to go to your father and tell him how you killed Gladys."

Samuel stiffened, and his brow twitched at the thought. "I beg you," he whispered. "Don't tell my father."

"Then sign the paper."

"I can't sign it, Inspector."

"You can't write your name? We can help you."

"Yes, I can write my name, but . . ."

"But what?" Fiti handed him the pen. "Just write your name there on the bottom. You're not really signing—just writing your name."

Samuel held the pen for a moment, but then he put it down. "No."

Fiti glanced at Constable Bubo, who delivered such a hard blow to the back of Samuel's head that the boy was thrown forward and his face bounced against the table. Bubo planted a foot in Samuel's side and sent him hurtling to the floor.

Fiti stood. He would not be staying for this. As Bubo picked

Samuel up by the neck, the inspector said, "When you are ready to sign your name, just tell the constable."

As he returned to his office, Fiti heard the heavy thuds of Bubo's blows and the crash of Samuel's body against the walls of the small room as he screamed and begged for mercy. After each round, Bubo could be heard asking the boy if he would sign the confession. He would not, and so the next round of beatings began. *The boy would confess. He had to.*

32

TIMOTHY SOWAH ASKED THAT his lawyer be present during his interrogation, but it turned out that counsel was in Lagos and wouldn't be able to make it to Ho before the next day at the earliest. So Timothy would be spending the night in jail, and Dawson decided to find somewhere to stay overnight in Ho rather than go back to Ketanu. He called Chances Hotel but found their prices were far beyond his reach. *Hence the name,* he thought wryly. *Chances are you can't afford it.* He should have known. That hotel was every tourist's first choice when visiting the Volta Region.

He found another place called Liberty Hotel, an establishment of dubious credentials, but he wasn't that bothered. After filling up with a meal of yam and fish stew, Dawson spent some time in his hotel room looking over Gladys's diary and the two letters from Timothy that she had kept with it. The more Dawson read, the more it became clear that Gladys was smitten with the kind of infatuation that makes a person blind to reason and reality. The more she closed in on Timothy, the more he drew back in alarm, and that hurt Gladys, as it always does in these cases. Pain quickly turned to anger.

Something troubled Dawson, though. It was Timothy who had pressed for a detective from Accra because he doubted the abilities of the CID man stationed at Ho. If Timothy was the murderer, why would he have done that? Wouldn't he have wanted a *less* competent investigator, to increase the chances that the case would go unsolved and he'd get off scot-free? The question didn't blow Dawson's case apart, but it did make him uneasy.

The mobile signal was strong in Ho, and Dawson called Christine to let her know how things were going. Hosiah was doing fine and spoke to Dawson briefly before his bedtime story. Six-year-old boys are short on phone conversation. After he had hung up, Dawson had a smoke and felt good, and then he played his kalimba. Marijuana made his fingers more nimble. He took a shower and then turned in to bed. He was bone tired.

Reindorf Bannerman, Timothy Sowah's lawyer, was supposed to arrive by nine o'clock in the morning but did not show until almost noon. While he was waiting, Dawson bought the *Daily Graphic* from a newspaper boy. On the second page he came across a small article that made him curse with disgust.

Madina Traditional Healer Released

ACCRA—Well-known herbalist and traditional healer Augustus Ayitey has been released from Madina police custody. Charges of assault on a child being treated for illness have been dropped. Chief Superintendent Theophilus Lartey, of the Criminal Investigations Department, stated that an investigation would be carried out as to whether Mr. Ayitey was improperly detained.

One of the Ho police constables came up to Dawson. "Please, sir, Mr. Bannerman has arrived and we are ready."

They went into the interrogation room. Timothy was seated at the table next to Bannerman. He was tense and did not look like he had

had much sleep. Nervousness had replaced his self-assured air, but Bannerman, despite his resemblance to a squat bulldog, had a warm voice and a calming effect on his client.

"You'll be all right," he said quietly to Timothy, touching his arm.

He shook hands with Dawson and said, "Are you ready to proceed?"

"Yes, thank you, Mr. Bannerman. Good afternoon, Timothy."

Dawson wasn't going to take any chances that the suspect might get off on a technicality, so he was careful to recite verbatim the police advisory statement, known to some as the Judge's Rule, that cautioned Timothy that he didn't have to say anything, but that what he did say could be used in evidence against him.

"I've been looking through Gladys Mensah's diary," Dawson went on, "and in several places she talks about how she feels about you.

"Here's one from early this month: 'I can't stop thinking about Timmy. Can't wait to see him when I go up to Ketanu.' By 'Timmy' she means you, is that correct, Mr. Sowah?"

"Yes."

"Were you having sexual relations with Gladys Mensah?"

"Is that necessary, Detective Inspector?" Bannerman cut in.

"The type of relationship is important in establishing motive."

Bannerman conceded and nodded permission to Timothy, who hesitated before he said, "We did have sex, yes."

"How often?"

"*Please,* Mr. Dawson," Bannerman said. "There's no need for prurience."

"That wasn't my intention. I'll rephrase. Where and when, Mr. Sowah, did you rendezvous with Gladys?"

"Sometimes I went to Accra and booked a hotel in town and Gladys would come to see me there."

"What about in Ketanu?"

"I had access to the Ministry of Health guesthouse, and she would join me."

"The same one I'm staying at now?"

"Yes."

"I see. Did you ever meet in the forest around Ketanu and Bedome?"

"Once or twice."

Dawson flipped through Gladys's diary entries. One in particular caught his eye.

I despise Togbe Adzima. I want to get the trokosi wives away from him, but there has to be a place for them to go, somewhere they can make a living.

That was an important paragraph, but for the moment, Dawson was more concerned with what was going on directly between Gladys and Timothy.

"On the fifteenth of March," he continued, "Gladys wrote, 'Timmy says he doesn't think he can spend Easter Sunday with me. I can understand that he may not be able to take the whole day, but I don't believe he can't reserve a couple of hours for me. I feel he's pulling away from me.' What would make her say that, Mr. Sowah?"

"I don't know why she thought that."

"Tuesday, the eighteenth of March: 'He won't answer my calls.' Was that true?"

"I never deliberately tried to avoid her calls."

"But something was wrong, Mr. Sowah," Dawson pressed, "because here's what she said just the following day, the nineteenth: 'Went to Ho to Timmy's office since he won't answer my phone calls. He was meeting with some VIP from Accra, and when I came in, Tim looked as if he would faint. Then he called me "Miss Mensah" as though he hardly knew me and said he couldn't talk right now. That was a hateful and cowardly thing to do. You don't abandon your loyalties just because you're afraid of what people may think.'

"Thursday the twentieth: 'Love has to grow. It can be secretive at the beginning, but it can't stay that way. I should not need to play hide-and-seek with the man I love. He doesn't love his wife, he's told me that. Then why can't he leave her?' So now Gladys was putting a lot of pressure on you, Mr. Sowah, not so?"

Timothy took a deep breath. "I loved her, I loved being with her, but little by little it felt as if she had me by the throat."

"What did you decide to do about it?"

"I knew I had to sit down and have a serious talk with her before it got beyond control. When I received her message on Thursday threatening me that she would go to my wife, I called her back and agreed we should meet in the forest the next day to talk."

"Why the forest and not the guesthouse?"

"Because at the time it was occupied by an official visiting from Upper Region."

"How did you feel, Mr. Sowah, when Gladys threatened you with confronting your wife?"

"I felt sick. I didn't know whether she would really do it or not, but the thought that she should go to the length of making a threat like that made her seem a very different person from the one I'd known. It was very disturbing."

"Did you have an impulse, even if slight, to kill her?"

"No."

"She's becoming obsessed, maybe even dangerous to you. An affair can be exciting, but it's the routine life with your spouse that gives stability, and stability is comforting even if dull. The prospect of losing it can be frightening."

"I know that, but I would never kill her."

"Did you set a time to meet on Friday, the twenty-first of March?"

"We said no later than five because no one wants to be in the forest after dark, but I had a meeting that kept me, and I didn't leave Ho till about quarter to five. I was running late."

"What time did you get to Ketanu?"

"I didn't."

Dawson frowned. "What do you mean you didn't?"

"Just as I was getting to Sokode, which is only about five kilometers from Ho, I had a flat tire, and I didn't have a spare, so I had to limp into the town to see if someone could repair the puncture. It took me a little while to find someone."

Dawson felt momentarily derailed. This had come out of the blue.

"Did you try to ring Gladys to let her know you were delayed?" he asked.

Timothy nodded. "Yes, but I kept getting that 'subscriber out of range' message. By the time my tire had been repaired, it was dark and there was no point in going to the forest. Gladys would not have waited until then because it simply isn't safe. So I had no choice but to come back to Ho."

"Weren't you worried about her?"

"But of *course* I was. I tried all night to reach her on her mobile."

"Why didn't you go to her house in Ketanu to check if she was all right?"

Timothy sighed. "Look, in retrospect I know I should have, but at the time I thought . . . I'm not sure what I thought. I think I thought she might be so angry with me, she might have decided she didn't want to talk to me. Would I go to her house and risk creating some scene?" He closed his eyes and rubbed his forehead. "I feel like I've been such a coward. From the very beginning, everything I did in relation to Gladys was cowardly."

"I think we've established that my client could not have been responsible for the murder of Gladys Mensah," Bannerman said. "She was found the following morning in the forest, and clearly that's where the murder took place. We can't be sure of the exact hour, but obviously my client was not present at either the time or the place. You therefore have no grounds on which to hold him any longer."

"I don't think we've established your client's innocence at all," Dawson said firmly. "And as for the murder taking place in the forest, that isn't necessarily the case. Her body could have been brought from elsewhere and dumped."

Bannerman became exasperated. "You're clutching at straws, Detective Inspector Dawson. Come now, this is preposterous. I demand that you confirm my client's alibi immediately and release him forthwith. Is that understood?"

Dawson refused to be rattled. "Timothy, are you able to show us the location of the repair shop in Sokode?"

"Yes, of course."

33

INSPECTOR FITI WENT TO see Samuel and found him lying on the floor of the cell with his knees pulled up to his chest. His back was bruised where Bubo had whipped him, and there was one small telltale cut below his left eye.

"Get him a shirt," Fiti ordered Bubo, not wanting anyone else to see evidence of the thrashing.

Bubo brought one from the storeroom where they had a pile of discarded clothes. He stood Samuel up and helped him put the shirt on.

"Are you going to sign the confession?" Fiti asked Samuel.

Samuel shook his head and went back to the floor to curl up.

"Do you want us to beat you again?"

Samuel shrugged.

"I'm going to tell your father what you've done," Fiti said.

Samuel looked up as if about to say something, but he lowered his head again and closed his eyes.

Boateng was sitting outside the house and jumped up eagerly as he saw Inspector Fiti and Constable Bubo walking up. He pulled over two stools for them.

"Bring them some water," Boateng told his wife.

Fiti waited for her to return with two battered tin cups of water. She disappeared quickly to leave the men to their meeting.

"How are you today, Inspector Fiti?" Boateng asked deferentially.

"I'm fine, but your boy is not."

"Please, what is wrong, Inspector?"

"He killed the girl. Gladys Mensah."

Boateng squirmed. "He killed her?"

"Yes. Someone saw him go with her into the forest, and that was the last time she was ever seen."

"Who saw him?"

"I can't tell you that, but I believe what the person says. So your boy did it, but he won't confess. If he confesses, he will get a light sentence from the judge. So talk to him. Tell him to confess and sign the paper. Okay?"

Boateng's shoulders slumped. He was devastated.

Fiti stood up and patted him on the shoulder. "Go and see him now, understand?"

One of the Ho police constables drove Dawson and Timothy the five kilometers to Sokode. They bumped over an unpaved, gravelly road full of potholes.

"Turn at the next right," Timothy instructed.

They bounced along a little farther, and Timothy pointed. "There it is."

In God We Trust Motors was aptly named, being not much more than a wobbly shack amid scores of large and small engine parts scattered about the yard. A wiry man in his forties was tinkering with a chunk of equipment on a table and looked up as the car approached and stopped about fifty meters away.

"Is that the man who did your repair?" Dawson asked Timothy.

Timothy was squinting out the window. "I don't think so. He doesn't look familiar."

"Wait here," Dawson said, getting out.

He walked over to the man. "Ndo na wo."

"Ndo. Any problem?"

"I'm Dawson, from Accra police." He showed his ID.

"I'm Quaye."

They shook hands. Quaye's palm was rough as sandpaper.

"Am I in trouble, sir?" he asked.

"Not as far as I know," Dawson said. "Are you the owner here?"

"Yes, sir."

"I need your help. Do you see that man sitting in the back of the car? Do you recognize him?"

Quaye took a look for a few seconds and then shook his head. "No, sir. Why?"

"He says he was here last week Friday."

"I wasn't here at that time. Only my cousin."

"Is your cousin here now?"

"No, sir. He went back to Cape Coast."

"You work here alone?"

"My son helps me, and he was working last week. Do you want to talk to him?"

"Yes, please."

Quaye turned his head and yelled, "Ato! *Ato!*"

A skinny, bare-chested boy of about ten years old came around from behind the shack wearing threadbare oversize Nikes.

"Yes, Papa?"

"This is Inspector Dawson from Accra. He's a detective."

"Good afternoon, sir."

"How are you, Ato?" Dawson said.

Ato's attention was momentarily drawn to the police car, and he suddenly smiled and waved.

"You know that man?" Dawson asked Ato in surprise.

"Yah, I remember him," he said. "He came last week with a tire puncture."

Dawson's stomach lurched. "What day last week?"

"Friday, sir."

"How are you so sure it was Friday?"

"Because it was my birthday and I was conversing with him and when I told him it was my birthday he gave me some extra dash." Ato grinned.

Dawson's mouth had gone dry. "What time of day was he here?"

"I don't remember exactly, but it was getting to evening time."

"And he left when?"

"He was our last customer and it was already dark. After him, we closed, so I think maybe about almost seven."

"What kind of car was he driving?"

"Audi Eighty. "

"Color?"

"Like a silver or gray color."

That was what Timothy drove. A silver Audi 80.

"And you remember that was his car for sure?"

"Oh, yes." Ato's eyes went wistful. "I love that Audi Eighty toooo much."

Dawson was shattered. His heart was pounding as he went back to the car.

"Do you remember that boy over there?" he asked Timothy.

He nodded. "I do. I gave him a couple cedis for his birthday—as he claimed it was."

"What kind of car were you driving?"

"My Audi, of course. What else would I be driving?"

Dawson was asking these questions in the futile hope that he could somehow stitch his case back together, but he knew he couldn't. The brutal fact was that Timothy's alibi was now established beyond a reasonable doubt.

"What's going to happen now?" Timothy asked.

Dawson stared at him, feeling chilly even in the hot afternoon sun. "You're free to go," he said.

"Oh, super. Um, if it's not too much of a bother, can I have a ride back to Ho?"

34

SAMUEL DREAMT HE WAS trying to get away from his father, but he seemed to be running in place and Papa got closer and closer to him, reaching with grasping fingers as he called out his name.

"Samuel. *Samuel!*"

He started awake and realized it was Papa calling him in real life. He got up and went to the bars. This time, Mama had come too. Samuel ached to be on the other side with her.

Constable Bubo leaned against the wall and watched them with folded arms.

"Mama, Papa," Samuel said, "I'm so glad to see you."

He could tell his mother had been crying, and it made tears prick the corners of his own eyes. Papa looked sad, but it wasn't like anything Samuel had seen before. This was deep, and there was pain and anger.

"Papa. What's wrong?"

"Why have you brought us this shame, why have you disgraced us?"

"Papa, I'm not trying to—"

"*Quiet!* Do you hear me? Keep quiet. You have always been a troublemaker and a liar. Tell the truth just for once, eh? Tell the inspector what you did to that girl. They already know you did it, eh? Someone saw you going into the forest with the girl, so why are you trying to deny it?'"

"Papa, it's not *true*," Samuel said desperately.

"Confess, Samuel, please. If you confess, they will give you a lighter punishment and the gods of Ketanu will forgive you."

"But Papa, *I didn't do it*." His voice broke and rose to a high pitch that bounced off the cell walls.

"Samuel, stop," Mama said. "You can't hide it anymore."

Samuel hit the jail bars with his open hand and turned away in fury and despair. He put his forehead against the dank wall and wept.

"Take me out of here, please, Papa, take me out. They're going to kill me, I swear, they're going to beat me to death."

"Then tell them the truth!" Papa shouted. "*Tell* them!"

Samuel stopped crying and sank to his knees with his head bowed. Mama was weeping now.

"I'm sorry, Mama," he whispered. "I'm sorry."

Bubo said, "Time to go."

They left, and the cell became ghostly quiet again.

Timothy was released and cleared of all charges. Dawson drove despondently back from Ho to Ketanu. For the first time since beginning the case, he was starting to doubt himself. What if it *was* Samuel who did it? Maybe Dawson didn't want to believe it because Samuel was *Fiti's* suspect and not his. Was he perhaps prejudiced against Fiti because the man was just a "bush policeman"? Wouldn't it be ironic if it really was Fiti doing the solid detective work and not Dawson?

Now that he had no case against Timothy, Dawson wanted to find out more about what Auntie Osewa had told Inspector Fiti—or what he *said* she had told him.

All of a sudden, Dawson felt a powerful need to talk to Christine. He pulled over and got his phone out.

"What's wrong?" she asked, even before he had the chance to tell her how miserable he was.

"Everything," he said gloomily. "Not getting *any*where with this case."

"No leads?"

"I'm either following them wrong or they're just not the right ones."

"Are you and the local police chief or head or whatever he's called getting along?"

"No."

"Something you think you can smooth over, or has it gone beyond the point of no return?"

"I don't know, quite honestly. I was supposed to be here to clear up this case, but I'm beginning to think it's really me making the blunders."

"I wonder if . . ."

"If what?"

"If you might call Detective Armah, see if he has some ideas. After all, he was in Ketanu himself those years back—maybe he has some tips."

"You see? This is why I married you. For your brains."

"Oh, *really*. What's wrong with my looks?"

They both laughed.

"You know what I want right now, don't you," Dawson said, lowering his voice.

"I have no idea," she said airily.

He groaned. "Christine, I'm dying."

"Focus, focus. Don't you men ever get past adolescence?"

"Well, obviously I'm not getting any sympathy out of you," Dawson said in mock resentment.

Christine giggled. "Sorry."

"I'll be going now. You'll find me sulking in a corner."

Christine let loose a peal of laughter.

"I'm glad you find it amusing," Dawson said. "Good-bye, and kiss Hosiah for me."

"Yes, of course I will. Be careful, Dark."

"I will. Bye, love."

After he hung up with Christine, he tried to reach Armah on his mobile, but the circuits were busy. He would try again later on.

No one was around as Dawson entered the station. The front desk was unattended. He heard an odd, low-pitched thud rather like the impact of a bass loudspeaker. Gyamfi suddenly appeared from somewhere in the back of the building, walking quickly and looking distressed.

"Gyamfi? What's wrong?"

Gyamfi stopped, shoulders slumped, arms limp at his sides, as if all vigor had been flogged out of him.

"I tried to stop them, sir," he said. "I swear I tried."

Dawson heard another thud and then a muffled scream, and now he realized it was coming from the interrogation room. He moved fast. The door was shut. He shoved it open.

Bubo was whipping Samuel with a thin bamboo cane frayed at the tip to deliver maximum sting. He drew his hand back to strike again. Samuel, torso naked and trousers almost coming off, leapt away and collided with the wall. The cane hissed through the air and made contact, raising an instant stripe of inflamed flesh. Samuel cried out, lost his balance, and fell.

Inspector Fiti was watching from a corner of the room. "Are you ready to confess?" he asked Samuel calmly.

Bubo raised the cane, and Samuel cringed. "I beg you, stop, please. *Stop.*"

The cane landed again, and Samuel jumped as if jolted by an electric shock.

Dawson felt a tidal wave of rage rising and sweeping him along on its deadly crest. He knew the sensation well—the muffling of sounds around him, the crimson heat erupting deep in his chest and spreading quickly up into his neck while the surface of his skin turned cold with a thousand icy pins and needles. He could seriously hurt Bubo this instant. A good choke hold, he could kill him, and he felt a strong impulse to do it.

He moved in close behind the constable. "Beating him won't bring your mother back."

Bubo swung around like a whirling flywheel.

"*Hey!*" Fiti shouted at Dawson. "What are you doing?"

But Bubo was frozen in place. His eyes had gone wide with distress and astonishment. His eyelids twitched as he began to speak.

"You s-s-s-say what?"

"It won't bring her back."

"How do you know about my m-m-mother?"

"I lost mine too."

Bubo jerked his head back, and his eyes narrowed as if an eerie suspicion was slowly dawning.

"Are you a w-w-wizard?" he whispered.

"Maybe."

Bubo dropped the cane on the floor and scrambled for the exit, giving Dawson as wide a berth as he could in the small space. He pushed past Gyamfi, who was standing in the doorway.

Fiti gaped at Dawson. "What did you do?"

Dawson didn't answer. He went to Samuel, who was on his feet again.

"Are you all right?" Dawson asked.

Samuel nodded.

"Let me see. Turn around."

There was a crisscross pattern of welts and bloodied streaks of raised skin all over his back.

Dawson looked at Fiti. "You see this? You see what you've done?"

Fiti glared back defiantly, and without taking his eyes off Dawson, he said to Gyamfi, "Take the boy back to the cell."

"Leave him alone," Dawson said.

"*I say take him back!*" Fiti shouted.

Samuel's face contorted with pain, and his body seemed to shrivel like a shrub dying under the scorching sun. "No, I beg you, please. I don't want to go back—"

"Then confess and we will send you to a better place to stay in Ho," Fiti said.

"Samuel, don't say anything," Dawson warned.

Gyamfi took Samuel by the arm to lead him away, but he crumpled to the ground weeping.

"I did it," he moaned. "I did it."

"Did what?" Fiti said.

Dawson crouched on the floor near him. "No, Samuel, *stop*."

Samuel slapped his head repeatedly with both hands. "I killed her, I killed her, I killed her."

Fiti knelt beside him. *"Killed whom?"*

"Gladys. I killed her." Samuel's body shook with sobs.

Fiti looked at Dawson and stood up with a grim smile. "There. Now you have heard him confess."

"Because he doesn't want to be beaten anymore," Dawson cried.

"Look, I know this boy and I know how these people are in Ketanu."

"You're just a bush policeman, Fiti," Dawson shouted. "You don't have a clue. All you know about is children stealing chewing gum from the market—"

Fiti banged his fist on the table in fury. "Get out! *Get out!*"

Gyamfi looked pleadingly at Dawson, and at the same time he flicked his head to one side with an oblique glance meaning *Meet me outside.*

Dawson leaned close to Samuel. "I'll do everything I can for you, do you hear? I'm not going to let anyone hurt you anymore. I know you can be strong."

As he stood up, Dawson got his phone out, pointed the camera at Samuel's back, and took three photos in rapid succession.

"What do you think you are doing, Inspector Dawson?" Fiti said.

Dawson brought his face within six centimeters of Fiti's. "I'm reporting you for this, photographs and all. And if you lay one finger on Samuel again, I'll drag you to jail."

"Don't make me laugh," Fiti said, without flinching. "You're a fool. You're not above me. You think you are smart, but you are nothing but a fool. Now, get out."

35

OUT OF SIGHT AT the side of the station, Dawson waited for Gyamfi. He paced, his pulse still racing from the confrontation and the pain of seeing Samuel being whipped.

Gyamfi appeared a few minutes later. He glanced over his shoulder to be sure he wasn't being followed. "I want to make sure you believe me, Dawson. I tried to stop them from beating Samuel, but I couldn't do anything against them."

"I believe you."

"But I don't understand what you said to Bubo. You say he lost his mother? How do you know that? He's never mentioned such a thing."

"It was just a lucky guess. Something about him made me think he might have had some sort of tragedy as a child. And even if I was wrong, it would have been such a strange thing to say to him he would have stopped to ask me what I was talking about."

"You're right," Gyamfi said. "And by the way, he still thinks you're a wizard."

They laughed, grateful for a chance to relieve tension.

"What are you going to do now, Dawson?"

"I want to work on getting Samuel's name cleared, but for now I'm going to get him transferred to Ho Central. It's too dangerous for him to stay here with Inspector Fiti."

He pulled out his mobile and called Ho Central Prison. The constable who answered said the commanding officer wasn't in. After some persuasion, the constable released the commander's mobile number, which Dawson tried immediately. No answer. He left a message and made a note to himself to call again later.

When Dawson arrived, Auntie Osewa was outside hanging clothes on a line. "Darko!" she exclaimed, smiling broadly. "How are you? I thought maybe you had forgotten about your poor old aunt again!"

"No, Auntie," he said, stooping to kiss her on the cheek. "Not at all. I had to go back to Accra on an emergency."

"Oh." Her expression changed to concern. "Is everything all right?"

"Yes, thank you. Took care of it."

"Good. Come. Uncle Kweku is inside."

He was listening to a news bulletin on a tiny portable radio, but he switched it off as Dawson and Auntie Osewa walked in.

"How are you, Darko?" he said, smiling broadly. "How is everything? Have a seat."

They chatted for a few minutes.

"So," Auntie Osewa said, "any news on the investigation?"

"That's partly what I came to talk to you about," Dawson said.

"Is that so?" she said.

"Inspector Fiti told me you've reported that Samuel went into the forest with Gladys that evening. Is that true?"

Kweku shot his wife a quizzical look. "You did? He did?"

She nodded. "I was collecting firewood when I saw them."

"You never told me," Kweku said evenly.

Osewa shrugged, unperturbed. "I didn't even think it was important until some of the women collecting water at the pump said they had heard Samuel had been arrested and the police were looking for information about him."

"Auntie, do you mind if I ask you a few questions and write down your answers?" Dawson asked.

"Of *course* I don't, Darko. You have to do your job."

He fished his notebook from his shirt pocket. "Can you say about what time you first saw Samuel?"

"Well, I don't wear a watch," she said apologetically, "but the sun was soon about to go down."

"So maybe around five thirty or five forty-five," Dawson said. "And where were you exactly when you saw them?"

"There is a place between Bedome and Ketanu where I get my firewood. I was collecting it when I heard some people talking. I went to see what was happening, and that's when I saw them."

"How far away from you were they?"

"When you were coming, did you see the two houses before ours?"

"Yes."

"From here to the one farther away from us."

"I see." That was about three hundred meters. "Do you remember the clothes they were wearing?"

She laughed. "Ei, Darko, you are giving me a tough test. The boy—well, you know his clothes are nothing special. Just some torn khaki trousers and something like a red shirt, or orange, with no sleeves. And Gladys was wearing a blue and white skirt and blouse with Adinkra symbols. Very pretty. She always wore beautiful clothes."

"You couldn't hear what they were talking about?"

"No, too far away. Do you know the firewood place?"

"No, I don't."

"If you're walking from Bedome, before you come to Mr. Kutu's compound you will see it on this side." Osewa indicated her left.

"I see. Thank you."

"But anyway, after Samuel and Gladys had been conversing for a little while, Isaac Kutu came from his compound and told Samuel to go away and leave her alone."

"I thought you said you couldn't hear anything from that distance."

"I could hear some of it now that Mr. Kutu and the boy were shouting at each other, and I could see what Mr. Kutu was saying because he was shaking his finger at Samuel like he was warning him. And so the boy went away."

"Which way did he go when he left?"

"In the direction of Bedome."

"And then what happened?"

"Mr. Kutu and Gladys conversed for a little while, and then he went back to his compound and she started walking back to Ketanu."

"And then?"

"And then I saw Samuel come out of the bush and accompany her on the path."

Dawson's hand froze. He had picked up a tremor in Auntie's voice, a ruffling of its smoothness. An eerie sensation came over him like a thousand creeping spiders. *This has happened before.*

The scene came flooding back. The evening Mama, Cairo, and Darko had visited Auntie and Uncle.

The game of oware was nearly over. Auntie Osewa had just come in from outside. Uncle Kweku asked her where she had been. "I went to set the rabbit traps," she said. Her voice felt so strange to Darko that it jolted him.

Back then, he had not wanted to think she was lying, and now Dawson had the same disturbing feeling.

He recovered. He didn't want Auntie Osewa to sense anything was amiss.

"And what happened next?" he asked.

"The boy held Gladys's hand and tried to put his arms around her, but she didn't want that. They stood there talking some more, and he was trying to persuade her. She would make as if to walk away, but he would always come around in front of her, begging her not to leave. And after a while, they went into the bush."

"He didn't take her by force?" he asked.

"No, nothing like that. "

"After they went in, did you see anyone else around?"

"Not anyone close by that I can remember."

"Okay, thank you, Auntie."

"Not at all, Dawson. Anything you want to ask, just tell me."

"Oh, yes, now that you mention it, there *is* something else. Do you know if there was anything going on between Isaac Kutu and Gladys?"

"No, I don't know anything about that."

"I heard that she wanted to steal his medicines from him," Kweku said.

"Really?" Dawson said. "Who told you that?"

"It was just some talk."

"I don't think it's true," Osewa said, shaking her head firmly. "She wasn't like that, Kweku. She was a very good, honest woman. You shouldn't say anything bad about her now that she's dead."

"I'm just telling you what I heard."

Auntie Osewa turned dismissively away from him. "Stay with us and eat, Darko, will you?"

His salivary glands sprang into action at the thought of Auntie Osewa's cooking.

"I'd love to," he said.

And for now, he put the worrying questions out of his mind.

36

DAWSON LEFT AUNTIE OSEWA around seven that evening after a meal of goat meat stew and rice, and he made his next stop the Mensahs' house. Lights were on inside. Dawson tapped on the side of the front screen door, which was tightly shut to keep the mosquitoes out.

"Who is it?" Charles's voice answered.

"Inspector Dawson."

Charles came to the door and opened it with a smile. "Good evening, Inspector. Come in. You are welcome. We're having a family meeting. Gladys's funeral is tomorrow."

"Ah, I see."

The front room was packed with people, and it was noisy and stifling with the heat of bodies. Several discussions were going on at once over the funeral preparations—the food and drinks, the drum and dance troupes, where the body would be placed, the seating arrangements, and so on.

Elizabeth spotted Dawson and walked over. "How are you?" she said, smiling sweetly.

"I'm well, Elizabeth. Can I talk in private with you and Charles and his parents?"

"But of course."

Elizabeth extracted Mr. and Mrs. Mensah from the tumult, and they went into a room off to the side.

"I want you all to know that I've found Gladys's diary," Dawson told them. "At least for now, I won't say exactly where I found it, but it's safe with me and I'll return it to you as soon as I can. I haven't located the bracelet yet, but I'm still looking."

"Thank you," Elizabeth and Charles chorused, and Gladys's parents echoed them.

"Please, Inspector Dawson," Mr. Mensah said, "Inspector Fiti was here earlier on and he told us Samuel has confessed to killing Gladys."

"I'm not so sure about that," Dawson said.

"Not sure about what exactly, Inspector Dawson?" Elizabeth asked.

"I have a problem with how the confession was obtained."

"We don't want the wrong person to be arrested," Charles said, "but at the same time we want to be able to say who killed my sister, because the longer we don't know who did it, the more people say bad things."

"What kinds of bad things?"

Charles glanced at his aunt.

"Why do you have to bring this up?" Elizabeth asked frostily.

"Because it's important," Charles said. "Inspector Dawson, there's a rumor that Auntie Elizabeth is a witch and that she used her powers to kill Gladys."

"It's all talk," Elizabeth said with a toss of the head. "They can't do anything to me. They are jealous of me, and that's all there is to it."

"We're just saying be careful, Sis," Mr. Mensah said. "Don't go anywhere without someone accompanying you, all right?"

"Come on. I'm not a child, Kofi."

Mr. Mensah looked at Dawson and shook his head. "That's the way she is. Stubborn as a goat."

All of a sudden, Mrs. Mensah broke her silence, and it startled Dawson. She looked at him directly with soft but intense eyes.

"You must go after Isaac Kutu, Mr. Dawson. He is the one who started all these rumors about a witch, and I know he's doing it because he doesn't want anyone to be suspicious of him. He's a dangerous man, a liar who pretends to be as good a healer as his father was. I warned Gladys to stay away from him, but she didn't and now she's dead. Samuel did not kill her. He is a harmless, useless boy. They should let him go and lock Isaac Kutu up instead."

37

Early saturday morning, dawson got dressed, grabbed a quick breakfast of oatmeal at the corner kiosk, and then headed for the other side of town. After Mrs. Mensah's stunning words last night, he was most certainly going to pay a visit to Isaac Kutu.

The Mensahs' house was along the route, and as he approached he saw a crowd outside, along with three parked minivans. Dawson spotted Elizabeth and pulled over.

"Morning, Dawson," she said as he came up.

"Morning, Elizabeth. What's going on?"

"We're getting a delegation together to pick up the body."

It seemed to Dawson like a lot of people to carry out this one mission. There was much animated discussion until it was finally decided who would go to the VRA Hospital mortuary. They piled into the vehicles and sped off.

"Where are you going?" Elizabeth asked Dawson.

"To pay Isaac Kutu a visit."

"I hope you'll be able to attend the funeral?"

Dawson loathed funerals, but he said, "I will be sure to pay my respects."

Dawson stopped at the police station on the way to Isaac's compound. He intended to see Samuel and was mentally prepared for a confrontation with Inspector Fiti if he was there.

Fortunately, neither the inspector nor Constable Bubo was in the station, although Gyamfi was at work at his desk. It seemed sometimes that Gyamfi ran the place.

"Morning, Dawson." He appeared subdued.

"How are you, Gyamfi?"

"Fine, sir."

Dawson searched his face. "Everything all right?"

Gyamfi flashed one of his brilliant smiles. "Yes, everything is fine."

"Can I see Samuel, please?"

Gyamfi hesitated. "Yes, all right. But you have to hurry before Inspector Fiti gets here. I don't want trouble."

"I'll be quick. Thank you."

Samuel was pacing in his cell, as if he had new energy.

"Are you okay, Samuel?" Dawson asked

He came to the bars. "I'm fine, sir."

"Have they been treating you well since yesterday?"

"Yes, sir."

"Did you have something to eat?"

"A little bit."

"What about your family? Did they come to see you?"

Samuel shook his head. "They don't want to talk to me anymore, sir. Well, my father doesn't."

Dawson said nothing to that, but he made a mental note to visit Mr. Boateng and persuade him that his son needed him.

"I want to ask you about that evening you talked to Gladys," Dawson said. "Do you remember what she was wearing?"

"I remember it was a blue skirt and blouse. Very nice. With white."

"Blue and white? That's all?"

"And with Adinkra symbols on it too, sir."

Samuel had just confirmed Auntie Osewa's description of Gladys's outfit. It was a strange conflict for Dawson. He didn't want his aunt to turn out to be a liar, yet he wished it wasn't true that Gladys had gone into the forest with Samuel and that it had been the last time she was ever seen.

Dawson tried another angle. "You know the place people like to get firewood?"

"Yes, I know it. Why?"

"Did you see anyone cutting firewood there that evening?"

"No. Not that there wasn't someone there, just I didn't notice anyone. Have you found something that will free me?"

"Not yet," Dawson said, "but I want to move you to Ho Central Prison as soon as possible. At least I know one or two people there who will make sure you're treated well."

"Ho Central?" Samuel's face fell. "I don't want to go to another prison. I only want to be set free."

"I know you do, Samuel. Believe me, I want that too, and as soon as I can make it happen, I will. In the meantime, I want you somewhere safe where neither Inspector Fiti nor Constable Bubo can lay a hand on you."

"I see," Samuel said dejectedly. "Okay. You know best, sir."

"Just tell me something and I will never ask the question again," Dawson said gently. "Look at me and tell me the truth. After Mr. Kutu had told you to leave Gladys alone, did you secretly come back and kill her?"

Samuel's eyes locked on his. "I didn't, Mr. Dawson. If only someone, just one person in the world, would believe that I didn't kill her."

"That one person is me." Dawson put a curved finger through the bars. "Shake."

The detective and the prisoner locked their fingers together.

"I'll be back to see you," Dawson said.

But just as he was about to leave, Gyamfi put his head around the corner.

"Wait there," he said softly. "Inspector Fiti is coming."

He hurried back to his post. Dawson heard Fiti barking an order.

"Yes, sir, Inspector," Gyamfi said. "I'll bring it to you in your office."

He returned. "I'm going into his office," he whispered. "Wait till you hear the door close."

Dawson waited, listening to the conversation between the inspector and his constable. Thirty seconds later, the office door shut with a bang and Dawson got out fast.

He walked to Isaac's compound. Tomefa was outside sorting firewood. "Isaac is out," she told Dawson, "but he'll be back soon."

While waiting, Dawson went to take a look at the spot where Auntie Osewa said she had been gathering her firewood the evening she'd spied Samuel and Gladys together. It was a cluster of trees ravaged by overcutting. Dawson stood at the edge and confirmed that Auntie Osewa would have had a good vantage point to observe Samuel and Gladys entering the forest. From Isaac Kutu's description of where he had seen them together that same evening, they would have been about three hundred meters away from where Dawson stood.

Dawson walked back to Isaac's place wondering how to resolve the conflict between Samuel's and Auntie Osewa's stories.

Isaac Kutu was standing in the middle of his compound as Dawson walked in.

"Woizo, Darko."

"How are you, Mr. Kutu?"

"I'm fine, sir."

"I would like to look around your compound, if you wouldn't mind."

"What for?"

"I'll know when I see it," Dawson said. But he thought, *A silver bracelet would be nice.*

"What if I say you cannot search this place?"

"If you attempted to stop me, I would have to arrest you."

Isaac laughed drily. "I don't believe you would do that."

Dawson took out his cuffs. "Try me."

"You'll have to catch me first."

"You won't run. You're not the kind of man to run, so we will fight."

Isaac smiled tightly and his eyes darkened. "Where do you want to search?"

"Everywhere."

The first room was small, dark, and close, and had one of the strangest smells Dawson had ever experienced. Hanging on the walls were many things he didn't recognize. The ones he did included snakeskins, mummified lizards, roots, bark, and dried leaves of several kinds. On the floor were clumps of powder of different colors.

Dawson spotted a box full of small animal skulls that made his skin crawl.

"Would you empty that, please?" he asked.

Isaac turned the box over, and the skulls rattled out. They smelled ghastly.

"What are those for?"

"Snake skulls," Isaac said. "You crush them into a powder and use it to cure snakebites."

Dawson peered into the box. There was no silver bracelet.

They moved to the second room, and Dawson poked around where he could. He was becoming ill from the odors, and he realized that, if Isaac had Gladys's bracelet, there was an infinite number of places he could have hidden it.

"What are all those things on the wall?" he asked Isaac in a third room.

"Different things for different sicknesses. I can't tell you all of them."

"Give me one or two examples."

"There is a root called asreetsopoku—that one over there. We use it to cure hernia. You cut it and wash it and drink it with gin. We have another one there, *nereyu,* that we use for heart trouble."

"Are any of these the ones Gladys was interested in?"

"She was interested in all of them."

"Did you try to hide anything from her?"

"I didn't tell her everything."

"Were you working on something secret she wanted to know about?"

"Secret, like what?"

"I don't know. I'm asking you."

"Yes, I was."

"Can you tell me?"

"Then it won't be a secret anymore."

"I can't steal it from you, so what do you care? A certain disease?"

"Of course."

"One that has no cure."

"Yes."

"You've discovered something for AIDS?"

"I can tell you a little about it, but I need something in return."

"I don't pay people for information."

"Not money, Darko. Just a promise that you won't go and tell someone in Accra who will come to try to steal from me."

"You have my word."

"First, Gladys told me one of Togbe Adzima's trokosi was suffering from AIDS."

Dawson's stomach plunged. That almost certainly meant Adzima had HIV. He thought of Efia and the other four wives. *The new wife.*

"Gladys wanted her to take a government-supplied medicine," Isaac went on, "but the trokosi refused and Nunana brought her to me instead. I gave her some traditional medicines, and she got well for some time, but she died later."

"What did Gladys do then?"

"First, she went to the wives to ask them to take a test for AIDS. Second, she asked me if I could go back to Accra with her to meet some scientists at her school about my medicine—maybe it could be made to work better."

"What did you say to that?"

"I told her I would think about it. I wasn't ready to give her an answer."

"Did she try to get Togbe Adzima tested for AIDS too?"

"Why should she?"

Dawson frowned. "The trokosi come to him as virgins."

"And so?"

"And so if one of them got AIDS, she can only have got it from Adzima."

"No, AIDS can come from a curse, or witchcraft."

Dawson shook his head. "You should stop believing that."

He turned to leave, and Isaac was surprised. "Where are you going?"

"To see Togbe Adzima."

38

BEFORE CONTINUING ON TO Bedome, Dawson took a slight diversion to talk to the handful of farmers toiling on their plots at the side of the forest.

He called out, "Good morning. *Ayekoo!*"

They responded appreciatively, and Dawson introduced himself and asked if any of them had witnessed the argument between Isaac and Samuel. Two of them said yes.

"Where were they when you saw them?" Dawson asked.

The farmers pointed, and as he turned to look, Dawson realized something that he hadn't before. Although Isaac and Samuel would have been within view from this spot, the Bedome-Ketanu footpath was obscured by a clump of bushes. It meant that the farmers would not have been able to see whoever accosted Gladys on her way home.

"Did Samuel come back this way?" Dawson asked.

The older of the two farmers nodded. "He came and helped us for a little while."

"Did he leave you before it got dark?"

The farmer shook his head. "No, sir."

"Did he seem angry after the quarrel?"

"He was annoyed, yes, but I told him not to let it trouble him, and I think he was all right after that."

Dawson thanked the two witnesses, and took down their names in case he needed to get back in touch with them.

As he walked on to Bedome, Dawson wondered, *How could Samuel have been in two places at one time—working on the farm and talking to Gladys on the path?* It wasn't physically possible.

Togbe Adzima was sitting outside bouncing one of his children on his knee, but as soon as he saw Dawson approaching, he got up and retreated into his house.

"Don't come in here," he shouted from inside. "Get away from me!"

But there was no door to stop Dawson from entering.

"What do you want from me?" Adzima snapped.

"I need to talk to you."

"About what?"

"I'm not here to do anything bad to you, but Togbe Adzima, your life may be in danger."

"What are you talking about?"

"One of your trokosi died."

"Who told you that?"

"Mr. Kutu."

"All right. And so what?"

"Have you had that blood test Gladys Mensah was giving?"

"I don't need any kind of blood test."

"Was the trokosi a virgin when she came to you?"

"Of course," Adzima said contemptuously.

"Okay, listen to me. I have come to ask you to use condoms, especially with your new wife. I can get you some."

Adzima threw his head back and roared with laugher. "For what? Mr. Detective Man, I'm not going to use any condom."

"I'm begging you."

"You are begging *me*?" Adzima spat. "You came here and did all kinds of bad things, and now you say you're begging me. You are too funny, Mr. Inspector."

After several more futile attempts to talk sense into Adzima, Dawson left abruptly, annoyed and despairing. Even if he did find a way to put the priest behind bars *today* and get him away from Efia and his other wives, it might already be too late. He may already have transmitted HIV to some or all of them.

Dawson walked quickly back toward Ketanu. He passed a mango tree laden with ripe, rosy fruit and badly wanted to climb up and pick a few. He used to love doing that as a boy. The only problem was that fire ants, just as fond of mango trees, made ingenious nests out of clusters of leaves. If they were disturbed, these vicious little creatures the color of fire launched an attack with bites that felt like a thousand red-hot needles.

As he passed by, Dawson heard a hiss from somewhere behind the mango tree. He stopped and turned.

"Mr. Dawson!" A loud whisper.

He moved back toward the tree. "Who's there?"

"Can you come, please?"

He circled around to see who it was.

"Nunana? What are you doing?"

She was crouched behind the tree trunk.

"So sorry to disturb you, please, sir," she said, still speaking in a whisper. "I saw you coming from Bedome. I have to tell you something, but I don't want anyone to see me talking to you."

He knelt down beside her and dropped his voice in the same way. "What is it you have to tell me?"

"You are looking for a silver bracelet belonging to Gladys Mensah."

"Yes, I am! You know something about it?"

"Please, I have seen one, sir."

"Where?"

"In Togbe Adzima's room, sir. In a tin he keeps with his drink." She swallowed hard and looked around nervously, as if convinced they were being watched. "I was cleaning his house, and I saw it."

"When was that?"

"On Tuesday."

Dawson's heart surged. That was the *day before he and Fiti had searched Adzima's room.* This could be the lead he had been praying for.

"Inspector Fiti and I didn't find the bracelet," he said. "Do you think he's hidden it somewhere?"

Nunana shook her head. "I don't think he has it anymore, sir. I think he has sold it."

"To whom?"

"I don't know, sir."

"How do you think he got Gladys's bracelet?"

"I don't know, but when Efia came to tell us Gladys was dead, Togbe went to see where the body was, and he went alone." Nunana dropped her voice even further. "Maybe he stole it at that time."

"Do you remember what the bracelet looked like?"

"Yes, sir."

Dawson took his notebook and pen from his top pocket. "I want you to draw it, if you can. Just do your best."

"All right, let me try."

She rested the notebook on her knee, and with her tongue sticking out with the effort, she painstakingly drew the bracelet, laughing with both embarrassment and pride as she finished her rendition. It was rudimentary, but it showed clearly enough that the bracelet was a double strand of loops.

"Beautiful," Dawson said.

She laughed again, pleased.

"Now, Nunana, tell me the truth," Dawson said. "Think about this carefully and tell me the truth. That evening before Efia discovered Gladys's body, did Togbe go anywhere? Did he disappear somewhere?"

She looked away for a second. "I . . . I don't know. I'm not sure."

Her voice was stretched tight like a rubber band at its limit. *Lying.* She knew, or had seen, something.

"You're afraid," Dawson said. "Afraid of Togbe, not so?"

Her eyes swung back and forth like a pendulum.

"If you're so afraid," Dawson pressed gently, "why come and tell me anything at all? Because, Nunana, you have honor. You can't just let it be that a man takes a bracelet from the wrist of a dead woman. Is that right?"

Nunana nodded. Dawson waited as she gathered courage.

"After Togbe quarreled with Gladys that evening and she had left Bedome, he was angry and he started to hit all of us. Then one of his friends from Ketanu came and he went with him to have beer."

"Do you know that friend?"

"No, I don't know him."

"Can you describe him?"

Her description was not the best in the world, but Nunana was certain that Togbe's friend was fat, short, and had speckled, graying hair.

"Do you have anything else?" he asked Nunana.

"No, sir. Please, I beg you, don't tell him—"

"That you told me about the bracelet? I won't."

She was shaking. He touched her shoulder. "Don't be afraid."

Dawson went looking for Constable Gyamfi while praying he would not bump into Inspector Fiti. He sidled up to the front entrance of the station and briefly put his head around the door to see who was inside. Bubo was leaning against the counter picking his nails, but Gyamfi wasn't there. Dawson circled around the side and ducked down below Fiti's office window. He peeped in from one corner. Gyamfi was standing up talking to the inspector, who was seated with his back toward the window.

Gyamfi spotted him, and Dawson quickly pressed an index finger to his lips. The constable acknowledged him without giving him away, and Dawson went to the rear of the building.

Gyamfi joined him about five minutes later.

"Dawson, how are you?" he said. "What's happening?"

"I need your help. Here is the situation. I've just found out it may have been Togbe Adzima who stole Gladys's bracelet."

Gyamfi raised his eyebrows in surprise. "Is that so?"

"After Gladys's death, someone in Bedome found it in Adzima's room. What we don't know is whether he killed Gladys and then took it off her wrist or whether he just took the bracelet after she had been killed by someone else."

"Yes, I understand. What do you want me to do?"

"I can't interrogate Togbe anymore. We hate each other so much now, and he's afraid of me. You're more charming than I, so I want you to work on him. There are two things: how he got the bracelet, and where he went on the evening before Gladys's body was found. I have a witness who says he went to Ketanu with a friend, but we need to find out if that's accurate—who is the friend, was he with the friend all the time, could he have doubled back and accosted Gladys, and so on. You get what I mean?"

"Of course, Dawson. I'm on it."

"Thank you. One other thing—the bracelet looks something like this." He showed Nunana's drawing to the constable. "It's silver."

Gyamfi studied it a moment. "All right. I have a half day off, and I can go and see Togbe after I leave here in the afternoon."

He and Dawson slapped hands. As they parted, Dawson briefly watched Gyamfi walking away with a long, rolling lope. He liked Gyamfi. *He* was the kind of partner Dawson would like alongside himself at CID.

It was past eleven o'clock in the morning, and a dense crowd of funeral spectators and mourners had collected at the Mensahs' home. Dawson parked away from the house, closer to Elizabeth's dress shop.

A dancing and drumming troupe was performing in a courtyard at the side of the house. The collective driving beat of the *sogo, kidi,* and *atsimevu* drums was irresistible. A young woman came out and began dancing the Agbadza, her arms rotating rhythmically from her shoulders while her torso swung back and forth in opposing motion. Another two women soon joined, and then a man. They kicked up red dust with their steps.

Dawson saw someone handing out beer to several men at the back of the crowd. *Freeloaders.* They would be thoroughly drunk by early afternoon.

For the short funeral service, a seating area under a canopy had been set up in front of the Mensahs' house. There was a long line of people waiting to get inside to view Gladys's body. Dawson wormed his way to the front and went in. It was packed with people in a sea of black and dark brown mourning cloth. It was oppressive, and Dawson was bothered by the tight space. Gladys lay in state in the front room. The men stood back, but several women were wailing loudly over her casket while the procession of viewers slowly wound its way past her body. In the midst of all this was a videographer filming everything, and a few people were snapping photos of Gladys's body with their mobile phones and digital cameras, which Dawson found quite bizarre.

A woman in red and black had worked herself into quite a state, sweat pouring off her as if she had been in a rain shower. She was weeping and moving frenetically around the casket like a roaming insect.

"Why have you left us?" she shouted hoarsely, gesticulating at Gladys's body. "What will we do now?"

Dawson wondered for a moment if she was a professional mourner. Families sometimes hired these, but he doubted the Mensahs would do that.

Gladys had been dressed in iridescent blue and her casket supplied with items she might need for her journey to the other side: makeup, perfume, jewelry, and a large roll of yellow and white fabric embellished with Adinkra symbols. In case she needed a change of outfit, Dawson supposed.

Everyone who entered the room was obligated to pay their respects to Kofi and Dorcas Mensah and the extended family. There was no way for Dawson to avoid it. He had no idea who 99 percent of these people were, but he had to shake hands with every single one of them. After a while he stopped counting.

He stood near Gladys's casket for a moment. She had been heavily made up, and Dawson felt disturbed by that. A dead body at a crime scene or in the morgue meant something to him, but a decorated corpse in a casket left him cold. Gladys's body was a shell. The whole person was gone, and no amount of makeup could bring her back. Feeling suffocated by the atmosphere, Dawson went outside to watch the dancing.

A new set of dancers was performing to distorted music blaring from a pair of speakers.

"Did you get some refreshments?"

He turned at the voice. "Hello, Elizabeth. No, I didn't have anything to drink."

She was dressed in a beautiful burgundy wax print with black velvet trim. She raised her voice above the din and beckoned to a boy a few meters away.

"Would you like some beer?" she asked Dawson.

"No thanks. How about some Malta?"

"Go and bring a bottle of Malta for him," Elizabeth commanded the boy.

He obediently ran off.

She smiled at Dawson. "Are you all right? I saw you in the wake room, and you seemed uncomfortable."

"I don't do well at these kinds of things."

"Sometimes it gets too much," she acknowledged. "But traditions die hard."

"Do you believe in all of it? Putting things in the casket, for instance?"

"It's symbolic, that's all. It means we care about her even to the point of her leaving us. Providing her with the things she liked."

Something suddenly occurred to Dawson. "The cloth in the casket with the little Adinkra symbols—is that the yellow version of the blue one she was wearing?"

"Yes, that's right," Elizabeth said. "She loved that pattern, Inspector Dawson. She had a yellow, a blue, and a red. We didn't want to put the blue one with her, so we chose the yellow because it's so nice and bright."

The boy came back with a bottle of half-chilled Malta, and Dawson thanked him. He took a couple of swigs.

"Elizabeth, I want you to do something for me," Dawson said, raising his voice above the noise. "Can we go over there where it's quieter?"

They walked a distance until the music was less intense.

"That's better," Dawson said. "I'm going to show you a diagram someone drew of what might be Gladys's missing bracelet. Tell me if you think it looks like hers. Take your time. Don't hurry to any conclusion."

He took Nunana's diagram from his pocket and gave it to Elizabeth. While she looked at it, he downed some more Malta, Heaven's elixir.

"It had two rows of silver loops the way it's drawn here," Elizabeth said, tapping the paper with a manicured index finger. "It could be it. Who did this? Where did you get it?"

"I can't say right now," Dawson answered evenly. "Tell me this, if I stole a bracelet like this and I wanted to sell it quickly, where would I go?"

"The best place would be to one of the jewelry traders at the Ho market."

"Would they buy one like this?"

Elizabeth nodded vigorously. "By all means, because the traders know how to shine it up and then sell it at a profit."

"How many jewelry traders come to the Ho market?"

"Lots of them. I know a few. I can take you there after the funeral is over."

"Thank you."

"I have to go now," Elizabeth said. "They're going to close the casket, and then the service will start. Would you like to come?"

"I'll be all right here, thank you."

After some time the casket was brought out. Dawson watched the service from a distance. It was performed in both English and Ewe, using a microphone so people could listen if they weren't in the seating area. It was hot even under the canopy, and people were fanning themselves somewhat uselessly with the funeral program. Older men wore the traditional style mourning cloth, while the young could not be bothered and dressed in shirts and slacks, some quite casually.

The service lasted forty-five minutes and went like clockwork. Finally, the pallbearers raised the coffin and a chorus of women began to sing and clap. An elderly woman with bare shoulders led the procession, pouring libation along the way. They would walk a short distance through Ketanu to the hearse that would take the coffin to the cemetery.

Dawson realized they were heading in the direction of his car, so he hurried to the Corolla and backed it well out of the way beside Elizabeth's shop. He leaned against the trunk and watched as the long line of black-clad marchers moved forward like a giant millipede.

Just before the pallbearers passed the shop, the coffin seemed to veer off course. It was as though a magnet was attracting it, but then Dawson realized that two or more of the pallbearers were deliberately pulling the coffin to one side. He couldn't understand what was going on. Some of the men lost their balance, and the coffin tilted and pitched. Cries of alarm went up: *Don't drop the coffin!*

An older man stumbled and screamed, "What are you doing? *Heh!* What are you doing?"

Several funeral attendees ran in to help steady the coffin as a pushing and pulling match began. Members of the crowd began to shout and jeer, but then another cry gradually became prominent as a collective chant.

"Witch, witch, witch!"

As the coffin got closer to the shop, a fistfight broke out between two men. Elizabeth appeared, yelling at the pallbearers to get back on course, and several people jumped in front of her and began to scream the word in her face. She looked shocked and backed away. *Witch!* spread through the crowd like a firestorm.

Charles and three other men came to Elizabeth's side to protect her. The coffin had swung and swayed back to its route. Dawson realized what had just happened. When a casket was drawn "mysteriously" toward a particular house, it was said that the person most associated with the dwelling had caused the death of the deceased through witchcraft. In other words, someone was trying to frame Elizabeth. It was an ugly, nasty turn to a funeral that had otherwise been proceeding smoothly. Who could have arranged this stunt?

The disruption died down, and the procession got back to normal. Elizabeth, not one to be intimidated, returned, head high, to her position near the front. About a minute later, a boy of about thirteen ran up to her and whispered in her ear. She was obviously puzzled as the boy pointed backward at something, and Dawson could see he was asking her to come with him in that direction.

She followed him and disappeared between her shop and the building next to it. Dawson circled around and looked down the length of the space between the rear of the buildings and the bush.

Elizabeth appeared with the boy, and waiting to meet her were a half dozen young men with sticks. Elizabeth turned to run. They pounced on her like a pack of hyenas and clawed her down. She held out her hand defensively as they began to club her.

Dawson opened the trunk of the car and got the cricket bat out. As he ran toward the melee, Elizabeth was trying to get up, but the youths struck her down again.

"Witch! Witch!"

"Beat her, beat her!"

She screamed as blows rained down. For a moment she got to her knees, but a strike to her head flipped her over sideways.

As Dawson got there, two of the youths shot away, but the others turned to fight. The first to come at Dawson got the cricket bat forehand and went down. The second got it backhand to the side of his head and a second strike square in the face.

Dawson moved forward to take care of another two, but they dropped their sticks and escaped.

"Elizabeth." He knelt down next to her. "Are you all right?"

He lifted her head, and she groaned. A gash in her forehead was spurting blood. Her right forearm was bent, obviously broken as she had tried to defend herself.

Dawson ripped the bottom of his shirt and folded the length of cloth to press it firmly against Elizabeth's forehead.

"Can you hear me?" he asked.

"Yes," she whispered.

"Hold on, all right?"

One of the youths was out cold; the other was groaning and attempting to get up. Dawson wasn't worried.

Charles and four other men came running. They knelt down beside Elizabeth.

"I'm okay," she said, but her face was creased with pain. Her forearm had rapidly swollen to the size of Dawson's leg.

"She has to get to the hospital," he said.

"Take her to Isaac Kutu," someone suggested.

"*No!*" Dawson shouted angrily. He was sick of this. "You take her to the VRA Hospital *now.*"

Charles looked at him and nodded.

"Run and get the van," he said to the youngest man there. "Tell the driver to be quick."

39

DAWSON'S TWO PRISONERS COULD not have been much older than eighteen. Both of them quickly came to, and Dawson was able to question them. Someone in town by the name of Dzigbodi had paid them off to beat Elizabeth "because she's a witch."

"You are such stupid boys," Dawson told them. "Get up."

He cuffed them to each other and got them up, pushing them in front of him to the car. He opened the trunk.

"Get in."

"What?"

"You heard me. Get in before I knock your heads off."

They struggled in, one uncomfortably on top of the other, and Dawson slammed the trunk shut.

When he got to the police station, Constables Gyamfi and Bubo were there but not Inspector Fiti.

"What happened?" Gyamfi asked in surprise as Dawson came in with the two disheveled youths.

"Book them," Dawson said. "Assault, battery, conspiracy to murder, attempted murder."

He gave a quick version of the story. Gyamfi listened attentively, but Bubo avoided making any eye contact with Dawson.

"We'll take care of them, Inspector, sir," Gyamfi said, shooting a disparaging look at the two boys.

"I'll write my report in a minute," Dawson said. "Can I see Samuel?"

"Yes, no problem."

Dawson went down the two-stair drop to the jail.

"Samuel?"

The young man had fashioned a rope from his shirt and was hanging from the bars of the jail window, his toes about an inch from the ground. His head was slung forward, and the bucket was on its side on the floor along with the excrement it had contained.

"Gyamfi!" Dawson screamed. "*Gyamfi!* The keys, *bring the keys!*"

The constable came quickly. He saw Samuel hanging and gasped. "Oh, *no.*"

The key rattled against the lock, and it seemed too long before Gyamfi got the door open.

"Hold him up, hold him up," Dawson said.

Gyamfi lifted Samuel's legs, and Dawson flicked open the blade of his Swiss Army knife and cut above the knot.

Live, please live.

They got him down. His body was limp, his neck had been stretched, and his face was swollen with engorged blood.

Bubo came down with the two new prisoners just as Dawson tried blowing a breath into Samuel's mouth. He pumped on Samuel's chest and gave another breath. He had forgotten the correct number for each action, but he performed the sequence just the same and repeated the cycle for he didn't know how long and until he was pouring with sweat.

He thought he heard someone say, "Dawson, stop," and then a hand squeezed his shoulder.

"Dawson, you can't do anything more."

It was Gyamfi talking. Dawson looked up at him and then down at Samuel.

He was dead. It was all over.

Dawson jumped up with fists clenched and cried out in the purest anguish. He hurled himself against the wall and then crumpled to the floor with his head in his hands. He didn't make another sound.

"Inspector," Gyamfi whispered, touching his arm. "Inspector Dawson, it wasn't your fault, hear? You couldn't have done anything wrong."

40

DAWSON TOOK THE NEWS to the Boatengs. This was an ordeal he had to go through. He blamed himself for Samuel's death, and he wanted the family's pain to be his punishment. He wanted them to whip him with their fury and lash him with words that cut like barbed wire raked across the skin.

But it didn't happen that way. Mrs. Boateng let out a single shriek of shock and collapsed. Mr. Boateng supported her, and she pressed her face into his chest and began to utter a high-pitched keen like a lost kitten crying for its mother. And all the children in the house stood and watched with big, round eyes.

Mr. Boateng said nothing. He stared unseeing at a point on the wall. He may have seemed without emotion, but Dawson saw where all the pain was. It was deep in those sad, bloodshot eyes.

"I'll be outside if you need me," Dawson said quietly.

He stood in front of the crumpled house and watched people going about their daily business. He wished he could start over again. He wished he could have forced Inspector Fiti to free Samuel for lack of evidence.

Instead, what had he, Darko Dawson, done so far? Arrested the wrong man, antagonized the local police, beaten up a few people, and lost an innocent boy to suicide.

He turned as Boateng's soft voice invited him back in. "Do you want to drink some water?"

"No, thank you, Mr. Boateng." *I don't deserve water.*

Dawson sat with them in silence for a long time until Samuel's father asked him if he would tell them the whole story.

He left them late that night. By then he knew for certain Samuel had not murdered Gladys Mensah. He had been a troubled boy, vulnerable even while trying to make a show of toughness. The time he had stolen a packet of chewing gum at the market, it had been on a dare from his friends. That was when he had been hanging around with the wrong crowd, but that had become history. Samuel had shunned them and expressed his intention to go back to school. He had had a strong love for animals, particularly dogs, often sacrificing his meals to feed a stray.

Dawson didn't sleep. He sat outside the house and smoked until he was higher than a soaring eagle. The smoke from the marijuana kept the mosquitoes away. He became quite numb to pain, although not completely dead to it. At some point he thought he felt tears running down his face, but he couldn't be sure. He kept seeing Samuel hanging from the jail window, and he cringed and cried out each time the image hit him like the strike of a puff adder.

He had no idea what time it was until the cocks began to crow back and forth like echoes as light came quickly to the dark sky.

In the distance Dawson saw smoke rising from the forest. More illegal fires. But it was a little different from the time he had asked Inspector Fiti about it. This smoke was white rather than black or gray, and there appeared to be a pattern to the puffs as they went up. It took him a little while to get it. One puff, two puffs, two puffs, one. Dawson laughed a marijuana giggle. It seemed unreasonably comical that smoke should rise this way. Look, there it was again. One puff, two puffs, two puffs, one.

Now it seemed stupid and not at all amusing. Dawson went back inside the house floating on air. He wanted to ring Christine, and then he didn't, and then he did again. He debated. Normally he would have turned to her in this kind of situation, but he couldn't call her in his marijuana-suffused condition. She would *immediately* detect he was high, and that would quench any sympathy she might have for him. Christine loved her husband, but she did not like him on drugs.

Call Armah. That's what he should do. Armah could help him through this.

Dawson looked around for his mobile, forgetting where he had put it. After a few minutes, he found it in his pocket.

His call went through.

"Hello?" It was a woman's voice—Armah's wife, Maude.

"Hello," Dawson stammered. "Is this . . . is Armah there, please? May I speak to him?"

He was shocked at the sound of his own voice. He might as well have been talking through a mouthful of cotton balls.

"Who is calling?" Maude asked after a second's hesitation.

Dawson was about to say his name, but he lost his nerve. It would be embarrassing and insulting to Armah, a man Dawson revered, to talk to him from out of this mind-altered miasma. Dawson was about as lucid right now as Ketanu mud.

He ended the call and flung the phone across the room, cursing fluently in Ewe. He needed a shower.

He suddenly remembered Elizabeth and wondered if she was okay. He would have to visit her later on, he thought.

He fell asleep upright in the straight-backed chair. It had always mystified Christine how he could do that. He started awake at the sound of a car pulling up. He looked out the window. Chikata was alighting from a Corolla, and directly behind him Chief Superintendent Lartey was getting out of a shiny black BMW marked CRIMINAL INVESTIGATIONS DEPARTMENT.

My God. Lartey was *here*? This was serious. Dawson's heart sank like a lead nugget. There couldn't be a worse time. He opened the door wide before they could knock. It was past eight in the morning, and the day was already buzzing with people shopping and running errands.

"Dawson," Lartey said.

"At your service, sir. Come in. Hello, D.S. Chikata."

Lartey looked quickly around and then back at Dawson. "Is something wrong with you? Are you drunk?"

"No, sir, I'm not."

Lartey sniffed. "Is that marijuana I smell?"

"No, sir, just some strong cigarettes."

"Since when do you smoke?"

"I do sometimes."

Lartey grunted. "You look horrible."

He took a seat. Chikata remained standing, scrutinizing Dawson but trying not to be too obvious about it.

"What are you staring at?" Dawson said to him sullenly.

"Sit down, Dawson," Lartey said sharply.

He did.

"What's going on with you in this place?"

"What do you mean, sir?"

"I've received more complaints about you in the past few days than I have had about any other detective in several years. Is it true you insulted Inspector Fiti by calling him a bush policeman?"

"He was having a prisoner beaten up, sir. That prisoner is now dead."

"As a result of the alleged beating?"

"Indirectly, yes, I would say so. And it's not alleged, sir. It did happen. I witnessed it."

"Have you filed a report?"

"I was about to, sir."

"At the same time it appears you've been doing your own share of beating up, doesn't it? You assaulted Augustus Ayitey, a respected herbalist, and put him in jail for supposedly hurting your boy when he went for treatment. Which is a conflict of interest. The correct procedure would be to file a report as a citizen and let someone else in the department handle it. Seems to me you were just looking for an excuse to take revenge on Mr. Ayitey, isn't that right?"

Dawson didn't answer. Quite frankly, he was too tired and too high to care that much.

"You also managed to falsely accuse a Ghana Health Service official of murder and throw him into jail."

"I made a mistake—"

"Wait, I'm not finished."

"Sorry, sir."

"You also beat up the fetish priest at Bedome. So my question is, What is wrong with you? Why are you so out of control?"

Dawson dropped his face into his palms. His head was throbbing.

"I don't know, sir," he said finally.

"Is it drugs?"

"No, sir."

Lartey grunted. "You're only sabotaging your own progress, Dawson. It's folly, and it is giving my department a very, very bad name. That's what I detest most. I hate it. Do you understand?"

"Yes, sir, I believe so."

"The reason I've brought D.S. Chikata here is to have him take over the case. I'm suspending you. Three weeks' suspension without pay, and then you face the Disciplinary Board."

"Sir, wait, please. Please, I have to solve this. I promise I'll be on my best behavior—"

"Pack up your things and get out, Dawson. Chikata is moving in."

41

SAAC KUTU HAD BEEN preparing a potion for a woman who had come to see him for her weak blood. It was still warm as he poured it into the bottle she had brought with her.

"Wait for it to get cool," he instructed her, "and drink half of the bottle today. Tomorrow you drink the rest."

She thanked him profusely and went away happy. For payment, she had left him two live chickens.

Isaac joined Tomefa in the courtyard, where she was cooking goat stew on the firewood stove. He sat on the stool and watched her quietly. She was a very good wife, he often reminded himself—faithful, hardworking, and fertile. She had borne seven children, and lost two, so now there were five and that was just fine. It was funny that he didn't love Tomefa. He *liked* her well enough. In fact he could go as far as to say he was fond of her, but it wasn't love. His father, Boniface, had arranged Isaac's marriage to her, yes, but couldn't love sometimes grow like a planted seed? He assumed it could, but with Tomefa, it hadn't. Take Osewa by contrast. Even after all these years, whenever he saw her, he felt something in his chest, like a surge of joy, warm and wet. Why was it so? It was such a marvelous thing. And he would never give Osewa any kind of command the way he would Tomefa. There was no need for that. He and Osewa flowed together like two streams converging to form a single river.

Isaac got up and went to stand at the entrance of the compound, leaning against the side contemplatively. Some ten minutes later, he saw puffs of white smoke rising over the forest. One, two, two, one. He didn't know why he even bothered to count. He knew when he was being signaled.

"Tomefa," he called back, "I'll be back soon."

She nodded obediently.

He walked quickly. Off the footpath to Ketanu, he made his way into the bush and found Osewa harvesting plantain. The quenched fire was off to the side.

"Aren't you afraid?" he said, half jokingly.

"Afraid of what?" she asked, pulling over a nice bunch of the plantains she had just cut down with her cutlass.

"This is where Gladys Mensah was killed."

Osewa stopped. "Here? I thought it was the other plantain grove where they found her."

"No. Right here."

She shrugged. "There's no reason her spirit would be angry with me. Anyway, my juju protects me just in case."

"Yes," he said, desiring her. "Come here."

He took her hand and led her deep into the forest to where he had built another of their love shelters. Intimacy in the forest was all right with the gods provided it took place under a roof of some kind.

He sought her thighs hungrily, marveling at how tight and moist she still was after all these years. Her walls milked him quickly to climax.

They rested for a while, and then she said, "I have to get back soon."

He nodded drowsily. "Me too."

"Did you hear Samuel Mensah killed himself?" she asked.

Isaac sat up frowning. "Yes. That's a terrible thing."

"Maybe he couldn't live any more knowing that he killed Gladys. Confessing couldn't take away his shame."

"But Inspector Fiti beat him," Isaac said. "If someone beats you enough, you might confess to anything."

"I still believe he did it."

"I wish Darko Dawson saw it the same way. He's still hunting me."

"He thinks *you* are the one?"

"He searched all my rooms yesterday."

"Ei! This boy." She sighed. "I love him, but I'm sorry, this police business does not suit him. Is he worrying you a lot? I can talk to him, if you like."

"No, he'll wonder why you're defending me like that, and he might get suspicious."

"All right."

He pulled her to him.

"I love you," she said.

On the road to Kumasi, Dawson counted four serious accidents, the crushed carcasses of vehicles lying on their sides or overturned completely. He drove with both care and assertion, staying clear of speeding drivers, tro-tros packed with people, and trucks top-heavy with merchandise.

He made it to Kumasi in something over three hours. Alongside Kejetia, Ghana's claim to the largest open-air market in West Africa, traffic crawled, rendering cars prey to kid traders hawking fruits, cold drinks, ice cream, and worthless trinkets.

Dawson finally escaped the congestion and got to a quieter part of town, where he managed to find a parking spot between two rusting minivans.

Taking his tote bag with him, he walked through a maze of small houses, getting progressively farther from the street until he came to a cul-de-sac occupied by a neat yellow house. Daniel Armah had built it from scratch, and second only to his wife, children, and grandchildren, it was the pride of his life.

The door was open, and Dawson called out to announce he had arrived. Having got through to Armah by phone earlier in the day, he was expected, and Armah knew what the topic of conversation was to be. Before all the developments of the past day, Dawson had planned only to ask Armah's advice over the phone on how to "negotiate" the rural environment, but things had so radically and abruptly changed that Dawson now had to see him in person.

He heard quick footsteps as Armah approached, and when Dawson saw him, he felt even more elated than he had expected. Armah was still trim and compact, and though his hair had gone gray, there was still plenty of it.

"Darko, you made it!" he said, broad face alive with delight.

Dawson laughed as they embraced.

"Welcome, welcome," Armah said. "I'm so glad to see you, so very glad. Come in, come in. Here, let me take your bag."

Despite the heat outside, there was a nice cool breeze blowing through the house. The sitting room was spacious and relaxing.

"How was your trip?" Armah asked. "You must be exhausted."

"Well, you know how the roads are."

"Yes, yes. Maude went with the grandkids up to Mampong to stay with her sister for the weekend, and I insisted my driver take them because he's the only one I completely trust. Would you like something to drink, or would you prefer to freshen up a bit before you have your Malta Guinness?"

They burst out laughing at the reference.

"Aha, you thought I would forget?" Armah said, winking at him. "I have a whole refrigerator full of the stuff just for you."

"Thanks, Armah. I think I'd like to take a shower first."

"But of *course*. Come along, your room is all ready."

Dawson was a full-grown man in his own right, but Armah was still such a paternal figure to him that he caught himself making sure he didn't move anything out of place in the bedroom or bathroom, just like a "good little boy."

He showered gratefully; running water had never felt so good. With a change of clothes, he was revived as he rejoined Armah in the sitting room. Two bottles of ice-cold Malta were ready with a tall glass.

Armah served himself Star beer, and they drank and talked for a while about families and friends and the old days, but then it was time to get to business.

"So I gather you've had a rather rough time of it in Ketanu," Armah said.

"Yes, I have."

"I want to hear all about it. Maybe I can be of some help."

Dawson started at the very beginning and left nothing out. As he came to Samuel's suicide, Armah's face showed regret.

When Dawson was finished with his account, Armah leaned back in his chair and studied the ceiling.

"So," he said. "You've got all these things happening, all ingredients in a mixed-up soup. There's no solution to the murder yet, we think Adzima is connected to the silver bracelet but it's unconfirmed, this poor boy Samuel has killed himself, Queen Elizabeth is badly hurt, and you've been thrown off the case."

"That about summarizes it, yes," Dawson said with a bitter laugh.

"Something struck me," Armah said, "and I wanted to get it out of the way. About Samuel. Do we know for sure there wasn't foul play? This brute of a constable, Bubo—was that his name? Yes, him. Couldn't he have strung Samuel up out of vengeance and made it look like suicide?"

"I wouldn't put it past him, but Constable Gyamfi's account of the sequence of events makes that very unlikely. He took a meal down to Samuel, and at that time he was alive. Between then and when I found him, Bubo never went down to the jail cell."

"And you trust Gyamfi?"

"Completely. He wouldn't try to protect Bubo."

"All right, good. That's a relief." Armah reflected for a moment. "You feel very bad about Samuel?"

"I can't even tell you how terrible I feel."

"Good."

"Why good?"

"Darko, even though I don't think you're to blame, if you had come here defensively telling me it wasn't your fault the boy died, I would have been disappointed because it wouldn't be the Darko Dawson I know. It would say to me that you had lost a piece of your humanity. You see what I mean?"

"Yes."

"I remember when I was about your age, I arrested this boy—he may have been eighteen or nineteen. I say 'boy' because he was so small in stature, a tiny thing. Anyway, it was a petty crime, something utterly stupid. He begged me not to put him in a cell with other prisoners, but I ignored him. One of them beat him up that same night. He didn't die, but he was very badly maimed. Do you know I've never forgiven myself for that? I probably never will, but I'm glad of that, because if a day ever comes that I'm able to think back on that incident without any pain or guilt, then I might as well curl up in a hole and die."

"You may feel glad I haven't lost my humanity," Dawson said, "but I personally feel worthless."

"Because you're in the thick of it. I have the luxury of not being you."

Dawson laughed and began to feel a little better.

"What do you think I should do now?" he asked Armah.

"Who cares what I think? What do *you* want to do?"

"Solve the case, of course. I'm officially off it, but with three weeks of suspension to spare, I might as well use the time fruitfully." Dawson reflected somberly for a moment. "I owe it not only to Gladys, but to Samuel as well."

"There you are then. You think Chikata will cause problems if he sees you back in Ketanu? Run to Lartey and tell on you?"

"I don't doubt he will."

"I'll put a call in to Chikata's father, pull some strings, and make sure his boy keeps his trap shut."

"I didn't realize you knew his father."

"I know a lot of people."

"That's true."

"So what do we have so far on the case?" Armah said. "For practical purposes we've ruled Sowah out. We are not even considering Samuel, but we still wonder about Isaac Kutu and Togbe Adzima. I'm just worried we've overlooked someone. What about family? You always look at family."

"Their alibis all fit. There's nothing there, motive or otherwise. I need to pin down Adzima and Kutu."

"Something doesn't feel right about Adzima though," Armah said. "As both the murderer and the bracelet thief, I mean."

"How so?"

Armah shrugged. "If he killed her, we say the motive is his fear and loathing of her, not robbery. So, then, why does he steal her bracelet?"

"Because he's a swine?"

"Well, yes, he is," Armah said quite seriously. "But it still doesn't sit comfortably with me. Now, I could see him taking the bracelet off just as a petty thief with no respect for the dead."

"I get what you mean, but it would be a shame not to track him all the way down."

"You're absolutely right, and I shouldn't have implied it wasn't a lead to be followed. Now, to Isaac Kutu. I think he may have had a motive, but he's a difficult person to peg. When I was investigating your mother's disappearance, I had the strangest feeling about him, but I was never able to connect any dots that included him. You remember what I told you about solving mysteries?"

"That it's a matter of making a few of the connections and the rest will fall into place."

"A-plus. That *is* what solving mysteries is all about. Now, let's eat."

"Oh," Dawson said brightly. "You cooked?"

"Ha, you're funny. When have you ever known me to cook? No, Maude prepared it and left it all ready to be heated up. Which is about all I know how to do."

42

DAWSON RETURNED FROM KUMASI on Monday morning after breakfast with Armah. He was sorry he had missed Maude and the grandkids, and he invited Armah and his family to come to Accra and visit in the near future. Armah's last words were "By the way, my best advice is try not to beat so many people up." He had said it in a humorous tone, but Dawson knew he had meant it, and it was advice well taken.

Before he went into Ketanu, he took a detour to the VRA Hospital to look for Elizabeth. He found the female surgical ward and walked down the long row of stark metal beds looking for her. He found her in a vestibule that had been converted to accommodate a hospital bed, giving her more privacy than the patients in the general ward. She was propped up on ample pillows, and the bed was covered with a bright kente spread. He hesitated at the foot of her bed because it appeared she was sleeping, but she opened one normal and one swollen eye and said, "Detective Inspector Dawson. Come along, I won't bite."

Her head was bandaged, and her right arm was resting across her middle in a cast and sling. He sat on the edge of her bed.

"How are you feeling, Auntie Elizabeth?"

"Like I've been kicked by a set of donkeys."

"In a way you have, but I would call them asses. What does the doctor say?"

"My arm was broken, so Dr. Biney set it, and they had to sew my head up. I suppose to keep me from losing whatever little is inside."

She tried to chuckle but winced as she realized it hurt to do so. "Ouch. I've just been reminded I have two broken ribs."

"I'm not staying long," Dawson said. "I just wanted to make sure you were all right. Is there anything I can do?"

"No, Dawson, thank you. Dorcas and Kofi and Charles were here earlier, and they made sure I was taken care of."

"When will the doctor release you?"

"In a day or two," she said. "I'm so glad to see you, Dawson. I've been thinking over some things—since that's about all I can do right now. When I get out, I want to continue what Gladys started."

"Specifically?"

"She wanted to set up a shelter for trokosi women—somewhere they could escape and be protected from their fetish-priest husbands. I want to build a center to honor Gladys's memory."

"You'll have my complete support," Dawson said. "As a matter of fact, here's what I hope is your first private donation."

He dug into his pocket and peeled off some bills.

"It's not much," he said, "but it's a start."

"Thank you. You're a very good man."

Dawson was about to leave when Elizabeth said, "I haven't forgotten about the trip to Ho to see if we can track down the bracelet. As soon as I get out."

"Thanks, but get better first. Don't worry about me."

Dawson went to Auntie Osewa and asked if he could stay with them for a while.

"But of course you can!" she exclaimed, her face lighting up. "Stay as long as you like."

He would have to share Alifoe's room, but he didn't mind, nor did he care that the best mattress they had for him was made of foam as thin as a wafer.

He needed to go into town to look for Constable Gyamfi, but Osewa wouldn't allow him to leave without a full lunch of fufu and palm nut soup. They ate in the courtyard under the shade of a piece of canvas strung from the wall to a post. Alifoe and Kweku were at the cocoa farm.

"Auntie, you're going to make me want to take a long nap this afternoon," Dawson said as he ate.

"You should, Darko," she said firmly. "It would be good for you."

"I wish I could, but I have work to do."

"Are you still trying to find out who killed Gladys?"

"Yes."

"Samuel was not the one, then?"

"I don't think so."

"Why do you think not?"

Dawson took a mouthful and closed his eyes for a moment as he savored the flavor. "What did you say?"

"About Samuel."

"Oh, yes. There are many reasons why I don't think he did it."

"I see. Well, you know your job . . ." She paused.

"But what?" he prompted.

"But from what I heard, he was . . . No, I don't want to speak ill of the dead."

"It doesn't matter what you heard, Auntie Osewa. He didn't kill Gladys Mensah."

"Yes, yes, it's all right. I believe you. I'm sorry."

"Don't worry, it's nothing. Auntie Osewa, I might have to live with you and get fat."

She laughed, leaned over, and pinched his cheek. "You're a sweet boy."

He smiled. Still a boy to her.

Dawson did not have to tackle the police station to find Gyamfi because, as he was on the way into town, the constable called him to say he was headed to Auntie Osewa's to see Dawson. They met about halfway and found a quiet spot to talk.

"Did you find out anything?" Dawson asked.

"Yes," Gyamfi said. "The last evening Gladys was seen alive, Adzima had had a quarrel with her—you know that already. Now, after he got angry with his wives and started to beat them up, a cousin of his comes to Bedome and asks him why he's making so much trouble and tells him to come to Ketanu to drink beer."

"Who is the cousin? Do you know him?"

"Now I do. The cousin brought him to Jesus My Soul Chop Bar, and they ate *chinchinga* and drank beer and got drunk."

Dawson's heart was sinking again. "He was with the cousin all the time?"

"Yes. And that cousin has some friends who sat and drank with them also, and I found one of them and the stories agree. They drank till late, and then Adzima went back to Bedome drunk."

Just as with Timothy Sowah, the chance that Adzima had killed Gladys was dwindling quickly.

"What about the bracelet?" Dawson asked, without enthusiasm. It didn't make much difference at this point.

"That I had a little more trouble with," Gyamfi said. "I told Togbe that some boys from Ketanu got to the body first after Efia had left, and that when they heard Togbe coming, they ran and hid and saw him steal the bracelet. He denied and denied it until I told him Inspector Fiti and I would take him to Ho Central Prison. Then he confessed."

"What did he do with the bracelet? Does he still have it?"

"No, he sold it to a trader in Ho. I will try to get it back."

"Thank you, Gyamfi."

Dawson clasped the constable's hands, and their eyes met warmly.

43

AUNTIE OSEWA'S MEAL THAT night was rice and grilled tilapia spiced with ginger and hot pepper, with slivers of ripe plantain fried in palm oil until crispy. They ate outside by lantern light and talked. Alifoe was quite the comedian. As Dawson recovered from a stitch in his side from laughing, Uncle Kweku turned to his wife. "Darko sounds so much like his mother when he laughs," he said to her.

"Really?" Dawson said. "No one has ever told me that."

"I always thought the same thing," Osewa said quietly. "But I didn't want to say so in case it brought sadness to you, Darko."

"No," he said. "On the contrary."

"What happened to Auntie Beatrice?" Alifoe asked.

"Alifoe," Osewa said sharply.

"It's okay," Dawson said. "No one knows what happened, Alifoe. I was twelve years old, and you were a baby, of course. After you were born, she came twice to visit. The second time, she stayed a few days and then she said she was going back to Accra. She never arrived home."

"What could have happened? Maybe the tro-tro had an accident?"

Dawson shook his head. "That was checked by the detective assigned to the case. There were no accidents between Ketanu and Accra that day."

Alifoe looked perplexed. "Then she must have got off somewhere on the way."

"That we don't know," Dawson said. "But why would she do that?"

"Are we even sure she got *on*?" Alifoe persisted.

"Of course we're sure," Auntie Osewa said, sounding irritated. "How many times do I have to tell people that it was me who went with her to the tro-tro stop to see her off?"

"I'm sorry, Mama," Alifoe said. "I didn't know that."

"Tell us about it, Auntie Osewa," Dawson said. Now was as good a time as any.

"It was before noontime," she began. "She wanted to get home a little early, so she didn't want to wait until the afternoon to start out for Accra. Do you remember that, Kweku?"

He nodded in agreement.

"So anyway," Auntie Osewa continued, "we walked to the bus stop talking and laughing. She seemed so happy. Even when she talked about Cairo she was cheerful. Both of us were happy together, and we agreed I should visit Accra and bring Alifoe when he got a little older. When we got to the stop, I wanted to be certain she got a tro-tro that was safe, so I let the first one go on because it was a broken-down old boneshaker, but the second one was all right. I made sure she got a good seat at the front near the driver, and then we kissed good-bye."

"And that was the last you saw of her?" Alifoe asked.

"Yes," Auntie Osewa said sadly.

Dawson had stopped eating. He felt sick.

"Darko?" Auntie Osewa said. "Are you okay?"

He looked at her without seeing all her face. Had he heard her right?

"You said Mama sat at the front of the tro-tro?" he asked. His voice sounded distant and small.

Auntie Osewa looked quizzically at him, hesitating. "Yes, that's right. Why are you asking me that?"

Dawson's blood turned chilly. What his aunt had just said could not have been. She must have had a false memory of what had happened.

Or she was lying.

Mama had always been scared to death of sitting in the front section of a tro-tro. She wouldn't do it. What did she always say? *If there's an accident, I don't want you flying through the windscreen. Nor me.*

They went to bed late. Dawson lay on his back in Alifoe's room with one arm crooked under his head as he stared up in the darkness and his thoughts roamed. Nothing felt right to him. What Auntie had said was twisting in his mind like a fish on a hook. *A good seat at the front of the tro-tro . . . at the front . . . at the front.* That phrase over and over. Memories of his boyhood visit to Ketanu flooded back. Something had been wrong back then too.

Sitting at that table in Auntie Osewa's house and eating her delicious meal while the grownups chatted about things that bored Darko and his brother stiff . . . and then suddenly, Mr. Kutu's fleeting look at Mama. Dawson remembered it clearly. Mama's eyes had met Kutu's in a snatched instant so brief that no one would have expected it to bear a message. But it did, and Auntie Osewa had read it and understood. In turn, Darko had seen everything. One, two, three stolen glances whose meaning disturbed him without his quite knowing why.

What about later that evening, as they played oware? Auntie Osewa had disappeared for a while. *To set the rabbit traps,* she had said, and the quality of her voice had felt so strange to Dawson that he had looked at her in surprise.

"Cousin Darko?"

Dawson lifted his head in surprise. He had thought Alifoe was asleep.

"Yes?"

"You're not sleepy?"

"I never sleep well."

"Oh."

"Something wrong?"

"No, nothing."

Dawson waited. He knew there was more.

"Cousin Darko, have you ever kept something inside you that you wished you could tell someone but you didn't know whom to trust?"

"Yes, I think so."

"And when you find someone you trust, you feel like telling him?"

"Whom do you trust?"

"You."

"Thank you."

"What would you do . . . I mean, how would you feel if you knew your mother and father didn't love each other?"

"Mine didn't."

"Really?" Alifoe sat up in the dark. "It's the same with Mama and Papa. I want to see them love each other, but it never happens."

"And you can't make it happen either. That's what you mustn't forget. If they fell out of love at one time, only they can get themselves back in."

"Do you think I shouldn't care so much about it?"

"You can care as much as you want, but don't let it stop your life." Alifoe lay down again.

"Do you feel any better?" Dawson said.

"Yes, I do. Thank you, Darko."

As soon as the first cock crowed in the morning, Dawson's eyes popped open. He had been dreaming he was forcing his mother into the front seat of a tro-tro and she was screaming at him to let her go.

He looked at his watch. Five forty-five. Alifoe was still fast asleep.

Dawson got dressed and went out to the courtyard to find Auntie Osewa starting a fire for breakfast.

"Morning, Auntie."

"Morning, Darko. Did you sleep well?"

"I did, thank you," he lied.

"Good. Would you like to take some breakfast?"

"I would love to. Can I wash first?"

"Yes, I filled two buckets for you, and there is soap there too."

First he went to the pit latrine—a necessary evil—and then he took a refreshing bucket bath.

As he ate breakfast, Auntie Osewa was chatty and Dawson did his best to respond in kind, but he felt as though a two-way mirror had gone up between them. Auntie was on one side seeing her reflection and talking through it to Dawson, who was on the other side looking at her.

"So," she said, "what will you be doing today?"

"To start, I have to go and meet with Efia," he said.

"That's the one who found the body? One of Adzima's wives?"

"Yes."

"It must have been terrible for her when she found it," she reflected.

"It was. It's affected her deeply, probably for life."

He finished breakfast quickly and stood up. "Thank you, Auntie. It was delicious. I'd best be going now."

Dawson walked the footpath between Ketanu and Bedome, and as he came to the farm plots, he spotted Efia and Ama hoeing the soil along with a few other farmers. Efia waved at him as he came up to them.

"Morning, Efia. Morning, Ama."

"Morning, morning, Mr. Dawson." They spoke and smiled simultaneously, just like twins. Both were sweating, Efia a little more.

"How goes it, Efia?" Dawson asked.

"Fine," she said. "I'm so happy to see you. They told me you were going to leave Ketanu, and I was feeling so sad."

"Who told you?"

"That man from Accra—Mr. Chikata?"

"Oh, yes. He's my workmate. They told him to take over the case from me."

"Why?"

"Because . . . Well, it doesn't matter. Can you help me a little bit?"

"But of course."

"I hope you don't mind, but could you show me the way you left the forest after you found Gladys dead, and also exactly where you saw Mr. Kutu? Do you have time?"

"Yes, I can come."

She handed Ama her hoe. "I'll be back soon," she told her daughter.

Dawson and Efia walked back toward the footpath.

"I've been wanting to talk to you about Togbe Adzima," Dawson said.

"Yes?"

"Did one of his wives die last year?"

"Yes. Her name was Comfort."

"She died of AIDS?"

"I don't know. They said she was cursed."

"Efia, if it was AIDS, then it was Togbe Adzima who gave it to her."

She frowned as they turned onto the Bedome–Ketanu path, her head down as she thought about the implications.

Dawson's heart was in his mouth as he prepared to ask the next question.

"Efia, did Gladys do a blood test on you? For AIDS?"

"Yes, and she said it was okay."

Dawson breathed again. "I know it would be very difficult for you, but if there's any way you can avoid Togbe Adzima being with you, any way at all. You and all of the wives—especially the new one."

Efia was troubled. "I don't know what to do. The only thing that works sometimes is when he drinks too much."

"I'll buy him a gallon of schnapps then," Dawson said, "and you can feed it to him every day."

They looked at each other and laughed.

She slowed her pace.

"Mr. Kutu was somewhere here when I saw him," she said, making a circular motion with her hand.

Dawson nodded. "And how far away were you from here?"

"Down there." She pointed. "I'll show you."

"Was he walking toward you or away from you?"

"Away."

They went farther down the footpath. Two women talking to each other went by them with cassavas balanced on their heads, and Dawson and Efia wished them good morning.

"I came out from here." Efia showed Dawson.

There was a break in the bushy vegetation, and Dawson recognized it as the same access he and Inspector Fiti had used. He looked back the way they had come. "I noticed a place up there that might be another path into the forest. Come with me."

They retraced their steps to the spot. It was true there was a split in the vegetation, but it wasn't very pronounced.

"Could you go from here to the plantain grove?" Dawson asked.

Efia looked doubtful. "It looks tough. I've never done it."

"Let's try. You lead."

The going was not at all easy. They had to weave and duck to get through, and the underbrush was tangled and difficult to negotiate. They arrived at the plantain grove after about eight minutes.

They stood looking around the clearing.

"This is the first time I've come back here since Gladys died," Efia said.

"Are you okay?"

"Yes, I'm all right."

"I want to show you something," Dawson said.

He led her behind the plantain trees and stopped at the juju pyramid.

"Have you seen this before, Efia?"

"Yes, one time."

"Are you afraid of it?"

"No, but I stay away from it."

"What would happen if someone took all these rocks off to see what's underneath?"

Efia shook her head slowly and disapprovingly. "No one should do that."

"Do you know who built this?"

"No. And I don't ask."

He smiled at her. "Okay. Well, let's go back the way you went after you found Gladys's body. You say you ran?"

"Yes."

"Then let's do that. Try to run as fast as you did. I'll follow you."

Dawson had to admit Efia could tackle the forest a lot better than he could. At an all-out run he almost fell twice as he tried to keep up with her.

They came out on the path again, and both were breathing heavily.

"Ei, that was hard," Dawson said, looking at his watch. Four and a half minutes.

She smiled. "City man, that's why."

They laughed.

"I have to go back, Mr. Dawson."

"I'll walk with you. Thank you, Efia. You've helped me a lot."

"Not at all, Mr. Dawson."

On the way back to the farm, Dawson was thinking of a scenario. What if Isaac had killed Gladys that Friday evening?

Saturday morning, he returns to the plantain grove because he thinks he might have left an incriminating clue, or he wants to make sure he hasn't. While there, he hears Efia approaching. He escapes through the bush to the Ketanu–Bedome footpath by a route that takes him seven or eight minutes. Meanwhile, two or three minutes pass as Efia enters the grove, discovers the body, and screams for help. She runs back to the footpath, which takes another four and a half minutes. Add that up and we get about seven minutes. Isaac Kutu is emerging from the forest at about the same time. That's when Efia sees him and calls out to him.

"Let me ask you something, Efia," Dawson said, "and if you know the answer, I want you to tell me the truth."

"I will try."

"Gladys was interested in Mr. Kutu's medicine. Do you think she was trying to steal it from him?"

"I don't think so."

"Why not?"

"Gladys didn't need Mr. Kutu. She had everything in the world—what does she need him for? No, it was Mr. Kutu who needed Gladys."

"Do you think he was in love with her?"

"Once when she came to Bedome, I saw him looking at her with desire. I can't go inside his mind to know whether he was feeling love or not. Mr. Kutu does that with a lot of women. Sometimes he has looked at me the same way."

"And whom else has he looked at in that way?"

Efia hesitated.

"I have to know," Dawson pressed.

She was quiet for a moment and he waited.

"If I tell you—"

"No one will find out you told me."

"He loves one woman from Ketanu."

"Who? Do you know the woman?"

"Her name is Osewa Gedze."

Dawson stopped.

Efia turned. "What's wrong?"

He was stunned. "Osewa Gedze? Are you sure?"

"Yes, I am sure. You know her?"

"How do you know Mr. Kutu loves her?"

Efia visibly squirmed. "I've seen them together in the forest."

"What do you mean by *together*?"

"I mean they were . . ."

"Having sex."

"Yes." She looked disgusted. "To do that in the forest—it's terrible, Mr. Dawson."

"When did it happen?"

"Five or six days ago."

"Can you show me where they were?"

"Yes, but we have to be quick or Ama will start to get worried."

The spot Efia took him to was a clearing with a light tree cover.

"How did you find this place?" Dawson asked her, looking around.

"By accident. I got lost while I was looking for a different spot to pick plantains."

Dawson saw a little shelter—four short poles with a roof.

"Is that where they were, Efia? Under there?"

"Yes." The look on her face was as if she had just chewed a mouthful of quinine.

Dawson now spotted a bald area on the ground with a pile of ash and partially burned wood. He knelt down beside it.

"Were they cooking?" he asked.

Efia was slightly amused. "No, that's not the kind of fireplace to cook something. It's not a good fire." She picked up a couple of twigs and small leafy branches. "These are green. They don't burn well, they just make a lot of white smoke."

"White smoke," Dawson said with a sudden smile. "Thank you for that, Efia."

She was bemused. "What did I do?"

"You did a lot—in just one sentence."

He got up and went poking in the bush. He found a small raffia mat folded in quarters. He opened it out and saw burn marks.

Efia peered at it. "They must have used it to put the fire out."

"Eventually," Dawson said. "After they sent the signals."

44

DAWSON COULD NOT GET through to Chikata's mobile that afternoon, so he went looking for him. He tried the police station first and almost collided with Inspector Fiti as he walked in.

"Didn't Chief Superintendent Lartey tell you to go home?" Fiti said coldly.

"No, he told me I was on suspension without pay," Dawson replied, "so I decided to take a three-week vacation in your beautiful town and spend time with my aunt and uncle."

Fiti grunted and narrowed his eyes with suspicion. "And so what do you want here?"

"I'm looking for D.S. Chikata."

"He went to the guesthouse. Do you need something?" He was still suspicious.

"No, thank you." Dawson turned to leave.

"And by the way," Fiti said, "Chikata agrees with me that Samuel killed Gladys Mensah, so the case is closed and everything is settled."

"I see," Dawson said. "Congratulations."

He left Fiti and his smugness and walked to the guesthouse. The sky was setting up dark clouds near the horizon. It would probably rain by nightfall.

He knocked on the guesthouse door.

"Who is it?" Chikata's voice.

"Dawson."

He heard another voice, this time a woman's, then a lot of shuffling, and Dawson knew exactly what to expect. Chikata came to the door shirtless and let out a young woman with huge breasts and a dress so tight she could hardly breathe. She slipped past Dawson and quickly left.

"Hard at work, I see," he said drily to Chikata.

"I was lonesome," Chikata said feebly.

Dawson waved that aside. "I want to talk to you about the case."

He came in and took a seat. Chikata threw on a shirt and sat down on the bed.

"I hear you're going along with Inspector Fiti that Samuel killed Gladys," Dawson said.

"You have to admit the case against the boy is—or was—strong," Chikata replied. "He and Gladys went into the forest together and he was the last person seen with her."

"So Auntie Osewa's version of the story goes," Dawson said, "but two farmers who work at the edge of the forest told me that after his argument with Isaac, Samuel came back to their farm to work and never left their presence before dark. So how could he have waylaid Gladys on her way back to Ketanu?"

"Then what about your aunt's claim? You're saying she's lying?"

"Painful as it is to say, yes. I think she may be trying to protect Isaac Kutu."

"Why would she do that?"

"Because she's been having an affair with him—possibly for years and years."

"Are you serious?" Chikata asked, eyebrows up in surprise. "How do you know that? I'm sure she didn't volunteer the information."

"No, she didn't. I found out through another channel."

"Which I can see you're not about to tell me."

"Not right now."

"Then my next question is, Why would Kutu have wanted to kill Gladys?"

"Rejection. Kutu is the kind of man who gets any woman he wants—a bit like you—but Gladys was the exception. Her only concern was how she could work with him on his herbal medicines, but he wanted much more than that from her."

"And for that reason he killed her?"

"Crazed lust, jealousy? You act as though those aren't strong motives."

"They are—I know they are," Chikata said with some exasperation. "Okay. So now what?"

"I want you to take Kutu in for questioning—not here in Ketanu, but at Ho Central. I'll tell you exactly what to ask him when you interrogate him. I suspect he went to the scene of the crime just before Efia arrived that morning. I think he can be bluffed into confessing."

Chikata looked unhappy. "Ah, Dawson, I'm not at all convinced. It doesn't sound right."

"Your D.I. is telling you what to do," Dawson said evenly. "He's not asking you."

"Yes, sir, D.I. Dawson, sir—but Chief Superintendent has pulled you off the case and put me in charge. He outranks you."

"Come on, Chikata. Stop this nonsense. Work with me. What have you got to lose? You're not going to get in trouble over this. Lartey loves you. You're family."

"All right, but if you can't get anything out of Isaac Kutu, are you going to go back home and leave these Ketanu people alone?"

"I didn't say that. Now, get going."

45

ON THE WAY BACK TO Auntie Osewa's, Dawson noticed that Elizabeth's shop door was open. Peering inside, he was astonished to see who was there stocking shelves.

"Elizabeth! You're out of hospital already?"

"Dawson, woizo! Come in."

Her face was still swollen, but with artfully applied makeup and one of her elaborate and colorful headdresses, she looked just fine.

"Are you all right?" Dawson said.

"All right enough to leave the hospital. I was going mad in there. If Dr. Biney hadn't released me, I would have signed myself out."

"Don't overdo it, though," Dawson said. "I know you're tough, but . . ."

"Never worry, I'm fine. We have some new fabrics and dresses in, so I was just arranging them."

Dawson took a visual sweep, and his eye lit on something familiar. He went to the shelf and touched it.

"This is the same as the one you put in Gladys's casket. With the Adinkra signs."

"Yes."

"It's really beautiful. I'll get it for Christine."

"Oh, wonderful."

Elizabeth gift-wrapped a full-size length of the fabric and put it in a bag.

"This time I pay," Dawson insisted.

She smiled. "All right. Where are you off to?"

"Home—before the rain starts." He noticed how he had used the word *home.*

"I'll be closing up soon myself," she said. "I heard a rumor you've been asked to leave Ketanu. Is it true?"

"Yes."

"But you're still here."

"I'm still here. When Gladys's murderer is in handcuffs, I'll leave."

Dawson made it back just before the rain hit, and as he sat down to eat with his aunt, uncle, and cousin, the first grumbles of thunder began. The power was out, so they ate by lantern light. The meal was as marvelously delicious as any Auntie Osewa had prepared, yet what a difference a day had made. Eating with her just didn't feel the same. Dawson kept telling himself that he did not know for certain she had lied to the police about Samuel. Yet he could not shake the feeling.

"Why so quiet, Darko?" she asked. "Anything wrong?"

"Oh, no, nothing. Just a little tired today."

He had an impulse to ask her right now, point-blank, *Did you really see Samuel walk into the forest with Gladys, or did you lie to protect Isaac Kutu?* With a shock, Dawson realized he was seeing his auntie in a different light, or perhaps a new darkness: lying, deception. It was a horrible feeling.

Not yet, he told himself. It was not yet time to confront her.

Togbe Adzima told Ama to cook his soup inside his hut because of the rain. He was well on the way to becoming drunk. He had run out of schnapps, but one of his wives had brought him some palm wine.

He was hungry, so he decided to take a break to eat and then he would have some more to drink.

Everyone had gone inside in anticipation of the downpour, except Efia, who was trying to secure a tarpaulin to four wooden posts for the goats and chickens to take shelter underneath. The sky was black and angry. The first round of lightning flittered softly and was followed by a rolling, guttural rumble, like a giant cart being pushed across the heavens. The next was a bright, quick flash that showed everything in sharp relief, and the thunder that came after it was a deafening crack. Adzima watched the deluge of water outside the door and hoped it wouldn't rise above the first step into the house. That would mean a flood.

He turned to look at Ama as she spooned his soup into a bowl. He slurped it noisily and chewed loudly on the goat meat and vegetables. He chose a morsel from the soup and held it out to Ama.

"Here. Eat."

She seemed surprised that he was offering it. He seldom did. She ate it hungrily, and he watched her. She sat against the wall with her legs extended and crossed while she watched the storm.

Efia came in soaking wet.

"What are you doing in here?" Adzima yelled. "Get out."

"Sorry," she said and went back into the rain.

"Stupid," he muttered.

"Should I go, Togbe?" Ama said uncertainly.

"Did I tell you to? Stay there."

When he was done, she held the bowl out in the rain to wash it, and then she put it back in the corner with the rest. She made a move toward the door, but he told her to come back and sit down. He stared at her smooth black skin, the way it glowed in the light of the kerosene lantern. He turned the lantern off to save fuel, and it now was almost completely black inside the hut.

"Come here," he told Ama.

He drew her to him and felt for her breasts. They were lovely. He had been watching them grow over the last several months. But Ama was tense and stiff. He pulled at her wraparound skirt, groping for her flesh. She tried to get away, but he held her fast, and once she began to struggle, the fight was on.

Efia felt uneasy about leaving Ama with Togbe. The other wives were busy trying to catch leaks in the roof while the children played around, but Efia stood at the doorway waiting anxiously for Ama. Togbe's lantern had gone out, which worried Efia even more. She sighed, took a few steps toward Togbe's hut, and turned back again. What should she do? Should she check on Ama?

She decided she would. She was already soaked, so what difference did it make? She stepped out, trying to avoid the deepest parts of the water and holding up her skirt so she wouldn't trip over it.

Suddenly, before she could get to Togbe's hut, Ama came running out. Her mouth was open in a silent scream against the storm. Her top was torn. Her skirt was tangled and pushed up and some of her thigh was exposed. Efia knew immediately what had happened, and it stabbed her in the heart and seared clear to her back in between the shoulder blades.

She caught Ama in her arms. The girl was shrieking. Efia held her tight and cradled her head. Ama wanted to collapse, but Efia wouldn't let her fall. They stood in the rain until Ama was still, and then Efia took her to the wives' hut.

Nunana came to them. Efia looked at her in a special way, a way that said, *The worst thing possible has happened,* and Nunana nodded. She understood.

"Sit down with her and hold her," she told Efia.

Nunana turned around and ordered the other wives and all the children out.

"In the rain?" they said, incredulous. She must be crazy.

"Get out, *now!*" Nunana yelled furiously. "Go to the other hut. You can come back later."

They left hastily, crying children and all.

Efia was sitting on the floor holding Ama tightly, gently rocking her.

Nunana knelt down and put her arms around both of them as they began to cry.

After a while, Efia stopped, and then so did Ama.

"Ama," Nunana said, "did he make you bleed?" She spoke above the noise of the storm, but her voice still sounded gentle.

Ama nodded.

"We'll wash it with rainwater," Nunana said. "Did he go inside you?"

"I don't know. I . . . I'm not sure. I think so."

"I have to touch you, Ama," Nunana said. "I won't hurt you."

The girl cringed, but she let Nunana check her by lantern light while Efia held her tight and talked soothingly into her ear.

Nunana looked at Efia and shook her head. "There's blood," she said, "but no seed."

Efia kissed Ama, and into her ear she whispered, "It will never happen again, Ama. I promise you that."

The storm quieted down to a steady light rain, and finally everyone could get some sleep. Keeping her arms around Ama as she slept, Efia waited two hours. Her eyes never closed in that time. She was extra alert, her mind bright and clear.

She shook Ama gently. "We have to leave."

"Eh?"

"Shh. Come."

They stepped over the sleeping wives and children and went outside. A feeble flash of lightning lit up Togbe's hut for a moment, showing the way.

Ama wiped rainwater away from her eyes. "What's wrong, Mama? Where are we going?"

"Togbe will try to hurt you and me again. We're going to run away to Ketanu, and from there maybe someone can take us to another town far away, where Togbe will never find us."

Lightning illuminated Ama's face, and Efia saw how fearful she was.

"Wait for me here," Efia said, but thunder drowned her out and she had to repeat it.

"I have to get something from Togbe's hut first," she explained. "Don't come to look for me, do you hear? No matter what, you must not come looking for me. You understand?"

"Yes, Mama."

"But when I come out, we run, okay?"

Ama nodded. She was shivering from cold and fear.

Efia knew about how many steps it was to Togbe's house, and she found the edges of the doorway and went in. She waited for the next bit of lightning. It was less bright, but still enough to see Togbe sleeping on his right side the way he always did. He was a heavy sleeper and slept even better when it rained and when he was sleeping off his drunkenness.

Efia knelt down behind him and gently tapped his left shoulder. He grunted, moaned, and rolled onto his back, and she waited a few moments until she was sure he had settled back into deep sleep. Efia fumbled around for the bottom edge of his sleeping cloth. Some of it was tangled under his weight, and she had to gently peel it up and out. She looked nervously up at the door to make sure Ama wasn't there. *Good girl. Just a few minutes more.*

She had almost all of Togbe's lower section uncovered. He was wearing trousers, but she was still worried the exposure to the air would wake him. Now she had to be quick.

One burst of lightning, and then thunder. Good.

One button. The others had fallen off long ago.

Lightning. She spread the fly open. Thunder.

Don't wake up, please.

Her knife, the one she used to cut goat meat with, was under her cloth. She took it out. He stirred.

No, no, don't turn over.

Knife in her right hand, left poised steady over his penis like a runner on his mark.

A brilliant flash of lightning, and she saw it clearly, grasped the shaft, and pulled up. The knife blade arced silently through the dark, so sharp she did not feel it cut the flesh, but she felt his penis come cleanly up and away from his body in her left hand. He writhed like a worm on a stick and sat up, but she was already at the door, and she never heard his first scream.

For a moment she didn't see Ama. *Where was she?*

They bumped into each other.

"Run!" Efia shouted.

In pitch darkness, they held hands and ran over ground they could not see into a future they did not know.

46

"DARKO? DARKO, WAKE UP."
He started and opened his eyes.

Auntie Osewa was gently shaking his shoulder. "Good morning. I hate to wake you, but you have a visitor."

She left him so he could get dressed. He pulled on his jeans, threw on a shirt, and went outside, where he was surprised to find Elizabeth waiting for him. She looked grim and anxious.

"Morning, Inspector Dawson. Can you come quickly?"

As Dawson hurried with Elizabeth to her house, she explained what had happened. She had been in the shop early to set up for the day. Glancing out the window, she had spotted Efia and Ama walking by. Elizabeth did not know them well, but she recognized Efia as one of the Bedome traders with whom she had good-naturedly haggled at Ketanu's big market day a couple of months ago. Efia had struck her then as an extraordinarily lovely woman in pitiful tattered clothing, but this morning there was a special distress to her bearing as she led her trailing daughter by the hand. Sodden and miserable from last night's rain, they were looking around with wondering, confused eyes.

It took time and skill to get the whole story, but once Elizabeth found out that Efia and her daughter were on the run from Togbe Adzima, she didn't have a second's hesitation in taking the two women into her home for safety, a bath, and a change into dry clothes.

When Dawson and Elizabeth got to the house, Ama had fallen asleep in Gladys's room, but Efia was in the living room wide awake, tense and nervous. Dorcas Mensah was cooking breakfast, and Elizabeth joined her, leaving Dawson and Efia to talk.

"Are you all right?" Dawson asked.

"I'm better now, thank you, Mr. Dawson."

"You spent the whole night in the forest?"

"Yes, but as soon as it started to get light, we came to Ketanu. I didn't even know what we were going to do when we got here. The gods will bless Madame Elizabeth for what she has done for us."

"She's a very good person," Dawson agreed. "What made you decide to escape from Togbe?"

Efia cast her gaze down. "For a man to rape his own daughter . . ." Her voice trailed off. Tears welled up in her eyes. She shook her head as if she still could not believe it.

"It happened last night?"

"Yes, and I promised Ama it would never happen again. Nor will it happen to any other woman. Because I took away his manhood forever."

Dawson was uncertain what she meant. "You mean you put a curse on him?"

"No, I mean I used a knife to cut his manhood off."

Dawson's jaw dropped and he gazed at Efia with new awe, and then he smiled inwardly. *Sweet vengeance.*

He took her hand gently and gave it a quick squeeze. "You are very brave."

She nodded, but she was desolate. "Maybe now they will kill me for what I've done."

"Never. I won't let anyone kill you."

"I'm afraid."

"I know."

They were both quiet for a moment.

"You hid the knife?" Dawson asked her.

She nodded. "It's in a safe place in the forest."

"Good. Don't tell me where, and if the police come, don't say *any-thing*, all right?"

"Please, yes, sir."

Dawson took out his mobile. He hadn't charged it since leaving the guesthouse, and it had almost completely lost its juice.

Timothy Sowah answered on the third ring.

"Good morning, Timothy. This is Detective Inspector Dawson."

Silence for a moment.

"Morning, Inspector Dawson." He sounded wary.

"I need your help. I'm at the Mensahs' house with Efia, one of Togbe Adzima's trokosi."

"The one who discovered Gladys's body?"

"Yes. She and her daughter escaped from Adzima last night."

"Goodness."

"We need them moved away from here to somewhere safe."

"This is what Gladys and I prayed every day would happen," Timothy said, his voice trembling with excitement, all the aloofness in it now gone.

"Can you help?"

"Yes, I'll send a car to bring her here to Ho, and we'll go from there."

"Thank you, Timothy. Oh, and by the way, I'd like to officially apologize for my arresting you. No hard feelings?"

"None. You were doing your job."

"Good."

Once Efia and Ama were safely away, Dawson went to the guesthouse to look for Chikata again. He was just leaving as Dawson arrived.

"The bird has flown," he said as Dawson got out of the car.

Dawson stopped in his tracks. "Kutu's gone?"

"Correct. I went looking for him yesterday at his compound, and everyone there said he had left and they didn't know where he was. I checked inside his rooms to make sure he wasn't hiding."

"Have you searched for him in town?"

"I didn't have enough time yesterday to do a good job before the rain, so I'm going now."

"I'll come with you. I can't believe you're actually doing some work, D.S. Chikata."

"Thank you, D.I. Dawson, sir. You're very funny, sir, but thank you."

They canvassed the street, asking people if they had seen Isaac Kutu anywhere. No one had.

"I'm hungry," Chikata said.

They stopped at a street hawker's stand and bought some red-red—fried plantain and black-eyed peas in spicy-hot palm sauce—and a Coke and a Malta.

"You really think your auntie was lying about Samuel?" Chikata said, with his mouth full of food.

Dawson swallowed before speaking. "Last night I thought so, this morning I'm not so sure. I'm confused."

"I believe her story," Chikata said. "You read her police statement, right?"

"Yes."

"If she was lying, how could she know those details about the clothes they were wearing—Adinkra symbols and all that stuff? Every-thing she says checks out."

"Yes, I know." Dawson shook his head. "I'm frustrated."

"Drink some Malta," Chikata said with a snort. "Maybe it will help you think."

Dawson didn't answer. He stopped eating, and his blood turned to ice. *Adinkra symbols.*

Chikata was staring at him. "What's wrong?"

"Under my nose," he whispered. "Under my very nose."

"What are you talking about?"

"Let's go," Dawson said.

"Hey, man, I haven't finished eating."

"Can't you eat and walk at the same time?"

"Where are we going?"

"To buy me a skirt and blouse."

47

AT OSEWA'S FIREWOOD SPOT, Dawson instructed Chikata to turn his back and not to look until called. Dawson walked the approximately three hundred meters to the area at the side of the forest not far from the beginning of the path to Ketanu. It was here that Isaac had rebuked Samuel for talking to Gladys and had chased the boy away. That was well established. The unanswered question was whether Samuel had really rejoined Gladys on her way back to Ketanu after she and Isaac had parted. That was Auntie Osewa's version of the story, and if it was true, Samuel must have hidden behind a tree or bush and waited until the coast was clear. But how could he have done that if he had stayed with the farmers until nightfall?

Dawson had bought a skirt and blouse at Elizabeth's—extra large to fit him. He had lied and said it was to be a gift for a full-figured sister-in-law. The outfit was identical to the one Gladys had been wearing: blue and white with small Adinkra symbols. He had not shown it to Chikata.

With considerable ineptness, for which he forgave himself, he put on the outfit over his own clothes. Then he called out to Chikata to turn around. He stood in place for about three minutes and then walked toward the Bedome–Ketanu footpath. He went up as far as the mango tree laden with tempting fruit. He didn't know for sure, but he surmised Gladys would have got to at least this point before being accosted by Samuel.

A woman was walking along the footpath with yams on her head, and she looked at Dawson as if he was insane. After she had passed him, he heard her laughing convulsively. *Just jealous,* he thought.

He stepped into the bush, took the skirt and blouse off, and put it back in the bag. He trotted back to Chikata.

"You saw me clearly?"

"Twenty-twenty."

"Describe the dress fully."

"White, and some blue splashes all over."

"And what else?"

"There's something else?"

"I'm asking you. Think hard."

Chikata shook his head. "I don't know what you're talking about."

"This is your last chance. Think carefully what else there was besides blue and white."

"*Nothing.* How many times do you want me to tell you?"

Dawson took the dress out of its bag.

"Oh," Chikata said, surprised. "Adinkra symbols. I couldn't see them from this dis—" He stopped as the light dawned. "Aah, this time you hit it right. Your auntie could not have seen it either. But why did she tell you that? Why would she lie?"

When Chikata said that, Dawson felt tears pricking. His stomach had knotted up. The pieces were falling together one terrible step at a time.

"For the same reason anyone lies," Dawson said softly. "To hide what they really are."

"What is this place?" Chikata asked, looking about the forest clearing that Efia had introduced Dawson to.

"It's where Auntie Osewa comes for love and attention," Dawson said.

Chikata shook his head. "Sometimes I don't understand you at all."

"We need to build a fire," Dawson said.

"How are we going to do that?" Chikata demanded. "Everything is wet from last night's rain."

"We'll get it done," Dawson replied, undeterred.

But it did indeed prove difficult to engineer a pile of firewood dry enough to be set alight.

"Blow on it," Chikata suggested.

"What do you know about lighting a fire?"

"About as much as you. Nothing."

"Then shut up, D.S. Chikata."

A few minutes later a decent flame began.

Chikata collected more dry wood, and Dawson added it slowly to avoid killing the fire. Soon it was blazing and popping.

"Good," he said, pleased. "Now get me a lot of plants and branches with green leaves."

As Dawson put those on top, the flame dropped and white smoke appeared. He unfolded the raffia mat and covered the fire for a few seconds, smoke escaping laterally from underneath the mat.

"One puff." He covered for a few seconds and released again. "Now two . . . two again . . ."

"Smoke signals?" Chikata asked in disbelief. "Ah, but Dawson, who makes smoke signals anymore?"

"Nobody," Dawson said. "That's why it hasn't been noticed."

Dawson repeated the cycle several times. One puff, two puffs, two puffs, one. After a while, the fire burned itself out.

"Now what?" Chikata asked.

"We wait."

And wait they did. The more time passed, the worse Dawson felt. Even in the heat of the forest, he began to shiver.

I could leave now, he thought. Just go back to Accra, call it a day.

But he thought of Gladys and he thought of Samuel, and he knew he couldn't leave.

A light breeze whispered through the trees. Dawson caught the smell of the moist earth and the lingering odor of the smoke from the fire. He looked up as he heard the soft crunch of feet upon moist leaves. Judging by the interval between footsteps, it was a man approaching. A final rustle past an obstructing bush and Isaac Kutu broke into the clearing. He recoiled when he saw Dawson and Chikata.

"What are you doing here?" he said in surprise.

"Waiting for you and Auntie Osewa," Dawson said.

Isaac suddenly seemed to shrink. "Why?"

"Is this where you always meet, or do you choose a different place each time?"

Isaac's shoulders slumped, and he passed his hand over his face like a cloth across a windowpane. "How did you know?"

"Just when you think no one is watching, someone sees."

"You did?"

"Not me."

A soft footfall, lighter and quicker than Isaac's, came from beyond the clearing, and seconds later Auntie Osewa appeared. She went rigid and looked quizzically from Dawson and Chikata to Isaac.

"What's happening?"

"I saw the signal and I thought it was you," Isaac said.

"And I thought it was *you*." Osewa turned to Dawson, mystified. "Darko?"

"Isaac loves you, Auntie, and you love him. When you signal for him to come to you, he comes. Not so?"

"This is none of your concern, Darko."

"I'm sorry, Auntie. This isn't easy for me either, because I've loved you from the first day I met you. The way you treated Mama and Cairo and me, your cooking, how you've cared for us . . . I want to thank you. I'll never forget it."

She softened. "It's my duty as an aunt. I love you and Cairo, so I treat you with love."

"Did you love my mother too?"

"Of *course*, Darko. Why do you ask such a thing? Of *course* I loved her."

"But jealousy defeats love every time, doesn't it? They're opposite sides of the same coin, but jealousy always comes out heads."

"My dear Darko, what you are talking about?"

"Jealousy," Darko said softly, almost musing to himself. "And its twin, possessiveness."

"I don't understand."

"How did it feel the day Isaac came to the house with Gladys? Did it seem to you like they were close, Auntie? Like there was romance between the two of them?"

"They were working together on the medicines, that's all," she said. "I don't know why you or I should think anything else."

"I don't either, but that's our heads talking. What our hearts say is different. The heart makes an impression on the head, but it's never the reverse, and it's the heart that drives our passions and motives."

"All you're saying may be true, Darko, my love, but—"

"It was very threatening, Auntie. I know that, and I understand it. Gladys was so lovely, and although she was no lovelier than you, she was young, she was educated, and she was going to be a doctor. To see her with your Isaac, the Isaac who has done so much for you and whom you love more than any other man in the world—maybe the *only* one you love." Dawson shook his head. "Too frightening for Gladys to get so close. Who knows what they were doing together in Isaac's compound? Hours spent side by side. I would have gone mad myself thinking about it."

Osewa looked away.

"And that evening you were collecting firewood and you saw Isaac and Gladys standing together talking," Dawson continued, "they stood closer together than was comfortable for you. You couldn't bear it. Too much pain, too much."

The other two men were watching, transfixed.

"Once Isaac had left," Dawson continued, "you caught up with

Gladys on her way back to Ketanu and lured her to the plantain grove in the forest."

"Darko," Osewa said softly. "You are wrong. I already told you. I last saw Gladys with Samuel. She went into the forest with *him*, not me."

"You saw them from the firewood spot, not so?"

"Yes, that's what I said. I don't know what's going on, Darko. Is something the matter?"

"Auntie, what I'm getting at is how you knew Gladys's skirt and blouse had Adinkra symbols on it?"

Osewa shrugged. "Because I *saw* it. What do you mean, How did I know?"

"You could see the pattern on her outfit from where you were at the firewood spot. That's what you're saying?"

"*Yes.*" But he could see she was suddenly wary.

"Auntie, it's not possible. From that distance, you couldn't see the Adinkra symbols."

A wave of puzzlement and uncertainty passed across her face like a shadow. "What do you mean?"

"The symbols are too small to be seen from where you were. We've tried it ourselves, Chikata and I."

"*What?*" she said.

"It's true," Chikata said quietly. "It's impossible even for me, and my vision is better than normal."

"Then how did I know Gladys's dress had Adinkra on it?" Osewa challenged.

"You saw it only after you got close enough to see the pattern, but your mind played a trick on you and made you think you had also seen it from far off. You wanted to be sure we believed your story, so you gave us that detail and it was one too many."

Osewa swallowed. She stared at Dawson without blinking, and he stared back. "And you led Gladys to the plantain grove. Maybe you told her you had some special herbs to show her. How long did you wait before you killed her, Auntie?"

Osewa recoiled.

"She didn't do it," Isaac said suddenly.

Dawson's head turned. "What did you say?"

"Osewa didn't kill Gladys," he said. "I did."

"Isaac Kutu, are you confessing to the murder of Gladys Mensah?"

"You're right that Osewa lied about Samuel and Gladys going into the forest, but it wasn't herself she was trying to protect, it was me."

"How did she know you were the murderer?"

"She didn't know it for sure. She suspected it because she knew I was angry with Gladys for trying to steal from me, and then she got worried when she learned how you were after my skin. And as for the Adinkra symbols, that was easy. She simply asked me what Gladys had been wearing."

Osewa put her face in her hands and shook her head in disbelief.

Chikata stepped forward, cuffs in hand. "Isaac Kutu," he said, "I am Detective Sergeant Chikata. I am arresting you for the murder of Gladys Mensah. Please turn around and put your hands behind your back."

Osewa stood dumbfounded as the handcuffs clicked shut with staccato precision. Isaac bowed his head.

"Auntie Osewa," Dawson said, "are you really going to let Isaac be taken away to prison like that? Do you really love him if you can stand there and do nothing? After all he's done for you? Alifoe is your son with Isaac. *He's the father of your child.* You're going to let him go like this?"

Osewa's eyes had gone wide. "Who told you Isaac is Alifoe's father?"

"No one. Come on now. Kweku the father of a boy as beautiful as Alifoe? I don't think so. Kweku is, and always has been, as infertile as the Sahara desert. You know that, and so do I."

Osewa was looking from Isaac to Dawson and back again. She was torn.

"He loves you, Auntie," Dawson pressed. "But do you really love him if you can let him take the blame for what you did?"

"Don't judge me," she said coldly. "You have no right to judge me."

Dawson said nothing and waited. Chikata turned Isaac to face Osewa, and their eyes locked.

"Let him go," she said resolutely. For the first time, she shed tears. "He didn't kill Gladys. I did."

Chikata, confused, looked to Dawson for guidance. Dawson nodded his permission to unlock the cuffs.

"You've done the right thing, Auntie," he said. "Now tell me everything. I'm ready to listen to you."

Osewa turned to one side, arms folded across her chest. Dawson watched her in profile as she stared at an unidentified point somewhere in the distance. She was silent for a long time, and the calls of forest birds filled the void until she began to speak.

"I was collecting firewood when I saw Gladys and Samuel talking to each other at the edge of the forest," she began. "Then I heard Isaac calling out and saw him walk up to them and begin to argue with Samuel. I heard their voices, but from where I was standing, I couldn't hear much of what they were saying. Still, I guessed he was telling Samuel to go away and leave Gladys alone."

Osewa turned back to face Isaac, and now she addressed him directly.

"I didn't know why you told Samuel to go away, Isaac. Maybe you thought he was dangerous or troubling Gladys. But I was worried, because Samuel was not really a bad person, and so I was thinking to myself, Why has Isaac told the boy to go away? Is it because he likes Gladys and doesn't want another man near her?

"So I just watched you and Gladys talking and talking, and I was wondering what you could be conversing about for so long. And sometimes you were smiling, Isaac, as though you were enjoying her company so very much. I saw how close to you she was standing. One time she touched your arm, and another time I saw her laugh and I knew it was a laugh of desire for you, because I too am a woman.

"Then you left her and went back to your compound, and she went on her way back toward Ketanu and I was still wondering, wondering, because you always told me you were only working with Gladys on your medicines, so why did it seem that the two of you were so attracted to each other? When you had returned to your compound, I went after Gladys. I had to run because by now she was far ahead on the footpath to Ketanu.

"When I caught up with her, I greeted her and she was nice to me. And while we were talking, I kept thinking how beautiful she was. And I asked her how everything was going in her study of natural medicines. She told me everything was fine. And then she told me something I didn't like at all. She said she was trying to convince you, Isaac, to go to Accra with her to work with those doctors there. But really, I knew what she was trying to do. She was trying to take you away for herself and keep you in Accra."

"Osewa, no," Isaac said sadly. "She wasn't trying to do that."

"Maybe you didn't know that, my love. But that was what she was trying to do and I had to stop her. While I was talking with her, I was thinking to poison her. Maybe just to make her sick enough to want to leave Ketanu and never come back. I told her I could show her a place in the forest with some medicinal herbs, and I'm sorry, Isaac, I lied and said I knew which one you used to cure the AIDS. She was very eager to see it, and I took her to the plantain grove.

"When I got there, I was trying to think of a way to poison her, but time was going, the sun was about to sleep, Gladys wanted to leave, and she kept asking me which was the medicine to cure AIDS. I showed her a plant I didn't even know, and she began to laugh at me, saying that she didn't think that was it. And the more she talked, the angrier I became that she was telling me all these things she was planning to do for you. She even said she was going to make the Ministry of Health get you a nice guesthouse, and that's when I knew for sure that she wanted to live with you in that house. I wanted to tell her that you belonged to me, not to anyone else, that she couldn't have you."

Osewa turned to Dawson. "Isaac is everything to me in this world. He gave me everything. His very touch the first day I met him was like nothing I had known. He gave me the love I never had from Kweku or anyone else, and most of all he blessed me with a beautiful son. Do you know how much I wanted a son, Darko? Do you know how I felt when I saw women with two, three, four beautiful children while I had none?"

"I know it was painful for you, Auntie," Dawson said. "What did you do to Gladys?"

"I attacked her. I wanted to hurt her. We fell on the ground and she started to scream. I squeezed her neck to make her quiet, and she was looking up at me while I was doing it. She was struggling and I wanted her to stop, so I kept squeezing. Her neck was very soft. And when she stopped breathing, I felt sorry for her, and I didn't know what to do, so I just tried to make her more comfortable by moving her underneath a palm tree. And I rearranged her skirt and blouse so they were nice and neat again."

Osewa turned her palms up and looked at them as if she was seeing them for the first time. "I couldn't let her take away my treasure, that's what you have to understand. Not Gladys, nor any other woman."

"Even your own sister," Dawson said.

Osewa drew in her breath so sharply it made a sound of asphyxiation. Her right hand, fingers spread, went to her chest. She stood frozen. Dawson moved in close.

"Where did you bury my mother?"

He grasped her arm, but she threw it off and sprang away like a bush rabbit.

"Don't touch me!" she snapped. Her eyes blazed like red-hot embers. "You're just like her. Even your laugh is like hers. She was always better than me, that woman. Ever since we were children. And then she would rub it in my face. She had everything. She lived in Accra, she was more beautiful, she had you and Cairo while I was *barren,* and then she wanted Isaac for herself as well."

Her chest was heaving and her hands were trembling.

"Isaac looked at Mama that day we came to see you," Dawson said, "and she looked back at him. I saw it, and so did you, and you knew what it meant."

"Yes. That she wanted him. She was going to get him."

"When you said you had been outside setting the traps for the rabbits," Dawson said, "you really went to see Isaac, because you were afraid that something was going on between him and Mama, and you desperately wanted Isaac to reassure you that it wasn't so."

"Yes." She looked admiringly at Dawson for a moment. "How do you know everything? Then, when your mother came to see us just after Alifoe was born, a farmer mentioned to me that he had seen Beatrice go into Isaac's compound and that she had spent a long time there. And then I knew Beatrice was in love with Isaac, because if that wasn't the case, she would have told me she had gone to see him, maybe for some healing, but she didn't. She did not say one word about it.

"She came back to Ketanu again, and this time I challenged her. I asked her, 'Beatrice, I know you have been secretly going to see Isaac Kutu. Why are you doing that?' She told me she feared that she might have offended the gods in some way and that's why they had taken Cairo's legs away, that perhaps she needed to be purified, and so that was why she had visited Isaac's compound. And I asked her, Why not just find a healer in Accra to purify her? Do you know what she answered? She said that no one made her feel the way Isaac did. She said she just felt so *happy* when she was with him.

"And then your mother confessed something to me and begged me never to tell anyone. And I said, All right, I won't tell anyone. She told me she often dreamed that she was standing with seven or eight women who were Isaac's wives, and one by one they died around her. They just fell down on the ground one after the other and left only Beatrice standing. Once they were all dead, she became Isaac's new wife." Auntie Osewa shuddered. "That's when I realized."

"Realized what, Auntie Osewa?"

"Boniface Kutu had been right that one of my sisters was a witch, only he chose the wrong sister. It wasn't Akua who needed to be tried. It was Beatrice. *She* was the witch. It was *Beatrice* who had stolen my womb from me."

"Oh, no, Osewa," Isaac said, dismayed. "That's not the way it was."

"She had stolen my womb. Isaac got it back, and now Beatrice wanted to steal *him*. How *dare* she? What gave her the right to take so much away from me?"

Dawson's bottom lip was quivering. "Auntie, how did you kill Mama?"

"You already know," she said, suddenly weary. "You held the weapon in your own hands."

Dawson felt sick.

"Yes, Darko. It was the rope we make from elephant grass, the same kind I made for you when you were a boy." Tears streamed down her face. "I planned it. I knew I couldn't do it with my bare hands. Your mother was too strong."

"And when it came time for Mama to return to Accra," Dawson said softly, "you walked with her toward the tro-tro stop, but you never got there, did you? You led her to the grove—just like you were to do with Gladys twenty-three years later—and you killed her there. You told everyone the lie that you had seen Mama board the tro-tro, but this last time, when I was having dinner with you and you were telling us about it, you made another mistake. It's always in the lying that a mistake is made."

"What mistake?"

"Mama would never have sat near the front seat, even if it was the last tro-tro on earth."

"Oh," Osewa said dispiritedly. "I didn't even know that."

Dawson took her gently and held her close.

"Detective Sergeant Chikata is going to arrest you now, Auntie, and then he will be taking you away. Okay?"

"I love you, little Darko. I will always love you."

48

IT WASN'T A FETISH priest who had built the juju pyramid at the plantain grove. It had been Osewa's creation. Maybe it would indeed serve to keep evil spirits away, but its main purpose was to hide what was underneath.

With Constable Gyamfi's help, Dawson removed the rocks one by one from the pile. He felt a certain closeness to the constable. With Inspector Fiti and Constable Bubo suspended pending the investigation into alleged police brutality, Dawson had offered to stay in Ketanu and help at the station until a replacement inspector could be sent in.

All the rocks were down now, and the soil was exposed. Gyamfi had brought a shovel, and Dawson thrust it into the ground. Even though the soil was soft from the recent rain, it was hard work digging. Dawson had insisted on doing it without any help. When he got three feet down, he stopped and wiped the sweat streaming from his brow.

"Are you sure you don't want me to take over for a while?" Gyamfi asked.

"I'm sure."

As he continued, the shovel struck something hard, and he stopped and knelt down. Gyamfi moved closer to see. It was about the size of a thumb. It looked light in color but stained by the dark earth. Dawson used his bare hands to clear more soil away. It became clear that they were looking at a human bone.

Thirty minutes later, Dawson had the full leg and part of a pelvis. He freed the other leg and the feet, then moved up the spine. The body had been laid at a slight incline, so again he had to use the shovel carefully until he reached another level of bone.

He freed the arms. The skeleton was mostly intact. Around the bones of the neck, Dawson removed the soil in careful, thin layers until he found something again. It was coated with mud and the chain had been broken, but it was there—the gold necklace with its butterfly pendant.

"Mama," he whispered.

When her head was exposed, Dawson gently touched her skull.

Gyamfi turned away and retreated quietly. Dawson brushed soil out of his mother's head and eyes. In his mind, he didn't see her skull, he saw her face and her smile and felt her skin.

"I'll give you the burial you deserve, Mama," he said, "and Christine and Hosiah will be there. At last you'll see them and be proud. And then, Mama, you can finally rest."

ACKNOWLEDGMENTS

Thank you is a sufficient expression when someone holds a door open for you, but it is inadequate to express the depth of gratitude I feel for those who have in various ways helped me to write this book.

No one deserves the crown more than Marly Rusoff, my agent. When I first presented this novel to her, it was so roughly hewn I wonder how on earth she saw any potential shape in it. Marly not only has keen perception, she brings warmth and humanity along with it. She is a tenacious advocate for her authors. My tremendous thanks also go to Michael Radulescu and Jacqueline LeDonne in Marly's office, who worked magic with foreign sales of this novel.

I would never have come upon Marly Rusoff had it not been for Beverly Martin at Agent Research and Evaluation. An accomplished writer herself, she searched tirelessly for agents who might take me on, and she was really the first person to teach me how to write a good query letter. I am very grateful to her.

I was fortunate to meet yet another wonderful person in this process: Judy Sternlight, my editor at Random House. She infused me with excitement from the very start. She has an amazing grasp of character and story, seeing many things that did not even occur to me as the author. I consider myself privileged to have worked with someone of her caliber and brilliance. My thanks also go to production editor Vincent La Scala, sharp-eyed copy editor Susan M. S. Brown, and the marketing and promotion personnel.

I must not forget the first readers of the manuscript—Julie Mosow, in Marly Rusoff's office, and Mary Logue, both of whom gave me such invaluable guidance that I would not have been able to produce the second and third drafts without them.

Many thanks to Ken Yeboah, assistant commissioner of police and deputy director general at the Central Investigations Department in Accra. He was extremely helpful and patient with me in response to the scores of questions I had for him about police procedure in Ghana. Likewise, I would like to thank Edmond Vanderpuye and Patience Vormawor at International Needs in Accra for being so accommodating. I also thank Kofitse Ahadzi of Afrikania Mission; Moses Sowah, M.D., for getting me in touch with detectives and officers at CID; the incomparable and unflappable John Nkrumah Mills, M.D., at the Volta River Authority Hospital in Akosombo; Adukwei Hesse, M.B., Ch.B.; and Nii Otu Nartey, M.D. Many thanks to the always brainy Audrey Quaye for helping me make contacts in Ghana. I am very grateful also to Kwasi Asiedu, attorney at law, for his terrific assistance with tricky legal questions, and to David Asem for expert assistance with English-Ewe translation.

I cannot leave out my late father, K. A. B. Jones-Quartey, who taught me by example about the doggedness needed to write a book; my mother, Pearl; and my brothers, Kwatei, Nii Ofrang, and Kwatelai, to whom I'm grateful for their encouragement and support; as well as Joseph Adinolf, my physical trainer, who can always tell from my workouts if I've been doing a little too much writing for my own good.

Finally, thanks to Stephanie Cabot, who long ago suggested the story be set in real-life Ghana rather than a fictitious "Ghana-like" African nation, and to Marjorie Miller, who propelled me on my writing career in those early days. I will never forget Miss Mensah, my primary school English teacher, who inspired me to excel.

GLOSSARY

Pronunciation of Ghanaian words

- *gy, dj,* and *dz* are pronounced like *j* in *just.*
- *ky* is pronounced like *ch* in *church.*
- *e* is rarely if ever silent.

Terms

Abatasu: plant whose leaves are reputed to help rid a person of disturbing spirits.

Abeg (ah-beg): corruption of *I beg you.*

Adinkra: symbolic designs or logos used to decorate colorful patterned cloth, often expressing concepts such as bravery or loyalty. Originally used for funeral wear but now acceptable for other occasions and as a tourist item.

Akasa: porridge made from slightly fermented corn dough.

Ampe: a girls' rhythmic jumping and clapping game in which the participant scores points according to which foot she puts forward at the end of a sequence in relation to the other player's foot (reminiscent of rock-paper-scissors).

Ayekoo: congratulatory exclamation recognizing an achievement or hard work.

Banku: fermented corn-cassava dough mixed proportionally and cooked in hot water into a smooth, whitish paste.

Bulla: vulgar for *penis.*

Calabash: dried, hollowed-out gourd used as a container.

Cedi: Ghana's monetary unit, approximately equal to one U.S. dollar in this work.

Chaley: friend, familiar term only, as in *buddy.*

Chaley-wate: sandals made from old, discarded rubber tires.

Chinchinga: Ghanaian shish kebab.

Chop bar: a small food establishment where quickly prepared meals can be bought.

Cutlass: machete.

Dash: money given as a tip, gift, or bribe.

Durbar: ceremonial meeting of a Ghanaian chief and his subjects (deriv. Indo-Persian for "ruler's court").

Ewe: major language of the Volta Region spoken by approximately five million people in Ghana, Togo, and Benin (pronounced "eh-way").

Fien nawo: Ewe for *good evening* (short form: *fien*).

Fufu: cassava, yam, or plantain pounded into a soft, glutinous mass and shaped into a smooth ball, usually as an accompaniment to soup, particularly palm nut soup.

Ga: predominant language of the Greater Accra Region.

Gari: starchy carbohydrate made from cassava, approximately the consistency of couscous.

Kai: expression of revulsion.

Kawkaw-kaw: verbal representation of a knock on the door, used to announce one's arrival at someone's home and to request entry.

Kelewele: ripe plantain cut in cubes and deep-fried with ginger and other spices till crispy.

Kontomire: stew made with cocoyam leaves, palm oil, hot peppers, and other flavorings.

Libation pouring: at many important events, tradition of pouring small amounts of alcohol or other liquid on the ground accompanied by entreaties to the gods and/or ancestors.

Ndo na wo: Ewe for *good afternoon* (short form: *ndo*).

Okro: variation of *okra.*

Oware: a count-and-capture game of strategy played with pebbles on a wooden board with shallow pits.

Shai Hills: forest and grassland reserve fifty kilometers northeast of Accra.

Small-small: just a little bit.

Toto: vulgar for *vagina.*

Tro-tro: passenger minivan commonly used throughout Ghana for mass transit. (From *tro* for *three pence,* the fare charged during British colonial rule.)

Woizo: Ewe word for *welcome.*

Zongo: any of a number of communities in Accra with large Moslem populations.

ABOUT THE AUTHOR

KWEI QUARTEY was raised in Ghana by an African-American mother and a Ghanaian father, both of whom were university lecturers. When he was eight years old, Kwei began to write short novels that he bound by hand with colorfully illustrated cardboard covers. They were big hits with his family and friends. But his budding writing career was sidetracked during his training as a doctor and during the early days of getting his medical career off the ground. These days, Dr. Kwei Quartey practices medicine in Montebello, California, rising early in the morning to write before going to work. He is currently writing his next novel.

ABOUT THE TYPE

This book was set in Bulmer, a typeface designed in the late eighteenth century by the London type-cutter William Martin. The typeface was created especially for the Shakespeare Press, directed by William Bulmer; hence, the font's name. Bulmer is considered to be a transitional typeface, containing characteristics of old-style and modern designs. It is recognized for its elegantly proportioned letters, with their long ascenders and descenders.